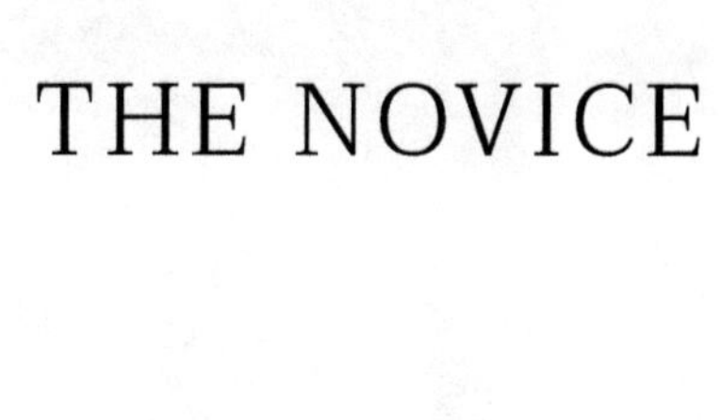

THE NOVICE

The Novice

The Tales of Zhava
Book 2

H. DEAN FISHER

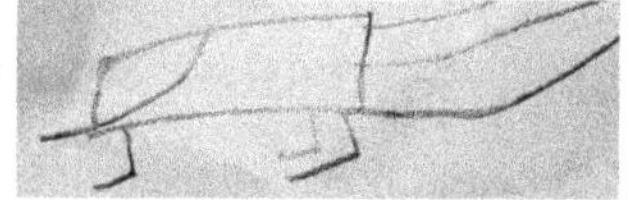

Seventh Battle Publishing, Nicholson, Pennsylvania

Author's Notes

Zhava and Plishka are two of my favorite characters, and they are a powerhouse team when they join forces. To grow, however, Zhava must discover who she is on her own. Just as we must all grow and become who we are when we're by ourselves and facing demons alone in the dark, so too must Zhava. It's easy to rely on those people nearby who tell us what to do or how to do it, but there comes a time in each of our lives when we must make those decisions on our own – and live with the consequences. Peter Pan refused to do it, and there are many people who fight it their whole lives. Unfortunately as happens sometimes in real life, Zhava was never adequately prepared for it – and therein lies the conflict. True growth is how we choose to deal with the problems we encounter.

Special thanks to my wife, Suzanne, who supports this writer's lifestyle; my most important reader, Freyja; my parents, Ken & Geri Fisher; publishing advisor Ann Lavendar, www.AnnLavendar.com; fighting advisor Robert Thomas of Tsunami Self-Defense Academy, www.Tsunami-SelfDefense.com; and trauma advisor Dr. Mark Hall.

For those so inclined, the soundtrack to "The Novice" is:
Lana Del Rey, "Ultraviolence"
Dana Fuchs, "Live in NYC"
Allison Sudol, "Moon"

To Freyja
Never be afraid to do the right thing

Contents

Prologue

Dawn broke with bird-song in the trees above, and Zhava slowly opened her eyes. She couldn't see the birds in the palm trees high above her, but their chirping melodies were so familiar that she had to smile. A dim glow of blues and yellows and reds filtered down through the colorful cloths strung between the trunks, the window ledges, and the hooks in the walls. Everything felt so normal, as if the Gods gave her this moment as reward for the good, hard work she and Plishka had done. Even the cool air smelled sweet, and she smiled and rolled onto her back on the prickly straw mattress beneath her.

Her body ached, but very few of her sore muscles, stinging cuts, and deep bruises had anything to do with sleeping on the ground in the open courtyard of her family's home. The fight against High Priest Viekoosh had been harder than anything she'd ever done, and her body now complained at the strains she'd put upon it. All of her training swinging a sword and throwing fireballs was wonderful, but there was nothing like the sting of real combat to make the aches and exhaustion somehow worse.

Beyond the battlefield, however, was the emotional sting of the night before, first all the screaming with her Mama and then the revelations from her Papa. Mama always treated her so differently from her brothers, criticizing her and chastising her and punishing her far more often and far more severely than she did the three boys of the family. Zhava tried to make things right, tried to do as she was told, but nothing was ever good enough, and she thought it was because she was a girl that her Mama did not like her. Last night, however, Papa told her of Viekoosh's treachery, of the curse he and Salient Kretsch set upon Mama almost 14 seasons back – that Mama would love Papa as she always had, but she would despise the adopted baby, Zhava. They placed that inside Mama's heart, and it had grown up within her and infected not only Mama's words and actions but those of Zhava's three brothers and her Papa. For fear of crossing Mama, Zhava had become the family pariah.

With a sigh of understanding she pushed up from the thin mattress and surveyed the courtyard where a few dozen children still slept. They had stayed up late into the night talking with Papa and swapping stories of how she and Plishka rescued them from her former betrothed, Ooleng, and a life of slavery across the mountains. The stories were mostly accurate, if a bit embellished with childhood enthusiasm, but those stories did more to change Papa's perception of Zhava than anything she had done in the 14 seasons of living in this very home. It was why he shared so openly with her the truth of how she came to live in this household.

She quietly stood so as not to disturb her friend Plishka who was still sleeping soundly on the ground next to her. Picking her way carefully around the children, she pushed aside the heavy blanket that served as a door between the courtyard and the kitchen – and stopped at the sight of Mama slicing fruit and arranging dates on a large platter. She had not seen her Mama since all the screaming last night, and it felt as if a hand gripped her chest in anxiety at being in the same room together. She had trouble breathing as she awaited Mama's scathing remarks. Instead, however, Mama pointed at the bench and table near the window in the corner.

"Sit," she said.

Zhava sucked in a breath. She was planning to get something to eat and sit at that table, but she did not like her Mama ordering her to do so. Whose idea was it?

"Or stand," Mama continued. "I don't care. You'll do what you want no matter what I say."

Zhava's jaw clenched as she held back what she wanted to say – what she wanted to scream. She reminded herself that Mama's words were not her own, but they were the result of a curse, one more reason to despise the evil High Priest Viekoosh and Salient Kretsch. Instead, she took a breath and went to the table with a loudly and clearly spoken, "Yes, Ma'am."

Mama set a small plate of fruit and nuts before her and went back to preparing the rest of the food.

"Thank you."

"You're a guest in my home," Mama said, with a heavy emphasis on the word "guest." "I will treat you well for the sake of the children who claim you saved them. Though it seems your friend Plishka is far more capable of rescuing children than you are."

Another deep breath, and this time Zhava shut her eyes for a moment. "As you say," she muttered, stuffing a sliced pepper in her mouth.

"As I say," Mama muttered. "If it had truly been 'As you say,' then you would be married to that wonderful Ooleng right now and living your life across the mountains where you belong, bearing him children and trying to do something constructive with your life." She tossed her knife across the stone counter, and it clattered to a stop against the wall. She sucked in a breath and examined her thumb, a thin line of blood dripping from a shallow cut. "Dammit, child, now look what you made me do."

She was ready to yell a reply, to scream at her mother that she had done nothing but sit at the table and eat her morning meal, but the heavy door to the outside banged open, and Papa and her brother Caleb walked into the room, smiles on their faces and dead rabbits dangling in their hands.

"We have more food for the children," Papa said as he plopped the limp animals on the side table. "Caleb helped."

With an instant smile, Mama quickly wrapped a strip of cloth around her finger and gave Papa a kiss and Caleb a hug. "That is wonderful," she said. "Thank you. And Caleb, my wonderful son, thank you for helping with this."

Zhava took a bite of fruit and shut her eyes. The only thing left would be to cover her ears to completely block out this moment, but that would draw too much attention to her pain. She reminded herself that Mama acted like this because of the curse, but that did not soothe the pain of this moment right here, right now.

"Did you really help those children?" Caleb asked as he approached the table.

"She claims she did," Mama said from the other side of the room, "but that second girl, Plishka, probably did most of the work."

Papa wrapped an arm around her and whispered in her ear, and Mama set aside her knife and towel and went outside. Papa smiled at Zhava and said to Caleb, "Your sister did indeed rescue those children from their mountain prison – with Plishka at her side, as I heard the children tell it last evening."

Caleb squinted at her as he casually flicked his favorite knife in his hand, the long, thin knife with the bone handle. He carried it everywhere, and from the streaks of blood across the blade and the back of his hand, he had likely used it to kill some of those rabbits. "So what Father told me is true," he said. "The King's people are really training you."

"Yes."

"To fight? Why?"

"It is the way of the Hibaro," she said with a shrug. "Not only to fight, but also to think more clearly, to push myself harder, to become more than I was. I am studying the Kandor."

He laughed. "You got these ideas from that crazy Marmaran woman Mother and Father hired to teach you. That was a waste of everyone's time. You were no better at cooking and sewing after a full season of her lessons than you were before she arrived."

"Caleb," Papa said, stepping forward and placing a hand on his shoulder. "Zhava is doing well. She is thriving, as we can see from the children she helped."

"I want to see," he said with a wave of his knife in Zhava's direction. "Show me this training of yours. Show me what you can do."

Zhava stared at him, a piece of fruit in her hand halfway to her mouth. What was she to do? Perform for him? Of her three brothers, he was the nicest to her, the one who would often speak to her as if she was a real person, but he still held far more traditional beliefs than Priestess Marmaran taught. Women were not warriors. Women were not thinkers. Women supported their husbands and sons, and they cared for the children, but they did not venture into the fields or fight wild animals – and they certainly did not fight evil men. Or any men. She could think of nothing to show him, nothing she could tell him that would persuade him she had grown since he'd moved away to his own home down the valley. She was only 9 seasons the last he'd spent any time with her, several seasons even before Priestess Marmaran arrived, and she suspected she would forever be that tiny girl in his eyes.

Before she could say anything, though, Caleb lunged forward with his knife. She didn't think, but her body reacted as she'd been trained, as Io Suleenuo trained her to respond. She slipped aside, gripped his wrist, and yanked him forward with her right hand. He stumbled forward into the table. With her left, she grabbed a handful of his hair and slammed his forehead to the table. The knife clattered to the floor as Zhava stood and darted away and out of his reach. She stood with her hands before her, palms open and ready for his next attack.

Caleb yelled and staggered, slipping to the floor even as Papa tried to catch him.

"What was that?" Caleb screamed. He leaned on the stone bench against the wall and rubbed at the red mark in the middle of his forehead. She did not want to hurt him, only to stop the attack and get away. He was her brother, and she would never try to hurt him.

"Caleb, you go outside," Papa said. He helped Caleb stand again and directed him to the door.

"What were you thinking?" Caleb screamed. "Are you crazy? Why would you do that?"

Zhava stepped away as Caleb continued yelling, continued insisting he was only joking and that she had overreacted, that if he really wanted to hurt her then he would have done so. Papa finally got him outside and slowly shut the door behind him. He turned to Zhava, and she saw both the anger and the sadness in his eyes.

"You have returned to us for only a short time, and already you have fought with your mother and now your brother. What am I to do?"

"Papa, you saw what he did," Zhava insisted. She retrieved the bloodied knife from the floor and handed it over. "That is not a practice weapon – it is a real knife."

"He would not have hurt you."

She threw up her hands and sat down hard on the bench. "He came at me with a knife, Papa. With his hunting knife. What was I to do? Let him cut me?"

Papa reached for a cloth hanging on the wall and slowly, ponderously began rubbing at the dried rabbit blood on the blade. "You are a woman now," he said. "You have been since you began the bleeding."

"I am a woman since Io Liori took me to train in the ways of the Kandor. Since my teachers began instructing me in service of the King."

"No, your training is irrelevant. It is only a small part of who you are. You will see when you have your first child what is so very important, and it will not be your training."

She opened her mouth to respond – to argue that he did not know her as well as he claimed – but before she could, he held up a hand to stop her saying anything, and he continued.

"You are young. You will learn. Now listen."

With a deep sigh she kept her mouth firmly shut, but her little flames began scratching at her palms, itching to come forth.

"Your brothers all care for you-"

She snorted.

"-but Caleb has shown more than the others that he truly loves you. He wants the best for you."

"By threatening me with a knife?"

"By testing you. But you should not have hurt him as you did."

"I was-"

"Stop." He held the knife between them, and she noticed the blade was nearly clean. "They may be teaching you some skills at the Hibaro – and believe me, I am so very proud of you for what you and your friend did in rescuing those children – but you cannot embarrass Caleb like that again. You cannot embarrass any of your brothers as you embarrassed Caleb just now. And when you get married, you should not do anything like that to embarrass your husband. It is not right."

"Papa," she gaped. "He came at me...with a knife."

"Do not argue." He tossed the blood-stained towel to the counter, reached down and patted her shoulder, and stepped to the door. "You may not accept the truth of my words now, but you will someday. I know you, daughter, and I know you will learn. I am so very proud of you." With that, he opened the door and headed back outside, leaving her to sit alone and in silence with the voices screaming rage within her.

Chapter 1

Four moons later....

Zhava sat with her back against the large stone, the after-noon sun high overhead, and stared into the dark, cave en-trance. As caves went, it was unremarkable. Set atop a tall rise with a set of steep, chiseled stone steps leading up to it, there was nothing much to differentiate it from any other nearby cave. It was dark. It was cool. It contained a large variety of plants peeking around the entrance, some moss along the chilly, damp stones just within, and a temperature that stayed relatively constant most every season. It was a little cooler now, with the winter months slowly approaching, but if she was to step inside and walk farther back, the air would be still and pleasant. There was absolutely no way, however, that she was going to step even one foot inside that cave.

This unremarkable cave at the top of the tall rise and ac-cessed by the terraced rock steps was home to probably the most vicious creature Zhava had ever seen. She called it "the bear." It wasn't exactly a bear, but that was the closest animal she could compare to it. The thing slinked across the ground when she first saw it, then it moved on four legs, and then it stood up tall, like a person. Bears walked on all fours, and they could stand up tall when they wanted to threaten or fight off an intruder – but she had never seen one slink across the ground. The differences didn't stop there. The creature in the cave didn't sound like a bear. It sort of...gurgled. Like a frog. Or a fish – if fish could make noise. It was also very fast, especially for its large size; it climbed down a sheer wall to get at her, and its eyes glowed red. Though that might have been simply the reflections of her little flames against the bear's own eyes. She wasn't sure.

As if that wasn't enough, however, the creature also seemed capable of stealing away her Gods'-given Abilities. She had to admit – that was the single scariest part about the creature in the cave. She used her Ability with the wind to send the bear flying back against a wall and – she thought – knock it unconscious. The thing got up, shook its black, bushy head, and flung a windstorm right back at her. That hurt. So she set loose her little dancing flames on the thing. Sent them scurrying across the ground to jump on the bear and subdue it and burn it down to a pile of ashes on the cave floor. That didn't work, either. Her flames knocked it to the ground, and they even began burrowing into the thing's black hide, but then it stole those flames away from her too. Somehow, the creature mesmerized her little flames, changed their eyes from bright, glittering red to a hollow, soulless black – and then they attacked her. Jumped on her, burned her clothes and skin, tried to burrow down within her. She shivered as she remembered the pain of her own flames attacking.

She hadn't wanted to be in that cave. She hadn't expected to be fighting for her life. She only just arrived at the Hibaro, and Io Kua sent her inside – to "test her" he said at the time. "A mistake," he said later – though he never did offer a real apology. Instead he agreed to be her Mentor, and then he presented her with the best gift she had ever received in her life – a Felton sword. A short, all-around sword meant mostly for self-defense and practice. She used it quite effectively to escape her captors far up in the Purneese Mountains – popped one man's kneecap in a fighting move that still made her smile.

She loved that sword, and her hand dropped reflexively even now to the belt at her waist – though she could barely feel the sword through the doe-skin coat she wore against the chilled air.

That sword, as versatile as it was and as fond of it as she had become, would do very little against the bear within this cave, this "Proving Cove" as everyone at the Hibaro called it. Io Kua told her several moons ago that she would be returning to the Cove again someday – and that day was fast approaching. She learned her Initiate philosophies until she could recite them in her sleep. She trained with Io Suleenuo until she could flick a knife into the center of a target from thirty paces, beat every other Initiate – except for one – during competition in the sword-fighting arena, and even stay her ground for a 10-count against one of the soldiers who sparred with the Initiates. She and Io Kua practiced with her Gods'-given Abilities several days each week, and he helped her focus and sharpen her mind until she could use her flames and her wind with ease. She no longer had to even think about them – she could simply call them to herself and will them to obey. They had not focused on her Abilities with dust and rocks, as her previous Mentor, the Priestess Marmaran, had done. But Io Kua said they could work on that later. No one else at the Hibaro had Abilities with three of the elements, as she did, and he said he was hesitant to push her too far too fast. As she seemed to have an almost natural affinity for controlling wind and fire, they focused their attention on those first.

A scraping noise to her left drew her from her reveries. Initiate Plishka – one of her best friends, and the only Initiate she could not beat with a sword in the practice arena – slowly climbed the cold, slippery steps to the mouth of the Proving Cove. She flicked back her own coat – bear skin, and a beautiful, deep brown color – leaned against the rock at Zhava's back, and scooched down next to her.

"Barae's looking for you," she whispered.

Zhava sighed. She loved Barae, but not in the way that Barae wished. She loved her as a friend – certainly one of the best friends she could ever have – but that never seemed enough for the young woman, and Zhava was at a loss how to convey that feeling without hurting her intensely. So instead, she avoided the topic altogether. And often avoided Barae.

"I'll see her at meal time," Zhava said, turning her attention back to the dark Proving Cove entrance.

Plishka stared at it too, and they sat in companionable silence for a long while, each lost in her own thoughts. That was a wonderful thing about Plishka, about the two of them sharing the bond of fighters. They competed against each other, they kept each other company, they both pushed each other harder, but in a moment like this, they could sit in the silence and enjoy being with each other. Zhava never had that before, with anyone. Barae was wonderful, certainly, but she wanted so much more than Zhava could ever give her. Their friend Posef was strong, funny, and irreverent, but he could never sit still and shut up. He had to be moving, doing something, even if it wasn't productive. Plishka, though....

"Io Liori returns in a few nights," Plishka said.

Zhava nodded. In the wake of High Priest Viekoosh's treachery, the King had appointed Io Liori as the temporary leader of the Hibaro. She was the highest ranking military officer on campus, and the King had developed a sudden mistrust of his religious authorities across the realm. All of that meant that Liori no longer went on patrol, spent far more time in her campus office, and traveled at least once a moon to report directly to the King about her ongoing investigation. Which had gone nowhere.

The Hibaro spy network had apparently belonged to Viekoosh, so they all seemed to vanish upon his disappearance; the files in the burned out Tower had all been destroyed, so there was no longer anything written down that could lead them to Viekoosh's whereabouts; and Salient Kretsch, the only other known confederate in the treachery, had apparently vanished from the land. No one had uncovered anything new, and the King would be furious. Which meant Io Liori would be furious. Which meant that everyone had better stay out of her way when she returned. She was a fighter, the First of the King's Third Salient. She was not meant to sit behind a desk to read and file reports, yet that was what she had been doing for several moons.

"You're lucky," Plishka said.

Zhava turned to stare at her. Lucky...?

"You've been in there." Plishka pointed into the dark entrance of the Proving Cove.

Zhava laughed. "That wasn't luck," she said. "It was torture. It was...a fight I couldn't win. Something I wasn't ready for."

"But you got to practice."

Ah, now Zhava understood. Plishka was being sent into the Proving Cove also, very soon after Zhava's second time.

"I didn't really learn anything. Except that the bear is mean and fast."

"But you've tested it. You've seen it in action."

"Yes, I have," Zhava said with a sigh. And she would be seeing it again very soon. She was, however, tired of dwelling on something she could only dread. She needed something to distract her, something that could make her laugh – and break through Plishka's stoic, antisocial attitude. She turned and, with a wide grin, asked, "So what's up with my brother?"

Plishka's jaw tensed, and her eyes grew ever-so-slightly larger, but she did not reply.

"Just wondered if he had sent any more packages." Zhava's brother Caleb met Plishka at the farm four moons ago, and he seemed to like her – a lot. He had given Plishka flowers and enough deer jerky to last nearly an entire moon; he offered

Plishka a team of camels if she wished to travel anywhere (which she did not); and he even sent that beautiful bear-skin coat Plishka was wearing at this very moment. It was a confusing situation. Even though Caleb was the most adventurous of her three brothers, he was still so conservative about so many things in his life. He didn't approve of dancing or loud music; like his brothers, he also believed women belonged only inside the home and tending to the household chores; and he strongly disapproved of any woman owning property of her own, including swords and armor. What would he find attractive in an independent warrior like Plishka?

As if that wasn't confusing enough, Plishka was an orphan; she had no Mama or Papa through whom Caleb could make his romantic intentions known. The Hibaro treated Candidates as wards of the King, but once they were promoted to Initiates, they became disciples under the guidance of various teachers and administrators – no longer under direct control of any one person, but not yet independent to be accepting or rejecting offers of affection. Sister Allenka, the woman responsible for Plishka's job and living quarters, found the whole thing hilarious, and she encouraged Caleb to send more gifts to win Plishka's affections.

"The coat looks good on you."

Without looking over, Plishka raised her hand and casually let a flicker of lightning dance between her fingertips.

Zhava burst out laughing and raised her own hand. A little flaming man danced between her fingers. She flicked him into the air, then caught him in her palm as he floated back down on the breeze. This was fun. This was what Zhava needed.

"Gods and iron at sundown," Plishka muttered, shaking her head. She wasn't smiling – Plishka rarely smiled – but Zhava could see the corners of her eyes crease, a telltale sign that Plishka was also enjoying the familiar banter.

"Oh, one little puff of wind, and down you go. I would hate to embarrass you like that."

"You would be too busy fending off my blade to even think about your Abilities."

"My flames would make that blade of yours too hot to hold. Can't swing a sword if your hand's on fire."

"Can't fling a flame if your hand's lying on the ground at your feet."

"Wow," Zhava laughed, turning to gape at her friend. "That got serious really fast."

Plishka glanced at her and gave a quick wink – no smile, of course – then turned back to stare at the Proving Cove entrance.

Zhava sighed, gripped Plishka's hand and gave a quick squeeze. "You're going to do fine. You probably won't even have to face the bear, because I will kill it before you get in there."

"No one's ever killed this thing. I asked."

"Then it's time I did."

"Ah, there you are!" someone yelled. Zhava and Plishka both turned to look down at the bottom of the stone steps. Barae was there, bouncing and waving her arm through the air. "I'll be right up," she called.

"Time for me to go," Plishka said, and she stretched her legs out before her and shifted against the stones.

"No, stay. Please."

"That girl's already jealous of me."

"I don't know why you say that."

Plishka turned and raised an eyebrow but said nothing.

"Okay, I know why you say that. But...there's nothing to be jealous of. You're my friend. She's my friend."

Plishka snorted at that, shook her head, and stood, shifting her hips and legs as she stretched out the kinks from the cold, hard ground.

"Hey, Plishka," Barae said as she scrambled up the last, tall stone. "I didn't expect to find you here too, but I'm glad I did."

Plishka frowned.

"Io Liori's back early," Barae continued, "and she sent me to find you two. She wants to see you both immediately."

Zhava tensed. This couldn't be good.

They all climbed back down the stone stairs, Barae talking the entire time. Io Liori and several soldiers arrived late in the morning, and she immediately began meeting with various Ios and army commanders. They worked through the midday meal, and then a Candidate runner was sent to find Zhava and Plishka; when he returned unsuccessful, they sent Barae. It sounded like an ominous morning, and Zhava couldn't believe she missed all the activity. They ran along the snaking path through the bare forest, their breaths steaming before them. Only a few, short moons ago, this path had been filled with enemy soldiers, confederates of the evil High Priest Viekoosh, who had lied about her, gotten her arrested and accused of murder, and then turned on their fellow Hibaro soldiers.

They reached the edge of the Hibaro grounds and headed for the Ios' barracks. The Tower that had proudly stood at the center of the Hibaro for generations had been burned beyond repair, and the King's engineers oversaw its demolition just last moon. Io Liori took over two spare rooms in the barracks, converted them into an office, and handled the daily operations of the campus grounds from there. It suited Zhava just fine, as she had never enjoyed climbing the nine flights of stairs to the top of the Tower, but she heard rumors that some of the Ios and army commanders felt Liori's new office failed to convey the "grandeur" of the position of the Hibaro Commandant. Zhava suspected that if that was true, Io Liori was probably doing it on purpose.

The three of them entered the nearly deserted barracks, their winter boots clapping against the hardwood floors down the center hallway. On each side, most of the doors were open to dark, empty rooms with rows of beds and supply chests shoved against the walls. Zhava had been inside the barracks only a couple times, but it had not been this still and quiet. She bit her lip as she glanced nervously at her friends. Barae gave a quick smile but, surprisingly, said nothing. Plishka gave a nearly imperceptible shrug of her shoulders but seemed otherwise unconcerned.

They reached the closed door with the engraved-metal insignia of the Ios attached to the door, and Zhava knocked.

"Enter," Io Liori called.

They opened the door and stepped inside. Unlike the Hibaro's previous Commandant, the treacherous High Priest Viekoosh, Io Liori arranged her office with an eye toward utility, not grandeur. In place of the large, plush chairs of his office, she had a row of five foldaway stools that could be easily set up and removed as the needs of any meeting required. Instead of the wooden shelves lined with expensive books and scrolls, she had a small chest of drawers tucked away in a corner – with one drawer currently open and various maps visible within. And instead of an ostentatious desk that took up nearly half the room, she had set up a field station against the far wall and sat behind a foldaway desk near the window. In fact, the window behind her seemed to be the only real concession she made to aesthetics, as she had angled the desk so she could see outside on her left and toward the door on her right.

"Excellent," she said as she glanced at the three and then back down at the paper she was reading.

Io Kua leaned against the far wall, his arms crossed and a scowl across his face. He gave a quick, curt nod of his head toward Zhava, then continued scowling at Io Liori. He was an intense young man, just a few moons out of his own Io training. An expert fighter and a trained field medic, he was also Zhava's

Mentor, tasked with overseeing her studies of the Kandor as well as testing her on her fighting forms and Gods'-given Abilities. It was he who had set the Proving Cove as Zhava's final test to advance to the rank of Novice.

A soldier also stood in the room, a captain by the rank insignia on his shoulder. He was out of his armor, though, dressed in his tan field shirt and pants with the tight, leather boots. He stood near Io Liori's desk, his hands clasped behind his back as he studied the three women entering the room.

"Barae, leave us," Liori muttered, not looking up from her paper. "Shut the door behind you and report to Sister Tegara."

"Yes, Sir." She didn't even try to hide the disappointment in her voice as she turned and walked out, swinging the door shut with a louder thud than she probably should have. The noise echoed through the small room, and Zhava cringed.

Something flitted at the corner of Zhava's vision, a blur against the wall, and she turned to look. The wall was empty. She glanced around, unsure what had caught her attention, then turned back to the others in the room.

"You two," Liori said, "sit."

They reached back and opened a couple folding chairs, then sat a few steps away from Liori's field desk. Zhava couldn't see the report she was reading, but it certainly had the Io's attention.

Again, something flitted at the edge of Zhava's vision. She held her head still and concentrated on the movement. It was a shimmer, like a heat wave, just at the corner of her eyes and against the far wall, the empty wall to her right. The tight, wooden beams of the wall seemed to bend ever so slightly. She turned to look. It was gone.

"Let's talk," Io Liori said.

Zhava turned back. Liori rested her hands over the paper before her, one finger pointing to the spot where she had been reading.

"Zhava, Io Kua has updated me on your Kandor studies. I'm very pleased."

"Thank you," she said with a nod. The shimmer at the edge of her vision seemed to move, but she tried to ignore it.

"And Plishka, Sister Allenka has reported that your progress is coming along remarkably well, especially considering you did only half the work while your sister was with us."

That was harsh, Zhava thought. Plishka's parents had been killed, and her twin sister had not been recruited by the Hibaro representatives, not even as a Candidate. As an orphan on the streets fending for herself, Plishka's sister, Vinaara, would have starved to death – or worse. They fooled everyone into thinking they were each "Plishka" and took turns living on campus and living in a cave just off the woods. Vinaara had been captured and likely killed by High Priest Viekoosh.

"Your attention to my progress honors me," Plishka said with a bow of her head.

Zhava caught sight of that shimmer again, but this time she did not ignore it. Io Liori began talking about something, but Zhava gave the words only a bit of her attention. She focused on that shimmer, that heat-wave bend of the wooden boards at the side of the room, and she really tried to see it from the edge of her vision. It was tall. It went from the floor up nearly two-thirds the height of the wall. The top of it was narrow and round, like a ball; the middle was thicker; but the bottom half was narrow and straight... shaped like a person. A head, a body, legs. She tried not to look directly at the shimmer. Each time she did that, it disappeared. She couldn't be sure that what she was seeing from the corner of her eye was even real. Was it a ghost? A spirit of a God? What could be so powerful as to hide itself like that, to appear invisible but for a small shimmer just at the edge of her vision.

Io Liori was still talking, glancing back and forth between Zhava and Plishka, and Zhava nodded as though she was listening. Her attention was riveted to that figure against the wall, and that's when it started moving. It was a slight shift, but definitely there. It seemed to turn, to move nearer to the window – and to Io Liori's desk. As it shifted more directly into Zhava's field of vision, it faded, and she had to keep turning her head away to keep the shimmer just at her peripheral.

"Zhava?" Liori said with a tap on the desk.

She jerked in her chair and looked up. "Yes, Sir?"

"Are you listening?"

"Yes, Sir."

"Because it seemed you were paying more attention to Io Kua than you were to me."

Her eyes had been turned to him, but she hadn't been looking at him – she had been looking at the shimmer, which seemed to have disappeared again – but there was no way to explain that to Io Liori. Instead, she ducked her head and apologized. "I'm sorry, Sir. I'll pay better attention."

Io Liori continued.

With her eyes directed toward the floor, Zhava could still see the shimmer. It had moved to stand directly behind Io Liori, and now Zhava began to worry. Whatever this thing was, she had no way of knowing its intention. A God? There were plenty of nice Gods, ones who might protect or help. However, there were just as many mean Gods, ones like the evil Coredor who worked to corrupt people's souls.

Or the shimmer could be some agent of High Priest Viekoosh, someone granted an Ability to blend in with the surroundings. An agent like that, working for the evil High Priest, could cause much damage. And it was standing behind Io Liori. Zhava had to do something.

She turned to Plishka who frowned in annoyance. Whatever Zhava saw, Plishka didn't.

The shimmer stepped closer to Io Liori, just behind her.

Zhava couldn't let this continue. She didn't know if it was an evil agent or a benevolent God, but it was her duty to protect her Io. She thought hard. No one else could see it. No one else would know what she was doing if she suddenly stood up and tried to stop the shimmer.

But one of her best friends, Posef, could help. He had a Gods'-given Ability that was incredibly fun, but it could be ever-so-helpful at a time like this.

She squeezed her eyes shut, tensed, and screamed within her mind, *Posef!* If he was anywhere nearby, anywhere on the Hibaro grounds, he would hear that thought. He would make his mind-connection.

A whisper, a faint but clear whisper, came into Zhava's mind. *That was loud,* Posef said.

Tell Plishka, Zhava thought. *She must protect Io Liori.*

What? came Posef's thought. *Why?*

TELL HER!

His mind-connection snapped away, and Zhava opened her eyes again. That last thought had probably been far too loud, but Zhava needed her friend to listen and obey. She needed him to help, not to question her.

Plishka sucked in a sudden, surprised breath and turned to Zhava, her brows furrowed.

"All right," Io Liori said, sitting back and rapping her fist against the table. "What is wrong with you two? What's going on?"

Zhava gave a quick nod. Plishka nodded back.

Zhava jumped from her chair and flicked a line of flames at the shimmering figure behind the desk. Plishka leaped forward and pulled Io Liori aside, nearly knocking the woman to the floor.

The flames sputtered and died in wisps of smoke in midair, and a tall man in flowing purple and red robes stood before the window.

"Get off of me," Liori snapped, wrenching her arm from Plishka's grip and stumbling back up.

Plishka's hand crackled in bright, blue lightning, and Zhava held a ball of flames in each hand. The man in the robes merely nodded at them and smiled.

"I told you she would see," Liori muttered, sliding her chair back to its place behind the desk.

"Indeed you did," the man said, his deep voice thrumming in the small room.

"You...know him?" Zhava asked. Her flames sputtered a bit between her fingers, and she glanced nervously at Plishka. She was a little disappointed that, though she had shot true, not a single flame landed on the man's robes.

"Plishka and Zhava," Liori said, gesturing to the man behind her. "Meet Ayaan, First of the King's First Salients."

Zhava gasped. This man was not just any Salient, but he was the most powerful Salient in the land, the man known throughout the kingdom as the most ardent observer of the Kandor, a man blessed by the Gods in multiple Abilities, the King's most trusted advisor...and she and Plishka had just attacked him. She clenched her fists and snuffed the flames, then sank to the ground on her knees and bowed her head, Plishka quickly dropping down beside her.

Chapter 2

"Zhava and Plishka," Salient Ayaan rumbled as he strode from behind the desk. "Io Liori told me your tale. Io Kua sings your praises. Sister Tegara commends your dutiful fulfillment of responsibility, and Sister Allenka calls you both...trouble-makers." At that last, he leaned down and spoke directly into Zhava's ear. She shut her eyes, certain that Sister Allenka had called her far worse than that in the past, possibly even to Salient Ayaan.

He gripped Zhava by the chin and yanked her head upright. He cocked his head and stared into her eyes, then frowned. "How do you mask it?"

"We are unsure," Io Liori began, but Salient Ayaan raised a hand to stop her speaking.

"Zhava," he said. "How do you mask it?"

"Sir, I'm sorry, but I do not know what you're looking for." He was a big man, especially towering over her like he was. His black hair was cropped short, and his eyes were a dark, intense brown. "I am not trying to mask anything."

He flicked his wrist to release her, then turned and gripped Plishka's chin. He looked into her eyes and smiled, but it was a dark, ominous smile. This man was scary in his intensity.

"Yes," he rumbled. "I can see it, deep within you. You have potential." He flicked his hand away from Plishka and stood up straight, striding around the room with his hands on his hips and his robes billowing around him. "One who can be read in a moment's time, and the other who masks herself…even from herself. Yet, if all of the stories are even half of the truth, both with such potential. This is a conundrum, is it not?"

Zhava glanced nervously at Plishka, but she was keeping her head bowed and her eyes aimed straight at the floor.

"The King's court has discussed you two. The King himself has been briefed on you two."

Zhava's heart clenched. To be known to the King…that was a little terrifying.

"You uncovered a traitor within our midst, you set the captives free, and you rode into the Hibaro with a winged killer out of legend – the mighty sengret, trained to hunt and to kill, and controlled by the whispered words of a boy barely able to complete his first lessons." The chair behind the desk groaned as the man sat and flicked his robes around his legs. The desk creaked as he leaned forward, and Zhava could feel the man's staring eyes as he looked down upon them kneeling to the floor. "You have both demonstrated your servility long enough. Arise, and sit back upon your chairs."

Zhava gently rose and sat in her chair. Plishka did the same. She licked her lips and fidgeted with her hands. She had been in the presence of many powerful people in just a few short moons, but this man was somehow scarier than them all, both in rank and in raw power. To so effortlessly flick aside her attack – not even High Priest Viekoosh had been able to do that.

"You," he said, pointing to Zhava. "How did you see me?"

"From the corner of my eye," she said, turning her head to the side. "Like this."

He pursed his lips and stared at her, then turned to Plishka. "And you? How did you see me?"

"Sir, I did not."

"And yet you rose to your Io's defense?"

"That was our friend Posef. He has the mind-speak. Zhava told Posef to tell me, and that's why I...did that." She bowed her head as if embarrassed. More likely scared.

Salient Ayaan steepled his fingers and leaned back in the creaking chair. Io Liori stood behind him, silently and with her hands held loosely behind her back. Io Kua was standing straighter now, near the wall, and the soldier in his field outfit and leather boots hadn't moved from his spot beside the chairs, his chest puffed out and his eyes straight ahead. Io Liori was the only one who seemed to have any comfort in the Salient's presence, and even she was tense.

"Yes," Ayaan rumbled, dragging out the word for several moments. "Io Liori, I understand your enthusiasm for this crop of students. There is potential here. Hope."

"Thank you, Salient," she said. The corners of her mouth edged up for just a moment, the Io's emotional equivalent of yelling for joy.

"Initiate Zhava, you are due to enter the Proving Cove," Salient Ayaan said. "You shall do so tomorrow."

Zhava tensed. Io Kua had told her she had several more nights to prepare.

"Upon successful completion of your trial – and the requisite time spent with the healers thereafter – you shall be promoted to Novice as your Mentor, Io Kua, has deemed appropriate."

"Thank you, Sir."

"Ever so polite, yes, to thank me for sending you to the grave. You are dismissed."

Zhava sat there a moment before she realized what had been said, then she nervously glanced up at Io Liori and Io Kua. Liori did not respond, but Io Kua gave her a quick smile and nodded his head toward the door.

"Of course, Salient Ayaan," she said, rising from the chair. "Thank you, Sir."

"Now, Initiate Plishka," the man continued as Zhava opened the office door and stepped out of the room. "We have other plans for you."

The soldier shut the door solidly behind her, and Zhava stood alone in the silence of the dark, empty barracks. The Salient's voice was a dull rumble through the heavy wood, and she could not understand any of the particular words. Something had just happened, she thought, but she wasn't sure exactly what. The King's most trusted advisor, the First of the King's First Salients himself, had left the capitol and travelled to the Hibaro...to do what? To question her and Plishka? To evaluate their potential? To stand invisibly at the side of the room and see if anyone saw him? To hide himself from everyone there?

But wait, she thought. He hadn't hidden himself from everyone in that room. After Plishka tried to shield her, Io Liori said, "I told you she would see." She knew the Salient was there. They planned that meeting, and Io Liori expected Zhava to see the man. She turned back to stare at the shut door. What were they saying in that room? She could easily drop one of her little flames to listen. A flame at the bottom of the door and another perched on her shoulder, and every word spoken within would be relayed back to her. Io Liori knew she could do it. Was this another test? If so, what was the correct response? Was she expected to break the rule and eavesdrop on the conversation, or was she expected to do as she was told and simply walk away?

She slowly, ever-so-slowly, stepped away from the door. She wanted to listen, but she wanted to continue gaining Io Liori's trust. So many at the Hibaro had seen her as a traitor, even after she told her story of freeing the children and fighting off the evil High Priest, but Io Liori – and Io Kua, her wonderful Mentor –supported her, spoke on her behalf to all of the soldiers and their commanders. She had been welcomed back as a hero, a young woman who survived against impossible odds. She would do right by Io Liori.

"Hey," Barae called, running down the barracks hallway.

Zhava strode toward her friend. Their chatter filled the empty rooms and corridors of the barracks as Barae asked question after question about what happened inside that room, and Zhava told the story with as much drama and excitement as she could. The mysterious shimmer at the edge of her vision; the frantic yell to Posef to pass a message to Plishka; the way the tall, powerful man so effortlessly snuffed out Zhava's flames; Io Liori introducing him as Salient Ayaan. Barae loved those details, and it was fun to see her friend get so excited.

But they did not see Plishka the rest of the afternoon. At the evening meal, they met up with Posef and told him the whole tale – with Zhava adding a few more details to make it even more exciting and to watch his beautiful, green eyes light up. It wasn't until much later that night, after Zhava returned to her second-floor room to do her evening studies and to begin preparing for her fight against the bear in the Proving Cove that Plishka showed up again and asked to speak with Zhava – alone.

She shut the door to her room, and the two of them sat on the floor, Zhava against the wall, and Plishka leaning against the small bed. This was so reminiscent of the night Plishka surprised Zhava, threatened to kill her because Plishka's twin sister, Vinaara, had been taken. Stolen away into the night in the giant claws of a bird out of legend – a mighty sengret. Unlike that night, however, when Plishka had been angry and filled with grief, she now seemed excited and eager. Her eyes sparkled, and her mouth was nearly upturned to a smile. She held her body tense, though. Even lounging on the floor, her muscles were taught, and flecks of blue lightning sparkled at the tips of her fingers. Her friend could mask most emotions from her face, but somehow the lightning energy still escaped through her hands.

"They've found her," Plishka said – and that produced a genuine, momentary smile. "She's alive, and they found her."

There was only one "her" who mattered in Plishka's life: her twin sister. "Oh, thank the Gods," Zhava said. She leaped forward and wrapped her arms around Plishka, squeezing hard. "Tell me everything."

The tale wasn't complex. The King's network of spies had been infiltrated by High Priest Viekoosh and his followers. With Salient Kretsch exposed as a traitor and Salient Noomira killed in the fighting at the Hibaro, it had fallen to Salient Ayaan, the only one remaining of the highest order of Salients, to build up a new network of spies and informants. After only a few moons of work, they had not only uncovered details about the underground trade network into which Vinaara had been dropped, but they managed to firmly establish the location of High Priest Viekoosh's camp deep in the Sineise Desert. The followers of the evil God Coredor would be stamped out, the kingdom would once again be safe – and Plishka would accompany Io Liori and a group of soldiers as they ventured into the desert to rescue Vinaara.

"That is incredible news," Zhava said. "When do we leave?"

Plishka's smile vanished, and she glanced at the floor. The blue sparks at her fingertips sputtered away. "You, um...won't be coming along. I'm sorry."

Zhava sat beside her friend, too stunned to reply.

"Salient Ayaan's orders," Plishka continued. "I'm to go, but not you. This will be my advancement test, instead of the Proving Cove. I'm to assist in the rescue of my sister, and then I will be promoted to Novice."

The arguments swirled in Zhava's mind. Vinaara was her friend too, a friend who had been nice to her even before Plishka. It was her fault Vinaara had even been taken by the sengret that night in the woods. She owed it to Vinaara to be there; she owed it to Plishka to help; she had promised Plishka she would do whatever she could to bring back Vinaara. Plus, she and Plishka were the best fighters of any of the Hibaro's Initiates – togcther, they were a powerful force. They had worked together to free those children in the mountains, they had become sparring partners immediately upon returning to the Hibaro, and they had pushed each other harder even than their teachers had pushed. They had learned to combine their skills with the blades and their Gods'-given Abilities – together, they could help in ways that neither was capable of even imagining when working alone.

"I'm all right with this decision," Plishka quietly said. She gripped Zhava's hand. "Io Liori is a brilliant leader. She'll see this through."

"Oh, yes, you're right," Zhava muttered. "Being a part of a mission with her...that's fantastic."

"You're jealous," Plishka said with a chuckle.

"Yes." Zhava nodded, though she didn't mean it. Jealousy was an easier answer than the truth, which was so complicated she wasn't even sure she understood it. She had promised to help, and she wanted to be with her friend, and she believed they were more powerful fighters when they were side by side, and Vinaara was important to her too.... But how could she say all of that?

"Let's go," Plishka said, standing.

"No, I can't go anywhere tonight. I have the Proving Cove at dawn." And apparently nothing else, she thought.

"That's perfect. Get your sparring rods. Loosen you up before your showdown."

Zhava wasn't sure she was in the mood for sparring, but she wouldn't turn down her friend's request. She retrieved her sparring rods from the weapons cabinet in the corner, and Plishka stood by the door, her own rods already in hand. Had she brought them along just for this, to soothe the sting of Zhava being excluded from the mission? That would be very much like Plishka. She might not know what to say, but a good fight could always clear away any unwanted feelings.

They quietly left the room and turned right, stepped lightly down the narrow staircase to the ground floor, and headed down the hallway toward the center of the building. They passed several open doors, and a general buzz of excitement began following them as the other Initiates caught sight of the two women carrying their sparring rods. By the time they reached the heavy, wooden front door, several young women followed close behind, and the news was already making its way down the men's side of the Initiate House.

The evening air was damp and chilled. They could just see their breaths as the last rays of sunset streaked through the bare trees and cast the open ground in bright and dark stripes. Plishka tossed aside her beautiful, bear skin coat, then stretched her neck and arms, casually flipping the sparring rods between her fingers. Zhava stepped across the hard-packed ground and dripped little flaming men from her fingertips as she paced out a large ring of fire. By the time she closed the flaming circle, more than half the Initiates stood in the evening chill, eagerly chattering with each other and watching her and Plishka.

"No Abilities," Plishka called out.

"Where's the fun in that?" Zhava returned with a grin.

"The fun is in the control." Her eyes narrowed, and her jaw went tense.

They paced, Plishka pretending to study the ground before her as she walked, but Zhava knew that was part of Plishka's act, pretending to look somewhere else when she was focused on the match. In a straight weapons fight, Plishka was a tough opponent. Zhava was likely to lose this, but she didn't care. Let

Plishka have her win before she headed out on a dangerous mission.

Zhava stopped walking, turned and faced Plishka, who also stopped and mirrored Zhava's stance. They flicked their wrists, and the short rods released their extensions in several sharp snicks. Within moments, each woman stood with a fully-extended, three-band sparring rod in each hand, the rods taught and pointed at the ground. They stood like that for a moment, smiling at each other and waiting for someone to make the first move. Zhava noticed Sister Tegara just outside the ring, her arms crossed over her long, buckskin coat, shaking her head at the two girls. She wouldn't stop this, of course, but she would be right here to use her healing Abilities on whichever of them might get injured. Even playtime could get rough.

Plishka used the distraction to attack, one rod swinging wide.

Zhava easily brushed it aside – CRACK – and smiled as she sidestepped around the ring.

"Pay attention," Plishka said. She casually sliced one sparring rod through the air before her. The wind whistled with each stroke, a too-familiar sound from hundreds of hours of practice.

Zhava lunged, and Plishka parried.

Crack-crack-crack.

The other Initiates murmured their excitement.

"Tell me again how you bring down the bear," Plishka said. She rolled her shoulders and head, loosening muscles and joints.

"A few well-placed shots of flames," Zhava said, watching for any sign of attack, "a little windstorm, and then I'll just let the ground swallow it up."

"Not a good strategy." She swung low.

Zhava jumped and swung high.

Plishka darted aside.

"Not enough swordplay?" Zhava asked.

"Not enough of a plan." She stepped in and swung low.

Zhava met the advance and countered, then aimed for her friend's arm.

Crack! Crack-crack-crack.

Plishka backed away. "And, no, not enough swordplay."

"What would you do differently?"

"More of this." Plishka danced in – crack – went for the legs – crack-crack – then swung wide for the arm-

Zhava yelped and spun away, her hand gripping the stinging arm.

Plishka pressed the advantage, and Zhava backed again. She blocked with her left, lunged with her right, then changed it up. A feint with the right, a quick swing with the left – she connected on Plishka's thigh.

After that, their sparring rods became a blur of swishing black against the dusk sky. Plishka advanced steadily, but Zhava let her in, pressed her back, then let her in again. The rods cracked and sung and slapped as they connected against each other and – rarely – against their opponents.

The cheers of the Initiates became a wave of deafening yells that mixed with the song of the match and the sweat flying from the women's faces and arms. They shuffled through the dirt, leaped into the air, rolled across the ground, and spun in flourishing pirouettes just for the simple joy of the chance to make their audience gasp.

And as quickly as it had begun, the sparring dance wound down, and Zhava and Plishka – both breathing hard and shaking loose their tingling arms – stepped away from each other. Zhava's grin was wide; she loved this, and she wanted her friend to know it. Plishka gave a slight bow of her head, snicked her sparring rods closed, slid them back into their sheaths, and stepped lightly forward. She grasped Zhava's hand and pulled her in close, her other arm wrapped across Zhava's back.

"May you succeed in the Proving Cove," Plishka whispered through Zhava's damp hair.

"Go and find your sister," Zhava whispered back, shutting her eyes and squeezing hard.

"With Io Liori leading the way, we will find my born-sister," Plishka said. Then she pushed away ever-so-slightly. Their breaths came out steaming between them, and Plishka looked Zhava in the eyes. "But know this before I leave: You are my fighting sister."

Zhava's smile spread even wider, and she gave Plishka one last firm hug. "I'll see you soon. Be safe."

"Always," Plishka whispered.

They stepped apart, gave each other the proper ceremonial bows to conclude the match, and turned and faced away from each other. Zhava walked, never looking back. To look back, to take that one last glance at her friend – at her fighting sister! – would have only invited the ill temper of the Gods, and Zhava knew that the Gods' favor would be needed if they were to reunite Plishka with her twin sister. She whispered a quick prayer to her patron Goddess, Preizhavan, to bless that journey.

Chapter 3

The Initiate House was loud, and Zhava found it hard to break though the press of her fellow students in the cramped, narrow hallways. She wanted to return to her room, to sit in the peace and stillness and dwell in the memory of that sweet embrace with her fighting sister, Plishka. To reconnect all the points of the match, to reflect on the joy of the competitive dance, the power and thrill of the sparring rods arcing through the air and cracking against each other.

Instead, her friends cheered her, slapped her on the back and shoulders, babbled loud questions at her more quickly than she could reply, and tried to press her into the commons room at the center of the Initiate House. She did not want to go, but then Barae stood at her side, gripped her by the hand, and pulled her along with the crowd.

"That was your best match," she yelled over the excited crowd. "I knew you improved since I watched you last, but I didn't realize you had gotten that good so quickly. Plishka could barely keep up."

Actually, Zhava thought, Plishka had seemed more to be keeping a rhythm with Zhava than trying to beat her. Less a contest of strikes and points, and more a chance to practice their skills. But there would be no saying that to Barae.

Another hand gripped Zhava and pulled her away, out of Barae's grasp and to the side of the hallway. Several Initiates streamed past, but no one got between Zhava and the woman who pulled her aside, Sister Tegara. The head of the Initiate House, the woman charged with keeping the Initiates safe and disciplined and focused on their studies – and she did not look pleased as she pulled Zhava into a small room and shut the door. The din of the hallway lessened, and Zhava's eyes had trouble adjusting to the dim light of the single lantern burning on the wall. Sister Tegara stood before the door and crossed her arms, her eyes hard and her mouth pressed tight.

Zhava bowed her head and folded her hands before her.

"Sit down," Tegara said.

Zhava glanced behind, then sat on the lone chair in the center of the room. Shelves of linens and glass bottles lined three of the walls, and rows of implements – needles, grabbing tongs, tiny blades – were arranged neatly on the far counter. This was Sister Tegara's mending room. She used it mostly for the difficult healings, those that required something more to supplement her Abilities, and Zhava thought this might be a bit extreme for a simple sparring match. But she wouldn't say that to Sister Tegara. She kept her mouth shut.

"You know I love you," Tegara murmured. "I love all of my Initiates, and I try to keep you safe." She tossed a metal hook across the counter, and it clanged against the back wall.

Zhava flinched.

"Io Kua is sending you into the Proving Cove first thing tomorrow – your second time inside the Cove, and this is how you prepare? By pushing yourself against the best fighter in your class?" She lit the two remaining oil lamps, one on each wall to Zhava's left and right, and rummaged through the storage bins. "You saw me before the match began. Yes?"

"Yes, Sister."

"And yet you ignored me. You knew I was displeased. Yes?"

"Yes, Sister."

"You knew that Initiate Plishka would strike you – several times. You knew the match would make you sore."

"Really, Sister, I'm feeling – ow!"

Sister Tegara had wrapped a hand around Zhava's wrist and squeezed. At the yelp of pain, Tegara stood back and smirked. "Yes, you're feeling fine. You're not that hurt. I'm glad to hear it. Remove your shirt and pants." She dragged a three-legged, wooden stool with a scrape across the floor, then sat beside and a little above Zhava. Once Zhava had removed her shirt and pants, Tegara took the wrist, more gently this time, and slowly rotated it in her hands.

Zhava flinched.

"I suppose you expect me to use my Abilities on this."

"No, Ma'am," Zhava said – though she really hoped Sister Tegara would do that.

"Good. I have no intention of encouraging this kind of fool-ishness." She rubbed something sticky across Zhava's wrist, then reached back and pulled a bundle of cloth off the counter. She set one end of the cloth into the stickiness at Zhava's wrist, then slowly wrapped the strip around several times before fastening it with a small, sharp pin.

She pressed into Zhava's arms, shoulders, neck, and back, finding the sore spots and either wrapping them or spreading a soothing jelly across them. Zhava had two bloody strips across her upper left arm where Plishka's sparring rod broke the skin. Sister Tegara glared and tutted at Zhava, then cleaned the wounds and pressed more bandages against them. The longer Tegara administered the healing bandages and ointments, the more painful it became for Zhava to sit. Her muscles ached, and the injuries to her arm and leg, though not severe, stung more than she cared to admit.

"Wouldn't it be easier-"

"No," Tegara snapped. "It would not. Now get dressed." She set the remaining strips of cloth back on the counter and sealed the jars of ointments and salves she had been mixing across Zhava's skin, then sat back and waited. When Zhava was dressed, Tegara sighed, leaned forward, and took Zhava's hand in her own. "Your friends, your 'Little Soldiers,' they would do anything for you."

Zhava wanted to argue. Her friends were wonderful, and she relished having so many — Plishka and Barae and Posef, plus all of the younger ones who had been rescued from the mountain. Weclin, Aaria, Sanama, the ones who dubbed themselves "Zhava's Little Soldiers"...all of them who followed her, talked with her whenever they saw her doing duties or going to her strength and stamina training, or her weapons training. What Sister Tegara said, it only seemed to someone at a distance that her friends would "do anything" for her, but she knew that was not true. They enjoyed being with her, and that was all it meant.

"Plishka is going away with Io Liori in the morning, and she knew you would be sad. She is not...the most skilled young woman when it comes to navigating people's feelings. She approaches problems as something to be beaten, something to be struck with either her sword or her lightning, and so she dealt with your sadness in the best way she knew how."

"By beating me?" Zhava smiled, but Tegara remained serious.

"Did she beat you?"

"Of course." She shrugged, and her shoulders only slightly ached from the gesture. "She always beats me."

"Then you must have been the only person not keeping score during that match."

Zhava looked into Tegara's dark eyes, but the woman was so serious that Zhava immediately looked away again. She was supposed to learn something from this conversation, she was certain of it, but she was having trouble understanding exactly what Tegara was trying to make her understand.

"Zhava, you won," Tegara whispered. "Decisively. I mended three cuts on you, one to that arm, and two on your right leg.

Plishka left that fire ring with at least eight cuts to her arms and another four to her legs."

"But...why would she let me win?"

Sister Tegara sighed and looked down at the floor. She sat back and rubbed her hands against a cloth in her lap, then tossed the cloth onto a pile of dirty rags in the corner.

"Go to your room," she said. "I will tell your friends that you are meditating for your time in the Proving Cove."

"Yes, Sister." She stood. The cuts on her arm and leg stung, and the skin at her wrists, shoulders, and back felt as if it was being stretched tight from the dried ointments and salves that Sister Tegara administered. As she left the little room, the yelling and laughter echoed down the hallway from the Initiate House Commons Room at the center of the building. Her own name was spoken many times as people recounted the sparring match, loudly retelling particular strikes or flourishes or even the little comments she and Plishka had made to each other. It was a fun match, but she didn't think it was worth that much excitement and laughter.

She reached the end of the hallway and climbed the dark, narrow steps to the second floor and to her room on the left. She slipped the bolt, entered the dark room, and locked the door behind her. With a casual flick of her fingers, she let loose a tiny, flaming man on the dresser against the wall. He leaped and danced his way across the polished surface, then jumped and landed on the wick of the oil lamp. With a spark and a smoky sputter, the wick caught, and the room brightened to a pleasant, flickering glow.

She gently replaced the sparring rods in the leather pouch she had strung from a bolt in the wall, then ran her fingers down the oiled sheath hanging next to it, the one that contained her Felton sword. A gift from her Mentor, Io Kua. The few moments it wasn't slung about her hips, it hung here, in her room where she could see it as she studied or rested. It was a simple sword, nothing fancy. About two hands in length, plus the hilt, it was one of the shorter swords on the market. But it was her sword – her very first sword – and she loved it.

Slowly, and with a few winces of pain, she stripped out of the damp clothes she had worn for the sparring match, tossed them in the corner where a pile of other dirty clothes lay in a tumble, and wrapped herself in a loose, woven robe. Sister Tegara had offered to lie for her, to tell her friends she was meditating before her return to the Proving Cove, but it would not be a lie if she actually did the meditating. She knelt to the floor and crossed her legs, gently rested her hands upon her knees, and shut her eyes. She ignored the tingling at her wrists and shoulders, the tight skin beneath the bandages.

Io Kua had taught her several new meditation techniques, but she found the one Priestess Marmaran taught her more than two seasons ago to still be the most effective at focusing her thoughts and putting her in touch with the spirits around her, sometimes even with the Gods themselves. The Kandor, Priestess Marmaran taught, was the beginning of all wisdom, and because of that, it was the perfect place to begin any evening meditation. She took in a deep breath, focused on the darkness behind her closed lids, and tried to still her aching muscles.

"The beginnings of all life prepared the ways to the ends," she whispered. The wick on the oil lamp sputtered, and she smiled. A stray mote of dust that crackled in the night, or perhaps one of the Gods already pleased with her devotion – it mattered so little because it was inspiring either way. "The ends of all life have paved the ways to their new beginnings. And the pathways through this life mark the passageways upon which we shall travel in the next. Kandor 23." Her favorite passage in all of the Kandor poetics.

She took another deep breath, then repeated the Kandor in her mind, focusing within herself. She let her mind wander through that Kandor, as Priestess Marmaran had taught, silently forming with her mouth into whichever of the individual words seemed to drift through and in whatever order seemed the most natural at this moment in time.

The flickering lamplight slowly ebbed away, but only within herself, because that was the part of her that was beginning to leave this room, the part of her that was drifting upon the meditations of the Kandor. She set herself loose upon the spiritual plain and allowed the winds of the Kandor to guide her, to pull her where they would. As her world ebbed to black, she also heard the distant sound of an animal crying...or yelling. It was faint on the whispers of the spirit, but it was there, and she felt herself drawn to it. She felt it was calling to her, that it echoed something deep within herself, and she had to know it. She had to find it.

Her head struck something so hard that spots danced before her eyes. She rubbed at her forehead with one hand as she tentatively reached out with the other. She touched something solid, cold in the darkness of this spiritual journey. That was unusual. She had meditated on the Kandor many times, but she had never before encountered a solid wall...except for that one other time.

She sucked in an excited breath, and all thoughts of the pain disappeared. She reached forward with both hands and felt against the cold wall before her, frantically searching the darkness for any glow of light.

"Priestess Marmaran," she called. She banged with her fists against the wall – a wall made of glass, if she was correct. A prison wall for her beloved teacher. "Priestess, please. Are you there? Can you hear me?"

A flickering glow sputtered to life on the other side of the wall – and Zhava grinned and pressed her face to the glass.

"Marmaran, I'm here," she called. She slapped the glass with her palm, the sharp sound echoing through the darkness. It had been more than four moons since she last communed with her teacher – the imprisoned spirit of her dead teacher – and she was so excited. Marmaran returned on the eve of the Proving Cove. Zhava couldn't wait to tell her about it.

The flickering glow grew brighter, than vanished as if snuffed out.

"No! Priestess Marmaran, I'm here. Come back."

A sudden, blinding light burst against the wall, and all went black again. Zhava stumbled away from the glass and rubbed at her aching eyes. The light had left the sudden imprint of a woman's form, but the brilliant flash blinded her.

"Priestess Marmaran, it's me – Zhava." She staggered forward, feeling ahead of her in the dark until her hands bumped against the wall. She carefully knelt forward.

Another flash from beyond the wall, this one a swirling ball of flames that stretched high into the blackness above her. The woman on the other side of the wall stood with her face pressed tight, her cheek and palms flattened against the glass, and her eye wildly flicking across Zhava.

The flames sputtered away, and they were left in darkness again.

"Marmaran?" Zhava said, leaning forward. The woman on the other side of the glass had been old, like her teacher, but she had never seen Priestess Marmaran look so...wild. So dangerous.

"Child!" the old woman screamed, and stars exploded from around the woman's body, flashing and jumping and flying and dancing through the darkness.

Zhava shielded her eyes from the pulsing lights, and she barely made out of the face of her beloved teacher, Priestess Marmaran. But so much had changed. Her eyes were large and strained against the glass. The fingers and palms of the hands pressed tight to the wall were cut and scarred. More scars criss-crossed her cheek and neck, and a thin line of blood was streaked across her forehead. Her mouth was twisted down, as if in despair, and tears were pouring from her eyes and smearing the glass wall as she slowly sank to the ground.

Just as suddenly as they had begun, the stars ceased, and the dark poured in on them again.

"Oh, Marmaran, what has happened?" Zhava whispered, leaning close to the wall. She rubbed her hands across the surface, and she felt long, thin cuts in the glass.

"Show me," Marmaran whispered back. "Show me the truth of you."

With a nudge of her will, Zhava made a dozen flames flicker to life in her palms. Their gentle, orange glow lit the glass wall and Priestess Marmaran's face and hands just on the other side.

The elderly woman took in a long, wheezing breath as she stared wide-eyed at the dancing men of flames in Zhava's hands. In this light, the scars across her face, hands and arms were even more pronounced, and the clothes were revealed to be nothing more than strips of torn rags hanging loose about her body. Marmaran shut her eyes, and her body relaxed.

"What happened?" Zhava asked.

"Child, tell me," Marmaran whispered, barely a raspy breath through the glass.

"Priestess, you've been gone so long, and now to suddenly appear again. What has changed? Why did you return?"

"You were always a good child, always so eager to learn. Tell me how."

"I don't know what to tell you." She pressed her own face against the cold, cracked glass. What did she want to hear? What would comfort her? Tales of her training? "I'm to return to the Proving Cove tomorrow. I'm to face the bear again, and this time I will succeed."

"No. You didn't?"

What did that mean? Should she not return to the Proving Cove?

"This is not your doing? But...it cannot be." Priestess Marmaran struggled to stand, her eyes wide and flicking back and forth.

"It is fine. I have faced the bear before. I know what I'm doing."

"No, it – not here. Why am I here?" Lightning flashed on Marmaran's side of the glass. It arced through the air and around her body and down upon the ground at her feet as she darted her head back and forth. Marmaran seemed to be looking for something just beyond Zhava – beyond the spirit world.

Zhava turned, but all she saw was the black of this vision world, the same darkness that had enveloped her since she arrived. What did Marmaran see?

"Child, you must stay away."

"What?"

"Stay away!" She flung her hands out to her sides as the lightning cast blinding sparks all around her – and in that brief instant, Zhava caught sight of a reflection in the glass. Something could be seen against the darkness behind her, a long, rectangular structure. A building with...two rows of windows...a building in the moonlit darkness, with trees all around...and a couple soldiers walking past.

"The Initiate House," Zhava realized.

Priestess Marmaran clapped her hands together, and a crack of shattering glass sounded through the darkness. The force of it shoved Zhava away, and she hurtled through the black, screaming from the pain and the sudden jolt-

-and she slid across the floor of her room and crashed into the wall, her head thudding painfully. Spots floated before her eyes, and she nearly fell over trying to pull in a breath. The back of her head throbbed. She braced herself against the end of her wooden bed frame and staggered up. She ignored the spinning of the room and stumbled to the window, flicked the lock on the shutters, and flung them open wide. She stared into the darkness beyond, scanning as best she could into the treeline.

Priestess Marmaran was out there. The bottle in which her spirit had been captured – out there, just in those trees. Zhava saw the reflection of the Initiate House in that glass prison; she saw the reflection of her own window.

She reached behind and yanked on her doe-skin coat and fur-lined boots, pulled the Felton sword from its scabbard, and vaulted over the window ledge and into the dark, cold night, ignoring the sharp sting of the pulling bandages as she bent her legs and absorbed the fall. She pulled a dozen flaming men into the palm of her left hand and sprinted across the open yard. If her Priestess was out there, she would find her. Her teacher had been captured more than four moons ago, and it was her duty to find her, to free her from that captivity.

She stopped and turned, looked back at the Initiate House. The angle was almost right, but the distance...she was still too near the building. She ran toward the trees.

Several men began shouting – soldiers to her right and left. She didn't care how many soldiers followed her, as long as she caught up with the man who had captured Priestess Marmaran's spirit – as long as they caught High Priest Viekoosh.

She reached the perimeter trail that marked the edge of the Hibaro grounds and into the bare woods beyond. She raised her left hand high and cast the light of her flames deep within the treeline. Nobody there.

"Where are you?" she muttered. She scanned the ground for footprints. She looked around the trees and farther back into the woods. She cursed, then turned around again and looked at the Initiate House. This seemed the right distance...but was it the right angle? The vision had already begun to fade, and she couldn't reconcile what she had seen with what she now saw.

Three soldiers, one with a torch and the other two with their swords drawn by their sides, ran up to her.

"Identify yourself," one of them barked.

"That's Initiate Zhava," another soldier said. "Just look at the flames in her hand."

"Someone was out here," Zhava said, turning back to the woods and darting between the trees. "I saw him...from my room." Wouldn't be good to discuss her vision – most people feared the spirits of the dead.

The soldier with the torch drew his sword also, and the three men slowly entered the forest. Zhava glanced around, at the ground and then between the trees, then back to the Initiate House as she tried to remember exactly the angle of the reflection. She turned back around – and stared at the ground. A small, square package wrapped in a sackcloth sat propped against the roots of that tree. The word "Zhava" was scrolled across the cloth in dark, running ink.

One of the soldiers approached and stood at her side as the other two continued deeper into the woods.

Zhava tucked her sword into the belt of her robe, and shut her jacket against the chill. She reached down and carefully unfolded the cloth from around the square box. The little container was made of carved, polished wood, and the top fit snuggly against the bottom. She pulled off the lid and looked inside. A single flower, a yellow, desert rose, lay inside. She plucked it from the box, then froze as she saw the word carved deep within the wood of the box: "Wife."

Chapter 4

The shock of finding that little gift – proudly proclaiming Zhava to be "wife" – made her world come to a halt. She expected High Priest Viekoosh and his confederates hiding in the woods. The last time she saw him, he carried the prison bottle that contained Priestess Marmaran's spirit. Who else would be carrying it now? He had a small group of loyal soldiers around him, and he was trading slaves for sengret eggs, building an army of the giant birds to cause who-knew-how-much damage to the kingdom.

But Ooleng...her betrothed. He had begun bartering with Papa for her hand in marriage when the Ios showed up and took her to the Hibaro. It was Ooleng and his family who supplied Viekoosh with the sengret eggs, they who pledged half a dozen eggs just to see Zhava returned as Ooleng's bride. Instead, Zhava and Plishka escaped. Freed the slave children and made off with three of Ooleng's wagons, half a dozen of his horses, and even one of the full-grown sengret. Ooleng himself, however.... She left him lying in a cold pool in a dark cave tunnel, blood running from a gash on his head and hundreds of her little flames lining the tunnel to keep him captive for several nights as she and Plishka made their escape. She thought herself so clever at the time, injuring and imprisoning the man who thought he could buy her.

But now, holding this little box with the word "Wife" carved into its base, she knew she only put him off for a time. She was not rid of him, and he had returned – sought her out at the very place she thought herself free of him forever.

She had no idea how long she stood there in the dark of the forest and staring into that box, but when the soldier beside her took it from her hand, she looked around to see a dozen more soldiers fanning out through the woods. They held their lanterns and torches high, their swords at their sides.

"If they're still out here, we'll find them," the soldier said. "Now you get back to your room."

Zhava didn't even argue. The night was cold against her bare legs, and the bandages Sister Tegara had applied were itching and stretched tight. She snuffed the flames in her hand, turned, and walked back to the Initiate House. A few people were still in the Commons Room, and they greeted her as she walked by, but she ignored them all. She found herself some time later standing in the center of her own room, her coat and boots still on and the shutters open wide, still dreading the face of Ooleng before her.

The last time she saw him, he was dressed in fine robes, and his hair was tied in a topknot. That hair had flown loose as she kicked his legs out from beneath him. That hair had become soaked in blood where he struck the cave floor. That hair floated around him just beneath the surface of the frigid water in which he lay. He had survived the attack. She left him there, assuming she would never see him again. But here he was now. At the Hibaro. Still claiming her as his own.

"No," she whispered into the stillness of her room. That would never happen. She would fight. She had her friends who loved her. The Ios and soldiers who would protect her – who would fight at her side. This man from the Purneese Mountains who had bargained – unsuccessfully! – with Papa for her hand in marriage would not frighten her.

She hung her winter coat on the peg on the wall, kicked her boots into the corner, and gently slid the Felton sword back into its scabbard. She shut and secured the window shutters, bolted the door. She left on the cloth robe and then wrapped herself in a thick blanket. Then she went back to the wall, retrieved the sword, and slid it between the slats of the bed post – just in case. She curled on the bed, the heavy blanket bunched around her and the robe a soft comfort against her skin, and stared at the tiny flame in the lantern on the desk. It was a terrible waste of oil to let that burn all night, but it made her feel better to watch the flame flicker and jump. To know she could see all around her small room. She reached beneath the blanket and set one hand against the hilt of the sword. That felt good too.

The next morning she was awakened by a pounding on her door and an excited voice babbling at her from the hallway. Barae.

Zhava was hot and drenched in sweat, and she shoved off the blanket and rolled out of bed. The robe stunk of dirt, sweat, and several of those salves Sister Tegara had rubbed on her skin. She tossed it in the corner with the rest of her dirty clothes, then rummaged through the baskets beneath the table until she found the dark pants and shirt she wanted to wear to the Proving Cove. Barae banged on the door again.

"Let me in," she called.

Zhava fumbled with the bolt until it released, and swung the door wide.

"Did you hear what happened last night?" Barae said. She rushed into the room and plopped on Zhava's bed. "The soldiers were searching the woods for half the night. Some people were out there, who knows how long watching the Hibaro, and they were trying to sneak onto the grounds and – how exciting! – trying to get to our own Initiate House!"

"Yes." Zhava got far too much enjoyment out of replying to Barae with as few words as possible. She ran a comb through her short hair. Not that it was long enough to get tangled – no one on the Hibaro grounds was allowed long hair – but it still felt good to keep good habits.

"You knew about them? How?" She turned and gaped at Zhava. "You were out there, weren't you? What happened? Did you see them? Did you chase them? How many were there? What were they trying to do?"

"Yes," she replied, tossing the comb back on the table.

"Yes?" Barae slapped a hand against the blanket. "Yes what?"

"I was out there, but only for a while. Now I have to get ready for the Proving Cove."

"No, you can't do that. You have to tell me what happened. You have to give me details. Why were you out there? Why were you helping the soldiers?"

"The soldiers were helping me, but now I really do have to focus on the Proving Cove."

"You're going to do great in the Proving Cove. You are the best fighter in the Initiate House – you'll kill that beast so we never have to fight it again ever."

"Like five moons ago, when you and Sister Tegara had to rescue me?" She cinched her belt at the waist, and pulled half a dozen throwing knives from the basket in the corner.

"What are you talking about?" Barae said. "I have never been in the Proving Cove. Not once. Sister Tegara said if I keep up my studies I might be ready by next moon, and then I could finally get promoted to Novice. Two whole seasons as an Initiate; I am really ready to do something else."

Zhava fussed with the belt's buckle, trying to get the fit just right, and turned to stare at Barae. "No, I wasn't talking about your own test. I was talking about when you and Sister Tegara had to come into the Proving Cove and rescue me. Right after I got here. Remember?"

Barae shook her head.

"What?" Zhava said with a chuckle. She stood straight and turned to her friend. "Io Kua was mad at me for requesting him as my Mentor."

She nodded.

"We sparred, and then he sent me into the Proving Cove to fight the bear."

Another nod from Barae.

"The thing nearly killed me, but Sister Tegara – and you – came into the Proving Cove and pulled me out."

"Hah! That wasn't me."

Zhava stared at her friend. She knew it was Barae who helped pull her from the cave. She had seen both Sister Tegara and Barae, right before she passed out, and Barae even talked about helping Tegara. Zhava nodded and said, "Yes, Barae, it was you. You and Sister Tegara."

"I don't know what you're talking about, but it's not funny. I have never been in there."

A knock at the open door. They both turned to see Io Liori standing in the hallway, her black and red riding clothes tight and polished clean, her sword at her hip, and a heavy coat folded over one arm.

Barae jumped up from the bed and stood with her hands folded before her.

Zhava stood a little straighter and tried to tuck in her shirt without being too obvious about it.

"Girls," Liori said stepping into the room, "this is a social call."

"Oh, thank you, Io Liori," Barae said, visibly relaxing her stance and smiling widely. "Could you tell us what happened in the woods last night?"

Liori turned, stared at her for several moments, and said, "Actually, I would like to speak with Initiate Zhava alone. Please leave."

Barae put her head down and darted from the room with a hurried, "Yes, ma'am."

Liori reached back and gently shut the door behind her.

"Am I in trouble?" Zhava asked.

"For what?" Liori hung her coat on the empty hook next to Zhava's, then turned and glanced around the small room.

"For last night. For running into the woods with the soldiers."

Liori shrugged. "I probably would have done the same at your age if I'd seen someone in the woods." She stepped forward, around Zhava and to the locked shutters. She flicked the bolt and pushed them wide, leaned out the open windows. "Beautiful view."

"Thank you." Zhava didn't know what else to say. Io Liori had never been in her room – she had hardly ever spoken casually with Zhava, so this...conversation?...was a little uncomfortable.

"I loved this view," Liori muttered.

"Ma'am?"

"This view." She glanced at Zhava and flicked a hand to the outside world. "Of course, the Tower made it far more impressive to sit and look out this window when I was an Initiate living in this very room."

"You lived here?" She edged up to Liori. In the many moons since first meeting this Io, Zhava had learned almost nothing about the woman. She was the best fighter in the kingdom – First of the King's Third Salients – and she had led many successful campaigns both within and around the kingdom. Her duties under High Priest Viekoosh had been primarily focused on patrolling the borders and overseeing the training regimens of the older Hibaro students. And that was nearly the sum total of what Zhava knew about Io Liori. To discover now, after all this time, that Liori once lived in this very room...that was a revelation. She leaned out the window beside Liori and looked at the Hibaro from a slightly different perspective...from this Io's perspective. "I never knew that."

"Which is why I also know you lied when you said you saw that man in the woods." Liori pointed into the distance, toward the treeline far away and along the patrol trail. "I would not have been able to see that far, especially at night. You did not see that far last night."

Zhava tensed. Not such a casual conversation after all.

"I leave with Plishka and a group of soldiers and Ios very soon," Liori said. "I want the truth. Now."

Zhava ducked her head. "Yes, Ma'am," she said, and then launched into the story. About the sparring match with Plishka; Sister Tegara tending to Zhava's wounds and then telling the others in the Commons Room that Zhava was meditating; how Zhava went to her room and began meditating so that no lie had actually been told; about...as difficult as this was to reveal to Io Liori...communing with the spirit of her dead teacher, Priestess Marmaran, and about the many times before that the Priestess had appeared in Zhava's dreams to warn her of danger or to give her instruction; then how Zhava jumped from her window and ran to the woods; how the soldiers followed her out there, and they all found the little box; and finally, how she left the box in the care of those very soldiers.

When Zhava finished the telling, Io Liori sighed and continued staring outside and across the Hibaro grounds. Zhava shifted nervously and glanced aside to see Liori bow her head and shut her eyes. Was she in trouble for leaving the Initiate House? She would certainly be in trouble for jumping out her window, even though that was the quickest way to get to the man in the woods. Were the soldiers mad at her? Io Liori was probably the most secretive person she had ever met, able to hide emotions behind a stony face. Yet...that face seemed a bit sad at the moment.

"I never had the privilege of being tutored by Priestess Marmaran," Liori said. "What was she like?"

"She was wonderful," Zhava said with a smile. This was a topic she would gladly discuss. "She helped me understand my Abilities. She showed me how to use them."

"Your Mama and your Papa, were they not blessed by the Gods?"

"No, Io. They were not."

"Your brothers?"

"No."

"That must have been hard for you when your Abilities manifested, not knowing what they were, what was going on within your own body."

"It was not. Priestess Marmaran arrived just as I was beginning to sense them. She arrived at our door one night, and she became a part of the family."

"Your...eleventh season?"

Zhava nodded. No one in the family had known to call Marmaran a "Priestess" back then. She was an old, traveling widow with dwindling sight who showed up on their doorstep, and then she offered to teach Zhava in exchange for food and lodging. The lessons included reading and writing in two languages, reciting the lessons of the Kandor, and understanding and harnessing her Abilities – well, one Ability. Zhava's manipulation of the earth. She kept her Ability with the flaming men a secret from Marmaran, and she had never even manifested an Ability with wind until she arrived at the Hibaro. Marmaran could see it all now, of course, now that she was a spirit...except she was a spirit trapped within a glass cage.

"When we were on the road and Priestess Marmaran died," Liori whispered. "Did she tell you what would happen when you collected her bones? Did you know you were binding her spirit to this world?"

"No." She had been told the words to say, but Marmaran never explained the meaning of those words. And if Zhava was being truthful with herself, if she had known then what she knew now about Marmaran's spirit remaining behind...she would have said those words anyway. It hurt her every day to be apart from her wonderful Marmaran, her beloved teacher, the only member of her family who had truly shown her love and acceptance. To have her bound to this world, to have her appear before Zhava and talk with her and give her instructions. That gave life meaning.

Io Liori reached over and gripped Zhava's hand. Zhava jerked a bit at the contact. For all of Liori's fighting skills, she was not one to just reach out and touch anyone. She gave Zhava's hand a quick squeeze.

"I said some awful things to you after Priestess Marmaran died. I regret that."

"Um...thank you." Was that the correct response? She couldn't remember Io Liori ever apologizing to anyone...about anything.

"I know you weren't planning a return to the Proving Cove today, but I'm confident in you. Salient Ayaan is confident in you. Io Kua agreed to the change in schedule, and you will learn from the experience. It will be valuable."

"I'm going to kill the bear."

Liori smiled at her – quickly, and for just a moment. Then she released Zhava's hand and turned from the window, retrieved her coat from the peg on the wall and opened the door to leave.

"I hope you find Vinaara quickly," Zhava said.

Io Liori stopped and looked over her shoulder. "If the reports are accurate, we won't have any trouble. I wish you all the success today – and listen to your teachers while I'm gone."

After Io Liori left, Zhava shut and locked her door, then continued dressing for the Proving Cove. Her belt and scabbard with the Felton sword sharpened and polished within. Her half-dozen throwing knives, their short handles bound in thin, tanned rope. One sparring rod tucked in a sheath at her back – but if things grew so desperate she needed that, she probably would not survive anyway. The small round, wooden shield that she never used – but if there was ever a time it might come in handy, it was this fight. She buckled the straps of her leather chestplate, tightened the leather cuisse around her thighs, and slid the dark, oiled gauntlets over her fingers and hands and secured them around forearms. Most of this armor wasn't hers; she borrowed the chestplate from Io Suleenuo, her weapons master, and borrowed the cuisse from Io Kua. The gauntlets, however, she could keep. They had been hanging in Sister Allenka's room when Zhava saw them, and the Sister traded them for a carved horse that Zhava made from the bark of an old tree. Sister Allenka said that if Zhava lived, she could keep the gauntlets; if Zhava died, however, Allenka would "Yank them off your cold arms." Sister Allenka wasn't always the most pleasant person to be around.

As Zhava left her room and went downstairs, Barae joined her and encouraged her on. Sister Tegara met her at the door with a hug, and then she assured Zhava she would be ready with whatever healing might be required. The three walked outside to find Weclin, Aaria, and Sanama waiting – even though they had early morning chores they were supposed to be doing. Zhava received hugs from all three of the younger Initiates, her "Little Soldiers." Weclin, the boy who could talk to animals and seemed the only one capable of controlling the sengret; Aaria, a young girl full of energy who could memorize entire passages of the Kandor with ease; and Sanama, a quiet girl who was just finishing her first season as an Initiate and who had found inspiration to be a fighter just by watching Zhava and Plishka rescue her from the mountain cave.

Sister Tegara sent the three younger Initiates off to their chores, then accompanied Zhava and Barae the rest of the way to the Proving Cove. Barae babbled at them, equal parts encouragement and random facts that seemed irrelevant to the moment. Zhava ignored most of it while pretending to listen to everything her friend said, though her thoughts were focused on the trial to come.

At the base of the Proving Cove, Zhava hugged them both again – and even received a kiss on the cheek from Barae – then she turned to climb the cold, hard stones. She had been up here only yesterday, considering how she would fight this monster. Plishka had given advice: more knives and swords, less fire and wind. Io Kua had been preparing her for the past couple moons with advice he claimed would help her to succeed, but really only served to confuse her more: the Proving Cove did not exist to beat her, but to test her; the creature that lived within the Cove had lived there since before recorded history, and it was deadly, but that did not mean she could not defeat it; and that her best way through the Cove was to consider all that she had learned up to that point and use it to her best advantage. Whatever that was supposed to mean. Because...maybe he thought she wasn't using her skills to her best advantage? Because he thought she had more skills left to learn? Because he had nothing better to say, and so he told her some cryptic comment to make her shut up about defeating the creature?

She reached the top of the steps and stared into the blackness within. White, sparkling frost had formed around the mouth of the cave. The moss hanging from the overhead ledge was tinged with it, and a hint of warmer air drifted out and into Zhava's face – as if the very cave itself breathed. She shucked her coat and tossed it into the corner of the steps. She would retrieve that soon enough, and it would only overheat her and impede her fighting. She secured the buckler on her left arm and drew the Felton sword with her right, and she stepped into the dark.

Chapter 5

With a whisper of her will, Zhava called a dozen of the little flaming men. They appeared along her shoulders and clinging to her arms. One even sat at the top of her buckler. Within just a few steps of entering the cave, the chilled, morning glow disappeared, and the darkness within seemed to swallow them whole. Unlike her first time stepping within this cave a few moons ago, this time she refused to let her flaming men get scared. She pressed her own convictions within them, forced them to remain bright, and refused to let them cower behind her. This was a fight she would win; she was sure of it.

She stepped forward, and the light from her flames flickered across the walls. The ground was packed firm. It had been squishy mud the last time, but the winter's chill seemed to have firmed it up enough for her to step upon it instead of sinking down into it. The smell seemed somehow better too, as if the winter air wiped away the stench of dead animals. Another, more tentative step. This was the point where Io Kua had collapsed the cave entrance last time, right before she saw the creature for the first time.

She turned around. The entrance was still there, wide open and brightly lit as the morning sun shone on the stones.

She took a step back, but the hard-packed dirt broke beneath her foot, and her boot sank up to the ankle in cold, damp mud. She lost her balance, flung her arms out wide, and toppled to the floor, butt first. She landed with a tailbone-rattling thud, her flaming men scattering around her and across the cave floor.

She cringed from the pain that ran from the back of her head, down her spine, and through her hips and butt. One leg was stretched out before her, and the other was bent at a painful angle where her booted foot was still trapped in the hole. Thin ice, she thought. Except the ice was made of mud. Her left arm tingled, and she shifted the strap of the buckler to see a long, thin scratch stretching from her shoulder and down almost to her elbow. She glanced up. A spindly plant grew along the cave wall, and several of the needles now glistened red from her blood.

"That was stupid," she muttered as she wiped away the blood. She turned and looked at the boot. "And that was stupid." She yanked on her leg, and her foot came flying out – the boot still stuck in the hole. "And that was really stupid."

She pushed herself away from the wall, sheathed the sword, yanked the boot from the mud, and stumbled as she tried to put it back on and lace it tight again, all while maneuvering the small shield to keep from cracking herself in the face with it.

"Look at me," she muttered. "One of the best fighters in Sister Tegara's Initiate House, and I'm beaten by a pile of mud." She looked up and yelled, "Are you watching me, bear? I'm coming for you!"

Only silence replied, so she finished tying the boot back in place. Once that was done, she wiped her hands on the bare stone, stood up, pulled her sword again, and looked around. The cave was darker now. Her little flames were scattered around her, still dancing on the floor, so she snapped her fingers to call them back. Even as they clambered up, the cave remained darker, as if any light at all was simply swallowed up. Outside had also grown darker, with less of the morning glow spilling in.

"Strange," she said. Io Kua was not there to close that entrance behind her, so there was no reason for the cave to get darker. Passing clouds? As she slowly turned in a circle, she saw a break in the shadows against the wall, a crack in the solid surface of the cave. Was that the cliff where she fell last time? She had landed in a large cavern, and the bear followed her down – climbing on the sheer stone walls the entire way. She had never seen an animal move like that.

Avoiding the not-quite-frozen mud, she edged her way to that break in the wall. Far from being a drop-off, though, it was a low, narrow passageway that sloped steeply down and angled off to the right and out of sight. She certainly had not gone down that the last time. She pressed her will, and one of the flames jumped from her shoulder, landed on the hilt of her sword, ran to the very tip, and clung on tightly. She dipped her makeshift torch/sword down, but she still couldn't see far. Cautiously, she took a step back and considered the narrow walls. She could fit, but it would be tight. It was wider near the floor than at the top, a strange way for the cave to erode. She would fit better without her armor, but she wasn't about to lose that protection. She slid the sword back in its scabbard and tested her footing.

She took a breath and a step forward – and something pushed her from behind. A heavy, solid shove to the middle of her back, and she fell forward. She flung her left arm down and tucked her head beneath the buckler. The shield landed with a crash that jolted her arm, and her head bounced against the solid wood. The momentum slid her forward along the slippery stone, and the path angled steeply down. Within moments, she was hurtling the narrow chute, the stones cracking against her back, legs, and even her head as she tried to wrap into a tight ball and protect herself. The path quickly leveled off again, and she slid to a halt, her flames scattering around her and dizzily staggering across the ground – seemingly as disoriented as she felt.

She rolled over on the ground and looked around. Her flames lit a small circle about her, and she could easily see the steep tunnel that had sent her careening down. Except it hadn't been the tunnel that sent her down. Someone – or something – pushed her. No dwelling on that now, though. She was down here, and with all the noise she made, the bear was certain to know her location.

She stood and inspected the buckler. It was scraped across the front and even a little dented on one edge, but it was still intact. She felt at her belt; all six throwing knives were still there, the Felton sword was in its scabbard, and the sparring rod was still securely tucked against her back.

The flames climbed back up and perched themselves across her shoulders and arms, and when she pulled her sword, the one ran along the blade and wrapped itself around the tip. She swung to the narrow tunnel and peered up. It sloped steeply, and though the walls were roughly carved by erosion, she could not see an easy way back up. She would need another exit.

But first, the bear.

She took in more of her surroundings. She had been dumped into a wide cavern, and she saw several smaller tunnels branching off. A pool of water sat at the center of the cavern, and more water dripped from the tall ceiling in high-pitched splashes that echoed around her. Zhava cringed as she realized that in all her excitement to confront this creature, she had never thought to pack something she could use to help find her way back. She should have brought some path markers.

She set aside that problem for the moment and began edging around the cavern and glancing into the tunnels. They weren't all tunnels, though. The first continued on and down for quite a way before she returned to the main cavern. The next, however, was nothing more than a narrow, empty hole. The third one she checked was not quite as small, and the fourth-

Her breath caught. The creature was lying on the floor of that fourth tunnel. Curled into a large ball, its black fur waved across its body with each breath it took. Its eyes were squeezed shut, and the claws on its legs glistened against the flicker of Zhava's flames. It let out a low, soft gurgle as it breathed – and Zhava shivered. She remembered that gurgle. It had haunted her dreams several nights over the past six moons. It gurgled like that when it circled her, when it attacked her, when it caught her own Abilities and used them against her. The creature had beaten her. It pinned her to the ground and opened its jaws wide to snap down on her, to kill her. If not for Sister Tegara and Barae arriving when they did, she probably wouldn't be alive today.

The creature seemed in a deep slumber. It had to be sleeping hard if it hadn't awoken when she crashed through that tunnel and onto the cavern floor. She stepped closer, but it did not stir. She waved her sword, the little flame flickering through the air, but the creature slept.

Zhava stood there, staring at the thing and suddenly feeling a little foolish. She prepared for this battle, she trained for this battle, she sat outside this cave worrying about this battle...and for what? The thing was asleep. Soundly. Could it be hibernating? Did it do that? And if it did, then why would Salient Ayaan and Io Kua and Io Liori – everyone! – send her into its cave now? Was this part of her test? Was she expected to decide its fate? She had spent several moons telling her teachers she was training so hard to kill the creature. Was this a test of her resolve? Certainly not her fighting skills, especially if they knew the thing slept through winter. Perhaps they had not even expected her to find it tucked away in its den?

Except that someone pushed her down that tunnel. She would have shown more caution on her own, and if she had seen the tunnel slope so steeply down, she would have turned back and found another way. Perhaps even found that ledge where she fell the last time she was here. No, if they meant to keep the creature's winter den a secret, they wouldn't have pushed her down the passage that led straight to it.

Zhava quietly stepped forward, and her boot pressed into a soft, fibrous mat. Brown tendrils lined the floor, and she bent down to inspect them. Shredded bark, made soft by the cool air and the creature's warm body. So, the creature did venture from the cave, at least often enough to yank bark from the trees and drag it back inside. Good bedding material. That would be useful information for her teachers.

Another step, and the flame at the tip of her sword flared brighter, lighting three small alcoves along the floor. She leaned down to inspect them. Long, curved gouges had been dug into the rocks, and the rubble lay scattered along the edge of the wall. The alcoves weren't deep, but more of the shredded bark had been shoved deep within them. Inside, she saw the skeletal remains of several small animals. Food storage? Traps? The dug-out spaces made little sense, like so much about this creature.

Zhava sighed and stood straight. She expected a fight. Instead, she intruded on the thing's winter nap, and now she was confused what to do. The creature was a menace, and it obviously ventured into the surrounding woods – no matter how many assurances her teachers gave that the creature did no such thing. It should be put down. She had seen animals slaughtered at the farmstead, and she knew it was a part of life. She even helped a few times. But that was livestock. Food. This thing? It was wild. And she had trespassed into its winter home.

"Compassion," she whispered, reaching her decision. That was what her teachers wanted her to learn. Find the creature hibernating, and she alone could decide its fate. They knew she was an excellent fighter. Perhaps they wanted her to display excellent judgment. As such, she could let the creature live, and she could tell her teachers she had the compassion and the judgment to deal with this new situation. But was that the right choice?

She turned to leave, and the light of her flames reflected in the creature's open eyes. Zhava froze. It lay on the floor, stretched out long and sleek – and now blocking her path back out of the den. It stared at her, watched her. Studied her.

A dozen thoughts raced through her mind. Panic. Flight. Fight. Her own death. The creature's power and beauty.

That last was a strange thought, but now that it entered her mind, Zhava had trouble seeing the creature as anything but beautiful. Its long, black fur rippled in waves down its body. Its round head and long, straight snout; its powerful jaws, and the points of its teeth peeking out beneath its nose. The large, black, soulless eyes. She never had the time to see the creature when it was attacking her, and now she found the thing stunning. Still a ferocious beast, but beautiful in its power and design.

It stared back at her, its eyes flicking up and down as if truly seeing her for the first time as she saw it. It stretched its long paws wide, the claws sliding out and then in again – all without shifting any other part of its body. It didn't seem the least bit interested in attacking. If anything, it was curious.

Zhava was stuck, though. The back half of the creature blocked the only way out of the den. The thing might be beautiful, but it was still a wild beast. She had thought to show compassion, but that might no longer be an option.

No sooner had the thought entered her mind than the thing lifted its head, narrowed its eyes, and gave a low, menacing gurgle from deep within its throat.

Zhava tensed, raising her sword before her.

From one blink to the next, the creature was up and towering over her. It pointed its snout at the ceiling, and its gurgles echoed between the walls. Its claws extended long from its paws, and the thing turned to her and snarled.

This was the fight Zhava had trained to win. Dozens of her flames sprang to life across her body, brilliantly lighting the den – fire, one of her Abilities. She pressed her will to the stone floor, and the mess of sand and small stones shifted beneath the creature's feet, knocking it off balance – earth and stones, another of her Abilities. A slight pressure of will, and she shifted the air within the den, slamming the creature face-first against the wall – wind, the final of her Gods'-breathed Abilities.

With the confidence that came from four moons of training, she raised her sword to her side, thrust forward, and pierced the creature's hide – that one flame riding the tip of her sword deep into the creature's body.

It howled a long, low moan as it slowly sank back to the ground. She yanked back on her sword, released the wind pressure holding the creature upright, and its body slumped into a pile. The muscles relaxed, the eyes dulled, and one last breath escaped its mouth.

Zhava wasn't fooled. She had thought the thing dead three times before, and it came back more powerful each time. She stood there, her sword at her side, the buckler raised high, and her flames burning across her body. She waited.

The creature lay there, its body limp, and after several long, tense moments, Zhava allowed herself to relax just a bit. She took a tentative step forward and tapped one boot against the creature's leg, but nothing happened.

"That was...easy," she muttered. This creature that had haunted her dreams, that tortured her the last time she ventured into this cave, and she killed it with one strike of her sword. Perhaps Plishka was right. Zhava's Abilities were powerful, but a sword – that could accomplish so much more. Was that the lesson her teachers wanted her to learn?

She sheathed the sword and looked around the small den. There was nothing more that could be learned from remaining here. She needed to find her way out of this system of caves. She stepped away – and heard a small, high-pitched gurgle.

Zhava spun on her heals, the sword drawn and her flames flaring bright. The creature's body lay still on the floor. She watched, but it didn't move. She gave it a quick tap with her boot, but it still didn't move. What did she hear?

Another soft gurgle, but not from the beast's dead body, and Zhava glanced around the den. Something skittered across the floor, something small and round and dark. She stepped back, ready to strike, but the thing rolled across the soft mulch and bumped into the creature's body. The little ball nudged the thing's leg and...almost chittered in its high-pitched voice. It bumped the leg again, and rolled further along the body, continuing its gurgles and its bumping motions. It was so small, a little fluff ball of black fur and tiny gurgles. Shaped and colored like it was, it could only be the creature's young.

It never occurred to her to think of it as anything other than a beast to be killed, a wild, uncontrollable animal living within the Cove. To discover it was a mother, though? She watched the little one bumble alongside the dead one, gurgling at it and rolling through its mother's black fur. She slipped the sword back into its sheath and knelt down to watch. So small, it didn't seem to have the exact form of its mother. It wasn't as clearly defined; its limbs were more squishy stubs than distinct arms and legs, and its snout seemed to be flattened to its face, as if it hadn't yet developed a full mouth. She had no idea what the things ate – besides people – and she wondered if the little thing could even survive on its own. A few tiny skeletons had been inside the alcoves, but that could have been fed to this little one, just as birds brought food to their nests.

The little one rolled to its mother's back leg, nearer to Zhava. Large or small, she still wanted nothing to do with the creatures, so she rose to leave.

The little one spun at her and snarled. Or it tried to snarl. It was more of a high-pitched growl and mewling, but its tiny face was scrunched tight, and its teeth – almost too large for such a small animal – shone bright against the light of Zhava's flames.

She backed away slowly, her hands before her – and that's when she saw two more of the small, black balls rolling from the remaining alcoves. Just as the first one, these two bumbled their way across the soft mulch to the dead body of their mother. Unlike the first one, though, these two seemed slightly more developed, just a little bigger, and their eyes were open wide.

It was time to leave, Zhava thought. She crept from the den and back into the main chamber with its numerous tunnels branching in every direction and its shallow pool of water in the center. One of those tunnels had to lead out of here, and she had to find it. She accomplished her goal of killing the bear in the caves, and now she wanted to go home.

But as she stepped lightly through the cave, the tiny mewling from the creature's den transformed to a growling and hissing. The young ones crawled from the den and followed her, their faces contorted and their mouths open wide to display their pointed teeth. They hobbled along through the bark, then slipped and skittered over the rough cave floor.

"I don't want to hurt babies," she muttered, and she reached behind her back and pulled out the sparring rod. She flicked her wrist, and the extensions snicked into place, giving her a good, long reach.

The little ones snarled at her, then spread apart, one angling to her left, the other to her right, and the third coming straight toward her. They were coordinating their attack – surrounding her. She rushed to her right and shifted the angles, but the little ones shifted with her. So she did it again, this time to her left, but the little ones shifted with her again. They were smart. All three hissed at her in unison, startling her with their ferocity.

She backed away, and they tracked with her, scuttling forward and snapping their tiny jaws. She wouldn't be able to do this for long before she ran out of cave, so she gave a quick press of her will and dropped a dozen flaming men to the floor around her. The flames scattered, charging at each of the babies. She didn't want to hurt them; she just wanted them scared and running away.

The young ones did not run, though. Almost as one, they leapt forward and pounced, opening their mouths wide and swallowing the flames down fast. They continued their advance.

Zhava licked her lips nervously. Her Abilities hadn't worked with the mother – why would they work with the babies? The cave system sprawled in all directions, but this main chamber was not very large. Tunnels branched off to her right and left, and even behind her, but she hadn't explored enough to know which were dead ends and which – if any – would lead her back out. The walls were slick with moisture and some slimy, stringy plants, and the floor around the pool was dusty with loose pebbles and small stones.

She swept her hand through the air and pressed her will to the floor. The dust and stones scattered away from her and into the open eyes and mouths of the baby creatures. They growled and snapped at the dust, then flicked their heads and rubbed their eyes to the floor and against their fur, trying to wipe it away.

Zhava used the time to toss more flames into the nearby tunnels and send them off to explore. Within moments their flickering, dancing lights went off in half a dozen directions as Zhava turned her attention back to the baby creatures – in time for one leaping at her. She raised her shield and knocked it aside. The force jolted her arm and set her a bit off balance. They were much heavier than they looked, especially for their small size.

A second one darted across the ground, aiming at her foot, and she swiped it away with the sparring rod. It screamed a high-pitched shriek as it tumbled away from her, then rolled to a stop and began licking its hind leg and limping in circles.

"I – I didn't want to do that," she said.

Another shriek, this from behind, and she ducked just soon enough to see one of the babies leap over her, clawing and snapping at the air where her head had been only moments before. With a flick of her will, she swept the wind away from her and sent the baby soaring across the cave. It landed with a dull thud and stumbled along.

"Stop," she said, raising her hands before her. "Just stop."

The bite into her leg surprised her with its intensity, and she swiped the sparring rod down and across the third baby's side. The creature yelped and released Zhava's leg, then snarled at the sparring rod and wrenched it from her grip. It darted away, the ends of the rod sticking from its mouth as it twisted and thrashed its head.

Zhava felt her stinging leg, and her hand came away slick with blood. She wiped the blood on her armor, then pulled the Felton sword from its sheath. At least the sword would bite them back.

Another leaping attack from her left, which she blocked with the shield, then one of the babies scuttled across the floor. She swept the sword along, and as it struck, the baby yelped in surprise and pain. The baby limped away leaving a trail of black droplets behind it.

It didn't feel right to harm the babies, she thought, but they were giving her no choice. She didn't want to hurt them – she had been here for the mother, not for them – and if they would just leave her alone, she would leave them in peace and find her way back out of the cave.

Two of the three raced at her, and Zhava whipped up an-other small dust storm, but this time they tucked their heads and kept coming. She swung the sword, and they dodged aside – then they were on her. One grabbed her right arm and bit down hard. The other ran into her stomach, its teeth lodged into the leather of her breastplate. The force of their attack staggered her back, and she stumbled into the cave wall. She swung the wooden shield across her arm, dislodging that crea-ture – its teeth tearing long gouges. She yelled at the pain, but clung fiercely to her sword. She would not lose her Felton. She pounded the hilt of the sword across the back of the creature stuck to her armor, and it opened its jaws wide in a shriek of pain and dropped to the ground before her. With a swift kick, she punted the two babies across the room.

She leaned against the wall, breathing hard and inspecting the damage. Her arm tingled, and streaks of blood trickled from the bites. She felt a little dizzy, which made no sense. She hadn't lost that much blood from either her leg or her arm. Probably just shock from the ferocity of the babies' attacks. She glanced down at the leather breastplate – and the eight tiny holes where the creature's teeth had sunk through. She shivered at the thought of what her stomach would look like if she hadn't been wearing the armor.

The creatures shrieked, and Zhava looked up again. The room was beginning to tilt, and she shook her head to clear her mind. The babies were arrayed around the cave just as before:

one to her left, one directly in front of her, and one to her right. The one to her right was dripping more of that thick, black blood from its mouth, and it limped every few steps. They shook their heads and snarled, their voices high and piercing. They pawed at the ground, scraping their tiny claws through the rubble and kicking dust behind them.

"Don't make me do this," Zhava whispered, raising her sword. Babies, yes, but they were as vicious as their mother. What they seemed to lack in size and strength, they more than compensated in numbers and determination.

The one to her left jumped first, and she raised her shield to knock it away. The one to her right, the limping one, stumbled forward second, aiming at her boot.

The thud to her shield confirmed she blocked the first attack. She swept her sword low, and the blade cut into the second creature's side. It rolled aside and splashed into the center pool, a thin trail of black blood behind it.

The third creature used the distractions to get in close, just under Zhava's arm, and it jumped up and clamped its jaws around her sword hand. She screamed as the tiny teeth pierced her fingers, but she held on tight to the sword. With her left hand, she gripped the creature by the scruff of the neck – like many young animals, the skin back there was loose, and she was able to grab a handful. The animal's muscles tensed. It curled itself tighter around her hand and brought up its rear legs. The hind claws sank in deep at her wrist, and the thing kicked away, slicing open more wounds.

Zhava had learned from her Papa, while dealing with small, wild animals on the plains, that to pull away would only hurt more. With a little one such as this, she had to make it gag – and that required going deeper. Instead of pulling, she pressed her left hand deep into the thing's neck. At the same time, she pressed her right hand deeper into the creature's jaws.

Its eyes grew wide, and its hind legs kicked harder, shredding the skin on the back of her wrist. She spun and slammed her hand into the cave wall, pinning the creature's legs tight.

It gagged and snarled, then loosed its jaws just a bit – and Zhava twisted her wrist and yanked hard on the animal's neck. She tossed it away, and it skidded across the cave floor and off into the darkness, shrieking and howling as it went.

Zhava's arm was shaking, and her grip on the sword was loosening. Thin streaks of blood ran from the bite marks across her palm, fingers, and thumb, and on to the back of her wrist where the animal's claws had slashed in deep. She tried to tighten her fingers, but that just made the blood flow stronger. She would drop this sword in a moment if she tried to hold on tighter, so she reached around and stowed it back in its sheath. She pulled a throwing knife from her belt and held tight to the blade's finger grooves.

One of the baby creatures stood before Zhava, watching her and snarling, its mouth open wide and its teeth bared to the flickering light of her flames. She twisted her hand and flicked the knife. The creature darted, but not quickly enough, and the knife sunk deep into its back leg. The animal thrashed across the ground and bit and tore at the knife's handle.

Zhava plucked another knife from her belt. Ignoring the creature's shrieks of pain, she stepped forward, raised her arm, and plunged the knife deep into its side. She felt the point of the blade scrape against the cave floor, and she knew she had pierced it completely through. She rolled away quickly, searching for the remaining two creatures. The room spun again, and she struggled to stand, her feet slipping from beneath her, and her sword arm shaking uncontrollably.

A hiss from her right, and Zhava turned. She saw nothing, but these babies were smaller and quicker than their mother.

The pool of water seemed to sparkle and glitter, its banks beginning to overflow. She squeezed her eyes shut, then opened them. The pool was dark, and the water rippled only slightly from the trail of black blood running down into it. She was beginning to see things that weren't there. Possibly from blood loss. Maybe something in the creatures' mouths, a poison – or even just their spit. Whatever the cause, it made fighting the babies much more dangerous. Two of the little things were still alive, one of which she hadn't even hurt. There was no way she could beat them both, especially if she couldn't trust her senses enough to see and hear.

She called forth more of her flaming men, surrounded herself with them, to make them stack up on each other to form a wall of flames. The babies might eat fire, but she hoped a wall of flames would make them more skittish. Smaller animals often fled from larger ones.

Behind her was a gap in the cave wall, and one of her little flaming men beckoned her to follow. Perhaps it found a way out? She shoved herself over and onto all fours and began crawling forward. Her walls of flaming men shifted with her, and she continued calling more to her side, building those walls of flames as high and thick as she could make them.

The baby creatures yowled from the other side.

Zhava shuffled along, the floor before her seeming to tilt and veer away from her. Her right hand slipped, and she stared in awe at the streaks of blood across the cave floor. She lifted her shaking hand before her and watched as the fingers bent forward and back, then side to side – and then vanish from her hand.

She squeezed her eyes shut again. This wasn't happening. Her fingers were still there. She had lost blood, yes, but she still had hands and fingers. There was something in the creatures' bites, something that made her see strange things. When she opened her eyes again, she saw her hand and all her fingers and thumb, though blood oozed from the bite marks.

The flaming man waved her forward, and she struggled across the tilting floor.

The creatures let out a high-pitched shriek, and her flaming men buckled down around her – and then they were scattered. One of the baby creatures rolled across the floor, knocking the flames in all directions and spinning to a stop next to where Zhava crawled forward. It leaped at her arm and bit down hard, piercing the leather armor.

Zhava toppled over, and the room turned around her. The ceiling slid to the side, the walls curved around her like a blanket, and the floor seemed to slip away beneath her. She felt herself float away, to begin to leave her body. Was this death, or was this more of the creatures' poison working its way through her body?

The remaining flames tumbled down and piled on the baby creature, burning into the thing's fur and thick hide. It yelped and howled and chewed away at the leather band around Zhava's arm. The second baby limped across the sloping ground, its teeth bared and its black eyes focused on Zhava's face. She tried to raise her shield before her, but her left arm seemed to have stopped moving. She blinked, hoping the baby creature was just an illusion, but it remained in place, steadily advancing across the floating floor.

The flaming men all cried in unison, their heads turning toward the limping creature.

Zhava screamed in pain as the one at her arm finally bit through the leather.

The second creature jumped forward, its mouth open wide...

...and Zhava sat up straight in the bed of the dark room. She gripped the night shirt with one hand and fumbled through the darkness before her with the other, trying to ward off the baby creature, but nothing was there. The air was still, and she heard the crickets sounding just outside the shuttered windows. She pushed aside the heavy quilt and swung her legs over and out of the bed, then leaned forward and shut her eyes as she tried to get her breathing under control. That baby creature had been running straight for her, and she knew she was about to die. But it was all just a dream...a memory...something from her youth. It all happened so very long ago.

Before she could even think it, a dancing, flaming man sparked to life on the oil lamp across the room. The light slowly grew, and Zhava stared down at her scarred, swollen hands. Her old hands with their dark spots and their wrinkled, cracked skin – the little finger missing from her left hand where...something had happened, but she could no longer remember what it was. She reached for the polished, wooden cane next to the low bed, and she used it to balance herself as she slowly, gently set her feet to the floor. Her back ached. Her joints popped. But she had lived a full life – an adventurous life! – and she was safe once again, back in her cozy home along the coast.

Chapter 6

Zhava shuffled from the small bedroom, her shiny, oak cane thumping along at her side. The hallway was lit by flames before she even reached it, illuminating her way to the narrow, steep stairs at the center of the home. That was one of the hardest things as she grew older, she thought, to pull herself out of childhood habits. She had traveled everywhere throughout her life, from the far side of the Purneese Mountains, deep into the Sineise Desert, as far as the southern edge of Go'aab, and now to live her final days near her grandchildren on the Storm Coast – but she still could not get accustomed to the layout of her home. It did not feel right. She missed the wide, center courtyard with its date trees and spring flowers. She missed the branching hallways that connected the family with the servants with the hired hands. She even missed the little kitchen with its heavy blanket for a door, the smells of the morning eggs rising gently to her bedroom. She missed the scalding heat of the midday sun as she lounged in the cool shade, one of her brothers or one of the servants – or even her own Papa – playing a loping tune on a weed drake.

These Storm Coast homes, she thought, were ugly in comparison. Ugly and cold, with their chipped-stone walls and their iron-banded, wooden doors. Their shutters were solid and heavy, and they were always damp. Narrow and tall, built along the steeply sloping coastlines, they were designed to keep the near-constant rain outside, which they actually did quite well.

She stepped onto the long, flat stone in the hallway and braced one hand against the wall railing while she rested her cane at her hip. She shut her eyes and smiled at the gentle pull of the tiny, rounded stones rolling beneath her. Wooden planks had been installed many seasons ago, covering the wall-side of the stairs, and her worn stone angled downward, and gently – with a clatter of pebbles on wood – rolled her down the steep stairs. She felt the pulsing of the dust and rocks within her very soul, linked as she was to the earth all around. She probably didn't even need the steadying hand along the wall, but it made Posef more comfortable to see her at least pretending to be cautious as she came down the stairs in her unique way, balancing as she was on the stone the way children balanced on thin boards when they played in the high mountain snows.

The stone leveled again as it reached the main floor of the house, slowed to a stop, and she gingerly stepped off. It always brought her into a joyous mood to use any little bit of her Abilities these days. Her adventuring days were over – too frail, everyone said, too much in danger of falling and breaking a bone that could no longer be mended – but these little moments of flexing her Abilities...ah, they felt good.

She turned to the right, to head toward the little kitchen, but something made her stop. Something drew her to turn around, to look behind her. Something that wanted her attention. She saw nothing out of the ordinary, though. A shut door to the storage room. The open doorway that led to the sitting room with its open hearth and crackling fire. The second shut door that led to...well, she wasn't sure exactly where it led. She stepped forward and inspected that door. Wooden, just as all the others in this coastal home, but it was stained dark, nearly black, and it was polished to a shine. A small latch held it in place, and a bolt kept the latch locked tightly – though she could see no hole for a key.

Something whispered to her through that door, something distant, high-pitched. It sounded like a voice. But then it sounded like a second voice...and a third. What were they saying? It was whispers. Overlapping whispers. They were speaking with each other, trying to stay quiet – but saying her name. She distinctly heard her name. Were they talking to her? Were they beckoning to her, or asking her questions? Or...were they speaking about her? Perhaps they did not even know she stood there, just on the other side of this door without any way of opening it.

She reached forward. Why would the door have no way to open? Who would build a door and then not include a latch, not include hinges? And...how long had this door been here? She did not recall ever seeing this door. Had she simply overlooked it? Had she forgotten it? Her fingers brushed against the polished wood, and –

"There you are," Posef rumbled from down the hallway, and Zhava turned to him and smiled. He shuffled toward her, his bright, green eyes sparkling even in the dim light of the hallway. He was dressed in his heavy, woolen pants and that dark blue sweater he got from some island he visited two summers ago. He looked so dashing in those, like his young, roguish self. He bent down and gave her a quick kiss on the forehead. "I thought you were still sleeping, my love."

"No, I was just...." She turned, but the wall was solid. There was no longer any door there, and no longer any whispered words seeping out to her. That couldn't be good, she thought. She shouldn't be hearing voices and seeing disappearing doors. What could it mean? Gods? Spirits?

"You were just...?" Posef said, looking the wall up and down.

Zhava smiled. "Thinking this wall needed something, maybe one of my old swords hanging here – to remember all the good fights we won."

"Hm. That would look good." He nodded. "But first, come outside. The grandchildren are here."

"Already? They weren't supposed to arrive until midday."

"They met a caravan and travelled most of the way with those folks. Come."

She shifted her cane and wrapped a hand around her husband's strong arm, and together they walked the stone hallway. They removed their woolen stormcoats from the pegs on the walls, helped each other into them, and ventured outside. The wind drove the stinging rain into their faces, and they leaned into it as they walked the short yard. A stray bolt of lightning crackled across sky, and distant thunder rumbled behind it, but otherwise the storm was a steady, beating rain. The stony path between the house and the barn was clear of mud, and the rain made only small pools around the closed flowers in Zhava's garden. Overall, it was a pleasant day on the Storm Coast.

Zhava grinned when she saw the half-dozen horses tied to the leeward side of the stone barn. She expected only her son and daughter-in-law, but if this many horses made the journey, then her two daughters and their families must have travelled with them. Oh, it would be good to have everyone home again. So long since she had seen the little ones.

They reached the barn doors, and Zhava gave a quick flick of her will to slide open the smaller door. The high-pitched chorus of "Onaa!" cut through the wind and rain before the door stopped sliding, and it made Zhava's smile grow even larger. Three children of varying heights burst from the barn and wrapped their little arms and hands around her and Onii Posef.

Zhava laughed and hugged them and let them usher her inside, each of the children animatedly babbling at her as they all shuffled out of the storm and into the warm barn. The grandchildren squealed and bounced in delight. Zhava and Posef's three adult children stepped around and leaned over the excited grandchildren for quick hugs and kisses, and then the grandchildren gripped Zhava's hand and pulled her down the barn's center lane. Lanterns were strung from long ropes every few steps, the light shining into the stalls and casting sharp, bouncing shadows across the watchful, wet horses within. As they did each time they visited, the three grandchildren seated Zhava on an upturned stump in the corner and told her of the grand adventures of their travels.

"The caravan was the biggest thing I've ever seen," said Stefaano, the youngest. He spread his arms wide, his fingers splayed and his grin stretching as he continued. "It went on forever. There had to be hundreds of horses."

"Thousands of horses," cut in Maia, the middle grandchild. Of the three, she was the most like Zhava, so full of energy and curiosity – and someone who would follow her passion wherever it led. Zhava was charmed by that every time she watched Maia bound across an open field or clamber up some rocky slope.

"Look what Papa gave me," said the oldest, Dymaan. She pulled a short sword from her belt and waved it through the air. "The boy in the caravan called it a Felton, and he wanted three reds for it, but Papa talked him down to one."

"A Felton," Zhava said, reaching for the sword. "Let me see that."

Dymaan handed it over, and Zhava ran her fingers along the grip and the cross guard. It was banded with old leather that had not been kept up well, and the blade was far from sharp. A falcon had been etched into the blade – a mark of the falconry blacksmithing shop deep in the heart of Go'aab. Their swords were shiny when they were new, but they always wore down quickly. Old, worn leather polished to look new, half-tang blades made of poor metal, and swords that were just a little shorter and a little narrower than they should be. Some people liked the falconry swords, of course, but Zhava had always found them to be more playthings for children or display pieces for the rich, but not serious weapons for long-term use in hard-fought battles. She smiled at her granddaughter and handed it back.

"Yes, it is a Felton," she said. "But I will get you a different one."

"Oh, may I have one too?" asked Maia.

"Me too!" squeaked Stefaano, grabbing Zhava's leg and squeezing tightly.

"Of course," Zhava said with a grin. "My grandchildren deserve only the best." She situated her cane in the dusty floor and pushed herself up with a grunt and a sharp pain in her hips. She winced, straightened, then smiled at the excited children. She slid aside the stump she used as her stool and shuffled to the back of the barn, leaving Posef and their grown children to tend to the weather-worn horses being led to their stalls.

She enjoyed the non-stop chatter of the grandchildren as they walked. They had seen a group of Ios camped along the road, and several of the Ios waved a greeting as the caravan passed. The caravan master made them all stop early on the second night because two of the traders' wagons broke wheels against a rock hidden beneath the muddy path. A falconer travelled several days with the caravan, and the children accompanied her on a hunt for stew meat. Rabbit, they exclaimed, was one of the best stews they had ever eaten. Much to their disappointment, however, there had not been a single bandit spotted along the entire trail. It led to a thoroughly uneventful trek, they said, and they fervently hoped the return home proved more exciting.

Zhava laughed at the tale as she swung open the gate on the final stall, the one at the back of the barn. It wasn't actually used for animals, and she and Posef had begun tossing old equipment into it almost from the moment they purchased their homestead. Torn strips of leather, an old saddle for camels, several tools they had used when they were much younger, and, what she was really searching for in the far back, a cache of old weapons she set in the corner in a bundle of old blankets. She sat on the little stool leaning against the wall, carefully wrapped a hand around the bulk, feeling for the sheaths within, then unwound the twine securing it all together and spread the blankets across the dusty floor. As she set apart the sheathed swords before her, a line of flaming men flickered across her shoulders, brilliantly lighting the stall – and producing a series of giggles from the middle grandchild, Maia, who reached up and began tapping and poking the little flames. Dymaan, however, gasped at the sight of the weapons being unrolled across the floor. Her eyes were wide, and she tentatively reached a hand down to brush against the gleaming metal handles.

"Those look old," Stefaano said, his young voice almost squeaking with excitement.

"I'm old," Zhava replied with a chuckle. She gently, almost reverently, stroked a finger along the centermost sheath, the oldest and shortest of the lot. Her very first sword, and the one that had held her through some of the worst of her earliest fights...such as that fight in the Proving Cove so very long ago.

"Is that a Felton?" Dymaan whispered.

Zhava gripped the sword and slid it free. The metal still held a shine after all these seasons. The blade glimmered in the reflected glow of her flames, and the memories of her youth came flooding back in. Her second, third, and fourth times in the Proving Cove, fighting off the creature and its babies, and in each season the animals becoming more ferocious. The time she took the Felton into a fight against desert nomads, when she had to fend off a flock of sengret. Each of those memories swam through her mind, and she relished them all. She and this sword had been through so much, and now she would pass on that tradition to the one child in the family most like herself. The one child most excited to gain a real sword, to use it and cherish it and find her own adventures.

"Here," she whispered, handing over the Felton to Dymaan.

The girl's eyes grew huge, and her mouth gaped open as she carefully took the sword from Onaa Zhava. "It is beautiful," she squeaked.

"Do I get one too?" Stefaano asked. "You said I could have one too."

"And me," said Maia.

"Of course, children, of course." Zhava casually flicked through the swords and daggers, picking out the smallest for little Stefaano – something good for him to use carving wood – and then a shiny dagger for Maia, though the only reason the girl would even want one was because the other two got one. Of the three, Maia was the most like her father-

"What is this?" Maia's father asked as he stepped into the cramped stall and looked at them all knelt over the blanket of weapons. The oldest of Zhava and Posef's grown children, he was the least like either of his parents. He preferred a solitary life of study, and he hosted small groups of pupils out of his home for several moons of every season. They studied the philosophies of the world, the religions of the world, the economies of the world, and they wrote lengthy, detailed reports for the King. But as for weapons and armor and sparring and going on long adventures? That was not for their eldest son, Torbis.

"Look, Papa," Maia said, holding up the old dagger.

"Yes," Torbis said, his jaw going rigid as he took in the sight. Maia and her cousins playing with weapons in a back stall of the barn. "Isn't that lovely, yes. Something you could use to hurt yourself, or others."

Zhava shook her head and began folding the remaining weapons back into the rolled blanket.

"Maia," Torbis said, "go find your Mama. And you two-" He pointed at Stefaano and Dymaan, though Dymaan was still ogling the Felton in her hands and giving her uncle little attention. "-go into the house and find a room. Leave the weapons by the front door."

The children gripped their swords and ran off, their boots pounding down the barn floor and out into the wind and rain.

"Mama, what are you doing?" Torbis said, squeezing his eyes shut and rubbing at his forehead.

Zhava finished rolling the blankets and weapons and began tying a new length of cord around the bundle. "I am indulging," she muttered. "Cannot an Onaa indulge?"

"They are too young."

"Dymaan is nearly 10 seasons. And little Stefaano? He is nearly 7."

"Stefaano just turned 5."

"Precisely. By the time I was 5, I was carving small branches into beautiful fish."

"I don't want Maia playing with a sword."

"It's a Felton," Zhava said with a wave of her hand. "It's barely longer than a dagger."

"It's a sword, and she's my daughter."

Zhava tossed the tied bundle of blankets and swords back into the corner and sighed. "You coddle her."

"Oh, Mama, not this again," he said a grunt and a glare at the ceiling. When he turned to her again, his jaw was set and his eyes were narrowed. "Maia is my daughter. I will raise her the way I please – and not in the Hibaro way." With a quick snort, he turned and stalked away, leaving Zhava sitting alone in the narrow stall, the little flames flickering and dancing across her shoulders.

She sighed and leaned back on the stool, resting her head against the stone barn wall. She shut her eyes and tried to let the frustration ebb away. She loved her children, but her oldest had always been the most difficult. He was the least like either her or Posef. He had never displayed any of the Gods' Abilities, never shown an interest in swords or adventures, never wanted to travel with them far from home or really do anything outside...and it seemed he was determined to raise his daughter that way too. He might believe himself doing the best for his child, but he was wrong. There was no nobler calling than that of the Hibaro. There was no living if not in service to the Gods and the Abilities they bestowed upon their children. There was nothing so fulfilling in life than to receive a charge from the King, to go upon that journey, to complete the mission. The land of Remmli had to be kept safe, the King was given that charge, and the Gods would see to it that their people were placed where they could best accomplish that goal. Zhava had lived her life in service of that creed, and she had no regrets...except that her eldest son so rejected that which fulfilled her life.

The creaking of the metal hinges drew her attention away from her own reveries. It wasn't that the hinges never creaked, but that the creaking she heard came from the wrong end of the stall. The doorway, where Torbis stood only moments before, was on her right. These creaking hinges were on her left.

She opened her eyes and turned. There should have been a wall. There had always been a wall. A solid, rock wall with a strong mortar holding it all in place – the standard for homes built along the Storm Coast. Instead, however, there was a door. A heavy, wooden door standing open wide, iron bands that hinged into those stones in the wall. Beyond the door, only darkness. Black, but with the sounds of children crying.

This was unnatural. A vision. The same vision that had tried to get her attention when inside the house, when Posef distracted her with a kiss and a hug and the temptation of her grandchildren awaiting her. Not this time, though. There was no such-

"Zhava," Posef called from the other end of the barn. "Zhava? Come, let's get back to the house. The children have already gone ahead."

She did not turn away from that door. She heard, and she knew this time that something was keeping her from looking. It was something good, of course, her children and her grandchildren, but then she would once again be left wondering what was on the other side of that door. Who were the children she heard, and why were they crying?

"Go on ahead," she called back. "Let me sit a moment, and then I'll be along." Instead, she pushed her aching body up, the flames on her shoulders waving eagerly at the chance to go somewhere new, the chance for one more adventure. She reached for her cane and stepped slowly. The darkness before her seemed to swallow up the light, so she called forth more of the little flames. They flickered to life up and down her body, clinging to her arms and legs and shining like a mighty fire. The darkness did not retreat, however, but seemed only to shrink back against the onslaught of heat and light.

She rubbed one hand against the wooden door, and it was slippery, wet and cold. The threshold along the ground was also damp, and rain pattered at it in slapping sheets. She spread one hand out before her, and the drops were icy against her palm. She shivered and called more of her flames, wrapping herself in a flickering blanket of heat and light, then stepped slowly forward.

The moment she crossed into the darkness, everything became silent. It was as if something stopped her ears, and she dug her fingers deeply inside the canals. They came away with flecks of brown and white wax, but still she heard nothing. The rain pattered at her body, and she saw the smoke and steam wisping away from the hundreds of little flames she wore. She had trained herself when she was far younger to continually renew the flames when she was in the rain, so when one fizzled out, another quickly popped to life in its place. They would renew themselves so she remained warm and dry, and the immediate path before her lit with the pulsing glow of the fires.

She turned to look back, and her breath caught. Though she had taken only a couple steps, the bright glow of the door into her barn was a sliver of light far in the distance. Lightning flashed dully above that door, outlining ominous clouds shaped like the faces of men and women, watching her, staring at her. The narrow gap between two clouds was the eye of one man. The billow of puffs along a cloud's edge was the nose of a woman. The cracked edge of another cloud was the split, uneven grin of a second man. Within moments, the lightning died away, but those faces remained burned into her mind. She tried not to imagine them laughing at her, but the distant cackle of voices that carried on the wind made her think it was not her imagination. She shivered, turned, and continued on.

Thunder rumbled overhead. The path before her lit in brilliant patches of blinding white and blue as the lightning arched all around. She did not dare look up again, but she knew those three faces were not alone. From the corners of her eyes, she caught sight of more men, more women, staring at her within the clouds. They watched her walk along, seemingly fascinated by the flaming woman braving the storm-edged darkness.

"Who are you?" a girl's voice said, and Zhava stopped, gripped her chest, and frantically spun around.

She nearly lost her balance, and the little flames wobbled and stumbled across her body, but she shifted with her cane, flung an arm out wide, and kept herself upright. She had no idea where she was in the blackened, storming world, but she did not want to stumble and injure herself. She did not know why, but she had the feeling the frail and lame were quickly eaten in this vision world.

A young woman stood on the path, her hair soaked and slicked around her head like a long cape, and her ragged clothes clinging to her body and draining pools of water at her bare feet. Her mouth was open, and her head was cocked to the side — but her eyes were the only bit of brilliant color on her otherwise blue and black form. Blazing a radiant white, they shone out from the pale face like twin flares on a shoreline. The dark, fur coat was stained in streaks of black that seemed to shift with the occasional flashes of lightning.

The girl reached out one blue, dripping hand toward the flames on Zhava's body, her bright eyes blinking so rapidly that the light seemed to strobe from within her. Even the girl's fingers were pale blue and streaked with mud and grime. As she reached toward Zhava's hand, the dozen little flames clinging there all leaned forward and stretched their own hands out to meet her.

But the girl's hand stopped.

The flames danced and leaped and stretched, but no matter how hard they tried, they could not bridge that tiny space between their bright fires and that girl's pale, grubby fingers.

"You are extraordinary," the girl whispered, looking up.

Zhava had no idea what to say to this strangely beautiful waif before her.

"Who are you?" the girl asked again.

"Zhava."

The girl squinted, cocked her head to the side, and seemed to study the ground between them.

"I don't know you," she finally said. She turned and gestured at the cloudy, lightning-filled sky. "But the dead most certainly know you."

Again, Zhava was struck by how there appeared to be so many faces in the shapes of those clouds, so many people all staring down at them in the flickers of lightning.

"Why are you known by the dead?" the girl asked, her shining eyes blazing at her.

But Zhava had no answer. She had thought herself on a spirit journey, and this certainly seemed like one. The spirits could become confused, and this little one certainly was. Undoubtedly drawn to Zhava by the brilliant flames alighting her body, this spirit alone had likely ventured down from the clouds to investigate. This curious in death, the girl must have had a powerful drive in life.

"I am not like the others," the girl whispered. "I am not dead. Not yet."

The statement startled her. Though nothing had been spoken aloud, the girl had responded as if those thoughts had been-

"Shh," the girl said with a wave of her hand. She turned and looked back down the path. "He follows."

Zhava looked, but she could see nothing in the dark. Perhaps a trick of this spirit journey, or perhaps an effect of her aged eyes. She wondered if she should be afraid.

"Posef," the girl whispered. "My young friend."

"My husband," Zhava corrected.

The girl turned back, and those eyes suddenly blazed brilliantly through the black gulf between them – nearly overwhelming the light cast from Zhava's own flames.

"You are not of this world, and this guise is not your own." The girl snapped her fingers, and the cane on which Zhava had been leaning vanished.

She stumbled forward, but quickly steadied herself. She began to protest, then glanced at her hands...but they were no longer the wrinkled, aged hands she knew so well. They had become young again, young as the day she entered the Proving Cove-

The threat of that memory sent a shock through Zhava's mind, as if someone had slammed a rod into the back of her head, and she staggered forward again.

The girl caught her, wrapped her in her arms and held on tightly, their faces pressed cheek to cheek and Zhava's flames crushed tightly between their bodies. The flames did not burn the girl, but a wave of frosted air crackled around them. The girl's grip was fierce, and her breath was like ice brushing across Zhava's ear.

"Posef calls to you," she whispered, "so you must be a friend. Find me."

"What? Who are you? Where are you?"

"I am Emsterold," she said-

-and Zhava sat up in the small bed, coughing and heaving. The bandages wrapped tightly across her stomach and around her back constricted her, kept her from pulling in a deep breath, and she almost tumbled over the edge of the bed. Someone gripped her shoulders, though, held on tightly and kept her from falling. A second pair of hands as someone else steadied her and helped her gently lean back on the mattress.

She blinked, and the dimly lit room came into focus. Her room, with only a couple of the lamps burning atop their wells. She was back in her own bed again, back within her room at the Hibaro – and her body was in pain. Her arms and legs stung from the dozens of cuts inflicted by the little creatures in the Cove, her back and head throbbed from them landing on her and knocking her to the ground, and her stomach, beneath the bandages, felt as if it had been sliced open and patched shut again.

"You're back home," a woman whispered as she gently cradled Zhava's head.

"Emsterold?" Zhava muttered.

Silence for just a moment, and then the woman said, "No, dear, it's Tegara." She backed away, and Zhava could clearly see Sister Tegara's kind smile framed by her long, braided hair. "And look who's here with me – your friend Posef."

Posef's face came into view, his green eyes sparkling in the lamplights' glow. Her first impulse, carried over with the power of her vision, was to smile and kiss him and tell him how thankful she was that he had been by her side all those dozens of seasons, to tell him how well their children were getting on and how lovely it had been to see their grandchildren again. But she kept her mouth tightly shut. No matter what the future might hold, they had not yet lived it – she wasn't even sure she was ready to live it.

"Welcome back," he said with a big grin.

She smiled back, as if it was the most natural thing in the world, and it felt...good.

Chapter 7

The morning arrived with too much noise, too much cold air, and too much light. Either Sister Tegara or Posef had left one of the shutters cracked open. Though Zhava rolled toward the wall and buried her head in the thick, woven blankets to block out the blinding sunrise, the winter chill drifted in, and the clang of the first bell and the din of people's morning routines conspired to drive sleep far away. Her body did not hurt as bad as when she first emerged from her vision. She still found it hard to breathe with the bandages wrapped tightly around her chest and back, but at least her arms and legs didn't itch anymore. Sister Tegara had removed the bandage from Zhava's stomach in the middle of the night, and she gingerly ran her fingers across the newly healed skin. She had seen many Abilities in Ios, teachers, and students since arriving at the Hibaro, but Sister Tegara's gift of healing always seemed the most humane – and perfectly suited to the loving, kind-hearted Tegara. Or perhaps Sister Tegara became more loving and kind-hearted because she could heal? If that was true, then what did it mean that Zhava's Abilities were so violent? That thought was a bit disturbing, and not one Zhava had the energy to consider first thing this morning. Her Abilities had kept her alive through that dark, lightning-filled vision and when she was attacked by those creatures living deep within the Proving Cove.

She had to speak with someone about those creatures. Everyone told her the animals stayed inside the cave, that they never emerged, and they certainly never hunted outside, but none of that was true. Bits of shredded bark lined the floor, bones were piled inside those alcoves where the young ones fed, and once again, the creatures tried to eat her. If not for someone getting her from the cave, she could have died this time just as she almost died the last time. Why would no one listen to her? Why did no one else see the danger? Students were sent into the Proving Cove all the time, and they always emerged beaten and bloody and torn apart. Sister Tegara or one of the other healers on the campus always spent long nights healing those students and bringing them back from near-death – why not simply march into that cave with a group of soldiers and Ios and slay every last creature within it? What did the students gain from it?

Io Kua said Zhava's second trip within the Proving Cove would be a better test of her skills – the first time being a complete disaster, he admitted – but she didn't feel she accomplished anything. Yes, she killed the mother beast, but now there were three vicious young ones roaming around down there with no mother to guide them. Or restrain them. What would happen when those young ones emerged from the cave some night, hungry and angry, to hunt for their own dinner?

The second bell rang across the courtyard, the high clangs drifting through those open shutters and making Zhava flinch with each strike of the hammer. She eased herself onto her back, careful to shift each limb slowly and slide her body gently across the straw mattress. As she did, she realized this was actually her last night on a straw mattress. Io Kua said that when she completed the Proving Cove again, she would be advanced to Novice – and the Novice House was stocked with feather beds. Not even her Papa and Mama had a feather bed. She never slept on one, but she heard they were softer than any bed she could imagine. Such luxury, and for nothing more than studying hard at her Kandor lessons, advancing in her fight and endurance training, honing her Abilities with the flames and wind, and then putting herself once more through the Proving Cove. Life at the Hibaro was far different than life at her farmstead – and certainly different than any life she had been promised as the wife of Ooleng.

She flipped back the woolen blankets, and the room's chill stopped her breath for just a moment. The Hibaro was farther north than her farmstead, which was just on the edge of the Sineise Desert, and all her friends had warned her the winters could be harsh. First snows hadn't even arrived, but already the falling temperatures made her body ached. As quickly as she could, she limped to the window where the shutter sat slightly ajar, pulled it shut and latched it tight. Then she lit a dozen flames across her body, leaned against the wall and shut her eyes, and let the heat soak in.

Within moments, there was a knock at the door, and Sister Tegara asked to come in.

"Oh, you are looking so well this morning," she said as she opened the door and entered, a polished brown satchel in her hand. She tossed the satchel to the bed and squinted at Zhava's flaming body. "Snuff a few of those, please. I would like to check your bandages."

Zhava let most of the flaming men flicker away, keeping only the two perched on her shoulders that were warming her neck so well.

"Your hand and arm first."

Zhava extended her sword arm. Tegara gently unwrapped the bandages and inspected the skin beneath, lightly running her fingers over the newly healed area.

"Oh, very nice. You'll have a few scars, but the cuts joined quite well. Now your stomach."

Zhava lifted her nightshirt, and Tegara leaned down and poked in and around Zhava's belly button. It stung, and Zhava's breath caught.

"Hmm. These weren't as deep as the ones on your wrist, but they were far longer. And jagged."

"They bit through my armor," Zhava said. "I was fortunate to be wearing the armor, or I would have been killed right then."

"Yes." She straightened, smiled, and sat on the bed. She smoothed her white skirt and sat straight and proper, as she always did. "Tell me about it."

So Zhava told her. Exploring the cove entrance, being pushed down the tunnel, killing the creature, being attacked by the babies, waking up as an old woman – and then she stopped. The first time she had been in the cove, just a few moons ago, the creature had attacked her. It could have killed her, and she felt herself lucky to escape with her life. She awakened back at her farmstead, and her Mama and her Papa were not acting like her Mama and her Papa. They were different. They were too perfect, too much the kind of people she always wished them to be. Even her betrothed, that oaf Ooleng, seemed a very kind-hearted, loving man. Not at all who he was in real life. That had been a vision. Another world in which she could live for just a time. Even Sister Tegara had said, "You came back," when Zhava awoke from that otherworldly vision, as if Zhava had a choice of where to live: a vision world or the real world.

This time through the Cove...had been much the same. She killed one creature, and three more attacked her. They came at her with such ferocity, leaping at her, trying to chew through her armor, trying to bite into her. Then she blacked out. She woke up as an old woman, and that had been a vision, she was sure of it. Each vision happened very soon after being attacked. She stared at Tegara, understanding dawning on her.

"Their bites," she said.

Sister Tegara smiled and waited.

"Those creatures...they bit me, and I had visions. You send us down there as Candidates, as Initiates, and we have to fight those creatures, but we never win. Do we?" Tegara sat on the edge of the bed but said nothing. "No, they always beat us. When they attack, they bite, and when they bite us, we have visions. That's why you send us into the Proving Cove. You want us to get attacked – you want us to get bit. You want us to have the visions."

"You have taken a step into a deeper understanding. That is very good."

"But...." She waved her bandaged arm through the air. "They could kill us."

"No one has ever died within the Proving Cove."

"No, you don't understand. I was in their nest. I was right there, where the young ones were being raised, and they hunted small animals and lined their nests with tree bark. They hunted in the woods around the cove and brought those things back to their nest. They don't stay in that cove. They get out, and they hunt. Someone could get hurt. Someone could get killed."

"Zhava, listen to me. The Hibaro has sent students into that cove for generations. No one – not one single person – has been killed. Injured, yes. Scratched and torn and bit, certainly. Never killed."

"But why? Why go in there? Why do it at all?"

"Tell me your vision."

"No, you don't understand."

"I understand, Zhava. I really do. I went through the Proving Cove four times when I was young. Now, tell me your vision, and let's try to understand what the Gods want you to learn."

Zhava sighed. She turned away and fidgeted with the bandages on her wrist. She thought the test was the fight. She thought she had to slay the creature in the cove, but that wasn't true. That wasn't the real test, and that wasn't fair. She prepared for that fight. She trained, bought and borrowed armor, prepared her mind and body to fight a creature, to fight a monster. But now she learned she would never be able to beat it. Apparently no one had ever beaten the creatures in the cove.

"Zhava?"

"Yes," she muttered with a shake of her head, "I'll tell you. It's just that...." She thought she knew what was expected of her. She thought the rules were fair at the Hibaro. That this wasn't like back at her farmstead where her Mama always criticized her no matter what she did, no matter how well she did it, no matter how hard she tried. She thought that here, finally, she found people who valued the truth, who valued being open and honest with each other – with her.

But how could she say all that to Sister Tegara. Would she even understand?

So she shut her eyes, clenched her fist, and began telling the story of the vision. Waking up in that bed and in that room, using her Abilities to maneuver the stairs of the stone house, seeing the door that had never been there, and then seeing...her husband. She skipped over the little detail of "husband Posef." Going out to the barn and briefly seeing her grown children before the grandchildren whisked her away to tell of their journey. She told of the cache of weapons and armor and supplies that she and her husband kept tucked into the back of the barn, how she distributed weapons to her grandchildren until her son discovered them and got angry. And then the second door appeared, but this time she was not distracted from it. She walked through it, walked into the land of the dead, was observed by the spirit people in the clouds, met a strange woman with glowing eyes who said she knew Posef, who said that, of all the spirits there, she alone was not truly dead. She said her name was Emsterold, and she wanted to be found.

Sister Tegara no longer smiled. She stared at the floor, her arms crossed and her brow furrowed. She sat like that for a while until she said, "Once more, please, describe the land of the dead."

"It was dark. I lit hundreds of flames all over my body, and we could barely see two steps in front of us. But the steps we took, they weren't real steps. Each step seemed to take me half a day's journey from the last."

"And the spirits?"

"They were in the clouds. Or...." She considered that again. The vision was beginning to fade a bit at the edges, and she was losing some of the details. She had noticed this, however, and it seemed an interesting detail, if a bit scary at the time. "The spirits actually were the clouds. Like when you're lying in a field and you look up at the clouds, and you can see shapes in them. A sword or a horse or something. It was like that, but it was the other way around. I wasn't seeing shapes in the clouds; the clouds were all the people floating in the sky above me, floating inside the thunderstorm."

"And the girl who called herself Emsterold?"

"She was wearing old, tattered clothes. She was soaking wet, and her eyes glowed. My flames were drawn to her, but she didn't want to touch them. When I slipped, and she caught me, she was icy cold, though."

Sister Tegara considered all of this. She leaned back on the bed and stared at the ceiling.

"Sister," Zhava asked. "Who is Emsterold?"

"A powerful student," Tegara said. "Her Ability was to commune with the dead. She could enter the land of the dead, speak with the dead – I even attended a demonstration of her Abilities when she brought a spirit over from the other side. He had been a soldier, and they were trying to discover who killed him. Of course we know now it was High Priest Viekoosh who was responsible, but then we were trying to find the answers from anywhere. We used the Apprentice House Commons Room, bolted all the doors, and had her bring him over to us. It was...scary. He never looked at any of us, only at Emsterold, and he seemed fascinated by her. His words were slurred, and he had trouble forming thoughts. She said that often happened with the dead, that they became confused."

"So," Zhava said, considering Tegara's explanation. "You're saying this wasn't just a vision. You think I met the real Emsterold."

"I'm not sure," Tegara said with a sigh. "There are two pieces to your vision, the future and this journey through the land of the dead. If you had only seen your future, seen your children and your grandchildren – and your future husband, whoever he was – I would have said this was like any other vision that people have from their time in the Proving Cove. Certainly, there is much we can discuss and learn from what you've seen. But this...is something different. We thought Emsterold was dead – one more person killed when so many others died before her. But if she was taken away instead of killed, if she is being held somewhere, possibly by the High Priest himself...well that would certainly be reason to worry."

Chapter 8

The pounding on the door startled both Zhava and Tegara. The excited voice calling, "Hello? May I come in?" from the hallway made Zhava smile and Tegara shake her head. Barae's unbridled enthusiasm made her a joy to be around, but it was also completely at odds with the serious conversation.

"Zhava, you should be awake by now," Barae called through the door. "I must talk to you. Right now." She didn't sound worried or upset or angry; she sounded excited, as if the smile on her face shown through every word she spoke. Which it always did.

Zhava glanced at Sister Tegara who sat up on the bed and shrugged her shoulders at the interruption. They could invite Barae in, or they could send her away, but Tegara was leaving the decision to Zhava. She went to the door, unlocked it, and opened it for her friend.

What she saw, however, made Zhava step back in shock. Barae stood leaning on a polished-wood crutch beneath her left arm, and she had bandages wrapped around her right arm, wrist, and hand, and another bandage secured to her left cheek.

"What happened?" Zhava blurted out.

"The best thing ever," Barae gushed as she hobbled forward. Then she saw Sister Tegara and clamped a hand across her mouth.

"You were to remain in your room," Tegara chided – but with a smile. "And yet you climbed all those stairs and pounded on Zhava's door. What if she had been sleeping? She needs rest too."

"I am so sorry," Barae said. "But I heard her moving around up here, and I had to come see her. I am just so excited. I know I wasn't supposed to climb the stairs, but I had to tell her, and the stairs really weren't as hard to climb as I thought they were. I just had to brace the crutch while I pulled with my other hand. May I tell her?"

With a chuckle, Tegara said, "You may certainly tell her."

"Oh!" She turned to Zhava, her face beaming with excitement. "I did it."

Zhava nodded. "You...did it?"

"Yes, I did it. The Proving Cove."

"Oh." The crutch and the bandages made more sense.

"People were saying I couldn't do it. Well, Io Suleenuo has been saying that since I met her, and Sister Tegara has been telling me to wait for at least a couple more moons, but I've already been here two seasons. There are many other Novices who have been here less than that, and they've already been through the Proving Cove a couple times. I don't know why people aren't believing in me, believing I can do it." With that, she cast a quick glance at Tegara.

"Honey, I've told you, your Abilities are not the best suited to the trials of the Proving Cove."

"I know, but that's what makes this so great. I did it!" She turned back to Zhava. "Well, you were my inspiration. You and Plishka. When I watched you two spar outside, I thought, 'I can do that. I can go into the Proving Cove, and I can fight just like Zhava.' So the moment you went in, I begged Sister Tegara to let me go too. She asked me so many questions about my Kandor studies – really hard questions – but I knew the answers. Most of the answers. So she agreed to let me through the Proving Cove just as soon as they pulled you out, and I did it. I survived my first time through the Proving Cove, and now I'm a Novice, just like you."

"Barae," Tegara said, "that is not quite true. I must still discuss with you the details of your time within the cove. Then we will consider promoting you to Novice."

"Of course, but I'm sure you'll see I did great," Barae said with a quick nod. Then, turning back to Zhava, "And it was exactly like you said it would be. I went to the back of the cove and found that ledge you fell down, and one of those creatures was there waiting for me. It attacked me. It was vicious! And scary. I shot a couple arrows into it, but those hardly slowed it down. I tried to fight it off with my sword, just like Io Suleenuo has been teaching us, but it was so strong it knocked the sword out of my hand. I thought I was going to die when it bit into my arm. What happened next was even more incredible, though. I had a dream that-"

"Barae, stop," Tegara said, one hand raised. "You and I must first discuss your dream."

"But I just wanted to tell her this one thing."

"No. Nothing more."

"Just one?"

"Barae, it is time for you to go back downstairs. I will be down very soon for another round of healing on your leg, and then you may tell me your dream."

"Yes, Ma'am. But then I can tell her?"

"We will discuss it. Go."

Barae leaned on her crutch and awkwardly wrapped her arms around Zhava for a quick hug, then turned and hobbled from the room. Sister Tegara followed her into the hallway and waited until Barae was clumping down the stairs, then returned to the room and shut the door behind her.

"Io Kua said I could evaluate you when you completed your journey through the Proving Cove, so you do not need to wait for his return to learn the outcome of your trial."

Zhava tensed. She thought Sister Tegara had been asking because she was curious, not because it was a test. Not that she would have said anything differently, but she would have prepared herself more if she had known she was being tested. She would have at least run to the toilette first.

"I believe you have shown extraordinary courage in the face of such an ominous foe. You put your training to the test, you slew the beast – just as you said you would do – your vision quest took you to the far future and left you with much to consider, and you may have provided us with good information regarding the fate of Emsterold. You have at least shown us that we must not give up hope for those who have been lost so long. However, I urge you to consider the two pieces of your spirit journey separately. What you saw of the future, with your husband, your children, and your grandchildren, I want you to consider what all of that means to your life now. Consider how you may best live now to learn the lessons that your older self believed you must know. Your time spent wandering the land of the dead...well, that bears further consideration, but first I must consult with the priests. We will speak of that again soon. Until then, please refrain from divulging anything of your journey with the dead except to me and your other teachers, and then only when you are certain no other students are nearby. We do not want to raise people's hopes if that part of your vision might be untrue. Can you agree?"

"Of course, Ma'am. Thank you." She heard everything Sister Tegara said, and she would always remember it, but right now none of it mattered. She wanted to know if she was being promoted, and she fidgeted with her finger, trying to find some way to expend her nervous energy.

"Initiate Zhava," Tegara continued, her smile broadening. "I will authorize your promotion to the rank of Novice."

The squeak escaped Zhava's mouth even before she realized it was within her. She shut her eyes and held her breath and screamed for joy within herself at what Sister Tegara said. The goal she worked so hard to achieve. The thing she spent the past several moons preparing to accomplish. Her goal, to be promoted to Novice, and she had achieved it. When she opened her eyes again, she had squeezed out tears of joy, but she didn't even care. She rushed forward and hugged Tegara.

"Oh," Tegara said, surprised, but she quickly embraced Zhava and squeezed tightly.

"Thank you," Zhava said as she stepped away and stood in the middle of the room, uncomfortably swinging her arms and glancing around at the floor and the walls and then back to Sister Tegara.

"You needn't thank me. This was you."

After giving three more hugs and receiving a few sets of instructions, Zhava finally let Sister Tegara leave to attend to Barae. Alone again, and overjoyed at her new status..."Novice Zhava"...she quickly gathered her belongings. She had few. Her sword, throwing knives, and armor. The wood carvings from home: a camel, a boat, and an elderly woman, her teacher, the Priestess Marmaran. Her three sets of white, Initiate clothes, which she would probably have to return; Initiates dressed in white, but Novices dressed in red, and Apprentices dressed in dark green. She wasn't sure when, or even if, she would be able to choose her own clothing colors again as long as she remained in service to the King. Even Ios dressed in varying arrays of colored armor, mostly blacks and reds. She smiled at the thought of herself atop a camel, riding into her farmstead, her black and red Io robes flowing behind her in the wind. Her Papa would be proud.

When she finished packing, she stood by the door and took one last look at the bare room. It was just as it had been on her first night at the Hibaro. A bed against one wall, a table and chair against the other, a row of pegs set into the wall behind the door, and another row of pegs in the wall next to the shuttered window. She strapped on her weapons belts, struggled into her winter, fur coat, tucked her bundle of carvings and clothes into her arms, and left her room in the Initiate House.

The other Initiates were all at their morning classes, so the hallway was empty. She limped and bumped her way down the narrow stairs, then got quieter as she passed Barae's room. Through the door she heard Sister Tegara muttering soothing words, but Barae was exclaiming in surprise and pain every few moments. Zhava was shocked thinking at the many injuries Barae sustained. Cuts and bruises and a broken leg...it was amazing the creature hadn't torn the girl apart. No matter what everyone said, Zhava believed more than ever that the cost of fighting the creatures in the Proving Cove was not worth the injuries. There had to be other ways to start a vision quest than being mauled by giant animals.

She left the Initiate House for the last time, turned, and stared at the long building. Two levels of mostly shuttered windows stared back at her in the bright morning. She had begun her new life in that building, and she felt a little sad to be leaving it. Change could be a scary thing, and though this was a small change compared to leaving her home and going into service to the King, this felt more significant. She had been taken from her home, with no choice in where she was going. Do as her Mama said and marry Ooleng, or do as her Papa and the Io Liori said, and join the Hibaro. This time, however, she initiated the change herself. She worked hard and trained and studied, and now she had become a Novice. It was sad to leave this house, certainly, but it was exciting to think where she was going.

Hefting her bundle of belongings a little higher on her shoulder, she turned in the direction of the Novice House and trudged across the grounds. Though most of the students were in their morning classes, the Hibaro was alive with activity. Soldiers and Ios and priests crisscrossed the grounds as they attended to their duties, and a crew of soldiers, engineers, and even a few volunteers were clearing away the last of the debris from the fallen, nine-story building that had housed the library, the priests' quarters, and High Priest Viekoosh's own office. A casualty of the attack on the Hibaro. She heard that the Novice House had also been hit, but she had never seen the damage herself. Always too many things to do, and visiting a place she did not live was not a priority.

Moments later she gasped in surprise when she turned a corner. The Novice House was smaller than the Initiate House – and it was built in the style of her farmstead, the desert plains style. A rectangular building with two floors and a flat roof, and, though Zhava could not see it from the outside, she was certain the building wrapped around a central courtyard of shade trees and lounging space. It felt like coming home, but so much better than that. This was a home without her Mama's judgments, without the berating and the belittling. This would be a home where she could grow into-

"Come along," a man said, elbowing her in the back as he passed by.

Zhava staggered forward, nearly dropping her bundle of clothes before she righted herself. She started to yell out at the rude man for nearly knocking her over when she looked up and realized it was Brother Y'Mey striding past with several wooden boards tucked under his arm. She had seen him around the Hibaro, but she never met him. One of the King's engineers, he supervised the reconstruction of some of the buildings around the Hibaro campus. But that was not the thing that most people noticed when they first met him.

He was a Duhaang, one of a group of people from far across the ocean. Everyone had at least heard of the Duhaang, even if no one had ever before met one, and they were rare in the Kingdom of Remmli. Zhava had no idea how typical Y'Mey was of his people, but there was no mistaking him for anyone else at the Hibaro. His skin was the whitest she had ever seen. Even during the hottest part of the season, he wore thickly woven shirts and long pants to avoid the sun. His white hair was cropped short, and he had a woven cap pulled tightly across it. He turned back to look at her, his eyes glinting red then blue then red again as they caught the morning light.

"You're helping me," he called, then turned and continued through the back door of the Novice House.

Zhava followed. It was a long, narrow room with a stairwell set into the wall and a door at the far end. This would have been the kitchen in her parents' farmstead, but the Novice House had no need of a kitchen when everyone met together for meals. Instead it was piled high with scraps of wood, tools, and various machines Zhava had never seen. Many were long, with sharp edges or blunt ends, and a couple of them even seemed broken.

"Sir, I'm Zhava," she said, rushing to keep pace with him.

"Yes, I know. One of my new Novices." He ducked through the door and out to the center courtyard.

Zhava stopped at the doorway and stared. The open-air courtyard was overflowing, but not with beautiful plants and flowers as she expected. Blackened, broken, and shattered pieces of furniture, walls, wooden beams, and metal hinges lay piled in a corner. The remains of a variety of plants and shrubs lay trampled down the center of the courtyard, branching paths winding in a jagged line to the far wall – or what remained of the wall. A tall, gaping hole had been covered over by a series of wooden boards, and now Brother Y'Mey was replacing them with new ones. The hole was deep, extending from the ground almost all the way to the roof. The top was narrow, barely wider than a person, but the bottom of the hole extended across at least two rooms.

"It was the fighting," Y'Mey called back as he set the pile of new boards on the ground. "You missed most of that when Viekoosh took you and Plishka. I wasn't here either, but I was told the fight was awful. Many people were injured, and several others died."

She picked her way slowly, carefully, across the trampled and littered ground. He was telling her nothing new, but she felt uncomfortable interrupting him. Though he was not one of the Hibaro teachers or leaders, he was head of Novice House while he supervised the reconstruction. The previous leader of the house had been killed. She scanned the jagged lines of the hole in the wall, the burnt and broken edges that marked where the explosion had occurred. She never heard the entire story, but everyone said something large was dropped into this courtyard during the battle. The wall collapsed, and people died.

"Yes," Y'Mey said, nodding as if he understood her thoughts. "This is where it happened. We covered over the hole several moons ago, but the boards have already begun rotting away. New boards, a temporary fix, and then we'll see to proper repairs when we reach the spring melt-off. But this isn't your task." He looked behind her. "You'll be helping them."

Excited voices began babbling from the other end of the courtyard, and Zhava turned to see three young people running toward her. They almost knocked her off her feet as they all slammed into her, wrapping her in their arms and squeezing in the biggest hug she had received since...well, since as long as she could remember. Weclin, Aaria, and Sanama, the three Initiates who declared themselves "Zhava's Little Soldiers," grinned up at her as they bounced around and talked over each other.

"You did it!"

"What was it like?"

"Did you kill the bear?"

"What did Sister Tegara say?"

"Was it hard?"

"Show us your Novice robes."

She laughed at their rapid questions and held them tightly to herself. She and Plishka rescued many children from the mountain caves, but these three had formed a bond with each other and declared themselves under Zhava's leadership. If Plishka had been a little nicer to them, they might have followed her too, but she tended to push them away when they wanted to be with her, and she glared at them when they got too excited and noisy – as they were right now. But Zhava didn't care.

Of the three, Weclin had been imprisoned the longest, nearly two full moons. Zhava wasn't sure if the time in captivity had changed him or if he had always been this way, but he was usually quiet and shy. The exuberance he showed now was the most excitement she had ever seen from him. He had an Ability to speak with animals, and he used it to care for the sengret, the giant bird they took from the mountain prison. Other than when he was with Zhava or the Little Soldiers, he was always studying and reading books, or he was training the sengret.

Aaria, however, was nearly Weclin's opposite. Easily the smartest of the three children, she learned concepts of fighting far quicker than the other two and could recite entire passages of the Kandor with more ease and accuracy than even Zhava. She also had a boundless energy that made her active almost every waking moment. Sister Tegara told Zhava once that Aaria's heart, even when she was sitting in a chair, beat at a rate nearly as fast as most people's hearts did when they finished a long run. It was a wonder the girl ever sat still.

Then there was Sanama. Of the three Little Soldiers, Sanama was the one who seemed to idolize Zhava. She watched Zhava with an interest that bordered on obsession. Quietly sitting in a corner or standing on the edge of the practice field or mimicking fighting moves and meditation stances, Sanama was always there. She hardly ever spoke about her life before the Hibaro. From what Zhava learned, the girl had grown up somewhere in the deep desert, a child of one of the nomad caravans that traveled from oasis to oasis, selling their wares and offering their services for trade. Sanama said little of the skills she learned as a child, except that they involved dangerous animals and spellcasting. She had been left behind on a job, either purposefully or accidentally, she was never sure. After that, she had been traded among a few different tribes before hearing of the Hibaro and walking away from her nomadic life one night when they were camped on the desert's edge of the high plains. Now she used her spellcasting in service to the Hibaro – and she was a frequent, silent presence somewhere nearby whenever Zhava had something to do.

"One at a time," Zhava said with a smile as she knelt down before the young Initiates. The questions started again, and she answered them as thoroughly and as quickly as she could. She told them about the fight in the Cove – leaving for later Zhava's fears that the bears might be wandering the Hibaro late at night – then a quick retelling of her future vision, the conversation with Sister Tegara, and finally how excited she was to see the three of them here, now.

Brother Y'Mey sent Aaria upstairs with Zhava's belongings, then put them all back to work. Their task: Clean up the courtyard before nightfall. All of it. He wouldn't give a reason, but the Little Soldiers grinned and covered their mouths as if holding in some great secret. So Zhava got to work as best she could with her recovering injuries, and together the four of them cleared away the debris, pulled up entire sections of dead plants and bushes, repaired any decorations that could be quickly put back together and set upright, washed the walls, and lit several torches and the two wall sconces that were still operating. Someone brought over a plate of fruit and nuts somewhere in the middle of all that work, and just as dusk was beginning to settle, they all stood in the doorway to the storage room and admired their work. The only remaining signs that a fight had occurred within the courtyard were the boarded-up wall and the lack of flowers and vegetation. Other than that, they had managed to brighten up everything, set up several places to sit or lounge, and made it something that could truly be called welcoming. It wasn't beautiful, Zhava thought as she stood with her hands on her hips staring at the courtyard, but it was certainly someplace that could become beautiful once again – given enough time and care.

"Why did this need to be completed before nightfall?" she asked Brother Y'Mey.

"Your Little Soldiers didn't tell you?" he asked with a grin.

She turned, and they all giggled. "What have you done?"

"Aaria," Y'Mey said. "Go get the musicians. Sanama, go retrieve Barae."

Zhava turned to him and stared, trying to decide what her new house master was planning.

"Weclin, go upstairs and tell him it is time."

"What's going on?" Zhava asked. The three Initiates sprinted away.

"They are good secret-keepers," Y'Mey said as he watched them go.

"Why do we need musicians?"

"An evening is not nearly as festive without musicians, and this is certainly an occasion worth celebrating – the first Initiates promoted to Novice since the fighting several moons ago."

Zhava didn't know that. She had been so focused on her own studies and training and preparations that she gave no attention to what was going on in the other houses. Initiate House received several new Candidates just last moon; she never noticed that no one left.

"And," Y'Mey continued, "your Little Soldiers kept a surprise for you." He pointed to the other end of the courtyard where Weclin opened a door to let someone through. A taller man stepped into the courtyard behind him, a loose-fitting shirt draped casually about him and a flowing sundyt wrapped loosely around his hips and legs. For just a moment, Zhava's heart stopped – not from excitement but from fear. Ooleng? But no, this man was far more handsome than her former betrothed. It wasn't...Posef, though she wasn't entirely sure if that thought was good or bad. As the man walked across the courtyard, his broad smile beamed at her, and she saw the waves of long hair draped down his shoulders – and she recognized him immediately.

"Caleb!" she called out in joy.

"I heard there was something to celebrate, but," he said with a laugh, "little sister, you are a mess."

She ran forward, wrapped her arms around her brother, and gave him a fierce, loving hug. She was overjoyed that he would travel all this way to see her promoted. Life was good.

Chapter 9

Zhava pulled away from him and immediately started talking. How was he doing? How were Papa and Mama? And her other two brothers, what were they doing? And their wives and children, were they doing well? And why hadn't Caleb found a wife yet? How did people keep it a secret that he was coming for a visit? How long could he stay? What did he want to do while he was visiting? The questions flew from her mouth almost faster than Caleb could answer. She felt like Barae.

When Caleb gave the briefest of answers to each question, Brother Y'Mey sent Zhava upstairs to clean up and get ready. The party would begin soon.

When she returned, proudly wearing the new, red Novice blouse and skirt she found lying on the bed in her room, the center courtyard was beginning to fill with people and get a bit loud – and musical. A trio of women stood by the far wall, one playing a wooden flute and the other two playing lyres. The music was festive, and it reminded her of some of the music her Papa and brothers would play late in the evenings after the day's work finished. There were at least a dozen red-robed Novices milling about, most of whom she had never met, a couple Initiates who would be going to the Proving Cove sometime before the next moon, and a few young Candidates standing in a corner nervously glancing at anyone who came near them. Several of the Hibaro's teachers, servants, and leaders, drinks in hand, were smiling and chatting with the students as they casually wandered the courtyard.

"Just like home," Caleb said as he stepped beside her.

"With you here," she said with a smile. "But why are you here? How did you know I would be promoted?"

"A messenger came to Papa last moon. Someone named 'Barae' wrote to tell him you would be promoted."

Zhava nodded. It was very much like Barae to do something like that, to announce to the world something that thrilled her, even if it hadn't happened yet, long before Zhava entered the Proving Cove. Even if the final decision rested with people who would not care how many people Barae invited.

"But the message said it wasn't supposed to happen for at least another moon," Caleb said. "What happened?"

So Zhava told her story again. Even though she had shared it with Sister Tegara, then with her Little Soldiers, this telling still felt new. Unique. Her brother wanted to know. Someone from her family was interested in what she was doing, was asking questions along the way, was curious why she did things and how she did them. He gasped – literally swung his head around, his eyes wide, and gasped – as she told how the baby creatures had bit her arm, her shoulder, and her stomach. She showed him the scars and bandages.

He was fascinated by her vision of the future, and he asked a dozen questions about her husband, the house and barn, and the children and grandchildren. Then he asked all about her training, mostly about her fighting and Abilities training, but he was also curious about her studies of the Kandor. His smile was wide, and his eyes gleamed in the reflected glow of the lanterns and torches scattered throughout the courtyard as she finished explaining the Third Couplet of the Kandor's King Stanza, a particularly beautiful narrative from the times of legends, and one of her personal favorites.

Caleb leaned in close so she could hear him over the noise of the crowd and the music. "Papa will never say, but he is very proud of you."

"I know he is," she replied. "And I know why he will never say it."

"He told you?"

"He told me." The pain of it still hurt. She had never before seen her Papa so emotional as when he described the curse placed upon Mama, and the many seasons of anguish he endured at the decision he made. She did not blame him, but it did not make it any easier to deal with the repercussions of that moment so long ago.

Caleb turned away and frowned. "I'm surprised. I didn't think he would ever tell you."

"Mama and I fought," she whispered, barely loud enough for him to hear. She still found the moment embarrassing, though it happened several moons ago. It seemed so important at the time, so necessary to yell and to raise her hand in anger and to come so close to lashing out with her Abilities. She never wanted to lose control like that again. "It was bad."

"Let's go outside and talk some more," he said, gesturing her toward the side door out of the courtyard. "It's too loud in here."

The crowd had grown much larger while she and Caleb talked, and the path from the courtyard wasn't easily navigated. The three musicians were playing a lively jig, and a few people were dancing near the pot of ferns Zhava had placed along the path to add a splash of color to the dirt. Several Novices she did not recognize patted her shoulders and commended her for advancing in her training. It felt good to be among so many happy, excited people.

"Zhava!" the squeaking voice called through the crowd.

She couldn't help but smile as Barae shoved people aside, gripped Zhava's arms and hugged her tightly. Sister Tegara trailed in Barae's wake, a smile on her face and a drink in her hand.

"The crutch?" Zhava asked when Barae stepped back.

"No crutch," she said, beaming. She hobbled in a quick circle and said, "Still a limp, but no crutch. Who's he?"

"My brother Caleb," Zhava said.

"The brother!" She lunged forward and hugged him too. "We sent letters. Well, I sent a few letters, but he was the only one who wrote back, and then he just sent back the one letter saying he'd come for a visit sometime. I told him you were sent into the Cove early – but I never saw a letter that you would be coming so soon. When did you get here?"

Caleb opened his mouth to reply, but Barae kept talking.

"It's great you got here when you did, though, because it's not just Zhava who got promoted. I'm a Novice now too!" She bounced on her toes, elatedly glancing at each of them in turn. "I took my clothes and weapons up to my new room already, but Sister Tegara said I could come straight back down because the party already started; I didn't need to change into my Novice clothes yet." She turned to Zhava. "Although you already did. Maybe I should have done that?"

"You look fine." She was happy for her friend. Barae worked so hard for many moons, training and studying and writing reports to Sister Tegara. She spent nearly two full seasons as an Initiate – never quite good enough to advance, but certainly displaying enough raw power and passion to let her continue on.

"Oh, Weclin!" Barae waved her arms until she caught the boy's attention through the crowd.

Tegara used that moment to slip away into the crowd just as Weclin joined their little group. He had a stern look on his face, and his eyes darted around at the people pressing in on him. This was the first time Zhava had seen him around this many people, and he looked miserable. Other than being with Aaria,

Sanama, and Zhava, Weclin preferred the company of his animals, especially the sengret. Being younger and shorter than just about everyone in the courtyard probably made him feel hemmed in, as if he couldn't easily escape.

"Weclin, this is Zhava's brother Caleb," Barae said.

The two exchanged greetings, but Weclin kept glancing around the crowd of people.

"Caleb's never seen a sengret," Barae continued.

That got Weclin's attention. He frowned at Caleb and said, "Then what animals have you seen?"

"He has a farmstead out near the Sineise Desert," Barae laughed. "He has seen many strange animals, but he's never seen a sengret. Go take him to the stables and show him yours."

"Sure," he said with a shrug. "Follow me." He turned and darted away, eager to get out of the crowd.

Zhava shrugged at her brother, then gestured for him to follow the boy. Whatever Barae wanted, she was trying to get Zhava alone. Once they left, Barae grabbed Zhava's hand and pulled her in close.

"This is exciting, isn't it?" she said. "You and me? Both promoted to Novice at the same time?"

"It is exciting." She let Barae lead her through the crowd. She had learned moons ago it was often easier to go along with whatever Barae wanted to do than to try to stop her – or lead her.

"It was supposed to have been Plishka," Barae continued, although it was difficult to hear as they walked past the musicians. "But Plishka had to go away, so they let me take her turn."

That explained much. Zhava wondered why Barae had been allowed to enter the Proving Cove when she did, when so many were recommending against it.

She stopped pulling Zhava's hand, turned and faced her, cocked her head, and smiled. "Dance with me."

"What?" The music was loud where they stood, and several people nearby were dancing the Tsiftoolio to the lively rhythm of the strumming and high, fluting notes. The dance was fun, and Zhava had seen a few people do it, but she had never tried it herself. What was Barae thinking?

"Come dance with me," she repeated, her smile large, and her laugh high and free. She lifted her hands into the air, snapped her fingers to the beat, and lightly tapped her feet across the uneven dirt floor.

Zhava raised her arms into the air, uncomfortably imitating Barae – and casting quick glances to see who might be watching her stumble through this dance she did not know. Nobody seemed to give her any attention.

"Feel the rhythm," Barae said as she took Zhava's hand in her own and led her in a loose loop.

She could feel the strumming beat within her chest – she felt little else being so close to the musicians – but it didn't seem to translate naturally to the rest of her body. She stumbled a bit across the floor, and Barae threw back her head and laughed, but it was a good-natured laugh, the laugh of a friend enjoying the moment. Zhava laughed with her, and she stopped thinking about the beat. She stopped thinking about how she was supposed to move and where she was supposed to step. In many ways it was like her last fight with Plishka. She could feel the rhythm of the song, just as Barae said, and she could almost anticipate what the musicians would do next. She felt herself going with the music, almost floating on the looping melody as she and Barae held hands and kicked their feet and circled each other in the press of the crowd. She had no idea how well they were actually dancing the Tsiftoolio, but she also didn't care. It was simply enough to be with her friend and let herself be free in the moment.

Two others hands reached in and joined them, and she looked down to see Aaria and Sanama dancing with them. She had never seen the Tsiftoolio with four people, but she didn't think it mattered. The two Initiates smiled up at Zhava, both of them thrilled to be included in the festivities, and she smiled back at them and laughed. Barae was glancing at the two, and if her face didn't seem quite as happy as a few moments ago, she was still smiling and dancing with her full energy. They released their hands, clapped a syncopated rhythm, then kicked their feet – nearly knocking into each other's ankles – then spun on their heels, grabbed hands again, and twisted away in the other direction.

The musicians stopped for half a beat, then resumed at a faster pace, and Zhava, Barae, Aaria, and Sanama started giggling. They tapped out their steps upon the ground, twisted their hips – and slipped their hands out of each other's grips. They staggered apart for just a moment, nearly knocking into several nearby people, and then they fell forward and wrapped arms around each other, hugging tightly and laughing uproariously at their failed attempt to keep up.

"That was so much fun," Zhava said, and she hugged them each in turn. When she got to Barae, she hugged a little tighter and said, "Thank you for inviting me to dance. You were right; it was exactly what I needed."

"It...really?" Barae asked.

"It was perfect. Thank you." She gave her friend one last, quick squeeze, then turned to go find her brother. She moved quickly through the crowd of people, many of whom smiled at her or congratulated her as she passed. This day started well when she learned she would be promoted to Novice; it got better when she spent all afternoon working with her friends; when her brother showed up, she thought the day was complete; but now that so many people from all across the Hibaro converged on their little courtyard to dance and celebrate, she was overjoyed. All the noise, the press of the people around her, the lively music spreading over everything...it was all so much fun. Her parents had thrown only a couple parties her entire life, and then it was only for her family, the aunts and uncles and cousins from across the valley, and then once even from deep in the Sineise, but neither of those had been anything like this.

She heard someone call her name as she worked her way to the storage room door, and she glanced back quickly. It was impossible to see who it was through the crowd, so she continued on. Even this little room with two lamps lit had several people sitting around an upturned barrel and talking, their drinks set before them and smiles on their faces. One of the men, the captain she'd seen with Io Liori, called a hearty, "Congratulations, Zhava!" as she passed, and she smiled and waved at him before she stepped outside.

The air outside was so much cooler than the long, narrow courtyard. The music, however, echoed off the courtyard walls and bounced up into the night, and she could still taste the rhythm of the fast-paced Tsiftoolio as the musicians brought it to a rousing end. The crowd inside cheered, and Zhava shut her eyes and smiled as she leaned against the outside wall. Yes, this was a wonderful night. She wasn't sure how it could get any better.

"Zhava," Posef said. "Didn't you hear me?"

"I heard someone calling, but I didn't know it was you," she said, as she turned to him. Her vision flashed before her again: She and Posef, elderly and living on the Storm Coast, their children and grandchildren coming to visit. A vision of what was to come...or a vision of what could come? If it was absolute, if it was ordained by the Gods...could she fight it? However, if it was her choice, if it was one future among many...would she even want to fight it?

Posef could be a braggart; he could commend himself for the slightest little accomplishment, and he could talk about all the incredible things he did, or that he would do; he was always so certain of himself, and if he ever failed, he laughed it off and said he planned to fail.

But he could also be one of the most compassionate and caring people at the Hibaro; he would go out of his way to help someone; he would go and stand watch with a friend until the middle of the night just to keep a friend company; he would give someone a hand in a competition and then claim he did nothing, that the other person simply exaggerated the assistance. What did it mean that the Gods had shown her this future life with him? What was she to learn about herself now that she would...or that she could...grow old beside this brash, compassionate young man? She would have to talk with Sister Tegara some more about these questions, find out her thoughts on the future. For now, however, for this present moment...she grasped Posef's hand and pulled him forward. She'd never held hands with a boy, and it felt good.

"Come with me," she said. "There's someone I want you to meet."

They found Caleb and Weclin in the soldiers' barn where the sengret was being boarded. Io Liori did not want the giant bird near the regular livestock where it would scare the other animals – or possibly fly off with one. She didn't trust the creature, and she didn't fully trust Weclin's ability to control it. He did well enough when the bird was calm, but when too many noises distracted it, or when it became too focused on any one thing, it stopped listening to him. With any other bird, that would be a manageable problem.

Sengrets, however, were creatures out of legend. They grew nearly as tall as a person; they could easily carry in their talons the weight of two fully armored soldiers; and this one alone could eat a dozen rabbits in a single day. They had not been seen anywhere on this side of the Purneese Mountains for generations, and most people believed them to have died off. This one was also quite intelligent, and with Weclin's Ability to speak with animals, it had already been trained to do some amazing stunts.

At the moment, however, the sengret was in its "cage," three horse stalls with their interior walls knocked down, their doors chained shut, and their open-air windows boarded across to keep it from flying away. Caleb leaned forward, his head pressed against a beam and his eyes wide as he viewed the bird between the slats of wood.

"But how does it listen to you?" he asked.

"That's my Ability," Weclin said. "I can talk to animals."

"Yes, you said that. But how? How do you speak to it, and how does it understand you? How does it know what you want it to do?"

Zhava smiled as she and Posef quietly approached. This was a familiar conversation. Caleb asked her similar questions when she was a girl, when all she could do was twirl around the dirt and rocks upon the farmstead's dusty ground. But HOW did she make the dust blow out the kitchen door when Mama said to sweep? But HOW did she make a rock skip down the creek – upstream! – until it went around the bend and out of sight? And WHY did the Gods bless her and not him with this Ability? So many questions she could never answer, and that last one seemed especially to bother him.

"I don't know," Weclin said with a shrug. "I asked my teachers, and they said I'll know the answer to that when I've mastered my Ability. For now, I must simply learn it."

Zhava knew her brother well enough that an answer such as that would never satisfy him. She chuckled when he said, "But that makes no sense."

"Read the Kandor, brother," she called to him from down the wide, center aisle. "'Do not question the wisdom of Vek, the Ruler of the Gods. He bestows upon some the servants' duties, and those servants must follow the rule of the Gods.'"

"Little sister, you have never followed anyone's rule," Caleb laughed. He turned from the sengret, and the smile disappeared almost immediately as he glanced from Zhava's face to her hand holding Posef's hand and pulling him forward, then up to Posef himself. Caleb's eyes narrowed, and his jaw clenched.

Zhava released Posef's hand, but it was too late. Caleb's smile remained frozen in place, but his arms tensed and his feet shifted in the dirt. No one else might notice, but Zhava did. Her Papa reacted that way when he got mad, when he expected to strike out at someone. Of all the members of her family, Caleb was the least likely to follow the old ways, the traditions of the elders of the desert. He spoke his mind at the family gatherings, even when his mind was different than that of Papa; he would not always follow his oldest brother's directions, especially if those directions did not directly benefit Caleb himself; and he had even requested his inheritance and moved onto his own land before he was married, claiming that a farmstead of his own farther down into the valley would allow him to grow up, become a better man, become the kind of man who would attract a more successful woman. Which made it that much funnier that the first woman to actually catch his attention, Plishka, was also the least likely to care about his success, his cattle, his large house, or his riches.

Though all of those things made him unique among those living on the edge of the Purneese Mountains and just off the border of the Sineise Desert, those older traditions were still bound up within his heart, within his very soul. He had been raised with them. Zhava had been raised with them also, but she never found them a comfortable fit. Priestess Marmaran showed her a different path, and Io Liori brought her to the Hibaro to walk that new path. Caleb, however....

Caleb would care deeply that his little sister held the hand of an unrelated man.

"This is my good friend Posef," she said, gesturing toward him.

"Hello," Posef said. He stepped forward, his smile wide and his arms outstretched.

Caleb gripped Posef's offered hand in his own, then wrapped his other arm around Posef and pulled him in close, clapped him on the back. As he did, he glared at Zhava, and she saw the fierceness in his eyes, the anger, the lack of understanding of the friendship she had with this young man. He saw only another man who held the hand of his sister.

"Wow, that is a strong grip," Posef laughed.

Caleb stepped back and released Posef's hand. Posef chuckled a few more times, but when Caleb did not laugh, he coughed uncomfortably and stepped back, nearer to the barn wall. Weclin stepped away also, his head down and his eyes glancing nervously at Zhava.

"Tell me," Caleb said, turning first to Posef and then to Zhava. "What is the difference between a 'friend' and a 'good friend'? What does that mean?"

"Posef is from the Highlands," Zhava started.

"Is he?" Caleb's eyes widened. "I had not noticed. His green eyes hid his heritage so well."

Zhava cringed. She apparently made things worse. She had known little of the Highlands before arriving here, and Posef's stories all seemed exotic and adventurous. Caleb must have...heard something different?

"Brother," she snapped, regaining his attention. "I would speak with you outside."

"Yes. Let's speak." He turned away from Posef and stalked past Zhava, not even looking at her as he made his way to the barn door and the glow of evening.

Zhava cringed, but Posef and Weclin were kind enough to step aside and begin a conversation between themselves. They laughed, stood before the sengret's stall, and pretended the tension of a few moments ago had not even happened.

Zhava clenched her jaw in anger and followed Caleb outside. They went around the side of the barn, away from the party at the Novice House. The sun was just setting atop the tallest trees, and the birds were fluttering and chirping in their roosts. A few sparkles of light flitted through the underbrush, star-bugs dancing among the tall grass.

Caleb suddenly rounded on her and said, "How dare you! How dare you embarrass me like that."

"Embarrass – you? You were the one being rude to my friend."

"At the Hibaro, is 'friend' simply another way of saying 'betrothed'?"

"Betrothed?" She stepped away, as if the word itself struck her. She had said nothing to him about Posef in her vision. This was from something else. "I'm not betrothed. How could you think I'm betrothed?"

"You were holding this man's hand. You were presenting him to me for my approval. Could you not have told me first?"

"Gods! This is just like that knife thing back home. You don't trust me." She stopped and took a breath. "Yes, I was holding his hand, but that is not such a problem here at the Hibaro, and he is from the Highlands anyway. It does not mean anything in the Highlands for me to take my friend's hand – even if he is a man."

Zhava realized the music had stopped, and she wondered how much their voices carried from the side of the barn. They were a fair distance from the Novice House, but she could hear people shouting. If she could hear that, others might hear her and her brother arguing.

"I know all too well what things mean to those people in the Highlands," Caleb blurted. "To them and their caravans. Their herds of goats and sheep. Their cold months traveling, all those men and women together keeping warm against their winters."

"What are you saying? What are you thinking of me?"

"I've heard the stories, Zhava, and you should have also. Those people in the Highlands, they don't treat women with respect."

Zhava just stared at him, her mouth open wide. Words like this she could have expected from Papa and her other two brothers, certainly from Mama with her curse. But from Caleb? He had always been the brother who was nicer to her, the brother nearest her age and the one who tried most to understand her.

"They don't...they don't value women. They don't respect women. Don't you understand? They take their wives, their daughters, and they go up high into the mountains, and they force them to work alongside them. They force them to labor in the bitter snows, to drive their caravans across the mountain passes. And when they are in those mountain villages, so high above the plains that even the Gods themselves have trouble seeing them, then they...well, they...."

"They what?" she whispered. She could not believe the things she was hearing. What was he saying about her friend? What was he saying about her?

"The parents will hold these...awful parties for the children. They'll build huge fires in the Highland forests, and the young men and women will dance naked beneath the full moon-"

Zhava shut her eyes and turned away. She wished she could shut out what she was hearing, the awful words her brother said. She had known Posef all these many moons, and he was a kind, caring, considerate young man. He had his weird qualities, of course – but who didn't? He flouted the rules, certainly. He was late to lessons, and he treated the Kandor with not quite the respect his teachers demanded – and he was sent to extra duties for those transgressions, but that did not mean he was the kind of man who would do what Caleb said. Posef might wink at her, and he might smile mischievously at her, but he always treated her with respect.

As for the work that was done? Zhava had done far more than simply toting and fetching and driving wagons in her time at the Hibaro. If Caleb did not approve of the labors of Highland women on their caravans, what would he say of the extreme lessons she endured at the Hibaro? What would he say about her strength training? Her weapons training? Her Abilities training? He saw it once, when he went at her with a knife, but apparently he didn't take that moment to heart, did not realize she did that kind of training all the time.

"Zhava, when you walked in holding the hand of a young man from the Highlands...what did you expect me to think?"

The shouting had grown louder, and nearer. She not only heard the sounds of young voices, the students from the various houses who were having fun at the party, but she also heard the barks of soldiers, the occasional clang of metal armor. One voice, however, seemed to carry above the others. It was a high-pitched voice, a pleading voice that was screaming out to be heard.

"What is that?" she said, turning from Caleb. Turning away from the awful conversation. And then she made out the words clearly, the name the hoarse voice screamed to be heard.

"Master Caleb!" the voice called.

Caleb heard it too. He pushed her aside and ran. Zhava quickly followed, rounding the edge of the barn to see a large crowd gathering along the northern edge of the Hibaro, just off the main road. Soldiers were running along the edge of the road, searching among the trees. Ios and priests stood at the edge of a small circle of people, and students were being ushered away by a dozen more soldiers. As Zhava ran, she saw a man on his knees in the dirt, one soldier gripping the man's dirty and blood-stained shirt to keep him from running away. One side of the man's face was purple and swollen, and his outstretched arms were dark with mud and dried blood. He knelt there, struggling to free himself from the soldier's tight-fisted grip, and screamed to the sky, "Master Caleb! Master Caleb!"

As she and her brother ran up, the battered and bloodied man seemed to get renewed life. He yanked himself forward, nearly knocking the soldier off balance, and tried to reach out to Caleb. Closer up, Zhava saw that the man wore servant's robes, but they were frayed and dirty, soaked and blood-stained. Whatever happened to this man, it had been violent.

"Master Caleb!" he cried out, struggling to shuffle forward on his knees through the dust. He turned his one, good eye on Zhava, and his face seemed to brighten at the sight of her. "Mistress Zhava! Oh, thank the Gods, I found you both!" He raised his arms above his head, sank to the ground, and slipped himself free of the tattered shirt and the soldier's tight grip. The soldier staggered away.

The shirtless man fell forward in the dirt and wrapped his arms around Caleb's ankles, crying and babbling uncontrollably. His back bore short cuts and bruises, further evidence he had escaped something awful. Beneath the injuries, however, Zhava could see tight, lean muscles and a deep, healthy complexion. This man was used to hard work in the hot sun, most likely a field worker or a mountain shepherd. For something to drive a man of such strength to this level of injury and despair must have been truly horrific.

"Master Caleb," the man said, his frantic cries finally subsiding enough to be understood. "Oh, Master Caleb, I am so sorry. I am so sorry. Please do not punish me. I tried to save them. I tried!"

Caleb knelt to the ground and gripped the man's shoulders, forced him to look up from the dirt, and said, "Tell me clearly. What happened? What did you try to save?"

"The Master's family, sir," the man cried out. He turned to Zhava, and his one, good eye brimmed with tears. "Your father and your mother, Mistress Zhava! They came in the night – bandits, they were! – but I could not stop them. I could not save your father and your mother!"

Chapter 10

Sister Tegara recruited Zhava to assist in tending the man's injuries.

He was Monh, someone Papa recently hired to break the horses in preparation for market.

Zhava went through the motions of helping. When Tegara told her to do something, she did it, but the man's words kept repeating in her mind: "Bandits! I could not stop them. I could not save your father and your mother."

Caleb kept asking questions, but Monh was so badly injured and in such distress that he could not give a coherent answer. The soldiers held back Caleb so that Tegara and Zhava could take the servant away and tend to his injuries.

Two deep cuts, one in Monh's left thigh and another on his left arm. The eye looked worse than it actually was. The dried blood and the swelling had sealed it shut, but when they cleaned around it, the eye seemed intact. He would likely keep his vision.

Bandits struck the farmstead. Papa and Mama were gone, taken away in the night.

Zhava applied healing ointments and bandages and sewed together some of the deeper cuts, Tegara used her healer's touch, and together they soon had the man patched back together.

They led him to the soldiers' barracks, to Io Liori's office. More than a dozen men and women sat or stood in the room.

Caleb, his whole body tense and his fingers fidgeting with a small length of rope, sat in a chair to the side of the window. Brother Y'Mey sat next to him, his white skin and short-cropped hair even more prominent next to Caleb's deep tan and rugged features. Brother Tymare, the custodian of the Hibaro's library, stood by the wall, shuffling his feet and glancing nervously at all the people in the small room. He much preferred his books and his work over anything that involved people. Sister Allenka, one of the few people at the Hibaro that Zhava simply did not like, sat at Io Liori's desk, her hand on a wooden mallet as she surveyed the people and listened in on their conversations. She wasn't an evil woman, but she enjoyed her position of power and used it to make others' lives more difficult – especially the youngest students. The remaining people were soldiers and Ios and priests Zhava had seen many times, but she had never learned their names. Posef and Barae stood in the farthest corner of the room, obviously tolerated there only because they were Zhava's friends. She could think of few gatherings with this many important people where they would be allowed to remain.

Sister Tegara led Monh to an empty chair next to the desk, whispered something into Allenka's ear, and sat nearby.

Caleb pointed at Zhava, then to the empty chair beside him. She would have preferred being with her friends at the back of the room, but she wanted to be as near to Monh as she could when he was questioned.

And the questioning began immediately. Sister Allenka smacked the wooden mallet to the table to get everyone's attention, and then she demanded that the servant speak.

Monh looked at Caleb who nodded his agreement.

Allenka sighed loudly and again ordered the man to tell his tale.

"It was six nights ago," he said.

"That was when I left to come here," Caleb whispered.

Zhava thought back. That would have been when Io Liori and Salient Ayaan told her she would be going early into the Proving Cove. About the time Plishka left. Gods, was that only six nights ago?

"I was in the fields since sun-up, working with the new horses." His voice was low and scratchy, and he tugged at his throat as if it hurt. It probably did, from all the screaming he did when he arrived. He wore a new set of clothes, a plain shirt and trousers, though Zhava could not remember when he changed into them. Her mind replayed his first words too often – "Your father and your mother...." Bandages bulged in odd places across his body, and a soft compress had been set above his eye, held in place by a cloth bound gently around his head. Cleaned up, he didn't look nearly as bad as when he arrived.

"They sent out a good midday lunch. Some cheese and some wafers, even a small cup of wine." He turned to Caleb and Zhava. "They were good people, your father and your mother."

"Yes, I'm sure they were," Allenka said, striking the mallet to the desk with a quick rap. "Continue."

"I...well, I didn't see nothing. I didn't suspect nothing. I finished my midday lunch and got right back to work, but the servant who brought that out to me...Ukah? Ukuh? I am sorry, but I did not know him well, I worked for your father such a short time."

"Ukuehr?" Caleb asked.

"Ukuehr? Possibly. I did not know him well."

Zhava knew him. One of Mama's household helpers. A sloucher who preferred not working.

"I found his body at the edge of the field when I returned that evening. Two arrows to the back, one in the shoulder and one center on. There was nothing to be done for him."

Zhava looked away. If the bandits had done that to a household servant....

"I knew there was trouble, but I didn't realize how bad it was. I thought I could help. I gathered up all my weapons from the shop, my hatchet and bow, my own knives, and I went straight up to the house. There were so many of them, though. There was nothing I could do. They'd already taken the house, and they were tearing out the valuables. I saw a couple more of the servants dead on the ground, and your father and your mother...your father and your mother were bound and set up alongside the house with gags in their mouths."

Anger rose in Zhava. Papa...Mama.... Her hands prickled as the flames itched to come forth.

"I was caught soon after. I fought and killed two of their men, but the one...the giant."

"Giant?" Allenka said with a laugh.

"He stood as tall as the mountain, and his armor shined in the sun. One punch from him, and I couldn't feel my arm. He laughed as the others caught me and beat me. I never saw him again, and I never want to."

Allenka rolled her eyes and sat back in the chair. "So they caught you?" she said. "Then how did you get all the way here? On foot?"

"Sister Allenka," said one of the soldiers – the new captain who arrived with Salient Ayaan. "Let the man speak."

"They took what they wanted from the house, they rounded up the camels and the horses, and they bound the three of us together, one after the other, tied together with ropes at our hands and feet – first your mother, and then your father, and then me. They led us away, and I could barely see, I could barely walk. But I managed to slip the ropes when they weren't looking. The one man who tied the knots at my wrists, he knew nothing of good knots, and I was able to slip the knot loose. I knew there was nothing I could do, but I had to get to you, Master Caleb. I knew you would have to do something. I knew you would have to be told."

"Me?" Caleb shook his head and bit his lip before he continued. He turned his fiery eyes on the servant. "I'm the youngest! Why didn't you go to my brothers? To Mitsel or to Alxindra? Their farmsteads – their families! – were just down the valley. Why travel all this way to me, here, when they were so near?"

"Please forgive me, Master Caleb," Monh said as he hung his head and stared at his bare, swollen feet. "I was so new to your father's employ, and he never said nothing about any other sons. He said his son Caleb was traveling to the Hibaro to visit his daughter Zhava. He said that to me not 10 nights ago. He never said nothing about a son Mitsel or a son Alxindra. If I had known...but I swear to you I knew nothing."

Caleb gripped the edges of his chair and shook his head.

"But I promise you, they were not going back down into the valley," Monh blurted out. "They were riding south, heading straight into the Sineise."

The desert. Her papa and her mama being driven on foot into the desert sands. Their horses and their camels being driven into the desert. That could only mean one thing.

"They're to be sold," she whispered. "Sold into slavery."

The captain asked the man dozens of questions about the bandits: How many were there? What did their armor look like? They wore no visible armor? Then what colors and patterns were their robes? What did their swords and bows look like? Their arrows? What markings or insignias did the man see? Were there any brands on the bandits' camels?

Sister Allenka demanded the man retell his entire story again, and she stopped him frequently when he mentioned the man as tall as a mountain, dismissing the description of the "giant" with a wave of her hand and another rap of the wooden gavel.

Sister Tegara asked many questions about his journey to the Hibaro. What route did he take? Did he come upon anyone else as he walked? How far was he able to travel in a day? How badly did his injuries impede his walking?

Caleb remained silent through most of this, his head down and his eyes studying the floor as he listened intently. He only interrupted the man when he told again of the damage to the farmstead, of the bandits raiding the home and the fields and the barns. The bandits sounded quick and efficient – but so audacious to conduct their raid in the middle of the day, in the open like that where they could be seen by anyone traveling nearby.

That was not the only thing that made so little sense. Through all of Zhava's childhood, their family had always kept good relations with the desert tribes. They hosted in their home's courtyard several of the desert lords and their families. They traded grains and livestock with the desert lords. Her Mama and Papa even traveled a day's journey into the desert with one of the lords, returning with wild stories of an ocean of sand and of the pools of rippling, silvery waters that could be seen in the distance – that always vanished before their very eyes as they approached. Why would this particular group attack her family? What was to be gained?

Monh was dismissed. A soldier escorted him out and to a barracks room where he could be kept under watch.

"Thank you for your hospitality," Caleb said to everyone. "I will take Monh, and we will leave at first light. I must tend to these matters."

"And I request a temporary leave to accompany my brother home."

"Oh, little bird," Allenka said with a laugh, "you are the noisy one, aren't you? You really think we would let you go?"

"I shall accompany them," Sister Tegara said, standing and staring down at Allenka. "The attack is several nights old, but there may still be injured who need tending."

"What?" Allenka said, turning from Zhava to Tegara with a frown. "But you can't possibly, you old jay. You're needed here."

"Zhava is under my command in Novice House," Brother Y'Mey said from his spot beside Caleb. "What has happened to her family is a tragedy, and I will authorize her temporary leave from the Hibaro – under the supervision of Sister Tegara." He turned to the guard captain. "And if your soldiers could accompany them? Those bandits might have returned in the intervening nights."

"I will bring my soldiers and travel with them myself, yes. I want to see this attack," the captain said, shifting back in his chair. "Several things about it seem wrong. If we are witnessing an increased threat from the Sineise Desert, or – Gods help us! – from the peoples of Go'aab itself, we must be aware."

Chapter 11

Before the dawn broke, Zhava walked to the Hibaro stables and began fitting a horse for the trek home. Caleb was already there, his pack set and his horse contentedly nibbling on the dewy grass. They ignored each other, just as they had done last night after they were dismissed. What more was there to say? They had grown further apart in only a few moons than Zhava thought possible.

Captain Redoly was also there with three of his soldiers, a woman and two men, and their mounts were nearly set with bedrolls, weapons, and field provisions. Sister Tegara was just brushing down her horse for the morning, several bags of medical supplies piled alongside her own bedroll and bow and foodstuffs along the dusty floor outside the stall. What surprised Zhava most, however, was seeing Posef and Barae at the far end of the barn preparing horses of their own. They waved and pointed to their meager bags set on the floor. Sister Tegara gave Zhava a wink and a nod as she pulled a blanket off the wall, then ducked back into her horse's stall.

"What are they doing here?" Caleb said, startling Zhava so much she jerked away in surprise. He pointed at Posef and Barae, his eyes narrowed as he considered them.

"Coming with us," she said. Then, because she was mad at her brother for his stubbornness and the way he judged her and Posef: "They are my friends."

The muscles of Caleb's jaw twitched, and he stalked back to his horse and yanked the bridle from the wall with a snap that made everyone, even the horses, jump.

"Settle down," Captain Redoly called from farther down the barn. "Angry riders, anxious animals, not a good combination."

The nine of them worked in silence after that, Zhava and Caleb because they would not speak to each other, Posef and Barae because they were trying not to draw too much attention to themselves, Tegara because she was content to hum softly to herself and her horse, and the four soldiers because they knew their duties and were simply going about them. A guard soon escorted Monh into the stables and pointed to a horse. He began tending the animal, his steps stiff and limping as he tried to see his way around the stall with his one good eye.

Before the sun peaked above the tree line, they mounted and headed down the main road from the Hibaro and into the surrounding forest. The perimeter guards saluted the captain and waved to everyone else. Within moments, the 10 of them were moving steadily along the trail and leaving the campus behind, the captain and one of his soldiers taking the lead while the two other soldiers rode in the rear. Caleb rode directly behind the captain, keeping his pace quick and steady, and the others spread themselves out evenly, Zhava riding as near to the back as she could. Let Caleb ride alone, she thought. The pre-dawn forest was coming alive with birds calling and flitting among the trees and small animals scurrying through the underbrush. The air had an early winter's chill to it that bit at Zhava's nose, and she rather enjoyed the quiet and solitude of riding at the back of the group.

It wasn't long, however, before the captain set Caleb in his place at the front and slowed his ride until he was even with Zhava. He paced his horse with hers, then waved forward the two soldiers at their rear. They passed, allowing Zhava and

Captain Redoly an amount of privacy now at the very end of the procession. He pointed forward, up the line of riders.

"These friends of yours, Posef and Barae."

She nodded.

"What are their Abilities? Give me your evaluation."

"Posef can hear thoughts and speak into people's minds, and Barae...well, she has an affinity for ropes and cloth."

"Not good enough," he said with a shake of his head. "I asked you to evaluate them. I need to know what I can use if we get into a combat situation. I know my people, and I know Sister Tegara. I observed you during weapons training."

She didn't know when he did that, but it felt good to know she was worth observing.

"But those two? I didn't want them along; Tegara insisted. Said they were your best friends and you would need your friends at a time like this. I need to know what they'll do in a fight."

So she explained Posef's Ability. He needed to be near another person, but that distance varied from one moment to the next. One time he could hear and speak with another person's mind from one end of the Hibaro to the other; the next time he could barely connect with that same person from across a small room. The priests worked with him to focus his thoughts, to hone his Ability, and he improved, even within the few moons she had been at the Hibaro, but his Ability could still fail him at any moment.

"But he can communicate with anyone?"

"He has to know you're there. They've tried to get him to find people hidden across the Hibaro, but he never can. If you tell him who is there and where she's hidden, though, he can usually do it."

"Hm." The captain shrugged his shoulders, thinking as he stared at Posef's back. "And the other one? Barae?"

"She's great. She's a wonderful friend who would do any-thing for me–"

"Stop." He turned and stared at her. "I know you're young, Zhava, but you are gaining responsibilities. I've heard of these children who follow you around, 'Zhava's Little Soldiers.' You might think it's wonderful or cute or...I'm not sure, maybe you thrive on the attention."

"I do not."

He waved away the comment with a flick of his wrist and a frown. "I'm not asking what's in your heart. I need your evaluation of the combat abilities of your companions. These friends of yours, the soldiers traveling with you. The ones who will have your back – or won't."

Zhava sighed and stared at her hands holding the reins and lazily resting on her saddle's horn. She lifted her hands. "Barae is weak," she whispered.

Captain Redoly leaned nearer and cocked his head to hear her better.

"She has been slow to progress through her training, taking nearly two seasons to advance from Initiate to Novice."

"You did that in only six moons."

"Yes. It is not from a lack of trying, however. She tries very hard, and she desperately wants to succeed."

"Desperate people are sloppy people."

"No, that's not what I meant."

"It is. It's what you said, and what I heard."

"It's not...I just don't think–"

"And her Ability? Her 'affinity for ropes and cloth'?"

"Rope and cloth, woven material, it responds to her touch. She can weave together some of the most beautiful clothes and tapestries. The teachers won't let her do it outside of her classes, however. I don't know why."

"Clothes and tapestries," he said with a sigh. "Not very useful in the middle of a fight. How is she with that little sword she's carrying?"

"She took it with her into the Proving Cove. She fought the beast with it."

"Yes, the Proving Cove. I heard that tale. The beast swatted the sword from her grip. She didn't even draw blood." Another sigh, and he straightened in the saddle. "So. Useless."

That stung. Her friend wasn't useless. She was a wonderful, vibrant, joy-filled young woman who tried her very best to do the things she set out to do. She might be slower than others to achieve them, and her Abilities might not be the best suited for a one-on-one fight, but that did not make her "useless." She opened her mouth to say more, to provide some amount of praise for Barae, but the captain suddenly turned to her and smiled.

"Well done," he said. "A good analysis." He snicked the reins, gave a quick order for the two soldiers to return to the rear of the procession, and rode forward until he caught up with Tegara and started talking with her.

Zhava watched his back, the folds of his outer robes blowing in the chilled breeze across the pieces of leather armor. She felt awful for the things she said about Barae. About her friend. It wasn't that those statements were false; everything she said was the truth. But being the truth did not make it less painful. Barae tried really hard. She studied, she practiced, she worked long into the night. She was not, however, very good at either her philosophies or her fighting, and her Gods-given Ability might help her produce beautiful clothes, but it would not win her any fights on the battlefield. She had passed through the Proving Cove, but to hear her tell the tale, she did not accomplish anything before the animal bit her and sent her into the vision world. Her arrow did nothing, and her sword had been knocked aside before she could land a strike. If Zhava was really being honest with herself, had she – not Tegara – been the one to evaluate Barae's performance in the Proving Cove...then Barae would still be an Initiate.

She shut her eyes, tried to push aside that thought, but now that it came to mind, it would not leave. Barae was not a good fighter. She was a good friend, certainly, but if it came to a fight, Zhava would prefer Posef at her side, not Barae. She would really prefer Plishka at her side instead of either of them...but that was not a nice thought either.

Her friends soon joined her at the back of the procession, and they began chatting with her, taking her mind off the honest analysis of their combat skills. They smiled and joked with her, assuming her downcast attitude was because of the attack on her home. They weren't completely mistaken, but when they asked why Captain Redoly spoke with her so long, she dismissed their questions, said he was asking about her family. The layout of the farmstead. Tactical positions that would be best for their approach. That seemed to make sense to them, and they asked nothing more.

The ride was fast-paced and long, and they soon left behind the forest of the Hibaro hills and entered the scrubby plains leading to the foothills of the Purneese Mountains. It was a solid 2-day ride to the farmstead, but Captain Redoly wanted to arrive with as much daylight as possible on the second day, so they kept up their speed, stopped only briefly for a midday lunch, and did not make camp until late into the evening. The skies were clear, so they simply made a low fire, roasted a couple rabbits they caught during the day, and spread their bedrolls in a loose circle. Captain Redoly took first watch, strolled into the darkness, and was soon swallowed up by the night.

Caleb, still silently chastising Zhava, set out his blankets on the direct opposite side of the campsite from her. The soldiers positioned their bedrolls around Monh, apparently still distrusting him, and then sat awake and polishing their armor and weapons as the servant fidgeted nervously and stared into the embers of the dying fire. Barea set out her blankets next to Zhava, and Posef sat between her and the soldiers, twining blades of grass around some sticks.

Sister Tegara stepped from the darkness and into the dim glow of the campsite, walked to Zhava, and whispered into her ear, "It is a beautiful night. Take Posef and go for a walk."

Zhava tensed. What was this? Was Sister Tegara trying to make things even harder with Caleb? This idea was probably the worst thing she could do to her brother, who already thought Gods-knew-what about Posef and her friendship with him.

"Thank you, Sister," she mumbled in reply. "But I'm tired, and I think I'll just bed down for the night."

"Clearly and distinctly ask him to go with you," she whispered, pointing to their left, "in that direction. I'll be your chaperone. Now go."

Zhava did not want to do this, but she recognized an order when she heard one – even if Sister Tegara did not use the words "I order you." Zhava sighed, stood from her place by the fire, smiled, and turned to Posef.

"It's a beautiful night," she said cheerfully, holding out her hand. "Let's go for a walk."

Every face around the fire turned to her and Posef. Monh watched, seemingly curious. The soldiers glanced at each other, but did not give away any reaction, positive or negative. Barae stared wide-eyed, her mouth gaping open. Caleb, however, barely contained his rage behind the hard-set line of his jaw and the piercing gaze.

"Great," Posef said with a grin. He jumped up and gripped her hand.

Zhava cringed at his enthusiasm. How could he be so oblivious to the emotions swirling around them?

"Pardon," one of the soldiers said as he stood from his place. "It's late and dark, and we know from the servant's testimony that bandits have been out here. It might not be the safest-"

"I will go with them," Sister Tegara said with a smile. "And I'm sure Captain Redoly will see us from wherever he has positioned himself out there. We will not stray far."

Zhava led the way, Posef close behind, his hand tightly gripping her own. She did not turn around. She did not want to see her brother's anger. As they stepped away from the circle of dim light that was their campsite, she saw that Tegara was right; the night really was beautiful. She looked up at the sky, and it was almost completely clear. A few wisps of clouds brushed the horizon to the east, but otherwise they could see almost every star glowing high above. The moon had not yet risen, but on a clear night like this, Zhava was certain it would be spectacular when it did.

"This is great," Posef said.

"Yes," she agreed, and she had to admit that it was very nice. Even holding his hand, that was also nice. When she had taken his hand at the party and led him to the stables, she thought nothing of it. He was her friend, she wanted him to meet her brother, and taking his hand and pulling him along had simply been the quickest way to get him there. Now, however, they had no place to go, no place she was trying to lead him. They did not need to rush anywhere. Yet his hand felt...good in hers.

"I'm sorry about your family," he said.

And suddenly the good feelings evaporated like wisps on the breath of his words. She released his hand and turned away, turned her eyes to the stars. "Thank you." What more was there to say?

"We'll find out what happened to them," he continued, his fingers brushing the back of her hand. "We'll find something, some clue as to where they were taken, or something about the people who took them. We'll go out to the desert tribes and get them back."

He had obviously never been to the desert. Why would he, raised in the Highlands of the north, among the tallest peaks of Remmli? What did he know of the southern desert? Of the tribes that moved through there? Of the people on the other side of the desert, the vicious fighters of Go'aab.

"Excellent," a voice said from out of the darkness, and both Zhava and Posef jumped and spun to the man standing in the deep shadow at their backs. He stepped forward – Captain Redoly.

"We must be quick," Sister Tegara said. "Your own soldiers did not like us leaving the camp."

"They know their orders. They'll stay with the servant." He turned to Zhava. "I watched you on the ride today. You're smart; you were watching our surroundings, keeping an eye on our perimeter. Very good."

"Um...thanks."

He turned to Posef. "You can read minds?"

"Well, some, sure. Yes."

"Excellent. That servant, Monh, is lying. I need to know what's inside his mind."

"Lying?" Zhava said. "About what? About my parents?"

"We do not yet know," Sister Tegara said. "But his injuries were not six nights old. They were more recent, perhaps three or four nights at the most. And did you see his feet? He did not walk all the way to the Hibaro. He traveled far, but not that far."

"We're the scouting party," Redoly said. "Investigate this attack – if there really was an attack – and send back word to the Hibaro. Possibly even to the King, depending what we find. But listen to me, you two."

Zhava and Posef nodded.

"We have decided to entrust this information to you two, but only to you two. Your friend Barae, she is not to know this."

"But-" Zhava said.

"Stop." Redoly held up a finger in front of Zhava's face. "Evaluate. She is not the best fighter, her Abilities are not suited to the battlefield, and she never stops talking. I will not trust her to keep this information secret."

"She can keep a secret," Zhava said.

"And this is not a discussion. This is my operation, and I have just given you my order."

"Yes, Sir. And Caleb?"

"No. I know he's your brother, but I've only just met him."

She nodded. She didn't like it, but she would obey.

"Excellent. And Posef? Do you understand, or have I made a mistake trusting you?"

"Yes, Sir, I understand. Don't tell Barae. Don't tell Caleb."

"Excellent. Let's be quick about this."

They knelt down among the small, prickly bushes. Posef shut his eyes and concentrated. It took barely a moment for the connection to be made, and then he described what he heard.

"He's scared," Posef said. "He can't...show it, but he's scared."

"Of us?" Redoly asked. "Of the soldiers?"

"Yes, but there's something more. Something...out there." He gestured to the darkness around them. "A person. No. Some people? Just one person. Is he out there? What was that noise? Where did he go?"

"His testimony never specified one particular person," Tegara whispered.

"Who is this person?" Redoly asked. "What's he look like? What's his name?"

"I can't see pictures. I can only hear thoughts, and he's not thinking of a name." He jerked suddenly, his body twisting to the side. "What was that?"

The others turned and looked into the darkness, but they saw nothing out there.

"Was that him?" Posef blurted. "Did they come back for me? No. Nothing. Calm. Stay calm. It will all be over soon."

"I don't like the sound of that," Tegara said, shaking her head.

"Excellent," Redoly said, gripping Posef's arm.

Posef shook his head, clearing his thoughts, and smiled at the captain.

"The servant is still worried. He's not safe, which means we aren't either. That's excellent information. Now you three had best get back to the camp. I don't want my soldiers getting too nervous about you."

They stood and dispersed, Captain Redoly sinking back into the dark of the night while Tegara led Zhava and Posef to the camp.

"Hands," Tegara whispered.

Posef took Zhava's hand and smiled. They had to keep up appearances. This had been nothing more than a nice, intimate walk between two friends...who were likely more than friends...just as Caleb had said, just as Caleb had feared.

Monh was lying beneath his blanket, his eyes wide as he stared into the darkness. Two of the soldiers were lying beside him, the woman sitting up and facing outward, into the darkness. Caleb had rolled over, facing away from the fire, and Barae had also crawled beneath her blanket, rolled over, and faced away from them all.

"Thank you," Posef whispered, just loudly enough that anyone still awake would hear. "I enjoyed that."

"Yes," Zhava whispered back, but with far less enthusiasm. "I enjoyed that too." She didn't know if anyone listening would believe her, and she really didn't care. Her brother had accused her of lying, of pretending that her friendship with Posef was more than she claimed. Her vision had shown her a future in which she and Posef were old and living out their final years on the Storm Coasts, being visited by their children and their grandchildren. What was truth anymore? Without a word to anyone, without a glance at anyone else, she yanked back the blankets from the ground, laid down and covered up, then turned her back on the small circle and tried to fall asleep.

***

It was the intensity of the darkness that made Zhava realize she was not yet awake, that she was instead drifting through a dreamlike fog. She had been here a few times already, and she knew what she would find, but she did not know how to reach it, how to quickly get to her teacher, Priestess Marmaran, and the glass prison that contained her, and so she swam aimlessly through the ocean of black.

Except, she realized, the darkness was not as complete as she would have expected from her other visits to this spirit realm. A faint glow seemed to spread around her, a bluish tint to the infinity of the nothing. She drifted through that blueish haze, and she caught a faint whiff of something burning, charred, as if left on the fire too long. The air around her seemed to hum its malevolence, to warn her of impending danger.

Lightning crackled before her, searing its jagged crack into her vision. More than that, however, was the long, distorted face that peered back at her through the cloud, the dead man whose giant hand reached through the lightning so slowly, so gently, reaching out to touch the living flesh of another being. To touch Zhava.

She stumbled backward and found herself again on the broken path through the spirit realm where she first met Emsterold. She staggered forward. This was not the spirit world of

Priestess Marmaran's glass prison, as she thought. This was the land of the dead. The vision began as she expected, like the other times she met her Priestess. What happened this time? How did she travel so far away?

More lightning, and she saw several more faces of the dead drifting through the clouds above, watching her, reaching down to her. She shivered. What would happen if one of them touched her? Would she die? Would she be allowed to leave?

She turned on the path, and before her stood a tall, glass bottle, its neck reaching to the sky – Priestess Marmaran's prison. The glass was splintered and cracked in a network of webs that sparkled blue-white with each lightning flash. It made no sense for the prison bottle to be here, though, in this vision world with Emsterold and the dead. Did Emsterold call it here?

"Ah, my child," Marmaran's voice echoed from behind the glass.

Zhava stepped closer. She caught her own cracked reflection, but she could not see Marmaran. One more step, and then another. Wisps of dark clouds circled within the bottle, obscuring her view. What happened? What was the prison doing to Priestess Marmaran?

She reached forward, touched her palm to the glass, and the dark clouds swirled away, blown as if by a gust of wind. Priestess Marmaran stood on the far side, her back to Zhava and her own palm pressed against the glass' interior wall. Her robes were tattered and frayed, and her hair was blackened, as if covered in soot or layers of dust. But there was a third person, another woman standing directly before Marmaran on the outside of the bottle. The woman with the long, wet hair and the ghostly eyes: Emsterold. Zhava stood there, her hand pressed to the glass prison, staring at Priestess Marmaran trapped within, as Marmaran stood facing away, her own hand pressed to the glass and mirroring Emsterold's stance on the opposite side of the bottle.

She kept her hand against the bottle and walked to her left. Without stepping, the images of Priestess Marmaran within and Emsterold directly outside shifted with her, remaining straight across, as if reality itself bent. Zhava turned and walked back to the right, and the two woman drifted with her, always opposite her, their own palms pressed against the glass.

"My child," Marmaran said. She did not turn around. She did not move. "This is a powerful vision."

"Yes, Marmaran," Zhava said.

Emsterold shifted her gaze, looked at Zhava through the two walls of curved glass.

"To visit with the dead, and not only once but twice. Child, you are growing."

"This is not my doing."

Marmaran laughed, but the laugh soon grew into a fit of coughing. She sounded as if she would collapse from the force of the coughs, but her body did not shift. She remained planted in her spot, palm to palm with Emsterold.

"Child, you must find this woman. Find this woman living among the dead, and you must free her."

"How am I to find her here? I don't even know how to get here."

"This woman is not dead. She is a traveler, but she does not reside here." She turned, the first time she moved since Zhava arrived. She cocked an ear to the sky, as if listening. "You must leave now, Zhava. You must go quickly."

The black clouds circled back within the bottle, once again obscuring the view.

"No!" Zhava yelled. She pounded her fists against the glass, but the swirling clouds only thickened. "Marmaran, no. Please come back."

She stepped away and tried to see as far up the bottle as she could. Reflections lit the glass – but not the reflections of the spirit world, not the land of the dead. She saw the night's sky, the thousands of stars twinkling back at her, the sliver of moon where it was rising just off the horizon. She saw spindly, scrubby trees and the orange glow of dying embers, and she recognized it.

"The campsite."

Several bodies lay wrapped in blankets around the circle, and one of the soldiers stood across the camp and with her back to the group as she stared into the night.

"He's here," Zhava whispered.

She saw herself lying on the ground, wrapped in her own blanket and sleeping soundly.

"Wake up!"

She opened her eyes. She stared back at herself in the reflection of the spirit prison. She sat up, raised her hand before her face, and called forth a ball of flames. She had never before known what that looked like from the outside. She had done it so many times that it was more habit, more instinctual now, but it actually looked quite -

- her spirit yanked away, and she fell back inside her body, looked out into the night surrounding the campsite, and panicked. Someone out there!

She threw the ball of flame straight out, and it connected with a solid body – a man standing directly in front of her. He yelped and jumped and beat at the flames, then turned and ran.

"He's here!" Zhava yelled. She threw aside the blanket and leaped to her feet.

Voices echoed behind her, startled voices and the shouts of someone giving orders. She crashed into the night, throwing more balls of flames before her. The man wasn't fast, but he kept ducking aside, turning just as she would reach out to him.

His movements were erratic, jerking first to the left and then to the right and then to the right again. Never consistent. Always changing his route. She gripped the hem of his hood and yanked back hard, but the fabric tore away, and she stumbled. Righting herself within a couple steps, she bolted forward.

An arm reached out from the darkness and gripped her around the waist. She tumbled forward, and the man spun her off to the right, kicked her legs out from beneath her, and threw her down hard to the ground. The breath was knocked out of her, and then he landed on top of her, straddled her across the stomach and fell forward on her. She pulled two hands full of flames, but the man flicked a dagger to her neck and pressed in hard, the point jabbing up into her jaw – and that's when the light of her flames lit his face.

"My bride," he muttered, his head shaking. "My – very bride. Snuff the flames. Snuff the flames!"

She stared into Ooleng's savage eyes. She recognized him, but only just. He had grown out his beard, but it was in patches, red and tender in spots where he it had been torn out. The right side of his head was shaved, and a bright, white patch of scar extended from just in front of his ear and halfway up his head.

"Snuff them – now!" He turned his head away, hiding the shaved patch and the scar from view. "Do not – see that. Do not look."

She shut her hands on the flames.

He calmed a bit, but he still jerked his head as if something forced him to look away.

"Did you?" he whispered. He bent even nearer to Zhava, leaned in close to her face. He smelled sweaty, dirty, as if he had not washed himself in days. "Is that – why you're here? Did you?"

"What?" she asked.

"The gift, of – of course." Another twitch. "Did you get – the gift? Is that? You're here because – the gift?"

She shook her head. What gift? What was he talking about?

He jerked away, pounded a fist into the ground, and screamed at her, "The box!"

Voices suddenly grew louder, sharper. They heard his shout.

"The box," he whispered, leaning in close again. "It was yours. It was – for you. You came – and you – you found it, where I...left it. Yes?"

The box in the woods. She gave it to those soldiers, and she pushed it from her thoughts. The ornate box with the word "Wife" carved into it.

"Yes, I got it," she said. "That was from you?"

"Of course – my bride. Of course." He relaxed his body, and he seemed to almost melt on top of her, his head lolling onto her shoulder, and his left arm collapsing beneath his own weight. "You – got it. Got it. Good."

She shifted beneath him, took in a full breath, prepared to fight him if she had to.

"My wife," he whispered. "He said – said you would come." He shifted away, rolled off of her, and sat on the ground beside her.

Zhava cautiously sat up and stared at him through the darkness. He looked so small, sitting there alone with his face to the ground. His body shook, just a little at first, and he put his hands to his face and sniffled. He was crying. He turned away from her, and that white scar flashed in the dim light of the moon, exposed by the shaved side of his head for all to see...and she now realized what had happened. When she escaped the prison cave. When she broke loose from her chains. She kicked Ooleng's legs out from beneath him, and he fell to the cave floor. He bashed his head against the rocks, and he bled into the frigid water pooling there.

"You – would come," Ooleng said through the tears. "Come for her. Come for them."

"What are you saying?" she asked. The voices in the distance grew closer, Captain Redoly and Sister Tegara, the soldiers. "Who said I would come?"

"Come – back to me." He turned and faced her again, and his face shone wet with the tears he had smeared. He pulled back the crease of his filthy, stained robe to reveal the top of a shiny, cracked bottle with a stopper burned into its end. "Come – for her."

"You have it," she whispered. Then, with her hand outstretched, she said: "Give it to me."

"You – you are my wife." He looked at her, his head bobbing in the dark.

"Yes, of course," she said with a smile. "I have always been your wife. Now give me the bottle."

"But – but you said-"

She leaned forward on her knees, made herself a little taller than him. "It doesn't matter what I said. I made a mistake. I have always been your wife. Now give me the bottle."

"So – your Papa – your Papa."

She grew still, reaching out, as she waited for him to finish. What did he know of her Papa?

"You are not – not coming to find – your Papa?"

She stared. She forgot to breathe, forgot to blink, forgot to move. Ooleng...knew that her parents were missing. He knew that she would be out here, that she would be traveling home. Knew that her parents were missing from the farmstead, and that she had to return to find them.

"What have you done?" she asked, her lips barely moving as the words slipped away.

He shuffled in the dirt, glancing first this way and then that. His head twitched, and he struggled to stand.

Zhava stood up first, her arms and legs locked tight, her eyes boring into the man.

"This – is very – good," he said, wagging his finger into the darkness. "Very good. We just need – find them. Buy – them back. One family – again."

The flames were rolling through Zhava's hands before she realized she called them. The flickering glow lit his patchy, disheveled face, made his twitching eyes sparkle in the reflected light. He turned and stared at the flames in her hands, and he stepped closer to her, reached out to take her fire-filled hands into his own.

"My – love," he said. "So – beautiful. A morning – star."

"Where are my parents?"

"What?" His head jerked up, and he stared into her eyes. He squinted, and his open, tear-stained face contorted into a snarl. His lips curled high, and his eyes opened wide. "You tried – to kill me!"

His scream startled her, and she jumped back, her flaming hands outstretched before her. He pulled his knife again and lunged at her – and then fell back, an arrow piercing his shoulder.

"Murder!" he screamed, spinning away through the dirt.

Zhava glanced back. The woman soldier – what was her name? – ran forward, her bow held high as she loosed another arrow. It snapped past Zhava, barely missing Ooleng's head as he stumbled.

"No!" Zhava called to her. "Don't kill him!"

Ooleng kicked away into the night.

Zhava turned to follow, but a hand snaked around her arm and yanked her to a stop.

"Let go!"

"No," the woman yelled back. "Stop and listen."

Zhava struggled to pull her arm free, but the soldier's grip was tight.

"Listen," she said again.

Zhava stopped. She stared into the woman's hard eyes and clenched her mouth shut. Ooleng was escaping, she thought. Ooleng was escaping, and she was being told to listen – and then she heard it. She turned her head and listened closely. There...just off in the distance...Ooleng was giving orders in that stilted way he spoke. A voice called back, and then a second voice, and a third.

"We don't know how many there are," the soldier said. "You and I, we're exposed out here. We get back to camp, and we prepare."

"That was Ooleng," Zhava muttered.

"That's good. Now we have a name for our enemy. Let's go."

She shut her hands and snuffed out the flames so she and the soldier could not be seen.

"Do you know why this Ooleng would want to harm you or your family?"

Oh, she knew. She knew all too well why he would want to harm them. She should have killed him in that cave, she thought. She would not make that mistake again.

Chapter 12

"Zhava, the next time an enemy attacks our camp, you do not go running off into the night to chase him down." Captain Redoly stared at her from his place sitting on the upturned stump, the pre-dawn glow just lighting the horizon beyond.

She nodded.

"You are not in command, and you left your spot, which was to be sleeping-" He pointed. "-just over there. I had been watching that man approach, observing him from a distance, but I lost him in the blinding light of all that fire you were slinging around – and then Brii-"

Ah, Zhava thought, her name's Brii.

"-had to go after you to ensure your safety, I had to go run down this lying piece of filth-" He pointed at Monh, now sitting propped against a dead tree with his hands and feet bound and a cloth wrapped tightly around his mouth. "-and your two little friends-" A quick flick of his wrist at Posef and Barae. "-had to be tackled before they could go chasing after you too. Your brother-" He glanced at Caleb standing on the far side and polishing his sword. "-was the only one of you with any sense. He remained at his spot, his sword drawn and ready to defend the camp."

"Yes, Sir," she said, her head down and her hands clasped in her lap. "I'm sorry, Sir. It's just that I saw him-"

"Yes, you said as much. Your betrothed. The spurned love of your life. The crazed man with the half-shaved head that you saw in your vision, but somehow he was here in the real world also, standing at the edge of camp and walking straight toward you. An amazing story." He leaned forward on the stump, clasped his hands together, looked Zhava in the eyes, and spoke slowly and quietly to her. "I have no Gods-granted Abilities, I receive no visions from the land of the dead, and – do not misunderstand – I have no time for such things when they serve no purpose in the fight. I believe in my eyes, my ears, my armor, and my weapon. You...." He licked his lips, clenched his eyes, then spoke even more softly, barely loud enough for Zhava to hear. "You threw around enough flames to light up our camp for half a day's walk in every direction, and for all that fire, you only. Hit him. Once." He held up one, shaking finger. "Once."

"Yes, Sir," Zhava whispered back, "but he-"

"Stop. This is my operation. I will get you home, we will tend to your wounded family, but this is my command. You follow my orders. Yes?" He watched her. Waited until she shut her mouth. "Excellent. I believe we understand each other." He stood, kicked aside the stump on which he'd been sitting, flicked a knife from his belt and stalked toward Monh.

The servant's eyes grew wide as he watched the captain approach with the knife, and he started moaning through the cloth in his mouth, kicking away with his bound feet.

Redoly flicked the knife, gripped a handful of the man's hair, slipped the blade beneath the cloth, and sliced it apart. He tugged the end, yanked it out of Monh's mouth and off his head, and tossed it into the dirt. Monh coughed and drew in a deep breath, then glared at the captain.

Redoly walked around the circle, picked up Brii's bow and quiver of arrows from her side, then waved the bow casually in Posef's direction.

"You. Be ready with that little trick you do."

"Yes, Sir." Posef's eyes were wide, and he grinned up at the captain.

Redoly stopped directly opposite the servant, propped the quiver against a rock, and knocked an arrow into place.

"How long has it been, Brii, since I last fired one of these?"

"Oh, a season or two at least, Sir," she said with a somber tone. "You're quite out of practice."

"I am at that." He turned and sighted along the shaft, let loose the string, and the arrow sailed high above Monh's head and embedded itself into a tree that was nowhere near their camp. He lowered the bow and squinted at the faraway arrow. "Well, damn," he muttered. "That was terrible."

Monh twisted around and looked at the arrow, then turned back, his eyes wide and his mouth gaping open as he watched the captain.

"Time to talk," Redoly said. He pulled another arrow from the quiver.

"I already told you," Monh said. "I don't know nothing else. That's the truth."

Redoly slipped the arrow into place, pulled back on the string, sighted along the shaft, and released. This one also went high, but it just nicked the dead tree, ricocheted off to the right, and skittered along the ground and into the underbrush.

"Brii, when did you last service this bow?" He flipped it around in his hands, studying the wood and the string.

"The night before we left, Sir. It's in fine condition."

"No, I don't think so. The tension must be off, or maybe this string is worn. I know I'm not this bad."

"As you say, Sir." She leaned back and watched.

"Monh, you need to think of something more," he said, retrieving another arrow. "Something we haven't heard. Maybe something about this crazed man with the shaved head? The one who thinks he's still married to Zhava?"

"We were never married," Zhava muttered.

"Very good, yes," Redoly said with a laugh. He slipped the arrow into place, pulled back, released. With a solid thwack it embedded deep into the dead tree's trunk, directly above the man's head. "Excellent! Just had to compensate for that loose tension. Brii, I want this bow serviced again. Soon."

"I swear to you, sirs, I don't know nothing!" Monh licked his lips and looked nervously around the circle of people. The soldiers looked bored, though Brii seemed the most interested, probably because it was her bow the captain was using. Caleb had put away his sword and stood watching the proceedings, his arms crossed and that perpetual frown on his face. Sister Tegara sat with Barae. She was glaring at the captain, but Barae watched with wide eyes, seemingly enjoying it all. Posef had his eyes shut, his brows furrowed in concentration. "Won't no one stop this? I swear I told you the truth. I told you all I know! I just work with the horses – nothing more!"

A third arrow. Slipped into place, string pulled back, released. It hit the collar of the man's frayed jacket, just above his shoulder, and stabbed the cloth deep into the dead tree.

"Aaaahhh!" Monh screamed, turning his head and jerking away from the arrow embedded alongside his head.

"Damn," Redoly muttered again, lowering the bow. "I was aiming for his arm. Did you see I was aiming for his arm?"

"You missed," Brii said with a shrug.

"Aaaaahhhh!" Monh continued screaming.

"I have several more of Brii's arrows," Redoly said, turning to retrieve another. "I know I will get better with each shot, but I do not have much more patience." He glanced at the lightening sky, the sun just about to peak over the horizon. "Or time."

"All right!" Monh yelled. "All right. His name's Ooleng. He just wants Zhava back. He wants to marry Zhava, and then he'll let her parents go free. I swear that is the truth. By the Gods, that is what I know."

Captain Redoly stood staring across the camp at the terrified man kicking in the dust and trying to tug his coat free of the arrow. He smiled and said, "Posef?"

"It's almost true," Posef said with a shrug. "He's Ooleng's man, and he's never worked for Zhava's parents."

Monh stopped struggling and turned to stare at Posef.

"Ooleng hired him," Posef continued. "Paid him pretty well too. Then they beat him up just enough to look bad and sent him walking to the Hibaro."

"No," Monh said. "No, that's not true. Not true! You're lying."

"And the parents?" Redoly asked. He slowly shifted the bow in his hands, slipped the arrow into place.

Posef glanced at Zhava, then at Caleb. He lowered his head and shifted in his spot, refused to look at either of them. "They're gone," he said. "That's the part that was mostly true. Sold to some man in the desert, just as he told us before."

"Now that is not good," Redoly said. "I did not want that part to be true." He slowly, carefully raised the bow and sighted along the shaft, the arrow aimed straight at Monh.

"No!" Monh said. He kicked and squirmed, tried to yank himself free of the arrow holding his jacket. "I can help you. I can help! I know his people. I know where they're hiding!"

"He's lying," Posef said. "He's only seen Ooleng and some woman mercenary from across the Purneese. Ooleng told him what to say, right down to the story about the giant, and she beat him."

"No! No, the giant's real. I swear to you, I can help!"

The captain released. The arrow shot true.

Monh screamed and ducked.

The arrow sailed above the man's head and struck the trunk of the dead tree, embedding itself directly next to the other one. Their shafts ticked against each other as they came to a rest.

"Good shot," Brii said with a yawn.

Redoly lowered the bow and frowned at the tree, the two arrows so close together they could almost be one. "Ah, when I was younger, I could have split the shaft," he said. "Too much time at a desk; too many reports. However, Brii, as always, your equipment...." He waved the bow at her and winked. "...is in excellent shape."

They struck camp quickly. Captain Redoly had Monh gagged again and tied to his horse – with a threat to sit still and behave, or he would be tied to the belly of the horse instead of its back. He gave Brii and one of the other soldiers some whispered instructions and sent them ahead, then he arranged a new order of travel: the captain and Caleb in front; Monh and Barae next – with Barae given instructions to lecture the "treacherous animal" at length on what was written in the Kandor about the punishments for lying, selling people into slavery, and dealing with enemies of the Gods; then he placed Sister Tegara and Posef together; and he set Zhava at the end of the line with their other remaining soldier, Ravid. He was a large man with bushy hair and a beard down to the middle of his chest, and Zhava had not heard him say two words since they'd left the Hibaro. Apparently Captain Redoly wanted Barae to talk and Zhava to shut up. Punishment, she decided, that's what it was. She hadn't done right when Ooleng attacked the camp, had messed up Captain Redoly's grand plan for somehow defending everyone by letting an enemy stroll into their midst while they slept, and now she was stuck at the rear of the procession that was heading to her own home. She would be the last one to see the farmstead – or what was left of it. It was spiteful and vindictive, she decided, and it truly showed how much the captain had grown to dislike her in such a short time.

The two fingers appeared before her face – SNAP!

She spun in her saddle, nearly tipping to the side, and glared at the soldier riding beside her.

"Whatever you were just thinking about," he said, his voice deep and slow, "stop it. Think about now." He pointed at the ground. "Think about here." He waved his hand in a broad circle that encompassed the trail they followed, the dry, dusty landscape around them, and the small clumps of trees that dotted the landscape.

"I know here, and I know now," she said. "I'm from here – we're near my family's farmstead."

"We're being followed," he said as he casually scanned the horizon to their left.

"We're – what?" She turned to look. She saw nothing.

"You're dangerous."

She turned back to him and stared. What was he talking about? He was silent the entire ride yesterday, but today he was talking about one thing and then another – and what did was dangerous about her? "My flames?" she asked.

"You're inexperienced with those," he muttered. "But that's all."

"Did Captain Redoly tell you to bother me as much as Barae is bothering Monh?"

The tones of Barae's voice had been carrying to them since they left camp, but Zhava couldn't understand what her friend said. As the captain instructed, however, she hadn't stopped talking since they left camp, and Monh's head hung low, his chin pressed firmly against his chest.

The soldier beside her chuckled now, low and rumbling in his throat. He casually glanced to their right.

"Think," he said. "You're rear guard now. Like me. Our duty is to ensure the safety of the people in front of us. Make sure no one sneaks up from behind."

The weight of this information seemed suddenly to press down upon her, and she found it difficult to breathe. She had been so busy getting angry at Captain Redoly for putting her at the end of the line, she hadn't thought it might be a responsibility – not a punishment. She considered their surroundings with that idea in mind, from the perspective of the suddenly chatty soldier riding with her. She looked again at the trail. The scrubby trees all around. Their lines of sight. She knew Ooleng was out there. She and Brii heard several voices in the dark, so he probably had people working with him, though Monh seemed to know only one other person with Ooleng.

She turned back to the soldier. "Who's following us?"

"Don't know."

She studied him and realized he was not randomly looking around as she thought; he was varying where he looked, first one way and then the other, then back again, then up. She could discern no real pattern to the way he watched their surroundings, but she was absolutely certain he was being methodical, that he watched all around as they travelled.

"Started following us as soon as we left the Hibaro," the soldier continued, his voice low. "We lost him about halfway to camp yesterday. Almost certain he's on foot. I think he's back out there now."

"Is it Ooleng?"

"No. Saw your man last night. He's too tall. This one's shorter." He glanced at Zhava. "Shorter than you."

That didn't help. She was taller than many of the people she met. She was taller than Mama, almost as tall as Papa. She was taller than two of her brothers and several of the students at the Hibaro. If she lined up all the people she knew by height, all the people at home, in the little village down from her farmstead, and from the Hibaro, she would probably be standing far nearer to the taller end. However, that did rule out Ooleng as the person following them; he was just a bit taller than she – much taller if he had his long hair bound atop his head. Although with half the hair on his head shaved away, that top bun would not be nearly as impressive.

She turned to the soldier and smiled. It was time she knew more about her traveling companions. "I'm Zhava," she said.

"Yes."

She waited. He glanced at her, then turned and continued looking around, observing their surroundings.

"And what's your name?"

"Tomaath."

That name sounded very familiar. Zhava thought back. It wasn't long ago she heard that name, that the name had been spoken by...Io Kua. It was during a lesson on the King's army, and how a great soldier, Tomaath, led the charge against a group of Go'aabite bandits who were disrupting trade along the caravan routes. Tomaath's unit found the bandits' camp, snuck in on a moonless night, and tied up all the bandits before morning. Not an arrow fired, not a sword drawn, and not a drop of blood spilled. For that work, the King had promoted Tomaath to-

"Oh my Gods," she blurted. "You're a Strike Force soldier." She looked up the line to Captain Redoly's back. The man was smiling and talking with Caleb, as if he hadn't a care in the world, but she began really analyzing his weapons and armor – at least as much as she could see from the end of the line. Fine lines of cloth, polished leather, gleaming bow. She turned back to Tomaath. His horse's tack was finely woven, the metal buckles and rings shining new. His weapons were shining, the pommel on his seemingly plain sword engraved with the mark of the fox – an excellent and very expensive craftsman who worked out of the capital.

The Strike Force soldiers were elite groups of fighters who worked under direct orders of the King. Those soldiers could come from any branch of service: the regular army, Ios, the priests, the brotherhood or sisterhood. They most often came from the ranks of Salients, but not always. The King wanted men and women who consistently achieved results, people he could trust to go out on their own and accomplish the impossible. Which meant....

"Why are you here?" she asked. "Why are we being escorted by a Strike Force to my parents' farmstead?"

Tomaath shrugged. "This is Redoly's mission; not mine."

That was about the least helpful answer she could have received. What would a Strike Force want from her? From her farmstead? Or her brother? Her parents? Were they really there only to escort a few students and a Sister out to the edge of the Sineise? Did they know something more about Ooleng? Or the bandits who attacked her home?

"And you're wrong," he said. "You are not from here."

She just stared, unsure how to reply. His comments were so scattered she could hardly keep up. One moment about this, the next moment about that. He would obviously say only what he wanted to say and nothing more.

"It's in the face," he said, running his hand in a circle about his own face. "You don't have the face of a woman born to the desert plains."

She didn't want to admit it, but she was intrigued. She had learned only a few moons ago that her Mama and Papa were not her real parents, but other than the Salient who revealed that to her, no one had volunteered more information. She waited – biting her lip the entire time – and he soon continued.

"You look more...high forests. Much further north than here."

With that, he turned away and continued studying their surroundings. Zhava did the same, now far more focused than she had been when he first began talking with her. She rode beside him in silence after that, though the trek itself was far from silent. Sister Tegara and Posef talked occasionally, and

Posef asked Zhava a couple questions about the trail. Barae, however, took her assigned task seriously, moving seamlessly from one topic of conversation to the next in her non-stop monologue to Monh.

From the end of the line, Zhava could not hear the details, but some of the phrases she caught had to do with Barae's childhood. She told the man things from when she was a young girl. Her mother died early, and her father took her and her siblings to the open seas to help earn a living fishing. Her oldest brothers now had fishing boats of their own, and all three of the men went out to sea daily. Her older sister married a merchant, and her younger brother worked with horses on a valley farm. Zhava knew all of this, so though she was not a part of the conversation, she only had to hear a bit to know what was said. Monh, however, with his hands bound to the saddle horn, his feet strapped to the stirrups, and a gag looped around his mouth and head, only sat on his horse and hung his head as the stories unfolded. The couple times he seemed to nod off, Barae poked his arm to rouse him.

They stopped only the briefest of time for a mid-morning lunch and to water their horses. Soon after that, however, Captain Redoly turned their group off the main trail and farther toward the north, angling around the farmstead instead of directly toward it. Before Zhava could ride up the line to tell him of his mistake, however, Tomaath set a hand to her arm.

"Your brother's up there," he said. "The captain knows what he's doing."

Zhava wasn't lost, even as they veered so far from the trail that they could no longer see it behind them. She had wandered the low hills and played in nearly every copse they passed for all the seasons of her childhood. Captain Redoly led the procession to the base of a low hill and brought their group to a stop. He set Sister Tegara and Barae to guarding the bound servant and called forward Zhava, Tomaath, Caleb, and Posef to follow him up the hill. As they neared the top of the rise, he had them all crouch down, and they crawled on their bellies through the dirt and short, dry grass as they crested the hill. They were only a short distance from the farmstead, and Zhava knew she could be there soon if she just ran the whole way. Captain Redoly, however, lay there, his head propped in his hands as he studied the way before them.

"All right, children," he said. "What's different out there?" He spoke quietly, just loud enough for them all to hear.

"I have not been here since the last moon," Caleb said. He shielded his eyes from the sun and looked across the low hills before them. "I helped Father move some of the cattle to the north hills, and then I went home. I have my own farmstead down the other end of the valley."

"Zhava?"

She studied the land. The hills and trees. The swaying grasses. The looping paths that wound subtly across the farmstead where she grew up. A breeze blew across her, ruffling her hair and bringing with it the damp, earthy scent of a well-tilled field. It all seemed so normal.

"Nothing," she said with a shake of her head.

Captain Redoly reached around his back and pulled forward a small satchel. He untied the woven cord and pulled out a smaller pouch and a square of hardened leather. The leather had two thin rows of short cloth sewn into the ends. From the pouch, he pulled two bound cloths and carefully unrolled them, revealing thick circles of gleaming, polished glass. They were some of the finest bits of glass Zhava had ever seen — not that she had ever seen much glass in her lifetime, mostly jars for storing herbs or oils, but those were usually cloudy or ripply or bubbly. These pieces of glass contained none of the imperfections she saw in those.

He set the pieces of glass within the cloth rows, rolled together the stiff leather, and looped short cords around rivets to bind the thing together. He held one of the ends to his eye and looked back over the rolling plains before them. He sat like that quite a while, leaning his elbows into the dirt and slowly turning his head from side to side as he stared through the leather tube. After a few moments, he offered the tube to Caleb and explained to him how to hold and look through.

"I see no one," Caleb said. "There is much damage to the house, though. We should go. Now."

"Soon," Redoly said. He took back the leather tube and held it out to Zhava. "Hold it here. Put your eye here. Point it toward there."

She did as she was told, and she was amazed at what she saw. Her home was suddenly right before her eyes. Well, the one eye. Everything through her other eye was still the same as it had been, very far away. She started feeling a little dizzy, and she covered her one eye so she could look only through the tube. The back door of the house, the one that led into the kitchen. The door was hanging to the side on one hinge. The windows along this side, most of the shutters open wide to allow the afternoon breeze through. The rooms seemed empty, though the tube did not bring her close enough to be certain. The square patch of roof set high above the rest of the building, the home's watch tower. Empty. The dusty paths leading around the house, some to the empty field, one to the well out back, and another toward the animal pens and barn. The pens were empty; not surprising because most of the fences had been knocked down.

"Well, Zhava?" Redoly asked. "What's different."

She looked back at everything once more, moved the glass eye back along all the things she knew so well. The house, windows, trails, animal pens, empty fields. It all looked so normal, except....

"I don't see anyone," she said. "That's wrong. Papa has several servants, some in the house and several to work the fields. They're all gone."

She gave the glass eye back to Redoly who used it to look back across the plains. "No people," he muttered. "No animals. No bodies. No movement at all. So, they were all killed, or they were all taken away?"

"Monh said they were taken," Zhava said. She didn't want it to be true, but that they might have been killed was far worse.

"Posef," Redoly said, pointing forward. "I sent Brii and Ravid to the other side of that house, about as far away as we are. I need you to do your trick with them. Find out what they see."

"Sir, it doesn't work like that," he said with a shake of his head.

"You told me. Almost every time you've tried, you've failed." He set down the glass eye and turned to Posef. "Try now. Maybe you'll succeed."

Posef took in a long sigh, gave Zhava a nervous glance, faced forward, and shut his eyes. He sat like that for several moments, his eyes tight and his jaw tense, before he finally shook his head.

"I don't – I can't. I'm sorry."

Redoly pursed his lips, turned back to the house. "What about that farmstead? Can you tell if anyone's there?"

"Sir, I just said–"

"Yes, I know. It doesn't work like that. Try anyway."

Another sigh. He shut his eyes and concentrated again. He dipped his head to the side, and his eyes shifted behind their lids. His breathing quickened, and his mouth opened and shut. Beads of sweat popped across his cheeks and forehead. He gasped and fell forward with a sharp cry.

"Ouch," he muttered.

They all waited, staring at him.

"There is...something inside that house. I don't know what." He shook his head. "The thoughts were loud, but I couldn't understand them. Several images, though, like roaring pictures, one after another. A mountain pass. A cave on fire. Drowning. Anger. But it was more than anger. More like pure rage. And then just...empty. Hollow. Like there was nothing left."

Captain Redoly turned to Zhava and smiled. "You left your husband to drown in a fiery cave, did you not?"

"He's not my husband," she said. "We were never married. But...yes, I left him to drown." She ducked her head. "In a fiery cave."

"Excellent," he said, and he started crawling backward through the short grass. "Let's go visit your husband."

They tied Monh to a tree ("If we're still alive when this is over," Redoly said, "we'll come back for you."), explained the plan to Sister Tegara and Barae ("We're walking up to the kitchen entrance and demanding to speak with Ooleng."), and set off at a leisurely pace ("They'll see us coming, but they can wait for us."). When Barae pointed out to the captain just how foolhardy it was to stroll up to such an obvious trap in the middle of the day, he flashed a huge grin and said, "You're absolutely correct!"

As the horses plodded across the uneven dirt, Zhava took in the state of her family home. It seemed so empty without the animals and servants. A blackened scorch marred the back of the nearest barn, evidence of a recent fire that had been stopped before it destroyed too much. The wind stirred a dust devil across the open field, lending the farmstead an abandoned, forlorn air. They neared the house itself, and Tomaath kept Sister Tegara, Barae, and Posef back. Captain Redoly led Caleb and Zhava forward. About halfway between the broken horse paddock and the house, he dismounted and stepped forward, his arms spread wide at his sides.

"Ooleng!" he called. "Your man, Monh, was terrible at his job. I saw through his little story by about the second time he told it, and so we left him for dead back along the trail. I, however, am a man you can trust to see things through to the end. And as proof, I have hand-delivered your bride to you today."

Zhava stiffened in the saddle and glanced at Caleb. His eyes widened as he watched the captain.

"Come out of there, Ooleng!" Redoly continued. "Come out and claim the woman you want to marry, and then you can pay me for finishing the job your man could not."

They were being betrayed! Zhava spun in her saddle, ready to kick her horse into a desperate run.

Tomaath, however, had his bow out and an arrow pointing at the back of Posef's head.

"You like your friends too much," Tomaath said as he shook his head at her and pulled tighter on the bow's string.

"You traitors!" she yelled.

Redoly laughed.

Ooleng slowly, cautiously, stepped around the broken back door of the house. In the bright afternoon sun, he looked even more crazed than last night. He flinched, his right eye twitching as his head jerked to the side. The shaved, right side of his head was unevenly scarred, the white skin blotchy against the scraggly bits of brown stubble poking from around it. His clothes were dirty, and the hems were ragged. His right hand, which he held against his chest, spasmed in an uneven beat.

"You – You are?" he asked, his voice more a growl than the smooth baritone Zhava remembered.

"The name's Redoly." He stepped forward, his arms outstretched.

Ooleng jerked backward a step and ducked his head, and half a dozen men with bows appeared from within the windows along the side of the house. They leaned down, one arrow pointed at each member of the small group.

"Now that is not very friendly," Redoly said, stepping back and looking from one window to the next.

"What – Who...are you?" Ooleng rasped.

"Redoly. My partner back there is Tomaath."

"You're both traitors!" Zhava yelled. She glanced around, but there was no good way out of this situation. Not with an arrow at the back of Posef's head, and another six arrows pointed at them from the front. Her hands itched, and she fidgeted, tried to decide if she could hit enough of them with her little flames before anyone got hurt.

"I can see why you want her back," Redoly said with a grin. "She is a special one. Beautiful and brave and oh-so-fiery."

Ooleng stood up straight, and he took a shuffling step forward, his left arm clenched in a fist and his right hand tapping rapidly against his chest. "She – is – my wife!"

"Yes, I understand," Redoly said, quickly bowing his head. "No offense intended. None at all. I was merely complimenting your wife's beauty, that is all. Now...." He stood up straight again and held out his open hand. "Do you think we could start the negotiation? Zhava and the brother delivered straight to you, without injury, plus a couple additional people – excellent servant material, all of them – for...let's say, a certain weight in gold?"

Ooleng stood there, his head twitching as he looked from Redoly's hand to the man's face, then to Zhava and Caleb and the others arrayed behind them. He turned back to Redoly and stared, his head twitching occasionally as he focused. He licked his lips and kicked one foot in the dirt. After a long pause, he slowly unclenched his left hand and took a slow, shuffling step forward.

"Gold?" he rasped.

Redoly smiled and took Ooleng's hand. "I knew we could make a deal. Now."

Chapter 13

Zhava was so focused on her anger at Captain Redoly's betrayal that the first few moments of the ambush were lost on her. She saw the other two soldiers, Brii and Ravid, swing over opposite ends of the roof, ropes wrapped tightly around their wrists. Their momentum carried them in looping arcs toward each other and across the wall's outer face. As they crossed the first set of open windows, they jumped over the frames, knocked the men's bows from their hands, and stabbed them beneath their chests.

A voice screamed out to Zhava, but she sat and stared at the violence.

She had trained to fight. Practiced with her sword and her throwing knives and her shield and her Abilities. Killed the bear within the Proving Cove. She even fought High Priest Viekoosh and his soldiers in those mountain caves. But she never expected to see people killed in her own home. Through the open windows. The second floor...inside her own bedroom. The slain man slumped in Brii's arms. She flung him to the ground and ducked inside.

Again, the voice echoed in Zhava's mind. Who was it? Posef?

Zhava! he called with his Ability. The word echoed through her. He spoke directly to her mind again. *Zhava, now! Fight now!*

She shook herself and leaped from her horse. It jerked its head and sidestepped away, leaving her exposed where she stood.

Captain Redoly and Ooleng struggled in the yard, each gripping the other's arm, knives flashing in the sun.

Tomaath had ducked behind the low wall of the water well, and he loosed arrows into the open windows where Ooleng's soldiers fired back. Posef sat at his side, popping his head above the wall and firing his own arrows.

Sister Tegara, a sword in hand, traded blows with a man nearly twice her size by Mama's herb garden – and she seemed to be winning. Caleb marched forward, past all the fighting and straight into the house, his own sword at his side and angry determination on his face.

Zhava took it all in and smiled. Captain Redoly hadn't betrayed them at all – he distracted his enemy, diverted Ooleng's attention long enough for his team to get into position atop the house. Tomaath had an arrow at the ready, fooling them all into thinking he was aiming at Posef when he was ready to loose it upon Ooleng's soldiers. They had drawn much of the fighting outside, into the yard where fewer people could hide inside rooms.

This was a fight she could win.

Flames licked at her palms, and she balled them up, aimed at the armored woman darting around the side of the house, and threw them straight. They struck her shining breastplate and held on tightly, scattering across the metal armor and digging into her skin. She screamed and dropped her sword, waved her arms and tried to beat out the little flames crawling across her.

Zhava flicked a hand, and the dirt beneath the woman's feet brushed away. She lost her balance, staggered, and fell to the ground hard.

Before Zhava could enjoy the quick win, a pair of strong arms wrapped from behind and held on tight. She squirmed and kicked, but the man laughed in her ear and lifted her off the ground. She leaned forward as far as she could, then flung back her head. She felt the crunch of the man's nose, and he screamed and lost his grip. She dropped, clenched her fist, spun, and punched him across the jaw. He staggered to the side, clutching his face and yelling obscenities at her. She spread her hand wide and pushed her will into the ground; the dirt beneath the man's feet shifted, and he fell forward, his head hitting hard. He lay still.

Zhava turned and scanned the fighting throughout the yard. Captain Redoly had Ooleng pinned to the ground. Tomaath was leading Sister Tegara and Posef toward the far side of the house. Caleb had gone in through the kitchen door – she had no idea how many more people Ooleng had inside the house, but she needed to be at her brother's side. This attack was personal. Ooleng had struck at her family, kidnapped her Papa and her Mama. His people invaded her home, and it was her responsibility to get them out.

She slipped around the pockets of fighting and in through the open, kitchen door. The narrow table still sat by the window, but broken bowls and utensils littered its top. The shelves lining the walls were stripped bare, the jars of spices gone, the bundles of herbs gone, the statues of the household gods gone.

The sounds of fighting came to the kitchen from two directions: up the narrow, winding stairs to the second floor, and through the tattered remains of the heavy curtain that hung between the kitchen and the home's center courtyard. Brii and Ravid were fighting upstairs. They were highly trained soldiers, and Zhava had little doubt they could handle Ooleng's people. Her brother, however.... He could handle himself against the wild animals that threatened his herds, and he had even fought off a man stealing his sheep, but she did not want to leave him alone with the mercenaries who hurt their family.

She drew her sword, stepped forward, and brushed aside the curtain's torn remnants. The courtyard was at once familiar but also completely different. The trees that provided shade – almost all cut down and scattered against the wall. The decorative flowers Mama worked so hard to cultivate – trampled into the flattened ground. The colorful canopy on its ropes and hinges that they could pull from one side of the courtyard to the other for mid-day shade – tattered, the gears smashed, and the ropes slapping against the walls.

Caleb stood at the far end, near the wooden, double doors shut against the outside. His sword rang in quick strikes against the swords of two men, both bigger and faster than he. At the other end of the courtyard, though, her other brothers Mitsel and Alxindra lay bound in ropes and gagged upon the ground. Their eyes were wide as they watched the fighting, and they squirmed upon the ground, desperately trying to loose their bonds.

The wonderful thing about her Abilities, Zhava thought, was that she could do two things at once. She called a bundle of her little flaming men to her palm and tossed them upon the ground, willing them to burn through her brothers' cords. Confident that task would be completed, she turned her attention to Caleb's fight. The two men had backed him into the corner of the courtyard, and they were quickly overpowering him, their sword slashes raining down, knocking him off balance. He staggered and slipped to one knee, barely keeping his sword up to protect his head.

She didn't even think about it; she reached her will into the dirt at their feet and shifted it from beneath them. Both men toppled over, one flat upon his back on the ground, and the other smacking into the wall. She stepped forward and kicked away the sword of the man lying on the ground. Caleb staggered back up, grabbed the other man by the collar of his cloak, and slammed his head into the wall again. That man sank to the ground.

Zhava smiled at her brother, thrilled at the chance to help. He did not smile back. Instead, his face twisted in anger as he leaned against the wall, breathing hard and gripping his elbow. Blood oozed from between the plates of leather on his arm.

"What are you doing?" he said with a scowl.

"I'm helping you. I'm fighting."

"You could get hurt. Get out of here."

The chastising was cut short, however, as another of Ooleng's soldiers dropped from a second-floor window to land between them. Before either of them could react, the black-clad woman slammed the pommel of her sword into Caleb's cheek. A loud crack from his jaw, his head snapped back and bounced against the wall, and he crumpled to the floor, blood running from his mouth. Zhava had just enough time to raise her sword before the woman spun and slammed a booted foot into her chest. The power of that kick sent Zhava flying backward. She fell hard on her tailbone, skidded across the ground, and came to a hard stop against the spindly bark of a fallen date tree. She knelt to the ground, coughing, and tried to draw in a breath.

She struggled to stand again. Her sword had gone somewhere, so she called her flaming men to her. The ground and the plants all glowed from the light of the flames wrapped about her body. Her chest throbbed, but the leather breastplate had absorbed much of the impact. She turned to face the woman in black – and saw dozens of balls of water flying at her. Of all the strangest things, Zhava thought each of the balls had arms and legs, a bead of water for a head, and a huge grin across its watery face.

The water balls crashed into Zhava and knocked her back to the ground. Her own flaming men were doused in tiny sizzles of anguish. She heard the gurgled snarling and snapping of wet jaws as the living balls of water rolled across her body. They ran beneath her armor, soaked through her clothes, and bit into her skin. They gouged down her arms and legs. They chilled her fingers and toes. They swam across her face, obscuring her vision and plugging up her nose and ears. She opened her mouth to scream, and one of the water balls jumped in and ran along her tongue, slid quickly down her throat and stopped any sound from escaping – stopped any breaths.

She gripped her neck. She rolled over on the ground and tried to suck in a breath, but that only lodged the water deeper.

Her heart pounded. Her chest burned. She shook her head and tried to cough out the water, but it clung steadfast to the inside of her throat.

She crashed into a wall, and her head smacked against the stone tiles. Pain ran through her head and down her neck and back. Her vision began to blur at the edges, clouds of black slowly rolling before her eyes.

Zhava had met many people with Abilities in the past several moons, but she had never met someone who could move water the way she moved fire. Had never met someone who could make water bite and burn the way her little flames so naturally did. And now, upon first meeting this woman, Zhava was going die – was going to drown from the little balls of water. She collapsed to the floor.

The woman in black stood by the double doors and lifted the wooden crossbeam off its mount. The beam tumbled to the floor, and she pushed open the doors to the narrow entryway. She turned and glanced back at Zhava, then frowned.

She was getting away, Zhava thought.

Her fingers tingled. A flaming man sparked to life before her eyes.

She could not let the woman in black get away.

Several more flames sprang to life. They started dancing a jig in her palm.

If she did not stop this woman, then who would?

The pain burst from within. The heat of the little fires rose up from her belly. They clawed their way up, shoved against the water in her throat, and pushed onward – upward. The water clawed at her insides as the flames pressed on, into the back of her mouth, across her tongue, and then spewing out upon the ground, a dozen little flames tumbling out behind them.

That first breath came as a wave of relief. It had never felt so good to breathe. The dark clouds before her eyes drifted away, and her own thoughts rushed back into her mind – the woman in the black armor!

Zhava shook herself, and a hundred flames sprang to life across her body. They perched on her shoulders, clung to her arms, and roared their fury. She stumbled back up and took in the courtyard scene. Caleb, lying in a heap and unmoving along the south wall. Mitsel and Alxindra, their legs now free – but they were edged along the west wall, their eyes wide in fear as they furiously kicked their feet, trying to stamp out Zhava's flames.

She had no time to worry about her brothers. The warrior in black stood at the outer door, pushing aside the wooden beam that secured it as she watched Zhava get to her feet. She shoved at the door and darted into the bright, afternoon sun. She was getting away!

Zhava pushed forward and grabbed her sword from where it had fallen. She stumbled past the inner doors and held a hand before her eyes to shield against the bright sun cutting through the shadows. She gripped the door handle, yanked it fully open and charged outside. She heard the fighting happening around the other side of the house. She saw the long road that led to their home's front courtyard. She turned to see where the warrior in black had run – and that's when the hand came at her head.

It wasn't any normal hand. This hand was massive. Wider then her head. Fingers thicker than her arms.

She had just enough time to turn aside before this huge hand struck her – the blow landing on the right side of her head. The impact was as if a field stone had been chucked against her. The world turned black. Her body spun through the air, and she crashed to the ground, skidding through the dirt and rocks. Her head felt as if it had been torn from her body. Her right ear throbbed – and she realized she could hear nothing through it.

Her eyes focused. The dirt path came into view, but it was on its side. Dozens of little flames lay scattered before her, tumbling and spinning, sputtering their last breaths before disappearing in wisps of smoke upon the ground.

That great hand swam into view again. It gripped her around the neck as a second hand yanked hard on the armor at her back. The world spun. She floated high into the air, and then flew suddenly backward. She slammed into a wall, her head cracking against the mortar wall behind her.

Lights danced before her eyes, and she blinked fast, trying to make them go away, trying to see straight again.

That hand still gripped her neck, and she could just make out the blurry outline of dented, metal armor extending down from the hand, along an arm, and meeting the shoulders of the largest man she had ever seen. His rounded face seemed to have been shoved inside a helmet far too small for him. A black scarf covered his mouth and nose, but his wide eyes stared curiously at her.

"Is this her?" He bellowed so loudly that even hearing him through only one ear, Zhava squinted at the sound.

"Yes," the woman in black yelled back at him. "You get her to camp. I'll rescue Ooleng."

The woman ran off, disappearing around the corner of the house. Now that she could think a little clearer, Zhava realized how far above the ground she was held. The giant had lifted her high above his own head, almost level to the second-floor windows. The hard wall dug into the back of her head, and his rough, powerful fingers held tight around her neck, nearly encircling it in his grip. She gasped for breath, trying desperately to tear at his armor, but he seemed not to feel her struggles. She called several of her flaming men, and they skittered off her shoulders, ran down his arms, and started biting into his armor. He reached up and casually swiped them away. The flames sputtered out as they fell to the ground.

"You stop that," he said. He yanked her forward, then slammed her against the wall again.

The back of her head ached, and a piercing whistle shot through her right ear. She squinted at the pain, unsure which was worse, the throbbing through her skull or the high-pitched sound piercing her ears.

"He wants you alive."

She twisted her hips and kicked out. Her boots struck at the metal armor, but he seemed not to feel them. He tilted his head and squinted at her through his too-tight helmet.

"You're a fighter, though," he said. His voice was higher-pitched and smooth, and he spoke slowly, precisely. He sighed and clenched his jaw, his eyes narrowing. "Jezza's a fighter too. You won't make this easy for me."

He released her.

She gasped, the air rushing back into her body. She flung her hands to the sides, to catch the wall as she fell, but her hands scraped the rough surface. She hit the ground, and a loud pop sounded just as her body crumpled into the dirt. She tried to push herself up, but her body wouldn't obey. She needed more air, but her body was already full, and she couldn't take in a deeper breath. She tried to think what to do, but the loud ringing in her right ear shoved away any clear thoughts and drowned out the sounds of fighting.

The giant's large, metal boot casually tapped her in the side, and then he kicked her over and onto her back. She pushed herself upright onto her elbows and tried to kick away from him, but her left foot wouldn't obey. Instead, her left foot stuck out at a severe angle from the rest of her leg. It pointed to the side, and she couldn't move it, couldn't feel it.

"Now you won't run," the giant said. He reached down and gripped that left ankle –

– and Zhava felt as if her foot, her ankle, her leg exploded in pain.

He pulled her along behind him as he ambled through the open yard and toward the fields beyond. She screamed and cried so much at the jostling, jabbing pain running through her leg that she barely felt her head bouncing over the hard-packed earth and stones. More dirt and rocks scraped along her back as her armor dug into the ground beneath her. Her vision began to blur, and the ringing in her ear reached a pitch and volume that threatened to drive away all thought. She desperately reached to the sides and tried to grab anything she could use as a weapon, but each twist of her body yanked harder on that left leg and sent another stab of lightning-pain through her.

He stopped with a grunt.

He dropped her foot, and she yelped and tried to roll away.

"Come back here," the giant said.

Zhava turned and tried to focus. Her entire left leg seared with pain, felt as if it would fall off at any moment. The giant stood with his back to her, his large, round shield in his left arm and his sword close by in his right. He slowly, tentatively scanned the fields around them.

Zhava struggled to roll over and stand, but nothing wanted to work. Her left leg refused to obey, and her arms wouldn't hold any weight, kept slipping out from beneath her. She swiped at her eyes, and she could just make out the dried stalks left standing from the harvest. Papa always planted the grains to the south of the house, which meant she would be in that first field. The giant had not taken her far. Yet.

A flash of movement, and she jerked her head. Something small and fast darted out from the dried stalks, gripped the giant from behind, and slashed at the back of his exposed neck.

The giant roared and spun, his sword high, but the small creature leaped away and scurried back into the crop rows.

"I do not want to hurt a child," the giant yelled, "so stop this now." He turned away again, searching the ground.

The fast-moving creature scurried to Zhava's side – and it was Sanama, the Initiate from back at the Hibaro. She leaned in close.

"I'll distract him," Sanama whispered. "You get back to the house."

"There you are," the giant bellowed.

"Take this." She shoved something into Zhava's hand, then leaped away just as the giant's sword flashed down and sliced through the air where she had been sitting.

Zhava rolled away and tucked her hand to her chest. She now held a sparring rod. What good was a sparring rod? She needed a weapon. And a new leg.

Sanama darted past again.

The giant howled, his rage and his pain mixing as Sanama used a knife to slice away one of the straps of armor at his waist. A thin line of blood quickly spread across the small of his back. He swung his sword in a wide arc that nearly clipped Sanama's arm as she sprang away.

"Come back and fight!" he roared. He took a couple thundering steps, then turned back and glared at Zhava. "You stay there," he said.

Sanama bounded in from behind him, her knife drawn, but he spun around and slammed his shield into her. He followed through and slammed her into the ground at his feet.

She lay there, her head and hands sticking out from the edges of his metal-banded shield, and she gasped for breath. Her eyes grew wide as she stared into the giant's face. He leaned in closer, pressing the shield deeper against her small body.

"Who are you?" he said.

She could barely drag in a breath as she squirmed beneath the weight.

Zhava tried to push herself up. Sanama had risked her life in this rescue attempt, and she couldn't leave the little Initiate to die. The throbbing in her left leg made it hard to even think as she struggled to roll over, tried to do anything to help her friend – her Little Soldier.

"I think you are trouble," the giant rumbled. "And I think you will cause more trouble if I don't stop you now." He swung his sword around and laid it against the shield, level with Sanama's throat.

Zhava panicked. From that angle, the giant could kill Sanama in one, quick slice of that sword. She had to do something.

"Leave her alone," Zhava rasped. Her throat burned from the effort, burned from the water that had clawed at her from the inside.

The giant looked over but did not shift his shield or his sword. Sanama scrunched her eyes shut and tried to squirm from beneath the weight. She got nowhere.

"A deal then, Zhava," the giant rumbled. "I will spare her, but you will no longer fight. No more fires. No more kicking and screaming. You will come willingly and quietly as I return you to Ooleng."

Zhava slipped back to the ground, her breathing ragged and fast. She thought she felt pain inside the Proving Cove, but that was nothing compared to this giant and his partner, Jezza.

"Oh, Sanama," she whispered. Her Little Soldier. Her little cub, doing everything possible to fight, to protect. She had followed Zhava all the way from the Hibaro and watched the fight unfold. She saw the giant attack Zhava and jumped into the fight without a thought of her chances against a creature so large and powerful. Zhava had only ever amused her Little Soldiers, patted them on the head and smiled at the adorable way they showed their devotion, but this was something completely different. This was life and death for one so young. This was, as Sister Tegara tried to tell her, the responsibility Zhava carried for those who followed her. For her own cubs.

"Yes," Zhava said, but her words got lost in the dirt and mud. She opened her eyes and shifted her head up, above the crop rows so she could see the giant's face. "I'll come. Let her go."

"I do not believe you."

Zhava stared through the pain and tears. She swiped at the mud and the blood across her face and tried to make sense of what he had said. He offered her a deal. He would let Sanama go – would let her live – if Zhava stopped fighting. But now that Zhava agreed...the giant would kill her anyway?

"You are too much a fighter," the giant said with a smile, "and you are hiding a new weapon. This child gave you a new weapon."

Zhava tightened her grip on the sparring rod. Through her pain and through her concern over Sanama, she had actually forgotten she held it. It was a weapon, certainly, but not one that people took to the battlefield. It was a practice weapon. It was strong, and it was flexible, but it was meant to sting and draw a little blood. It had never cut deeply into her skin; it could not slice through even the shoddiest of leather armor;

though she had heard of people breaking fingers from sparring rods, she had never experienced even that.

"This child dies, and then you come with me."

She couldn't let that happen.

The giant turned and shifted his weight. Sanama whimpered.

Zhava had to do something – even as an old woman in her vision she had been able to get around. She had used her Abilities with the rocks to move, and with the wind to hold herself steady. If she could do something like that as an old woman, she could certainly do it now. She called to the wind and the rocks around her. She pressed her will into the tilled soil beneath her body. She pulled the whisper of the wind across her, and she felt her body shifting. Felt the wind like a firm hand upon her as she was lifted off the ground.

She opened her eyes to the swirling storm of wind and dust and rocks that enveloped her. It pulled her upright, and she turned to the giant – who was now staring in awe at her, his eyes gaping wide and his mouth hanging open. He still held the sword to Sanama's throat, and he still pressed her to the ground beneath the weight of his strong arm and shield, but his attention was on Zhava.

The needle-sharp pains pierced her left leg, but she pushed that aside to focus her will on this one, simple task. To press forward with a quick attack that would save Sanama.

Zhava swung her arm wide and flicked her wrist, and the sparring rod sprang open, tripling in size with a couple sharp snaps. She screamed to the wind, and the force of it struck her from behind, pushed her forward in a rush of dirt and rocks.

The giant jerked backward and raised his sword to her, but not quickly enough.

She snapped the sparring rod across his sword hand with every bit of strength she had. She felt the cracks of his fingers breaking beneath the rod. He dropped his sword and shrieked.

She felt the life quickly leaving her, saw the edges of her vision blurring. But Sanama was not yet safe! The giant could still harm her! She must finish this quickly. Decisively.

With a final call of her will upon the elements, Zhava wrapped her arm in a spinning tunnel of wind. She had seen the power of the storm winds throughout her life on the farm. She knew the damage a powerful gust could cause, how the wind could knock over a fence, how it could topple a small building, how it could level an entire field of grain. She forced the wind to her will. She called to that damaging storm, and she pressed all of its strength behind her arm, and she swung once again – and struck the giant across the face with a force so powerful the sparring rod splintered into half a dozen pieces.

The giant flew backward, his powerful body arching away. Blood sprayed from his nose, showering through the air above them all and splattering across the front of his armor. He fell to the ground with the thunderous crash of his weight and the resounding clangs of his weapons, his shield, and all the metal striking and denting against each other.

The pull of her Abilities sapped the last bit of strength from Zhava, and she collapsed to the ground in a heap. The wind sputtered away, and the dust and dirt rained down upon her. She couldn't feel her left leg, and the rest of her body tingled as if she'd run around the Hibaro a dozen times. She fell across her arms, and she felt them twisted at odd angles beneath her, but, strangely, they didn't hurt. It actually felt really good to lie on the ground. It felt peaceful, restful, and Zhava could really use some rest.

The giant, now screaming and thrashing in agony, stumbled back up and staggered away, one hand to his bloodied face and the other hanging limp at his side. He tripped on the field ruts, and his shield dropped away. His wailing cry grew louder, and he yanked off a leather band from around his arm, then broke into a run as he fled.

"Zhava," a high, distant voice called. A face swam into view before her, and Zhava smiled. Or...she tried to smile. She wasn't sure if she actually smiled, but she knew she felt relief, she knew she felt happiness. It was Sanama's voice she heard. It was Sanama's face now floating before her.

"Zhava, don't die!" Sanama screamed. Well, it seemed like the girl was screaming, but the words sounded so distant, as if she was screaming from far away. As if her voice was getting lost in the rush of the evening waves.

Sanama looked away, off into the distance, and yelled even louder, loud enough that Zhava could hear it quite clearly across those rolling waves: "Help! Someone, please! Zhava needs help!"

That wasn't right, she thought. She was doing fine. She was drifting in her little boat on the evening tide. She felt perfectly fine now – she could just drift away because little Sanama, her Little Soldier, was alive and well. Sanama hadn't died at the hands of that evil giant, so the world was good again, and Zhava could enjoy the cool breeze and the darkening, evening sky.

When Sanama turned back, tears were rolling down her cheeks, and her voice – her distant, hollow voice – was pleading, "No, don't die. You can't die. Please don't die." But that made no sense. Zhava wasn't going to die. She was enjoying her time drifting out to sea. She would simply float away as the sun dropped slowly to the horizon, and she would spend the night sleeping in her boat, and when the morning arrived again, she would set the sail and head back to land...and she would greet Sanama once again...because Sanama was alive, and that mattered most....

Chapter 14

The lightning flashed across the black sky, outlining the clouds high above. Zhava slept in her little boat as she drifted to sea. She didn't know how long she had been out here. Did the storm come up suddenly, or did she sleep so long it moved in without her notice? No rain fell on her, though the lightning flashed angrily, highlighting the roiling puffs of clouds, the edges that blurred and formed and then reformed, as if dozens of faces looked down upon her.

She tried to shift, tried to stretch out on the deck of the small boat, but her body seemed to have stiffened up. She couldn't move her legs, and her arms and hands only tingled as if she'd been lying in the cold all night. That scared her a little, that she couldn't move. She had been stiff like this a few times before, especially in the depths of winter when the cold rolled in swiftly, before Papa brought in enough fuel for the fires. She remembered burying herself in the pile of wool blankets upon her bed and shivering uncontrollably, her body refusing to move quickly until she warmed up. And yet, this still felt different. On those cold mornings in her bedroom, she had been able to move something. Even with the blankets weighing down, she could still shift. Now, here in this boat and staring up at the crackling sky, she could not even –

Her thoughts scattered as a high-pitched note sounded through the air, and she clenched her eyes shut. It was as if someone stood beside her and blew hard into a flute, as if this person fingered the highest note possible and then played that note long and loud. The sound dove deeply into Zhava's ear, seeming to pierce through her head and into her very soul. It drove away all thought and brought only the pain of that one, single note that enveloped her.

As quickly as it began, it stopped. Zhava sucked in a breath, unaware she held it. Her temples were wet from the tears that streaked down and into her short hair. She tried to reach up and wipe them away, but her arms still would not move. She twisted her head – and realized that her head could move. Had she tried earlier to move her head? She couldn't recall.

She couldn't quite make sense of what she saw. She wasn't lying in a boat on the ocean, as she thought, but she was spread upon a glowing path that cut through a world of darkness with only the clouds above and the streaks of lightning providing any light.

A rain-soaked woman with long hair sat on the path nearby. Her hands clamped to her ears as she scowled at Zhava. Slowly, tentatively, she moved her hands and looked around at the darkness, and Zhava recognized her. She was the lost girl, Emsterold, who had shown up in her visions.

"What was that sound?" Emsterold asked.

Zhava heard it only once before, but she was unsure how to explain it. It was the ear-splitting note that sounded when the giant struck her across the side of her head. That note stayed with her as the giant slammed her against a wall and dragged her away from the farmstead. It rolled through her mind as Sanama tried to rescue her, and as she called forth the wind to launch a devastating attack upon the giant, the attack that sent him running away and screaming in agony. But how to explain all that?

"It's...inside me," she finally whispered.

She studied Emsterold then, looked around them to take in the glowing path, the blackened world, the flashing lightning, and the swirling clouds shaped like faces staring down at them from high above, and she knew where she was. This was not the ocean. This was not a pleasant ride on the evening tide.

"Am I dead?" Her throat burned as she spoke, the remnants of the water spirit that had crawled down inside her. She swallowed hard, but the ghost of its presence remained.

"Not yet." Emsterold pulled her knees up tight and peered over them with large, inquisitive eyes. Her damp hair clung to her cheeks and shoulders.

"Then why am I here?"

"I had nothing to do with this," Emsterold said with a shake of her head. "You appeared on the path. You looked dead." She turned her eyes to the swirling clouds of spirits far above. "But they wouldn't take you, no matter how much they wanted to."

Zhava's left leg twinged, and her foot spun around in a circle, then came to a rest again, back at the same odd angle it had been when the giant broke it. She saw it all happen, but other than that first moment, she felt nothing. No pain, no relief. That lack of feeling frightened her. How could she not feel her foot spinning on the end of her leg?

"Someone's trying to heal you," Emsterold said. "Someone out there." She pointed behind her. "But they're not very good."

"Sister Tegara is a great healer."

"Sister Tegara is an excellent healer, yes." Emsterold hugged her legs even tighter to herself, and her voice dropped to a whisper. "This is not Sister Tegara. This person is hurting you almost as much as she's healing you."

Zhava felt nauseous. Her stomach churned within her. The dark sky seemed to tilt and spin. The narrow path beneath her felt as if it lifted her away, as if she was rolling head-first through the night, though she did not move at all. She shut her eyes. The feelings remained. She tried hard to think of anything else that could distract her, but the only images that floated through her mind were terrible ones. Sanama being squashed like a lizard beneath the giant's shield. Her brothers squirming and bound in the dilapidated courtyard. Herself, choking on the water spirit sliding down her throat.

As quickly as it began, the nauseous feeling disappeared. She kept her eyes shut for several moments, expecting it to return. When it did not, she slowly, carefully opened her eyes again. She was now standing. She turned her head. She moved her arms and flexed her fingers. She felt almost like herself again.

"That healer finally did something right," Emsterold said. She stood up and smiled, relief on her sunken, wet face. "You might actually live."

Zhava smiled, then tried to take a step. She lost her balance, swung her arms wide, and toppled forward. Emsterold caught her, then staggered beneath Zhava's weight. Her cold body shook as she struggled to help Zhava stand again – until they both toppled to the ground in a painful heap.

Zhava clenched her jaw tight to keep from yelling out as the hard, stone path bit into her arms and shoulders, her back and her head. She tried to roll over, but her left leg just wouldn't do what she wanted. She looked down and saw that her left foot – was gone. She stared, trying hard to reconcile the image of her leg simply stopping where her foot should have been. What happened to her foot? Then it appeared again. Reattached. Facing forward as it should.

"That's not real," Emsterold said. She took Zhava's face in her hands and forced her to make eye contact. "This is the land of the dead – but you're not dead."

"My foot...?" She tried to look down again, but Emsterold held on tight, wouldn't let Zhava turn away.

"The real world is an illusion here. It's an echo. Like when you woke up, but you couldn't move. Your body – your real body – was almost dead, so this body here could not move."

Zhava started to shiver. Emsterold's hands were so cold, and the things she was saying so strange. How could a body have an echo? How could she be in the land of the dead again even though she hadn't really died?

"Or it's like me," Emsterold continued, this time in a whisper, and Zhava had to lean in to hear. "My body here is wasting away. I'm soaking wet – all the time, but it never rains. I've been living here for... I don't know how long I've been living here. Forever? But I just won't die." She stared into the sky.

Zhava looked too, and she saw the swirling faces up there, the clouds outlined by the lightning. Sometimes those faces looked down, and sometimes they looked at each other, and sometimes they seemed to all be speaking at once. The real spirits of the dead, Emsterold had said. She wasn't up there yet, so...she must still be alive. As alive as Emsterold, which wasn't much of a comfort.

"Will I die?" she asked.

"You came so close," Emsterold said, still watching the clouds. "That healer of yours is not very good, but she is trying-"

Zhava never heard what Emsterold said next. The high-noted trumpet blasted into her ear again, and the pain of it dropped her to her knees. It drowned out the words, all thoughts, all other feelings but the sharp stab as the sound pierced her ear, went through her head, and rang down her body. She clenched her hands to her head and toppled back over. She rocked on the ground as that long, shrill note blocked out anything...everything. She felt Emsterold's wet, freezing arms wrap around her and squeeze hard, but it didn't matter. Nothing mattered but that resounding tone. The tears streamed from her eyes, and she realized her mouth was open and a scream was probably escaping, but she couldn't even hear that through the noise in her head. She felt Emsterold convulsing against her, also crying and yelling, though she heard none of that either.

A sound of clapping thunder echoed all around, and everything grew still. The note faded away. The lightning subsided to only dim flickers.

Zhava opened her eyes. The ground beneath her was shaded dark in the outline of a person. Not Emsterold, though, who still knelt beside her and held her. Someone else stood on the rocky path. She lowered her hands, afraid that the piercing note would sound again, but she heard only the still silence all around. She looked up – and sucked in a gasping breath at the sight before her.

"Marmaran," she said.

The old priestess stood there, one hand gripping the knobbly head of her cane and the other reaching forward, stretched out to help Zhava stand.

Emsterold backed away and stared in confusion at Marmaran, but Zhava took the offered hand, stood as straight as she could on that backward foot, and wrapped her arms around the old woman. She shut her eyes and hugged, never wanting to let go, never wanting to lose her teacher again. She had no idea how Marmaran found her, but now that they were together, she never wanted to be apart again.

"My child," Marmaran whispered, "you should not be here."

"It's all right. I've been here before, and Emsterold is nice."

Marmaran gently pushed Zhava away and stared at her – and Zhava saw the old woman's clear eyes. She was no longer blind.

"Thank you for coming back," Zhava smiled.

Marmaran smiled back, but it did not last. She frowned as she looked up and down Zhava's body, her bruised, battered, and broken body. She stared at Zhava's backward foot for a long time. "Your healer is gifted, but untrained." She gripped Zhava's chin and twisted her head to the side to stare at her right ear. "She has not even tried to stop the ringing in your ear. She probably does not know the ear is damaged." Marmaran leaned forward, gripped Zhava's shoulders, and stared intently at her neck. "And what has gotten inside there?" she whispered. "No healer would find that."

"Who are you?" Emsterold said.

Marmaran turned and studied the girl a moment. "I know you." She stepped around Zhava and advanced on Emsterold. "I saw you once before. You were with Viekoosh."

"I am not with him," she said with a shake of her head.

"You are his sleeping seer, the one who guides him."

"He kidnapped me several moons ago. He makes me live with the dead, tell him the stories of the dead." She pointed up into the clouds where the faces flew and twisted and lit sparks of lightning between each other.

"So you are an unwilling helper?"

"He wakes me occasionally and lets me eat, and then the other one, the Salient, puts me back into a dead sleep. They make me do this every night."

Marmaran glanced between Zhava and Emsterold, and her eyes lit with understanding. "This is what we need. This will help us."

"What will?" Emsterold asked. "Being half dead?"

"You called to Zhava, didn't you?" Marmaran asked.

"I never called to anyone."

"You are trapped here. You want nothing more than to leave this land of the dead. Zhava is nearly dead now, and she-" She turned to Zhava. "When were you first here?"

"I was in the Proving Cove, and then I was with – well, I had a vision. But the vision changed, and then I was here."

She turned back to Emsterold. "You are crying out for help, and Zhava answered that cry. She met you in a vision. You can lead us to Viekoosh."

Zhava's foot twisted again, and she stumbled. It pointed forward, then blinked to the side, then back to the front again.

"Quickly now," Marmaran said. She gripped Emsterold's arm. "That healer is finally doing something right. We have little time."

"What do you want?"

"You provide visions of the dead for Viekoosh. Now provide us with visions of the living."

"I...I don't know how."

The trumpet note blasted through the air again, and Zhava fell to the ground. She gripped the right side of her head in agony – and with a clap of thunder, the noise disappeared.

Marmaran stood before Zhava, her hands clasped around Zhava's head. "This injury will be with you a very long time, Zhava. You must learn to master it." She looked back at Emsterold. "Now. Show us."

"But how? What?"

"Open your eyes. You are not yet dead – open your eyes and show us the world of the living."

Emsterold shut her eyes and shook her head, her wet hair flinging around her. "I don't think...I can't."

Zhava sucked in a breath, and she smelled something wonderful, something that made her mouth water for a taste. Stew. Someone was making stew.

Marmaran grabbed Zhava's hand and squeezed. "Do not leave me yet. Zhava, do not go."

"But...that smell."

"Emsterold," Marmaran yelled. "Open your eyes – now!"

Emsterold spread her arms wide, and a whole scene opened along the pathway. Several men stood before a small table where a handful of scrolls were spread open. Lanterns hung from hooks pounded into sun-red rocks, their flickering glows casting deep shadows on the faces of those men. The man at the table, however, was unmistakable – High Priest Viekoosh.

He moved his finger along the scroll as he recited the words that were there, the words of the prophecies of the God Coredor. His voice droned, and the men regularly chanted their praises. Just behind him, though, just out of reach of the lantern light, there was movement. A pair of people stood watching the ceremony, stood behind bars of a cage. It was Zhava's Papa and Mama.

While the gateway to the land of the living remained open, intense heat drifted out, hotter than Zhava had ever felt. It seemed to burn her face. A searing wind blew through from the cave, and red sand drifted across the stone pathway. The sand grains flickered briefly, then popped in tiny sparks. This window between the land of the living and the land of the dead did not want to remain open, and Emsterold's hands began to shake as she gripped the edges.

The beef stew Zhava smelled was so in contrast to the heat drifting from the hole, and she shut her eyes, drew in a deep breath. It smelled so good. Was Mama home already?

"Zhava," Marmaran snapped. "Wui-sha'Olm, in the deep desert."

Zhava opened her eyes and frowned at her teacher. What did the desert have to do with stew? And what was Wui-sha'Olm?

"That is where you must go," Marmaran continued. "Wui-sha'Olm. That is where you will find your parents. That is where you will find...." But her voice faded as Zhava simply drifted away. She floated in darkness for a time, the delicious scent of stew swirling around her. She reached to grab hold, but she could not find it.

A twinge of pain began in her left foot, and she worried it might be flipping around again. She couldn't see it in the dark, so she twisted it – and cried out at the sharp throbbing that ran all the way up her leg. The foot most certainly pointed in the correct direction, and it did not want to be moved.

Now that the foot throbbed, other parts of her body began to ache, sting, and itch. Her back felt as if it had been scraped raw with a bucket of rocks. The back of her head felt hot and itchy, as if something wrapped around it. Layered across all of those small aches and pains was a general feeling of exhaustion. Every part of her felt weak and heavy. Her arms and legs no longer wanted to move. It was hard to draw in a breath, and the sides of her body throbbed when she tried.

There was light. It was soft, just off to her left.

She slowly opened her eyes. She lay facing straight up and staring at a dark sky full of twinkling stars. Shadowed walls loomed to her right and directly above her head, and she realized she was lying in a corner. She recognized it, though, as the corner of her home's inner courtyard. The branches of one tall palm waved lazily in a slight breeze. Soft, warm blankets were piled beneath her, and another was spread across her. The scent of stew lingered in the air, but it was an old smell, and it did not seem as good as it had when she was...dead.

Emsterold. The winding path. Priestess Marmaran. It was all still there, deep within her. She had died, and she had traveled to the deep desert. No, that wasn't right. She had been in the land of the dead, and now she had to go to Wui-sha'Olm. But where was that?

A stirring to her left. Zhava tried to turn, but her neck ached, and the pile of cloth beneath her head would not let her move.

Someone small appeared at her side, a young girl with short hair and a dirty, white tunic. Sanama. She looked intently into Zhava's face, and she smiled.

"Zhava?" she whispered.

Zhava opened her mouth to reply, but only a soft croak escaped. Something stung down deep within her, something that wouldn't let out any more sound – but that did not stop Sanama's enthusiasm. She practically leapt forward as she wrapped her arms around Zhava's shoulders and gave a tiny hug. She gripped Zhava's arms and squeezed, and she pressed their faces close together.

"You're alive," she whispered. "Thank the Gods, you're alive."

Chapter 15

Dawn broke gently in the courtyard. Sanama was snuggled against Zhava's side, and they were both covered in a heavy, wool blanket. She heard someone working with a chopping knife in the kitchen, and a few low voices sporadically broke the rhythm of the cook's breakfast preparations. They spoke too quietly for her to make out their words, but she recognized a couple of the voices: her brother Caleb and Captain Redoly.

Someone nearby coughed, gasped, and wheezed.

Zhava turned her head, and that was when parts of her body really began to complain. The back of her head stung. Her back, slick with sweat, itched and burned. Her left foot throbbed steadily with the beat of her heart. She tried to suck in a deep breath – but her right side was tender and had been bandaged tightly. How many of her bones had been broken in that fight?

Slower this time, she eased her head a bit to the side and strained to look out the corner of her eye. Three other people lay sleeping in the courtyard, their heads propped on piles of cloth, and torn, bloodied bandages covering exposed parts of their bodies. Barae was nearest, her arm wrapped and tied tightly across her chest – likely broken. The woman soldier, Brii, coughed and gripped her chest, a bandage around her head and across her left eye. The farthest away, Sister Tegara, lay sleeping peacefully beneath a heavy blanket. Zhava was relieved to see that Tegara did not look injured. If anything, she slept soundly, her breaths regular and deep.

Sanama shifted beside her, yawned, stretched and looked up. She smiled, and her eyes lit as she saw Zhava was awake.

"My commander," she whispered.

"Little soldier," Zhava whispered back with a smile. The tickle in her throat made her voice catch, and she coughed. The coughing made her ribs ache, and she sucked in a breath. Her leg started throbbing again, and she shut her eyes and tried to push away all the pain. She lay like that for several moments before she realized Sanama was no longer at her side. She looked around to see Sanama pulling a woman from the kitchen – it was her sister-in-law, Yenl. Her oldest brother's wife. She carried a small bag that bulged at the sides.

"Sister," Yenl said with a smile as she knelt at Zhava's side. Alxindra's wife was a wonderful woman, always willing to help anyone in the family, and she had so many talents. She kept her household servants in order, managed their four children, and helped Alxindra with the livestock. That she would be skilled in the healing arts was not surprising, though Zhava never knew that.

Sanama sat next to her and started pulling things from the bag, needles and cloth and lengths of rope, and setting them on the ground beside Zhava. Yenl lifted the end of the blanket and began inspecting Zhava's left ankle.

"Sanama found me last night and told me you woke up," Yenl said. "But by the time I came downstairs, you were asleep again. How do you feel now?"

"It hurts," Zhava said with a cough.

"As it should. You nearly died." She lifted Zhava's foot and unwound the bandages.

She sucked in a breath at the sharp pain.

"Broken foot," Yenl said. "Broken ribs. Rocks and sticks in the back of your head. More rocks beneath your armor and shoved into your back. Bruises all around your neck, more bruises along your leg."

"Did Sister Tegara-"

"No. Your teacher is not yet awake."

Sanama leaned in close and whispered, "She's been asleep for three nights."

"That water witch did something to her," Yenl said. "It is beyond me. But this." She twisted the foot, and Zhava winced. "This we can mend." She plucked a bottle from Sanama's hand and pulled the stopper from the top. She dipped her fingers and pulled out a sticky, red paste. The smell was immediately overwhelming but not altogether unpleasant, filling the air with the distinct scent of crushed peppers, mushrooms, and even a hint of lilac.

Zhava tilted her head and looked across the folds of blanket to where Yenl worked. She had never seen Sister Tegara spread an ointment on a broken bone. How would it help? Would it numb the pain?

"My own recipe," Yenl said as her hands gently smoothed the paste. "I've used this on Xindr a couple times, and it speeds the healing."

Zhava had never seen a paste that could speed the healing of a broken bone. What else was mixed with the peppers and the flowers?

"I also used this on your ribs, two days ago. They weren't hurt as badly as this foot, though, and they healed quickly."

Two days to heal broken ribs? That was amazing.

Yenl finished spreading the paste around Zhava's foot and lower leg, and she cupped her hands around the ankle. The power that pulsed from Yenl's hands was unmistakable. Zhava had felt it many times before, though from Sister Tegara the effect was far more powerful. The healing thumped through her foot, around her ankle, and up her leg. The bones stung deep within her as they knitted back together.

Zhava turned wide eyes on her sister-in-law and opened her mouth to speak, but she was not given the chance.

"You probably feel it already," Yenl whispered, her eyes narrowed as she slowly nodded her head, urging Zhava to agree. "The paste seeps down through the skin and starts working right away."

"I felt something," Zhava whispered back.

Yenl smiled, and another healing pulse moved through Zhava's foot.

"Your brother and I have spoken of the Hibaro. I think it's brave of you to do the things you do. Xindr, though, he doesn't trust the Gods'-chosen. You're his sister, so he knows – deep down – that they're not a bad person." Another pulse of healing, and the tingling began to ebb away. The foot started feeling better. "But he also told me what that water witch did to you, how she tried to drown you. How she tried to drown your teacher and put her into the sleeping sickness. When the Gods give people those kinds of gifts, well that's just not right. Most people cannot be trusted with the power of the Gods." Another pulse. Yenl smiled. "I have told Xindr that he's right. We both know there is nothing better than the old remedies. A stew for a sickness. Herbs and bandages for the cuts and broken bones. This recipe of mine – it works just as well as any of the Gods'-chosen Abilities. What say you?"

Zhava simply nodded. "Thank you for using your healing paste. My foot feels better already."

Yenl reached for the worn bandages and wrapped them around Zhava's foot again. "It soaks in quickly. This is the third day I've applied it, and your foot should be healed well enough to walk on it, though you should use a staff or a branch for support."

Sanama jumped up from her spot and ran through the door to the kitchen, the heavy blanket billowing behind her.

"She loves you very much," Yenl said.

"I know."

"Do you?" Yenl wrapped the bandage while looking into Zhava's eyes. "Your friends are devoted to you. Barae has been at your side frequently. The young man, Posef, asks about you at every meal, but your brothers will not let him through to see you. He seems very comfortable with you, though. Maybe too comfortable for a boy his age?"

Zhava looked away. He was a friend.

"That little one, though, Sanama. She loves you like a child loves her mother. She was badly hurt, but she would not let me do anything for her until I first worked on you. You should have heard her scream when Xindr tried to take her from your side."

Yenl secured the wrappings around Zhava's foot and leg and stowed her healing supplies as Sanama ran back into the court-yard carrying a short, stout branch. She grinned and presented it.

"A walking stick," she proudly said.

"Thank you," Zhava said, the words coming out with a cough and a tightening of her chest.

"Sanama, that is a wonderful idea," Yenl said with a smile. Then, to Zhava: "If you're feeling up to it, you should join us at the ancestors this morning."

After a moment, she simply said, "Oh." She knew people had died before they arrived, but they had driven away Ooleng and his hired soldiers. So that left...? "Who?"

"One of the soldiers," Yenl said. She picked up her bag and stood, dusting the dirt from her skirt. "I do not know his name."

One of the men. She heard Captain Redoly when she first awoke, so that meant either Ravid or Tomaath. "Of course," she said. She shifted beneath the blankets, pushing them aside with an effort that seemed far too much for such a simple ac-tion. "I'll be there."

"We'll be there," Sanama said. She rushed to Zhava's side and helped pull the blankets, offered her hand to steady Zhava.

"Only if you are able," Yenl said, and she turned and left them.

If pushing aside the blankets was an effort, shifting across the bedding and standing up was a monumental feat. With Sanama's help, Zhava finally managed, but her body did not want to cooperate. Everything felt whole – her foot, back, and head all seemed to be working – but she felt weak, and she struggled as she limped across the courtyard. Barae and Sister Tegara slept, but the soldier Brii was no longer in her bed. Zhava did not remember her leaving, but it was likely when Yenl tended the foot.

They moved slowly, quietly to Sister Tegara's side. Their teacher lay on the ground so peacefully that she could have been resting instead of seriously injured. Sanama pointed to the swelling on the side of Tegara's head, the cause of her sleeping sickness. Sanama hadn't been there when it happened, but Tegara had been engulfed in a floating pool of water conjured by that woman, Jezza. Tegara would have drowned, but she slipped and fell against a post, and the water spilled all around her. Jezza seemed to have as much control of her water Ability as Zhava had over her little flames.

"Sister Tegara's a great healer," Zhava said, resting a hand on Sanama's shoulder. "I'm sure she'll heal herself."

They made their way to the kitchen, Zhava becoming more confident with each shaking step. A servant she didn't recognize, someone from her brother Mitsel's house, was working at the stove, and she insisted Zhava eat a small bowl of baked eggs. The food was delicious, but after only a few mouthfuls, Zhava's stomach began to churn. She thanked the servant and hobbled outside. She stood in the morning sun, a slight breeze on her face, and shut her eyes, one hand supported by the thick branch and the other by Sanama. It took several moments, but her stomach settled. They continued around the house and across the field to where the ancestors lay.

There were dozens of burial mounds of the ancestors, and Zhava could name them all. Grandparents, great-grandparents, uncles and aunts, and a few cousins. Family members going back many generations to the first of her people who staked a claim to this land and began to till the soil, began to graze the cattle and the sheep. Her family was not the first to explore this valley, but her ancestors were the first to stay and make a home of it.

The new mound was still open upon the ground, ringed by dozens of good-sized rocks. Captain Redoly and Brii and Ravid stood at the head of the mound. Ravid was the only one of the three not in bandages. Captain Redoly and Brii both had broken arms, and Brii now wore a black cloth around her head and covering her eye. Next to them stood Zhava's brothers, Alxindra, Mitsel, and Caleb, then Yenl with her oldest son, Bec. Posef stood behind Captain Redoly, and after a quick smile at Zhava, he bowed his head and returned to a more somber expression. Caleb, who noticed the smile, narrowed his eyes at Zhava. Apparently going into a fight against a group of mercenaries and freeing their brothers had done nothing to ease the tension.

Brii cleared her throat and said, "This happened a couple seasons back. We were in some little village up the Storm Coast-"

"Monmount," Ravid said, a sad smile briefly lighting his face.

"Monmount, right," Brii said. She too smiled as she looked down at Tomaath and continued her story. "We were searching an abandoned building, trying to find where a group of smugglers had hidden a cache of weapons, and this young, tiny guy with long hair jumps out at me from the shadows. He had to have been a head shorter than me, and he was skinny. Long hair down to his waist." She chuckled and wiped her face with the back of her sleeve. "And he waved this broom at me and yelled at me that he would kill me if I tried to take his pigeons."

Redoly and Ravid both chuckled.

"I just stood there staring at him. I didn't know if he was telling the truth, if he was one of the smugglers, or if he was crazy. But then Tomaath walked up to him and-" She stifled a laugh, but it quickly turned into a few more tears. "He yelled at the man, 'Why aren't you working? There's enough dirt on this floor to grow next year's crops. Put that broom down and get to work.' And the crazy guy did! He apologized to Tomaath and started sweeping the floor like it was the most important thing he could do."

Brii stepped to the pile of rocks nearby, chose one of the larger ones, and returned with it to the mound. She gently placed it on Tomaath's arm and whispered, "I will miss that about you, my friend. Go with the Gods." She leaned down and pressed her forehead against Tomaath's chest, then stepped back again to stand by Redoly.

Posef stepped forward next. "I didn't know him very well, just this trip out here, but he really scared me when he pointed that arrow at my head."

Zhava nodded. Tomaath and the Captain scared them all when that happened.

"His aim was solid," Posef continued. "I thought he was going to shoot me between the eyes. But then everyone started fighting, and he started shooting all those other people, and as scared as I was, I sat there watching it happen."

Posef stepped away, chose a stone from the pile, and placed it next to the stone Brii had set in place. "Tomaath was an amazing fighter," Posef said. "I hope someday I can be as good as him."

The goodbyes continued, and the rocks piled higher across Tomaath's body. At some point, Barae limped across the field, squeezed Zhava's hand, and stood silently at her side, taking it all in. The three soldiers did most of the remembering, telling stories of Tomaath's bravery, his sense of humor, his skill in battle. The morning sun was higher, its golden light sharply cutting across the nearly complete mound, when Zhava's oldest brother, Alxindra, stepped forward and placed a stone.

"I never met Tomaath," he said. "But I am grateful that he came, that he gave his life to protect my own. To protect my brother and my homestead. He will be remembered and honored by us for as long as our family goes on. Thank you, soldier Tomaath."

Through all of this, Zhava said nothing, and she now regretted waiting as long as she did. How could her simple feelings, her gratitude toward Tomaath, follow what her brother just promised. She wanted to honor him for what he did, but she had nothing as powerful to present him in death as what Alxindra offered.

She could not, however, do nothing. She took a step toward the dwindling pile of ready stones, but Sanama tugged on her sleeve and handed her a stone instead. She hadn't noticed Sanama leave to get it, but she was grateful for the girl thinking ahead.

She stepped forward, the stone clutched in her hand, and set it gently atop the mound. "Tomaath, you were...." The words seemed so inadequate, but they were the truth. The truth was always most important in remembering those who had gone on to the next life. "You were nice to me," she whispered. "You rode beside me, and you talked with me. I didn't know you very long, but I believe we could have been friends." She shut her eyes and gently leaned forward. "I believe you were my friend. For that I thank you. Go in peace with the Gods."

Captain Redoly closed out the remembering with some memorized words about Tomaath's service to the King, service to the kingdom, service to his fellow soldiers, and then he offered a soldier's prayer to the Gods. When he finished, he stood staring at the freshly-built burial mound of rocks as the others dispersed. Zhava's brothers and sister-in-law, Brii and Ravid, even Posef and Barae, they all shuffled away in quiet conversation. Zhava limped around the mound, Sanama at her side, and stood beside the captain.

"It was inside him," Redoly said, his voice quiet. He tapped at his stomach. "Something broke, and he was bleeding inside."

"I'm sorry," Zhava said.

"Not the way a soldier wants to die." He sighed, scratched at the stubble on his cheeks, then turned to Zhava. "Yenl assures me her magical oils will mend our broken bones by tomorrow. So two nights from now, at dawn, we leave. You and your little friends are going back to the Hibaro."

"What? But, my family. They need me. And my Papa and Mama?"

"This was never about your parents, or anyone else in your family. This was always about you. Ooleng hired those mercenaries to attack your family's farm, hired Monh to pretend to be a family servant, and hired Nu the giant and that woman who was with him just to capture you."

"Her name's Jezza."

"I'll remember that name, thank you." He sighed and stared at Zhava's home across the field and the people slowly walking back. "We weren't ready for her. We were ready for Nu. We were ready for those sloppy mercenaries. But we weren't ready for a fighter who could conjure water out of the air. Someone who could drown you on the edge of the desert."

Zhava's throat tickled where that water spirit had lodged itself, and she reached up and scratched at her neck. The tickling subsided.

"I know where my parents are."

He turned and stared, waiting.

"Wui-sha'Olm."

He laughed and shook his head. "And where did you hear that name?"

"I...had a vision. When I almost died. Emsterold showed me the caves, and Priestess Marmaran told me the name."

"A vision? I told you: I'm a soldier. I'm not covering half the desert because a couple dead people you saw in a vision told you to do it," Redoly said with a shake of his head. He turned and walked away. "You're all going back to the Hibaro."

"But the vision," Zhava called after him. "It was true. I know where they are."

Redoly didn't even turn around as he called back, "The Hibaro. Two nights from now. Pack up and say your good-byes."

Chapter 16

"What did you see?" Sanama asked as she helped Zhava limp-walk across the field.

So she explained it all. Priestess Marmaran's death as they traveled to the Hibaro; the strange ritual and words she made Zhava memorize – all of which still so painful that it remained seared within her; Marmaran appearing to her as a spirit, kept from crossing over to the land of the dead by the ritual; Zhava meeting Emsterold in the land of the dead; and finally how Emsterold had opened a window from the spirit world back to the real world that revealed where her parents were being held captive: Wui-sha'Olm.

"Captain Redoly should have listened to you."

She squeezed Sanama's hand. "Thank you."

As they continued across the field, Barae ran back to meet them. She flung her arms wide and gave Zhava a tight hug that made her cough and wheeze.

"Oh, I am so sorry," Barae said, immediately releasing her grip. "Your ribs! I forgot."

Zhava leaned forward and tried to pull in a deep breath. It hurt.

Barae knelt before her and whispered into her ear, "Don't go home yet."

Zhava looked up. There was fear in her friend's eyes. She nodded her understanding and gestured for them to walk around the field and away from the house.

"Your brothers are scary," Barae blurted. "I walked Posef back to the house to keep Caleb from threatening him again. Alxindra is always angry. At everyone. And your other brother, Mitsel, he just sits and stares at everyone all the time. Like this." She stared ahead, her eyes wide, her brows furrowed, and her mouth set in a straight line.

"Barae, our home was just attacked."

"No, you have not been awake the past three nights. Alxindra does not want us here. He's said that several times – to everyone, including Captain Redoly. He said your father is gone now, and he's in charge of the household, and that the King's people have only ever brought trouble to his family, and he wants us all to leave. Except you. He said you must stay."

Zhava wondered how much Papa had said to Xindr about the night she'd been given to the family. Papa finally told Zhava a few moons ago, but that didn't mean Xindr didn't know long before. He was the eldest son, and Papa might have thought it right to tell him. If Papa had told Xindr, it could certainly make him distrust the King, the soldiers, and the Hibaro students.

They walked around the edge of the field and circled the house, and Barae put a hand on Zhava's arm to stop them. "That's not the worst, though. Come with me."

They entered the kitchen where Yenl and a servant were cooking the midday meal, slowly climbed the dark, narrow stairwell to the second floor, and went to the shut door that led to Zhava's old room. It was no longer her room. After leaving for the Hibaro, Mama removed everything of hers, the bed, the table, her clothes and blankets, even the wood carvings. The last she saw, it was strewn with cloth remnants, old shirts and robes, anything that needed repairing. Mama had turned it into a sewing room.

Barae opened the door, and Zhava gasped. The clothes had all been shoved to the edges of the room, and a long beam had been mounted between the far wall and the ceiling, pounded into place by spikes still protruding from each end of the beam. A man lay sprawled against the wall, his arms above his head and tied securely to the beam by rope. A length of cloth, streaked red with blood, was tied around his head. His arms were bruised, his shirt and pants torn and muddied, and his bare feet red and swollen. If Zhava hadn't been riding with Monh all the way from the Hibaro, she wouldn't have recognized him as the same man. She wasn't sure he was alive.

She knelt at his side and placed a hand in front of his mouth. He was breathing.

"After we rescued your brothers, a servant brought Yenl, and she started tending to everyone's injuries," Barae said. "Your brothers, though, rode out to where Captain Redoly had tied up Monh and brought him back here. They made him walk barefoot all the way, and then they brought him up here and yelled at him and hit him for half the night. I could hear Monh crying out in pain all the way down in the courtyard. We could all hear. When they finally came downstairs, Yenl wanted to tend to him, but Alxindra wouldn't let her."

"Why do this? What did they want?"

"They wanted to know where to find Ooleng."

"Captain Redoly already asked him that, and Posef listened to his thoughts. He doesn't know anything – Ooleng hired him, that's all."

Barae shrugged. "Maybe Posef didn't hear all his thoughts? He said Ooleng had gone to Castinthai."

"Castinthai? But that's across the Purneese...and another four or five nights...." Zhava quickly added the travel time in her mind. She had never been to Castinthai, but Papa and Mitsel went once when she was young. The stories they told when they returned, tales of the endless water of the ocean, the hundreds of white birds that lived in the city, the strange, "barking" animals that could live on land but had fins like the fish. Of all the places she had ever dreamed to travel, Castinthai seemed like the most foreign, the most exotic – and the one farthest from anything she had ever known. "Castinthai is at least a full moon away from here."

"Your brothers started packing yesterday."

Things were getting worse, Zhava thought. She had never before known that her brothers could be so cruel to another person, even someone as despicable as Monh, but here was the evidence. Needlessly hurting Monh to get him to reveal information that was probably wrong, information he probably said just to make them stop hurting him.

"Sanama," she said, "go find Yenl – quietly. Bring her up here, and ask her to tend to Monh."

Sanama nodded, jumped from her spot, and ran down the stairs.

Barae shook her head and said, "Your brothers won't like that."

"This is my house too." She gestured at Monh's unconscious body slumped against the wall. "And this is wrong."

Barae helped Zhava back down to the kitchen. They heard men's voices outside and followed the sounds. Out the kitchen door and around the back side of the home they found Zhava's brothers, Posef, and Captain Redoly. The brothers stood around a tall rock – the same rock Zhava played at when she was a child pretending to have her own home. They had spread a roll of parchment across the rock and were pointing at it and arguing about something. Captain Redoly leaned against a post behind them, interested in their conversation but not commenting on anything. He held a small stick and twirled it between his fingers, idly passing the time. Posef sat in the dirt at Redoly's feet, his back against the side of the post. He was doing nothing but sitting still and quiet as he tried to hide himself behind the captain.

As Zhava approached, she saw that the parchment was a large map of the region, western Remmli, the Purneese Mountains to the west, and the Sineise Desert to the south – the Go'aabite territories and their trade routes through that desert. They were arguing about the best path west and over the Purneese Mountains – whether the take the safer, longer route that skirted the lowland mountains or to take the more direct route along the Goat's Path. Winter had not yet struck their valley homestead, but those mountain passes would have been getting snow for most of the past moon.

They ignored her as she limped up to the rock and studied the parchment map. It wasn't large enough to show Castinthai far out on the edge of the world, but it was one of the cities listed on the side with a large arrow pointing farther west. She scanned down the map, deep into the desert where small dots were simply labeled with words like "water" and "shade" and "cave." She knew those labels had been placed there by the Go'aabite traders who ventured this far north and did business with Papa; her family had never actually traveled that far south, that deep into the Sineise Desert. At the bottom of the parchment map was a small grouping of rocks with the name Wui-sha'Olm written beside it. She pointed to it and looked at her brothers.

"That's where Papa and Mama are," she said. "Wui-sha'Olm."

Her brothers stopped talking. Captain Redoly stopped twirling the stick and studied her. Posef dipped his head and shifted in the dirt until he was hiding even more of himself behind the captain.

"Zhava, shut up and go away," Alxindra said with a glare.

"No," she said. "You're wrong. You hurt that man upstairs-"

"He deserved to be hurt."

"-until he told you something – anything! – to make you stop-"

"He told us what we needed to know."

"-but what you got was a lie. A lie you forced him to make."

"We got what we needed to know!" He gripped the edges of the large stone as he yelled at her, his jaw clenched and his muscles taught.

Zhava leaned forward and tapped the map again. She never would have stood up to her brother like this just six moons ago, but she was no longer that little girl. She would not back down from a fight, especially when she knew she was right. "Papa and Mama are in Wui-sha'Olm."

"You are not family," he spit out. "You are an orphan child abandoned on the doorstep of this house. Mother never wanted you, but she tolerated you because Father has a soft heart. Too soft!"

"Xindr," Caleb said, reaching for his shoulder. "Stop."

Alxindra slapped the hand away. "You all listen to me," he said, turning to each of the siblings in turn. "With Father gone, I am making the decisions for this household. We know where Ooleng took Father and Mother. And yes, I beat it out of him. He can thank the Gods I didn't kill him – yet. We will go to Castinthai." He turned to Zhava. "All of us. And then you will be that man's husband, as you should have been all along. This never would have happened if you had done your duty."

"That's not happening," Captain Redoly said with a broad smile as he stepped forward.

"Do not contradict me, soldier," Alxindra said. "This is my household, and she is my sister – unwanted as she is."

"The bride price was paid," Redoly said, shrugging. "Io Liori and your father – her guardian – negotiated that several moons ago. She is a ward of the King, the same as Posef and Sanama and Barae. I will be returning them all to the Hibaro two nights from now."

Alxindra turned to Zhava. He narrowed his eyes and spoke softly, slowly. "What say you? Where is your allegiance? To family?"

"I am a Novice of the Hibaro," she said. "Student to Io Kua and serving the King under the direction of Io Liori."

Alxindra shook his head and reached for the parchment map spread across the rock. He slowly rolled it together, bound it with a leather cord, and slapped it against Caleb's chest. "Zhava," he said without looking at her. "You have made clear whom you serve. What this family does – and where we go – is no longer your concern. As you have been directed, leave. Do not ever return."

He pushed the brothers away, and together they strode across the dusty ground, none of them glancing back.

Chapter 17

"Zhava?" Barae whispered. "Are you all right?"

She blinked. Her brothers were gone. Her friends and Captain Redoly all watched her, waiting for her reply. How long did she stand there, staring after her family? So long that her brothers had gone off to wherever they went so they wouldn't have to see her. Or speak with her. Or even hear her. So far that she could be cut off from them all. Did no one want her?

Someone squeezed her hand, and she looked down. Sanama stood there, holding her hand and looking up with big, sad eyes.

"I'm sorry."

"Thank you." She glanced at each of her friends in turn. "All of you. And to you, Captain Redoly."

Barae wrapped her arms around Zhava and hugged her. "Don't listen to them," she said. "We all love you. We'll be your family."

Zhava smiled and returned the hug. Sanama tried to wrap her arms around them both and squeezed hard. Posef took a step forward to join the hugs, but Captain Redoly slapped a hand against his chest and shook his head.

"We'll attend to the horses," Redoly announced. He gripped Posef by the shoulder and turned him around. Then, to the three girls, he said, "Order your belongings. Stay together. And avoid those three men." He kept an arm across Posef's shoulders, and together they walked off toward the barn.

"This is what you meant," Zhava said, "that my brothers are angry?"

Barae nodded.

"They really threatened Posef?"

Barae took a deep breath and turned to stare at the ground. When she spoke, her voice was soft, halting. "You presented Posef to your brother – for marriage?"

Zhava clenched her jaw and tightened a fist. Her little flames tickled her palm, itched to come forth. She had been so happy at that party, one of the best nights of her life. Newly promoted to Novice. Her friends surrounding her, laughing and dancing. Her brother visiting. And one little moment ruined it all. One little action that Caleb misunderstood. She never presented Posef for marriage. She presented him as a friend – she held his hand as a friend. As a fellow student of the Hibaro, someone with whom she studied and trained. Someone she might, possibly, someday in the future – only if she wanted to believe that vision – maybe marry. But that day was far off. That future was not yet written.

"No," she said. "I did not present him for marriage."

Barae's tension released, and she gave Zhava another quick hug.

"My brothers no longer understand me." She thought about that, then muttered, "I'm not sure they ever understood me."

"Brothers are stupid that way," Sanama announced.

Zhava and Barae both laughed.

"It's true," Sanama said with a scowl. "My brothers always laughed at me when I practiced sword fighting. Then an Io saw me fight, and he brought me to the Hibaro. He said I was a better fighter than either of my brothers, and he wanted me to train. My brothers were stupid, just like your brothers."

"You're right," Zhava said. "They are stupid. I know exactly what to do, but they won't listen." She looked down at the rock, where the map had been. Wui-sha'Olm was in the middle of the desert, but according to the map, it was almost straight south. She didn't know how far, but there had been several spots marked "cave" or "water" or "town" between her homestead and there. She had never traveled the desert, but she knew what was needed. Water. Shelter. Protective clothes. "I'm going to do this myself."

"Do what?" Barae asked. "Go to Wui-sha'Olm?"

"Yes. Without them."

"I'll go with you," Sanama said.

"That is a bad idea," Barae said, staring wide-eyed at Zhava. "You're only a Novice-"

"Please, can I go?" Sanama pleaded.

"-you have not been fully trained; you're hurt; and you don't know where you're going."

Zhava nodded as she thought through Barae's arguments. Each was true, yet none of them mattered. "They're my parents. My brothers are being stupid-"

"Yes," Sanama said with a firm nod.

"-and you heard Captain Redoly; if we stay with him, the only place we're going is back to the Hibaro. I can't do that. I know where my parents are being held, and I must do something. I'm going to get them out of there. Somehow."

Barae gave a big sigh. She clenched her jaw and rapidly tapped a finger against the stone table as she stared intently into Zhava's eyes. "Then I'm going with you too."

"What? No."

"We're all three going," Sanama said with a triumphant smile.

"No," Zhava said, taking a step back. "I can't ask that of you. Of any of you. This is my problem, and I have to deal with it."

"I don't remember you asking." Barae turned to Sanama. "Did she ask you?"

"Didn't ask me. I volunteered."

"Yeah, I volunteered too." She grinned at Zhava. "Guess you're stuck with us."

"Until the end, Commander."

Zhava reached forward and clutched their hands. "Thank you. You are both wonderful friends."

They had much work to do and little time to do it. Barae went to find Posef. He never liked following orders, whether those orders came from teachers or soldiers, and she felt confident she could recruit him to their rescue plan – especially when it meant defying Zhava's brothers and Captain Redoly. Sanama helped Zhava hobble back inside where they found Yenl and requested another treatment of "ointments" applied to their injuries. Sanama's ribs had already healed nicely. However, Yenl worked so hard to bring Zhava back from the edge of death that her broken foot had not been a priority. Now it was, though they couldn't reveal why. It seemed enough of an explanation to Yenl that Zhava wanted to walk without relying on the cumbersome branch.

Sanama became their errand runner. Younger than any of them, she could run from one end of the farmstead to the other and attract little attention. The couple times anyone asked what she was doing, she grinned and said she'd never before visited a farm. She ran to all of Zhava's hiding spots and stashed things they would need on the trip. Blankets and Go'aabite clothes, taken from Papa and Mama's upstairs room and hidden behind the rusted plow in the field. The desert tent, which Papa had been given by a Go'aabite trader just two seasons ago: removed piece by piece from the storage room in the back of the house and, after several quick trips, stashed inside a cave alongside the Goodspring and behind the tallest tree. Extra food, however, was much harder. Ooleng and his hired soldiers had eaten or trampled almost all the extra stores that Mama placed for the cold months, and Yenl was feeding them all with supplies she brought from her and Alxindra's home down the valley. Sanama was only able to sneak a few pieces of dried meat from the kitchen without anyone noticing – they hoped no one would notice for at least a couple nights. They would have to stop at a trading post soon. Were there trading posts in the desert?

The evening meal was uncomfortable for everyone. The brothers insisted on eating alone in the courtyard so they could plan their journey, which meant the four students, Yenl, and the three soldiers ate outside in the cool, evening breeze. Not yet cold as the nights at the Hibaro, but still cool enough for them all to be a little uncomfortable. Embarrassed by her husband effectively kicking out their guests during meal time, Yenl apologized to everyone and served them extra portions of fruits, meat, and bread to make up for the rude treatment. Sanama stuffed the folds of her robe with as many things as she could without drawing attention to herself.

The brothers left long before dawn the next morning, and Zhava did not bother to think about them – and she certainly shed no tears at their absence. Instead, the students used the quiet to get an early start planning. They decided it would be best to sneak out of the house during the mid-night watch, quietly take four camels from the yard, and ride away without anyone noticing. The plan was simple, but there were so many things that could go wrong. Captain Redoly set them to order-ing the horses for the ride home, so they had to sneak away to tend to the camels. Several of Yenl's household servants showed up at the farmstead, and she had them cleaning, fixing, and tending to the place as if it belonged to her and Alxindra – which would likely be true if Papa and Mama did not return. By the time the sun set, they had small bags packed and visi-bly set out for the trip they were supposed to take to the Hi-baro, and another, larger set of bags packed and hidden away for their real trip to the desert; they staked the camels to leads in the low pasture, just down the hill from the back side of the house and away from most of the light spilling out into the night; and they divided their tasks to get out of the house and as far into the desert as quickly as they could.

They finished their evening meal with little conversation, then obeyed Captain Redoly's orders for an early bedtime – each of them visibly sulking for the Captain's benefit. Yenl's servants cleaned up the meal, Brii remained on first watch outside the house gates, and Zhava buried herself beneath a heavy, wool blanket and pretended to sleep in her spot in the inner courtyard. Barae pretended to sleep just two bedrolls away, her form still and quiet beneath her own heavy blanket. It was strange to see Barae either still or quiet – and Zhava stifled a chuckle at that thought. At the far end of the courtyard, however, lay Sister Tegara, her breathing slow and steady. Yenl had made no further progress on waking her from the sleeping sickness. Some people never woke from it, but Zhava did not want to think about that for her teacher and protector. The woman loved all the Initiates in her charge.

As Zhava lay there, she counted silently to herself as she waited for the mid-night call. One of Yenl's servants stood watch on the roof tower. He set the sand vial and called out the hours of the night, mostly for the benefit of Redoly and his soldiers. Papa had never told his servants to call out the time, and though Yenl never complained aloud, no matter what she was doing, she always paused for just a moment and pursed her lips at the intrusion to the still night.

She coughed, tried to clear her throat again. As she did, the clear, high-pitched tone rose at the edge of Zhava's hearing, and she cringed. The giant's punch to the side of her head damaged something, and now she heard that dreaded note, as if a bell suddenly clanged but refused to die down. The tone interrupted her sleep, it interrupted her thoughts. Yenl tried to find the damage, but it wasn't the same as a broken bone or a gaping wound. Whatever came loose inside Zhava's head was too small for Yenl's Abilities. Maybe Sister Tegara...if she ever recovered.

"Third hour," Yenl's man quietly called from the roof.

Zhava tensed. Time to move.

She shoved aside the blankets and looked around the court-yard, blinking lazily into the dim light cast by the single lamp on the wall. She had heard no one enter the courtyard, and a quick look confirmed that she and Barae and Sister Tegara were alone. She pitched a small stone at Barae's back, then pulled out the extra blanket and fluffed it up along the ground. She covered it again and arranged the edges into a form vaguely like her own. Close up it was obviously not her lying there, but she hoped it could fool someone from a distance.

Rising, she saw that Barae had successfully formed a per-son-shape beneath her own blanket, and they crept quickly, quietly to the heavy blanket draped between the courtyard and kitchen. She gently shifted the folds. The kitchen was dark, empty.

Posef, she thought, hoping her friend was listening. This was his part of the plan, to help them all coordinate in the dark, and it was probably the most important.

I'm awake, he spoke back to her mind.

Go.

Wait.

Zhava stood still, waiting.

I can't hear Captain Redoly's thoughts, he continued.

Zhava bit her lip. That was unexpected. Posef had practiced hearing the soldiers' thoughts throughout the afternoon, and he never had problems. He needed to know where the person was to hear the thoughts, but simply knowing each soldier was somewhere on the farmstead had been enough. Now, though, if Redoly himself was missing....

The other two? Zhava asked.

Ravid is asleep in the loft, and Brii is sitting beside that big tree by the field.

"What's wrong?" Barae whispered.

Zhava held up a hand for her to be quiet. *What about Yenl's watchman? Or the other servants?*

The man on the roof is a good watchman; he's awake and doing his job. Everyone else is asleep.

And Sanama?

A pause, as he likely conferred with Sanama's mind. Then, *She's already at the camels. Says she has most of our gear stowed.*

She smiled at that. Sanama took her job as a "Little Soldier" seriously. *This night is the only chance we get, Posef. We go.*

Yes, ma'am. She didn't sense any difference, but she knew he'd left her mind. He might be a trickster, but he was too nice to keep listening when he wasn't supposed to – as he had reminded them all throughout the afternoon's practice.

She and Barae silently moved through the dark kitchen, carefully feeling their way along the wall and past the low table set before the shuttered window. The door was closed and latched tight, but the mechanism slid free without a hitch or a squeak when she gently pulled the lever. Her Papa took pride in all things working properly, even down to the smallest latch on the kitchen's rear door. They slipped outside, latched the door shut behind them, and darted into the long shadows cast by the few lamps along the outer wall.

"I'll see you down there," she whispered to Barae.

"Be careful."

Barae sidled back along the stone wall of the house, waited several long moments – that would be Posef sending her instructions – then rounded the corner and disappeared from view. Her part of the plan was simple: sneak down to the camels and help Sanama secure the gear. With Posef's help listening to the watchman's thoughts, it was relatively simple to send her along when no one was watching.

Zhava sat still and waited, concealed by the shadows. She saw the watchman pacing on the small roof tower. Posef was right in his assessment; Yenl's watchman servant was dutiful.

Zhava? he suddenly said.

Yes.

She's clear. Are you ready?

Yes. She watched the man on the roof as he slowly turned away.

He's watching the east field now, Posef said. *Go.*

She slipped from shadow to shadow in the long, flat yard. Her part of this plan was the most likely to be a problem, which was why she insisted she do it herself – that, and the fact that no one else knew her homelands as well. She had to make her way to the cave by the stream, retrieve the desert tent, follow the stream around the back side of the house, and meet every-one else at the camels. It sounded so simple.

Stop, Posef said.

She crouched low in the shadow of a small bush and waited. She blinked into the dark beyond, straining to see deeper into the night. Little had changed in the few moons she'd been gone, but it would be a stray rabbit hole she didn't see or a new rut in the ground that would most likely trip her.

And...he's turned away again. Go.

She rounded the bush and stepped into Papa's fallow field. If there was any spot on her trek where she might be seen, it was here. The field was wide open with only lines of scrubby grass cutting through. She moved slowly and methodically, careful to do nothing that would draw attention to herself. She had been through this field so many times as a child that she could almost walk it with her eyes closed – though she would not attempt that now. With each step, the line of trees that edged the creek seemed to remain at a distance, no closer now than a few moments ago. She knew that wasn't true; it was a trick of the dark that made it seem she was not moving. Another step, and then another. She kept expecting Posef to stop her, to tell her the watchman was turned her way, but he never did – and then she was in the treeline. She slipped around the nearest tree, her back to the house, shut her eyes, and breathed in deeply. She made it. The worst was behind her. From here, it was a quick walk between the trees, a few hops across the creek, and she could retrieve their tent from the cave.

Another quick breath, and she pushed herself away and deeper into the small woods. She loved this narrow band of trees that bordered the creek. She would watch the birds, count the leaves, and climb up high – when Mama wasn't looking, of course. She would get into trouble if Mama saw her doing anything she wasn't allowed to do. Of course, she would get into trouble if Mama saw her doing anything else too.

Um..., Posef suddenly spoke into her mind. *Zhava?*

I'm almost there, she thought back to him.

No, he's – Stop. Now!

She rounded a tree and ran straight into someone striding toward her. He gasped as her head slammed into his. She tripped over his leg, sprawled to the ground, and skidded in the damp leaves and dirt. Her flames sprang to life in her hands, and she rolled over, prepared to fight.

"What in the Gods' names," the man muttered, clutching his head and turning to her. Captain Redoly stood there, brilliantly lit by the glow of Zhava's little flames. He rubbed at his temple and shook his head, squinting at her. "Zhava?"

"Hello," she said, lowering her flaming hands and trying not to cringe. "You're...out for a walk too?"

Chapter 18

Her head hurt, and it wasn't all from cracking it against Captain Redoly. The little bit of ringing that bothered her earlier was now so loud she could hear nothing but that from her right ear. Posef was yelling into her mind, something about the loud noise – could he also hear the ringing? – and finally his yelling simply vanished. Thankfully.

"What are you doing here?" Redoly said. out He reached down to help her, and after dousing the little flames in her hands, she slowly, stiffly accepted.

"Me –?" She coughed, tried to clear her throat, coughed again, then continued, all of which made the ringing worse. "I live here. What are you doing?"

"I'm working. Keeping you safe. What's wrong?"

She squinted and pointed at her ear, the ringing getting a little softer by the moment. "It's still loud. In my ear."

"Oh, that," Redoly said. "I've seen it a few times in soldiers, when they get injured as you did. Don't worry. We'll get you back to the Hibaro and find someone who knows how to heal – not like your sister-in-law. Someone good with her Abilities, like Sister Tegara."

"Mm." The talking helped. The ringing was almost gone.

"Come," Redoly said, putting an arm around her shoulders. "Let's get you back to the house. You shouldn't be out here on your own."

"No," she said, shaking her head. "I was just looking around."

"As was I." He continued leading her back through the woods – away from the creek. Away from the cave and the tents and her mission to leave and rescue her family. "You were really fortunate to grow up here. It's beautiful. Me, though, when I wasn't working the pit mines, I was out on the streets, on my own. I never knew my father, and my mother never talked about him. But that made it tough for us. I had to bring home enough coins to survive – any kinds of coins. Copper or silver – sometimes a few gold."

He kept talking. They wandered aimlessly through the trees as he talked about his childhood. They shuffled through the dusty field as he talked about the beauty of the outdoors, all the regions of the world he'd visited in his travels, and the excitement of the large city-states.

The ringing had almost disappeared from Zhava's ear, and she managed to clear her throat enough that she could swallow without hurting. She could probably speak fine, but Captain Redoly didn't give her a chance.

As they neared the house, she saw the watchman on the roof stand and study them, his head glancing back and forth to be sure no one else waited in the darkness. Their conversation even attracted Brii's attention, and soon she joined Zhava and the captain on their slow walk back.

Zhava glanced around the empty yard. She heard nothing from Posef. She had no idea what her friends were doing or if they were worried about her. She didn't know how she was going to get away from the captain now. This was a disaster.

"Fourth hour," the watchman called from the roof. He reached to the wall and flipped the sandglass to count down the next hour.

"Fourth hour?" Redoly said. "So soon?" He yawned and stared out into the darkness.

"Sir," Brii said, "you should get some rest. We're leaving early."

"Too true," he said, clapping his hands and turning to Zhava. "And you, Novice Zhava, you also need your rest. Your family has a beautiful home, and I know you want to spend more time enjoying it before you return to your studies, but we have a schedule to keep. Thank you for the walk."

She turned from Redoly to Brii and out to the dark yard beyond. She had been so close, and now she was all the way back to the house – and two of the soldiers had seen her.

"What's wrong?" Brii asked. She turned and stared into the darkness. "Did you see something?"

"No," Zhava said. "Just...you're right. I'm going to miss it. Good night." She strode toward the kitchen door without a backward glance.

"Good night," Redoly called after her. "Sleep well."

She shut the door behind her. What now? There were two ways out of the house: the large front gates with their double entries, which were heavy and scraped across the ground and could not be locked from the outside, and this kitchen door, which – she ducked down and peaked between the window shutters – was now blocked by Brii standing guard.

Posef, she called in her mind. *Posef!*

Nothing. What was the last thing he said? She ran into Captain Redoly's head and fell to the ground, her ear started ringing, Redoly asked her what she was doing and if she was all right, and Posef yelled something.

Posef, she tried again. Still no response.

She was on her own. How best to get out of the house? The door was the easiest, but that option was gone. The windows in the upstairs rooms would be easy – unlatch the shutters, climb through, drop to the ground – but those rooms were occupied by Yenl and her family and servants. Zhava's own room housed a prisoner who certainly wouldn't keep quiet if she climbed out a window. And even if she managed to sneak out one of those windows without waking anyone else, that watchman on the roof could look down and see her.

The watchman on the roof....

She moved as quickly as she could without walking into the table or stubbing her foot on a stool. Up the stairs, down the hall, past all the closed doors of the people sleeping, and around the corner to arrive at the base of the heavy, wooden ladder that led to the trap door in the roof. Starlight filtered through that narrow hole above her, and she heard the low scuff-scuff of the man's shoes on the dusty roof. She waited until he walked away, then slowly, carefully climbed the ladder. She peaked over the edge and saw him standing by the far wall, his back to her and his hands resting on the ledge. She felt along the roof and rolled the gritty dirt between her fingers. It was perfect.

She wouldn't need much. A little wind from the right direction, some loose dirt willing to be blown around. She pressed her will into the air above, and the wind gusted across the roof. A little strong, but it would work. A quick flick of her wrist, and the dirt lifted off the roof and caught in the breeze. That was perfect, but it had better be; Priestess Marmaran taught her to do this several seasons ago. She let the wind swirl across the roof like a small dust-djinn, then twisted it into the watchman's face.

He cried out and rubbed his eyes.

She sent a second gust of wind and dirt at him, and this time it flew into his mouth.

He coughed and tried to spit it out, shook his head and rubbed his eyes more. He turned, squinted, and shuffled across the roof, one arm stretched out before him and the other still wiping his eyes and face.

Zhava ducked down and crouched in the corner of the dark hallway. The ladder shook as the man knocked his hand into the railings. He climbed down, shaking his head and trying to spit out the dirt, and shuffled down the hallway, around the corner, and down the stairs to the kitchen. She felt sorry for what she'd done to him – and he was likely to get into trouble from Captain Redoly in the morning – but she could think of no other way to keep him from seeing her leave. She was up the ladder, across the roof, and over the back edge of the wall in moments. She dangled from the second-floor roof for just a bit, long enough to wonder if this was really the smartest thing to do, then let go and dropped to the ground. Unlike when the giant dropped her, she landed gracefully, tucking her legs and rolling with the fall as she'd been taught. She knelt on the leeward side of the big tree facing the back ditch and listened. Satisfied that no one pursued her, she bolted from cover and half-ran, half-slid down the short embankment to the Goodspring gurgling along this side of the house.

She was about to head upstream to the cave and the tent when she heard someone cracking branches and stumbling through the water. Captain Redoly had been much quieter than that, but she did not want to risk being caught outdoors once more. She leaned backward against the slope of the ditch, slowed her breathing, and waited. The person stumbled toward her, a heavy load in his arms, and she recognized him at once.

"Posef," she whispered, standing up.

He jumped sideways, and his foot slipped in the mud. She gripped his arm and yanked him toward her. The large bundle in his arms – the desert tent and stakes – slipped to the ground at their feet, and he fell against her, knocking them both to the ground at the base of the hill.

"Zhava, what are you doing?" he said. "I almost jumped out of my skin."

He was lying beside her on the ground, his face right next to hers as he spoke, and she flashed back to the vision she'd had in the Proving Cove. Old and gray-haired, living in a little stone cottage along the Storm Coasts, their children and grandchildren coming to visit. He was skilled and handsome, and he made her laugh. He cared for her, too. He had volunteered to come with her to the farmstead when her parents were abducted, and now he was helping again, helping them all slip away into the night. She remembered the first night she'd been at the Hibaro, how he had strolled through the Initiate House, bare chested, his green eyes sparkling. He had an easy way with Barae, joking with her. He was a good friend.

"Zhava?" he said, quieter this time. "What's wrong?"

"I'm...listening," she said. How long was she staring? It couldn't have been more than a few moments. "I don't think anyone heard us."

"No," he said with a wide grin and a shake of his head. "You were staring at me. Like you did when we first met."

She shoved him away and brushed herself off as she stood. "You're imagining things. Let's go."

They collected the canvas and tent supplies from the ground, Zhava risking a little flame cupped in her hand so she could check for anything they may have missed. Satisfied they collected it all, they set off downstream to where Sanama had tied the camels. Barae was waiting beside the creek with a bag, and Zhava and Posef shoved the tent supplies inside. Sanama collected the bag and rushed to tie it to a camel.

"What happened?" Barae asked.

"Not now." Zhava pushed her along, afraid the girl would start chattering at them. Time was their biggest hurdle now, and they already lost enough of it with Captain Redoly catching her in the woods. She checked the straps of the four camels, none of the others having any familiarity with the animals, then helped them all get seated. Their camels lifted up with little complaint, surprising for the lateness of their journey. The lantern poles swung above them as they rode, but they kept the lanterns dark and set off single-file, Zhava in the lead. She knew the path well enough that she could guide them without the lights, at least far enough that the lanterns would not draw anyone's attention.

She turned in her saddle to be sure they were all there. Sanama was behind her, then Barae, and Posef at the rear. Sanama grinned and waved, and Zhava waved back, but no one spoke.

She turned her attention higher, to her home just above the little creek. The windows were still dark, shuttered against the night, and she could just make out the steady pacing of the watchman back at his post on the roof. There would be trouble at dawn, of course. Captain Redoly would chastise the watchman. Yenl would probably accuse the captain of not doing his duty in protected his charges. Brii...well, Brii would likely be disappointed, maybe a little mad at Zhava. Brii was nice. A friend? Probably not, but still a nice person. This was more important than any of that, though. This was about her family, her Papa and Mama. She knew where they were, and she knew how to get there. Mostly. No one else was willing to do this – not her brothers, not Captain Redoly – so she would do it herself. She would do it with her friends.

She turned to the south and focused on the path ahead.

Chapter 19

They travelled slowly until dawn, then urged the camels at a faster pace. They remained in their saddles and snacked on dried fruit but stopped to rest before mid-day. The mountains to their right slowly receded the farther south they went, and the dusty plains soon gave way to sandy ridges and then wind-swept dunes. None of them knew for certain when they had crossed the border, but the endless desert and sweltering heat that hit them soon after mid-day meant they were definitely inside Go'aabite territory. The Remmli king could claim the lands from the Storm Coasts up to the Highlands and on down to the desert plains where Zhava lived, but the high deserts to the south were inhabited by the Go'aabite traders and nomads. This was a foreign land to them all.

The desert clothes they had taken from storage were fancy – extraordinary gifts given to Papa and Mama. Brilliant blue robes with shining medallions on the sleeves, pure white head coverings that had obviously never been worn, and new sandals that did not bend comfortably when they walked. The clothes fit loosely on them, the sleeves allowing the desert breezes to flow through and cool them as they rode. There was even one small enough to fit Sanama.

The clothes were a problem, though. Zhava had met several Go'aabite traders who ventured near her home, and the only ones who ever wore brilliant colors such as these were the wealthiest of them. Most of the people's clothes were plain black or white. Barae assured them all she could work with the clothes when they stopped, though Zhava wasn't sure what her friend could do. She had never seen Barae use her Ability with cloth, though she heard the stories of Barae mending the ncts and fashioning the best sails for her father's boats. What could be done out here, though, with no sewing supplies or additional cloth?

The time seemed to pass slowly as they got into the rhythm of the camels' walking and the sun's steady trek across the sky. Zhava found her mind wandering and her body growing stiff and tired. They stopped late in the day and consulted the map Sanama had taken from Alxindra's supplies. The map was vague in its rendering of the desert, but they guessed they were at least another day, or possibly two, from the nearest city of any size. However, with a full day's ride south of Zhava's home, they felt confident they could rest the night. Zhava and Sanama tended to the camels while Posef and Barae set up camp. Once up, the tent was surprisingly large. There were three interior rooms, beautifully woven cloth curtains separating each, a cloth awning to provide shade outside the tent's main entrance, and rope ties on each side to allow the canvas walls to be rolled up and secured at the roof.

Barae took Sanama's blue robes and, insisting on privacy until she reemerged, went inside the tent to alter them. Zhava wanted so much to watch. She had never before been curious about her friend's Abilities, always assuming she was skilled with a needle and thread, but out here in the middle of the desert...how was Barae going to alter those robes? Some people used their Abilities in public, as she and Plishka did, while others kept their Abilities more private, concealed. Barae was neither private nor concealed about anything else in her life, and Zhava never questioned it. But, now...?

They finished unloading the supplies, and while Posef and Sanama began slicing some dried meat and dividing a bowl full of dates for the evening meal, Zhava emptied the sack of traveling supplies that Sanama had gathered from her brothers. There was the large map from across the rock, of course; some drawing tools; a vladar for measuring the distances between locations; a heavy satchel that Zhava didn't recognize; and a scroll labeled "Ways of the Go'aabites." She had sent Sanama into Papa's upstairs desk for the sole purpose of finding this scroll. Papa pulled out this scroll every season as the temperatures began to drop and the winter snows were on the way, right before the Go'aabite trading time began. It told him how to act around the Go'aabites, how to negotiate with them, how to recognize the different groups of traders. If Papa knew a certain Go'aabite Lord would be traveling to see him, he would review the history of that Lord's family, study that Lord's interactions with everyone else. This scroll was valuable, because Zhava had no desire to offend anyone and get into trouble as they made their way farther south.

She set aside the scroll and turned her attention to the brown, leather satchel. She wondered where Sanama found it and which of her brothers owned it. It was beautiful, the leather oiled and well maintained, hardly the kind of care that her brothers put into much of anything. She loosed the ties at the front and tossed open the flap – and stared, wide-eyed, into the depths of the satchel. It was filled with maps. She pulled them out. Dozens of small, square maps divided by regions that stretched all the way across Remmli and down into Go'aab. This was a wealth of information. Which of her brothers...?

She reached into the satchel and pulled out a leather pouch bound by a sturdy rope. She untied the knot, set the pouch on the ground, and unrolled the flaps, each layer revealing shining, well-maintained instruments. And not just a vladar and some drawing tools. This pouch was filled with a variety of instruments she had never seen before. Some were round, others had pointed ends, and one even had a small, metal dial that spun as she turned, the red-painted tip always pointing in the same direction.

"Sanama?" she said. "Come here."

She pulled another, smaller pouch from the satchel and untied the cord. This one fit in her hand, but it was heavy.

"Yes, Sir," Sanama said, striding to her and saluting. "Soldier Sanama reporting." She had taken to doing that since leaving Zhava's home, treating her like a commanding officer. Zhava found it cute, though she wasn't sure what Barae and Posef thought.

"Where did you find all–" She jumped up and tossed aside the thing in the pouch. "Captain Redoly!" The black cylinder lay gleaming on the ground. The same cylinder he let her use to see her home. The one that would make things far away look up close. The glass eye. She staggered back, gripping Sanama's arm and pulling her away.

Sanama yelped.

"You took Captain Redoly's satchel."

"What? No." She turned and stared at the satchel and all its contents spread across the ground.

"Where did you–? How could you–?" Zhava couldn't think clearly. Stealing supplies from her brothers, that she could justify. Her brothers were being unreasonable – and they were her brothers. But this...?

"What's going on?" Posef said, striding over.

"Sanama took Captain Redoly's satchel."

"No, I didn't." She tugged Zhava's hand, trying to free herself.

Posef's eyebrows rose as he took in the gleaming, well-ordered supplies. He smiled and said, "That's some good thinking, Sanama."

"No, you don't understand," she said, looking first at one and then the other.

"Stop," Zhava said, holding tight to Sanama's thrashing arm. "I understand. You didn't know it was Captain Redoly's satchel. Where did you find it?"

"I never found it, Sir," she said, her lower lip beginning to quiver. "I never took it."

Zhava sighed and glanced at Posef, her eyebrows arched in a silent question.

Posef shrugged and said, "Will you let me into your thoughts?"

"No!" Sanama yelled. She yanked her arm free and backed away from both of them. "You don't need my thoughts. I'm telling the truth." She turned to Zhava, tears pooling at the corners of her eyes. "Sir, why won't you believe me?"

"All right," Zhava said, lowering her voice and kneeling down before the girl. "I believe you. This is a real problem for us, though, and we need-"

"You don't believe me."

She believed the girl might have taken the satchel by mistake, but she didn't believe it was a complete accident. She had to have seen the valuable bag with Captain Redoly at some time and decided to stash it for the trip. Perhaps she forgot?

"I don't know why you won't believe me," Sanama said, the tears finally overwhelming her eyes and running down her cheeks. She spun and ran off as fast as she could, across the sand and over the nearest dune.

"Sometimes I forget how young she is," Posef said. "She's such a powerful little fighter."

"I suppose I should go after her," Zhava sighed.

"Where's she going to go in the middle of the desert?" Posef said with a laugh. "Let her calm down. She'll return."

The sun was just beginning to set when Sanama wandered back into camp, but she did not look at or speak to anyone. Barae had finished altering Sanama and Posef's robes, and they were perfect. Each was now bleached white and fit perfectly.

She assured a stunned Zhava that she would do the other two robes at their next stop – as long as she had privacy.

Barae and Posef took inventory of the equipment from Captain Redoly's satchel. As the stars popped out in the night's sky, they used the equipment and their navigation skills – Barae from her time on the ocean, and Posef from travelling the mountain passes – to locate their campsite on the maps, to chart a course to the nearest water, and to find the fastest route to Wui-sha'Olm. They presented their navigational plan to Zhava, who commended them both for such excellent work.

They were all surprised by how quickly the temperature dropped after the sun set, and they soon retreated into the tent. Zhava dug a shallow hole in the sand and dropped a dozen of her flaming men inside it so they could dance and play and heat the tent long into the night. With her friends safe and warm, Zhava bundled up in a couple layers of shirts and a blanket and went back outside for first watch.

An uneventful night led to a cool, quiet morning in which they struck camp, ate, and set off for their next stop before the sun even crested the first dune. Excited by the navigation equipment, Barae and Posef alternately led the procession. Zhava rode second in line, and Sanama rode the camel behind her, though Sanama remained quiet and sullen all day. Without the stress of leading their march across the desert dunes, Zhava used her time to read her Papa's scroll about the Go'aabite people. Nomadic traders, they were divided into three distinct clan groups, each living in a particular division of the country and rarely interacting with each other. Unlike Remmli with its one central capital, the Go'aabites maintained three seats of government, each ruled by a different High Lord, and they sent representatives to a central Conclave to work out matters of trade and justice. They frequently bickered with each other over the exact divisions of their territories, sometimes even going to war to claim – or reclaim – tracts of land said to be ancestral or sacred or anything else. Reasons need not be clearly spoken before any one group began fighting another. For all their squabbles, however, they were fiercely loyal to each other when it came to dealing with outsiders – especially hostile outsiders. An attack on any one group's territory was an attack on them all, and armies of soldiers were quickly sent from each corner of the country to repel invaders.

They were also related to each other. Far back in their histories, they had all been one large family.

"Sir, you should drink something," Sanama said when they stopped for the mid-day meal.

Zhava stepped away from her camel and stretched her legs and back. "I'm not thirsty," she said with a wave.

"You drank nothing all morning." She handed over a water bag.

Zhava cleared her throat as she took the bag. She didn't feel thirsty, even with the extreme heat and the sand blowing in her face. That seemed like a bad thing, to not be thirsty in the middle of a desert. She opened the bag and tipped up the spout to drink. The water tasted good, and it refreshed her. When she capped it and passed it back, however, she did not feel any better. She felt no worse. She felt as not-thirsty as she had when Sanama handed her the water. Before she could think more about it, Barae and Posef joined them, and they broke out the rations and sat in the shade of their camels to eat.

The remainder of the day's journey was a far slower trek. Posef and Barae argued about some fine point of their direction – something to do with the position of a star and the exact angle of their travel. Sanama frequently offered her water bag to Zhava throughout the ride, apparently refusing to believe that Zhava was not thirsty and felt fine. Late in the day they spotted another group of people in the distance. Zhava used Captain Redoly's glass eye to watch them. They seemed to be family group, several people on camels, a few children running around, and one person with a large sword across his back. The strangers were moving much slower than Zhava and her friends, so they continued on without worries.

As the sun neared the horizon, they crested a dune overlooking a low, muddy valley.

"I told you this was the way," Barae said, clapping Posef's arm.

A long, blue lake snaked a path through the valley, and several trees and bushes grew up along the water's edge. A flock of white birds milled along the opposite bank, scavenging through the mud and nibbling at something. The mud was a deep brown to the brilliant sand that rose up to the dunes surrounding the valley. They skirted the edge of the lake, taking in the scene below and the sandy crests above. Other than the birds, they seemed to be alone at this lake – a sabkha, according to Captain Redoly's map.

They tended to their camels, set up camp, and ate a light meal. Barae collected Zhava's blue robe and retreated into the tent with strict instructions to be left alone while she worked. Posef and Sanama peeled off their heavy robes and tossed them aside, glad to be wearing only their light, Hibaro shirts and pants.

"Have you ever watched her use her Ability?" Zhava asked. They sat on a wool blanket spread across the sand and tossed colorful, metal tabs into the woven circle. The game was simple: knock other people's tabs out of the circle, and keep as many of your own tabs inside. Posef was winning.

"I have known Barae for four seasons," he said, flipping another tab into the circle, "and I have never seen her use her Abilities."

"At least she has Abilities," Sanama muttered.

"You," Zhava said, "are an excellent fighter."

"Not as good as you, Sir."

"Why did you follow us?" Posef asked. "You know you'll be in trouble. Not just a little trouble, either. You snuck out of the Hibaro on your own to follow us."

"We'll all be in trouble now." She flicked a tab into the ring, tapping Posef's aside as hers stopped in the center.

"We'll deal with that later," Zhava said. She focused on her shot, but Sanama's words rolled through her mind. They would all be in trouble when they returned to the Hibaro. Would they even be allowed to return? It had seemed the only thing to do when she was at the farmstead – rescue Papa and Mama. But now, she wondered, at what cost? She flicked her tab, but the shot went wide. She missed the other tabs and landed at the edge, scoring only one point. Not that it mattered, as no one was keeping score.

"That's 12 to you," Sanama said. "I'm still ahead at 23, and Posef has 19."

"I'm sure I have 20," Posef said.

"Don't cheat," Sanama replied with a scowl.

"Am I the only one playing for fun?" Zhava asked.

"Yes," they both said.

Posef lined up his next shot. "You are only the second Initiate I've seen who didn't have any of the Gods' Abilities. How did you convince them to keep you?"

"I challenged Io Suleenuo to a duel."

Zhava and Posef turned and stared. They chuckled, waiting for Sanama to smile at the joke, but she never did.

"You're...serious?" Posef said.

"Our weapons master?" Zhava asked.

"I lost," Sanama said with a shrug. Then she looked up at them and grinned. "But I got her in the ankle with my sparring rod."

"No, you didn't," Posef said.

"I'm not lying." She scowled. "You both think I lie."

"Sanama, no," Zhava said with a sigh. "We don't think you're lying. But...we've never heard this. No one said anything about you dueling Io Suleenuo."

"It was private. You can ask her-"

"Stop." Posef turned and stared across the sabkha.

Zhava and Sanama sat up and looked around. The sun was just at the tip of the dunes, and it would be dark in moments. The light breeze had a chill to it. Most of the birds were nesting on the far end of the sabkha, chittering at each other, fluffing their feathers, and bedding down for the night.

"That family we saw," Posef said. "They're here."

Shadowy forms crested the dune. First two camels, then a couple people walking, a child running, and a few more camels.

Zhava scooped up the tabs – no gambling, that's what her Papa's scroll said. It also said-

"You two get into your robes – now!" She dropped the tabs into their leather pouch and rushed back to the tent. They hadn't expected anyone else – that was so stupid of them. They should have prepared to meet somebody; they should have been in their robes or inside the tent. The Sineise Desert was big, but many people lived here. It was only a matter of time before they met someone. A quick glance behind showed a steady stream of people, dozens of people, gathering around the sabkha. The children were running through the mud while several of the men began setting up tents. A few people stood near the water's edge and stared across at them. Posef and Sanama were both back in their robes. Zhava pushed past the tent opening, turned to her right, and shoved aside the canvas door to where Barae had the other robes –

-and Barae screamed. One robe lay spread across the ground at her feet, the top half white and the bottom half blue. She gripped the bottom hem tightly in her fists and stared up at Zhava.

And she was blue.

At first, Zhava thought Barae had blue dye on her hands and arms and face and legs – everywhere, really – but as she stood in the doorway holding the canvas curtain, she realized the dye wasn't on Barae's skin; it was inside it. The blue dye snaked its way through her fingers, along her arms, and spread throughout the rest of her body – at least as much of her body as she could see around Barae's own robe. The dye also moved. It pulsed, as if a pump pushed it along, stopped, then pushed it again.

Zhava noticed all that in the first moment she stood in the doorway before Barae flipped the half-finished robe over her head and sank to the ground beneath it.

"What are you doing in here?"

"Um...it's people." She pointed to the outside, a worthless gesture when Barae lay on the ground buried beneath the robe.

"But you didn't say you were coming in. You didn't warn me."

"I'm sorry," she whispered, kneeling down.

"I said I need to be alone. You weren't supposed to see me all ugly like this."

"Oh, Barae, no." She gently laid a hand on her back, and Barae flinched. "You are not ugly. Who said that?"

"Everyone." She spoke so quietly that Zhava wasn't sure she'd heard correctly.

"May I...?" She gently slid aside the half-finished robe from Barae's arm, still fascinated as she watched the blue streaks pulsing along. "Barae, this is amazing. Is this the dye from the robe?"

Barae pushed the robe back a little further until her one eye was exposed – with the blue pulsing across her brow and down the bridge of her nose. She peered out from beneath the cloth and gave a curt nod.

Zhava slid to the ground at her friend's side and stared into her face. Now she understood why she had never seen Barae's

Ability, because she was ashamed of the way she looked; she was ashamed to show off her gift. Zhava reached out and touched Barae's hand, traced her fingers and gently brushed the sand from her arm. The dye pulsed through her body, but Zhava didn't feel a thing beneath her fingers. She shut her eyes, and she couldn't tell what parts of Barae's arm were tinged by the dye and what parts weren't.

"It goes away when I stop." Barae slipped her hand out from beneath the robe and wiggled her fingers. The blue streaks had moved down to her palm, as if the dye drained away.

"Barae, this is amazing."

"Really?"

She pulled away the robe until it lay on the ground between them. "Absolutely."

Barae uncurled from her place on the ground. She tucked her legs beneath her and tugged her robe down to hide the blue swirling through them, but she sat up straight and let Zhava really see her. The pulsing, blue dye snaked like rivers beneath her skin, outlining the curves of her arms, shoulders, and face, and then disappearing beneath Barae's own robes.

"Is it...all over?" Zhava asked, sitting up.

"Yes, it's everywhere," Barae said with a blush. She held up her hands where the dye had drained away. "Until I stop."

Someone ran up to the tent and tapped on the canvas wall. "Zhava," Sanama whispered from outside.

"Don't come in."

"We need you out here. Now."

"I'm coming."

"I haven't finished yours," Barae said, standing up, "but turn around. I'll give you mine."

Zhava turned and gave her friend privacy. After several moments of shuffling cloth, Barae handed over the finished robe. As Zhava started to leave, Barae gripped her arm.

"You don't...," she started. "I mean, yes, I trust you. If, um, if you want to see...."

Zhava turned back. Barae stood in the center of the small room, dressed in her loose blouse and short skirt. The blue pulsed across her body, from her toes all the way up to where her hairline obscured it. She held the hem of the unfinished robe in her hands and quickly rubbed it between her hands. The dye from the robe seeped into her fingers, staining them a vivid blue before the pulsing rhythm began washing the color back into the rest of her hand and up her arms.

Zhava smiled, in awe of her friend's Ability. "Barae, you are beautiful."

Before Barae could reply, Zhava ducked through the curtain and into the wide, main room of the tent. She quickly threw on the robe and tied it around her waist, secured the hood around her neck and down her back, and rushed outside. Sanama grabbed her hand as they marched across the cooling sand to where Posef stood before two men in black robes.

She thought back to Papa's scroll and all the things she had learned. The black robes were important, but she couldn't remember why. They symbolized something. The men stood with their arms crossed, swords hanging from their belts. Across the sabkha five tents stood, and half a dozen fires had already been built into shallow, sandy pits. People milled around the firepits, many of them casting curious glances at the men confronting Posef.

"We don't speak their language," Sanama whispered. "They don't like that."

These people were fiercely loyal, and each one was related to another somehow. They had strict dress codes – such as these robes they had to wear – they did not like outsiders, and they did not like unrelated people traveling together. Families were the most important things to them. Large families, and extended families. It was likely that every person in and around those five tents was related somehow.

She stopped a distance away and knelt before Sanama, pretending to straighten the fit of the robe around the girl's head.

"What did you and Posef say to those men?" she whispered.

"Nothing. They just walked up and started babbling at us. Posef said he didn't understand, and that's when they got really mad. They speak Remmli, though, and they said they had to meet us all."

"All right, Sanama, here's what you do." She licked her finger and rubbed a spot of dirt off Sanama's forehead. "You're my daughter, and you're only 7 seasons old."

"They'll never believe that. I'm 10."

"You can pretend to be 7, just as I will pretend to be your mother."

"Then who's my father? Posef?"

She sighed. "Yes."

Sanama stared back at her, eyes wide.

"I am Mama, and he is Papa."

"But...Barae?"

"I don't know," Zhava muttered, straightening up. "My sister? Now let's go, and I hope this works."

Chapter 20

Zhava took Posef's hand as she stepped up beside him. The men in black robes were big. Not much taller than Posef or her, but they were wide and heavily muscled. They stood with their arms crossed over their thick chests and glowered, their long hair in braids draped across their shoulders. The one on the left was younger, but they looked similar enough they were probably father and son.

Zhava smiled and said, "Greetings. I am-" She doubted any of them would know her name, but she had no way of being sure they wouldn't know her family. If they knew her family, they would know she was unmarried – and that would get her and Posef both into trouble. "I am Allenka," she continued, "traveling with my husband, Posef, and my daughter, Sanama."

Posef shifted, and she squeezed his hand hard, willing him to shut up and play along.

The younger of the two men eyed the tent. "And who is in there?" he asked in Remmli. He had a thick accent, as if his mouth did not want to form the words, but he spoke them perfectly.

"That is my sister, Barae."

"We must meet her."

"I'm sorry, but that would not be good. She is very sick. She ate something that made her very sick, and now she is vomiting." The two men looked skeptically at her, so she went nearer to the truth. "She looks...blue now. Her skin is blue. I told her to remain in the tent."

That detail seemed to satisfy the men. They whispered to each other in their own language, and the younger man turned and ran back to the rest of their people. The older man stood where he was, his arms crossed and still glaring at them.

Zhava continued smiling. She wished she knew their language. There were teachers at the Hibaro who would teach her other languages, but she had always been more interested in her fighting skills and practicing her Abilities. Io Kua said there would be time for languages next season. Another language right now would be quite useful, though.

I'm your husband? Posef's thought intruded into her mind.

It's about family, she thought back. *The Go'aabites put family first. Always.*

Anything else I should know, "Allenka?"

The younger warrior was walking back around the sabkha, another man at his side. This man was dressed in flowing, purple robes with sparkling gold embroidery along the sleeves and chest. The young man had his head bent low, talking non-stop as they strode toward them.

Yes, Zhava thought back. *Tell them I was born in Go'aab.* She quickly spun a story for him in her mind. Nothing too complex, so they could easily remember it, but enough details to make it believable. She hoped.

The man in the purple robe smiled as he approached, his hands clasped behind his back. He stood between the two warriors, his hair long and straight, and his black beard bound in a series of knots evenly spaced down to the middle of his chest.

"Posef and Allenka," the young warrior said. "This is All-Father Ib'Dignas."

They bowed. Zhava wasn't sure if that was correct in the middle of the desert, but she had seen Papa do it when Go'aabites traded with him.

"Welcome to Sabkha U'Sholm," he said. He shut his eyes and inclined his head, but did not return the full bow. "The jewel of the central Sineise. You are foreigners. What is your business in our grand region?"

Zhava tensed. There was no hiding that they were foreigners, of course, but she didn't expect such a direct question so quickly.

"My wife," Posef said with a glance at her. "Her family was Go'aabite."

Ib'Dignas turned and studied her. "Allenka is not a desert name."

"I do not know my true name," she said. "I was raised far to the north, in the highlands of Remmli, and that is where I met my husband."

"And you are what? Fourteen years? Fifteen?"

"Nineteen, sir." She turned to Sanama and ran a hand down the girl's hair. "My daughter, Sanama. She is 7, and it is important that she meet her true family."

Ib'Dignas glanced at Sanama, who ducked her head, then back to Zhava and Posef. "Nineteen years is such a very long time to be away. How will you reconnect with your true family, especially when you no longer know your true name?"

"We're going from one village to the next," Posef said, "asking questions and gathering information. Someone must know what happened to her family, how they were killed so far north. We'll find the answers."

Ib'Dignas gave them a broad, toothy smile and clapped Posef on the shoulder. "I know just how to help. Come dine with us. We must talk." Then, to the younger warrior, "Show Allenka and her daughter to the women's tents."

Posef turned a panicked look at Zhava, but she only shrugged. Ib'Dignas pulled him around and started walking away with him, excitedly chattering about the savage beauty of the desert. The young warrior stepped forward, blocking her view, and gestured for her to follow. She hesitated, wondered if they were maybe being abducted.

"All-Father Ib'Dignas has extended to you his family's peace and protection," the man said. "You have nothing to fear."

Zhava blushed and ducked her head. "I meant no insult," she said. "I apologize."

"Not necessary," he said. He turned to the older man, and they talked briefly in their own language before the older man strode off toward Zhava's tent – where Barae was still working.

"What is he...?"

"No harm will come to your sister." The man clasped his hands before his face and gave a quick bow of his head. "My father would sooner die than allow any harm to one of All-Father Ib'Dignas' honored guests. Now I shall escort you to the women's tent."

She held Sanama's hand and followed the young warrior. His robes were open slightly at the collar, exposing the dark lines of his back and shoulders. His muscles moved beautifully – and Zhava turned her attention to the sandy ground between them as she felt the heat rise in her face. That did not help, however, as she found herself staring at his thick calves bulging with muscles from beneath the leather cords that twined around his legs, securing his flat shoes to his feet. She coughed, tried once again to get the tickle from her throat, and shut her eyes for just a moment. Just the bit she could see of this young man, he was...strong. That was a good, safe description. Strong.

"Are you all right?" Sanama whispered. "You're very hot."

"Yes," she blurted. She felt her face flush, and she fanned it with her free hand. "Just a bit overheated, Sanama. Dear."

"The women always get the first drinks," the young man said. "I'm sure there will be plenty of fresh water at their tents."

"Thank you, um...?" She looked up, focused on the top of his head, and that's when she noticed how his long, straight hair was parted, one part down his back and the other draped forward across his shoulder. He had beautiful hair.

"You may call me Garai."

"Yes, thank you, Garai."

"Your All-Father," he said with a quick glance at her as they continued their walk around the shores of the sabkha. "A northerner, but...he is willing to travel the Sineise with you?"

"It is very important that I find my family."

"And the clothes you wear? Those are from your family?"

"Uh...yes." She looked down at the robes and realized her story didn't work well with the clothing they had brought. If her family was killed when she was a baby, why would these robes fit her so well now? "I was found with them. The family that found me when I was a baby, they found these clothes also." The high-pitched flute began sounding in her ear again. She clenched her jaw and willed the noise to go away, but it stubbornly remained. "My family assumed the clothes were from...my family. I mean, my true family." She shook her head as if that would make her mind clear and the flute stop, then muttered, "I'm sorry. I'm not thinking well."

"You should have had more water today," Sanama said.

"I wasn't thirsty."

The man stopped at the covered entrance to a large tent. Music and women's voices carried through the heavy fabric, the noise – thankfully! – beginning to drown out the high-pitched flute playing inside Zhava's ear.

"All-Mother An'Iniga will greet you within." Garai pulled back the heavy curtain with a bow and a flourish of his hand.

As Zhava and Sanama stepped tentatively forward, they were met with the overwhelming jubilation of the women within. At least two dozen milled around, some standing in tight groups, a few sitting near the walls or in the corner, and several lounging on a spread of blankets around the tent's central support beam – as well as the four in the far corner playing various stringed instruments. There were many young women, a few babies in arms, a couple elderly women, and several girls playing in the sand at their mothers' feet. A few women had shed the outermost layers of robes and danced near the musicians, their silky underclothes flowing rhythmically around them. One woman, the only one wearing elegant, purple robes, sat up from her place in the center of the tent. She beckoned them forward and smiled as they approached.

"Welcome, guests," she said in fluent Remmli, her arms spread wide. "I am An'Iniga, and this is our family."

Several of the nearby women said greetings in their own language – at least, Zhava hoped the words were greetings. The smiles and bows seemed to convey friendly greetings even though she made no sense of the words. However, two of the younger girls behind An'Iniga exchanged fearful looks, then ducked low and snuck out of sight.

"How did you know to speak to us in Remmli?" Zhava asked.

"Good news travels fast, especially in a family as small as ours." She patted the blanket near her. "Come. Sit. You and your daughter must tell us all about the exotic lands to the north. And I must know what brought you back to your homeland after such a long time."

Zhava took a deep breath and sat, pulling Sanama down beside her. She hoped the girl remained quiet as she began telling her story: Her parents traveled far north, but she had no idea why. Bandits attacked her parents, and they left her to die. A nice couple happened upon the disaster, found her, and took her in. She was raised as their own daughter, given away in marriage to Posef, and had lived a pleasant life these many seasons in the far highlands with her husband and daughter. Now, however, she wanted to reconnect with her family – her true family from the desert – and pass along the traditions of her ancestors.

By the time she finished, the music and dancing had stopped, the other conversations wound down, and even the children ceased their playing. Zhava felt unnerved by so many eyes upon her, especially as the silence stretched on...and the high-pitched tone began sounding in her ear again.

"That is quite the adventure," An'Iniga finally said.

That broke the silence in the room, and the other women smiled and clapped and asked many questions. Were the people that far north really illiterate? (No.) How did parents treat their children? (Like all children, based on their behavior.) How did husbands treat their wives? (Fine. Posef was excellent.) Were women really required to do everything the men told them to do? (Not everything.) What was it like to live under a king? (Fine.) Had she ever seen the king? (No.) Did the king ever give her orders, and did she have to do everything he said? (No, and yes.) Why was there no queen? (There was a queen, and she was married to the king.) Why didn't the queen rule? (She didn't know.) And on the questions went....

The musicians returned to their playing, the dancers to their dancing, and the children to their games. Several water-skins made their way around the tent, and Zhava and Sanama drank their fill. That was soon followed by platters of food: freshly prepared small birds that were pleasantly spiced and cooked to perfection. Probably killed that very evening at the far end of the sabkha, but no one knew for sure.

With the stress of her fabricated life's story out of the way, Zhava began to enjoy herself more as the night wore on. She and Sanama played with a couple of the children, and they all danced for a while. An'Iniga invited them to participate in a late-night smoking of a pipe. Sanama was not at all interested, shaking her head and scowling as the smoking piece of carved wood was passed from one woman to the next, but with An'Iniga smiling graciously and all eyes on her, Zhava felt obligated to try. The smoke from the burnt leaves singed her throat and lungs and sent her into a coughing fit that seemed hilarious to everyone else but her. The tickle deep in her throat that had been troubling her for many nights grew worse, with sharp pains seemingly stabbing her from the inside. Someone passed over a waterskin, and after several drafts from it, the pain subsided.

She politely declined the pipe when it was offered again. The effects of that one pull on it, however, mixed with the increasing haze of smoke drifting throughout the tent, and Zhava felt her spirits lift. These women were so happy, all part of one big family, and the joy they expressed seemed infectious. A girl came up to Zhava and told a couple jokes, rude jokes in which the people of Remmli were dimwitted and too stubborn to do the right thing. She wasn't sure why, but Zhava found them the funniest things she'd heard in a very long time. Next, a young woman, a mother of two babies, invited Zhava and Sanama to dance, so they joined her at the side of the tent nearest the musicians, linking arms with the woman and twining circles with her. They sang and danced and kicked their feet through the sand, all accompanied by several women clapping along to the beat. They had more to eat, they joined the musicians in song, they swapped stories with several women, learning about their harsh life traveling the desert, and they laughed more in one evening than Zhava could remember laughing...ever. Though it felt far too soon, An'Iniga declared the mid-night hour had passed, and it was time for everyone to return to their own tents and prepare for the day-long journey from Sabkha U'Sholm to the city of Ving'Sa-wehn, the pearl of the desert.

Zhava wished everyone well, and she and Sanama shambled into the cold night. Four lanterns had been stuck in the sand around the sabkha's shore, lighting a path around the water and to their tent on the far side. The lights flickered in the gentle breeze, but they made it possible to navigate the moonless night with ease. When they reached the tent, they found Garai, not his father, standing guard. Zhava couldn't stop staring at him, that breeze pressing the robes snug against his body and outlining the solid muscles of his arms and chest.

"Welcome home," he said with a quick bow of his head. "An'Allenka, your husband is already inside."

"My husband?" she replied with a giggle. Her mind flashed back to her vision from the Proving Cove. She and Posef living on the Storm Coast, hobbling around their big, empty house and waiting for their grandchildren to arrive. She burst out laughing. "He's an old man!"

Garai glanced nervously from Zhava to Sanama and back again. "As you say, certainly," he replied. "But Ib'Posef is inside, and he did not look healthy when he arrived."

"Hmm." Zhava stopped laughing, not that she was getting Garai to join in anyway. She stood tall, straightened her robes as best she could, though her fingers did not want to do everything she told them to do. She studied Garai a moment, admiring him, and said the first thing she thought: "You're not an old man. You're a strong, solid man. I like that."

"Mama," Sanama said, gripping Zhava's hand and tugging her forward. "It is late. Come inside."

"She says it's late, strong man. Good night. Sleep well. See you at dawn."

"As you say, An'Allenka."

Zhava giggled at that. What would the real Sister Allenka say?

She stepped past the tent's curtain – and someone gripped her by the shoulders and yanked her down. She stumbled and landed on her knees in the sand. Barae held her head and looked her in the eyes. "What are you doing?" she whispered.

"You're not blue anymore." Zhava frowned. "When did you lose your blue?"

"What is wrong with you?"

"They smoked some kind of pipe," she said. "I only smoked it once, but I think it tasted good, um, by the third time...?"

"Oh, let the Gods just take us now," Barae muttered with a shake of her head.

"You were really pretty blue."

Barae pursed her lips and yanked Zhava into the side room of the tent, past a snoring Posef sprawled in the sand with a blanket tossed haphazardly across his back. He returned from the men's tent feeling sick, and she left him where he collapsed. She dimmed the lantern in the corner, muttering to herself the entire time about irresponsibility and scaring her half to death and what would they do in the morning and how she was the only one of them with any sense....

Zhava plopped down in the sand and stared at the tent wall. She wasn't thinking clearly, but she didn't know why. What was in that pipe? The tent wall shimmered, and it looked as if Emsterold was floating in the darkness across the room, her hair dripping wet and her hand extended and her eyes glowing, beckoning Zhava forward. But Zhava didn't want to go. Emsterold was trapped in that land of lightning and dead faces. She opened her mouth to speak, and she heard words coming out. What were they? If only she could think...

...and the next thing she knew it was morning, and she was lying on her side with a blanket draped across her. She coughed, and a cloud of sand flew up in her face. She shifted, wiped away the sand, and sat up. She felt good. Her thinking was a little slow, her thoughts just a bit fuzzy, but nothing at all like last night when she returned from An'Iniga's party. The high-pitched note in her ear had – thankfully! – gone away during the night.

The canvas tent walls were still dark, and the air had a chill to it. She wrapped the blanket tighter around her shoulders. Posef lay sprawled across the sand; he didn't seem to have moved. Sanama lay curled in a tight ball against Zhava's legs.

She slowly shifted away, careful not to disturb the girl, then stood and surveyed the ground. Where was Barae?

She gently pushed aside the flap to the central room. Empty. She checked the room opposite, but Barae was not there either. She peeked around the front entrance flap and saw Barae sitting in the sand just outside the tent and staring into the distance. The first glow of dawn was spreading above the horizon. She shuffled forward and sat beside her friend.

They sat in silence for a long time as the colors changed and the stars receded. At some point, as the morning's light awoke the birds nesting on the far edge of the sabkha, Barae reached over and took Zhava's hand. They sat like that, holding hands and watching the dawn break. Men and women from the other camp began moving around, tending to morning fires and letting their children run up and down the dunes behind their tents. When Barae finally spoke, it was in a voice barely above a whisper.

"No one has ever called my Ability 'beautiful.' Not my father. Certainly not my brothers." She gave a quick chuckle and stared at the sand. "Not even our teachers."

Zhava didn't know what to say. She meant it when she said Barae was beautiful. She had never seen anything like those blues swirling just beneath Barae's skin, the patterns they made, the pulsing rhythm as they moved through her. It looked like someone painted her, but the paints refused to remain fixed in place. How could anyone not see the beauty in that?

"That's why you never share your Ability in public."

"My father always wanted me to mend the nets and the sails. I'm so much better at it than my brothers. And faster. He even had me color them all, just a shade off red, something that would distinguish every bit of cloth and net he owned from what everyone else used on their boats. But I always had to go below-deck to do it. Or into the boathouse. Someplace where the other fishermen wouldn't see. He told my brothers it was because I was too much a boy, that I'm attracted to women, and he couldn't have the other fishermen spreading rumors about me. That might have been part of it – my brothers certainly believed it – but I always knew there was more. I always knew he was ashamed."

Zhava squeezed her friend's hand. It seemed what Barae needed most was love. She certainly understood. Her Papa was always so cold, so distant. Her Mama criticized her and condemned her constantly, for everything. She knew now why it happened, the curse. That was her story, though, and Barae already knew it. Though the circumstances were different, Zhava's own experiences helped her better understand what her friend felt.

"When were you going to tell me," Barae whispered, "that you plan to marry Posef?"

"Ummm...what?" She glanced over. A line of tears streaked Barae's cheek.

"You called me beautiful," Barae said, a slight hitch in her voice as she forced out the words. "But then you said you're marrying Posef."

"Barae, I never said that."

She turned so quickly, so violently, that Zhava jerked back. Barae's tear-streaked eyes narrowed, and her jaw set tight. "Don't lie. Don't ever lie to me."

She spoke with a fierceness Zhava had never before heard.

"You sat in that tent-" She pointed behind her, at the room where Zhava had slept. "-and you told me. You said you were going to marry Posef and have children with him-" She clenched her teeth and squeezed her eyes shut. "-have grandchildren with him. That you would live in a little stone house on the Storm Coast. In the middle of the night, you said all that. You said that me-" She lunged forward, her eyes wide and heat streaming off her body. "-even though you think Garai is...How did you say it? A 'God of the desert'?"

Zhava almost laughed at that, but the intensity of her friend's gaze squashed any humor she may have found in the comment. She slowly, gently, eased herself away from Barae, leaned back in the sand. She cleared her throat and spoke softly. "I do not remember saying that."

"But it's true?"

"Yes. Well, no. Not all of it. What I mean is, not most of it."

Barae swiped at her damp cheek, smearing a line of glistening sand across half her face. "All I want is the truth. Tell me the truth."

So Zhava told her story. Her time in the Proving Cove, her vision of the future – but a future that must happen, or a future that might happen? – and her time with Emsterold in the land of the dead. Then she talked about the young Go'aabite man. Yes, he was handsome – and so strong! She certainly did not remember calling him a "God of the desert," but...she had admired him, yes. The truth spilled out of her so quickly that Barae still hovered near her when she had finished. She reached for her friend's hand again, but Barae pulled away. She sat back, crossed her arms, and stared at Zhava. The intensity of her gaze was gone, replaced by a quiet sadness as she sat hunched in the sand, and they stared at each other in silence.

Zhava did not know what else to say. Barae asked for the truth, and that's what she gave her. Everything. Nothing held back. Would it be enough?

Just as Barae opened her mouth to say something, the tent flap flew open wide, and Posef stood in the doorway, one hand wrapped around the canvas door and the other shielding his eyes from the brightening morning.

"What in all the names of the Gods did I drink last night?" He slumped to his knees in the sand and glanced between them. "What's happening now? What's the...what we're doing?"

"Get yourself in order," Barae barked. She shoved herself up and glared down at him. "We have to leave with these people, and you'd better be able to ride." She stormed away without even a backward glance.

Chapter 21

It was amazing how quickly the Go'aabite family had their tents down, their camels fed and loaded, and their side of the sabkha so completely cleaned it was impossible to see that several dozen people had camped upon the site. Garai and his father helped Zhava and her friends pack their gear and prepare to travel. That meant Zhava had to intercede several times to keep the two Go'aabites from discovering the weapons and armor stashed in saddlebags. She and Barae claimed their Remmli upbringing would not allow them to sit idly by as the men did all the work, and Sanama heartily played at being a young girl and effectively distracted the men several times with her antics. Posef stumbled around the campsite moaning and complaining about his pounding head, and that further distracted the two men with hearty laughter at his expense.

The Go'aabites set off at a quick pace, swallowing up Zhava's small group in moments as they crested the dunes around the sabkha and ventured back into the ocean of sand. Zhava protested several times with anyone who would listen that they needed no guides, and they certainly did not need to visit this desert lord at Ving'Sa-wehn. Unfortunately, few of the Go'aabites spoke their language, and the ones who did simply stated that Ab'Dignas and An'Iniga knew what they were doing. Garai and his father rode alongside them, giving Zhava the impression more of guards on duty than friendly companions, no matter how many times Garai initiated conversations.

"Do you have no lhumir up north?" he asked Posef.

"Ugh," Posef replied as he wobbled precariously on his camel.

"I apologize for my husband," Zhava said. "He woke up feeling unwell."

"What's lhumir?" Sanama asked.

"It is a drink. Like your...um...." He waved his hand in the air as he stared into the distance, thinking. "It is like your wine, but it is not. It has more...how would I say it? More flavor? More...."

"You mean it's stronger," Zhava said.

"It can be," Garai said with a shrug. "But it does not have to be. Even the children drink it when we're far from a sabkha."

"Mama, may I try?" Sanama said, turning around on her camel to face Zhava, a sparkle in her eyes.

"No."

She pouted. "You never let me try anything."

Garai chuckled as she turned away. "Your daughter is very...forthright. Um...outspoken."

"Blame it on the northern influence," Zhava said with a sigh.

Maintaining the charade of An'Allenka, devoted wife of Ib'Posef, mother of Sanama, and sister of Barae was exhausting. As they rode their brisk pace, Zhava tried several times to speak into Posef's thoughts. She thought his name in a whisper and then a yell, but he did not look at her. Instead, he wobbled on his camel, looking several times as if he would puke, then righted himself and continued on without even a glance in her direction. When they finally stopped for a mid-day meal, she pulled him aside, next to one of the camels, and whispered into his ear as she pretended to rummage through a saddlebag.

"What is wrong with you? We need to talk. Why won't you answer me?"

"Headache," he said, wincing and pointing to his head. "I think Ib'Dignas can hear thoughts just like I can."

"You made your head hurt?"

"Got the idea from you," he said with a grin. "That ringing you get from your ear?"

She nodded.

"That was so loud I had to block off your mind. That's what I'm doing to Ib'Dignas. I think."

"So you drank too much of their wine."

"That was not wine," he said with another wince. "I don't know what that was, but it was stronger than anything I've ever had – and my father makes a strong drink back home."

"What did Ib'Dignas hear from your thoughts?"

"He knew where I was from, up in the Highlands."

She turned and stared at him, stunned that he would think that information was a secret. "Posef, you have green eyes and an accent. I knew you were from the Highlands."

"But you didn't know what town. He knew my hometown."

"Were you thinking about it?"

"I...well, I don't remember." He squinted, raised his hand and shielded his eyes from the high sun. "I must have been. Probably."

"Oh, Posef." She leaned against the saddlebag, took a deep breath, and tried to calm the anger rising within her. She needed Posef thinking clearly. She needed him focused on their problem – and the solution to the problem was clear from what she'd read in Papa's scrolls. She turned to him, gripped his wrist, and squeezed tightly. "Listen. In Go'aabite families, the men have the final say on everything. You're my husband. Remember? Go to Ib'Dignas and speak with him – one man to another – and tell him that we'll find our way without him. Tell him someone gave us directions. Tell him whatever you need to tell him to let us be on our way."

Barae and Sanama stepped around the front of the camel, each carrying a small cloth filled with an assortment of fruit and nuts.

"These are from An'Iniga," Sanama said with a smile, holding out one of the bags.

Barae, however, glanced at Zhava's hand on Posef's arm. Her eyes narrowed, and she thrust her bag into Posef's chest. "Here." She spun on her heels and stomped away.

"Is she mad at me?" Posef asked.

***

Posef never found Ib'Dignas before it was time to leave. Once back on their camels and continuing their trek, he asked those few people who spoke Remmli where he might find Ib'Dignas, but no one knew. So Posef started mingling among the other riders, letting his camel drift farther away from Zhava and the others – only to be escorted back by one of the men who claimed to be "concerned he might get lost."

As the sun rose high above them and the heat of the day made the sand seem to ripple in the distance, Zhava edged her camel nearer to where Barae and Sanama rode.

"How far is this taking us from...where we want to go?" she asked, as quietly as she could. She did not want to say the name Wui-sha'Olm, just in case one of the Go'aabites heard.

"I don't want to check the maps," Barae whispered back, "but we've been going southeast since we left the sabkha. Our...destination...was almost straight south, so not as bad as it could be."

"But a waste of time." She sat straight again on the camel and looked around. They were in the center of a sea of people and camels in every direction.

"I feel surrounded," Sanama said.

She couldn't argue with her "daughter."

***

Posef finally gave up wandering among the travelers and looking for Ib'Dignas when one of the men said he would lead Posef's camel for him if he could not get it to walk straight. Posef grunted about his head still aching, and the Go'aabite man and his friends all laughed. Zhava was almost certain Posef's head no longer hurt as she watched his face. He did not have the look of a man in pain, but in determination. His mouth was set in a grim line, and his eyes surveyed the riders, all the time keeping watch for Ib'Dignas. They had not seen the "All-Father" of the community all day, nor, Zhava realized, had they seen his wife, An'Iniga. Why would the two be in hiding?

"Your sister seems angry," Garai said, pulling Zhava from her thoughts. It was true. Barae stared straight ahead, her face framed by the white robes. Her jaw was clenched shut, and her eyes narrowed. She was happy almost all the time that the anger she showed now seemed unnatural for her.

"We had...an argument," she said with a dismissive wave of her hand.

"I am so very sorry, An'Allenka." He leaned nearer. "Is it any-thing to do with me or my family? Perhaps I should speak with her?"

A god of the desert indeed, Zhava thought. It would be the absolute worst thing for him to do, to go speak with Barae on her behalf – but it was so nice of him to offer. Handsome and caring!

"No, there's nothing you can do," she said, feeling her face blush. "This is between sisters."

"I understand," he said with a quick nod. "I also have a sister. Sometimes she is difficult."

"But never you?" she asked with a smile.

"Never." He grinned back. "I am the perfect brother." He burst out laughing, apparently quite amused at himself.

From the corner of her eye, Zhava saw Barae glaring. She sighed. Perhaps it had been a mistake to ignore Barae's feelings for her as long as she had. Even Plishka said she should talk with Barae, make it clear they were just friends – and nothing more. If they had talked at the Hibaro, they could have worked things out long ago.

Zhava turned the conversation to the topic of their destination. She and her husband had no desire to be rude, but they did not need to travel to Ving'Sa-wehn, and they did not need to meet this lord. They had been enjoying their time wandering the desert, seeing the strange sights, and slowly getting to know the land of her birth. Perhaps he could speak with Ib'Dignas? Perhaps he could explain the situation to his All-Father? They were thankful for the hospitality and the offer of assistance, certainly, but they really wanted to go on. Alone.

"No, the Sineise Desert is far too dangerous," he said, grimly shaking his head. "We will arrive soon at Ving'Sa-wehn very soon, and you will receive help on your quest."

***

As they rode on, the wind grew stronger, blasting dust into their faces. Conversations stopped as people secured their robes and wrapped their hoods more tightly against the elements. They bent heads into the wind and plodded on. Zhava considered leading her people away now, through the gusting wind, but it wasn't strong enough to obscure an escape – only strong enough to make their journey miserable.

She called out to Posef in her mind, and they spoke briefly. They could see no way out of this situation but to see it through to the end. Politely asking to leave didn't work. Insisting they needed no help didn't work. Seeking another audience with Ib'Dignas or An'Iniga didn't work. They could try fighting their way out, but what would they gain? They were significantly outnumbered, and there was nowhere to hide on the sandy dunes even if they got away. Their best option seemed to be traveling with this family.

As the sun touched the horizon behind them, they crested a ridge overlooking a long, walled city upon a hard-packed valley floor. Colorful towers of red, green, and gold shot into the sky, some as high as five stories with shuttered windows facing into the night. The sunlight had long ago left the valley, and torches burned brightly in a city center filled with tables and people.

The night guards opened the gates before the caravan arrived, and Ib'Dignas came striding out, his arms open wide as he greeted his family's arrival.

Zhava glanced at Posef, who only shrugged in return. The All-Father had rode on ahead. That was a convenient way to avoid confronting his guests.

As they approached the city walls, Zhava gaped. They were tall, with wide paths at the top where armor-clad soldiers stood guard, watching the surrounding valley. The gates themselves were thick beams of wood heavily banded with iron.

Servants appeared at the camels' sides, directed by Ib'Dignas, and they beckoned people off their mounts and into the city center. Zhava gave Barae and Sanama strict instructions to secure the gear – especially their weapons and armor – and then allowed herself and Posef to be led away to the tables set with plates of meat and bowls of fruit and vegetables.

The noise of the gathering overwhelmed Zhava, especially after the windstorm outside. Dozens of people – perhaps a couple hundred? – sat scattered around the tables in the city center. They talked and laughed and sang and ate. It was a party, but she had no idea the occasion.

She and Posef were seated across from An'Iniga who smiled warmly at them.

"Welcome," she said, handing over a couple plates. "Lord Su'Fyen is renowned for his celebrations."

"What are we celebrating?" Posef asked.

"The changing of the weather, of course." She gave him a puzzled look, as if she couldn't quite believe he didn't know. "The days will be growing longer again. That terrible chill in the air – I despise it."

Posef chuckled. "The chill? Out there?"

"It was awful, yes. Tonight will be even worse down here in the valley, but for now, the celebration will keep us warm."

Barae and Sanama joined them some time later, assuring Zhava their gear was stowed. Food continued to be delivered, more food than Zhava had seen in her entire life. She had no idea where it all came from, with these people living in the middle of a barren wasteland where nothing seemed to grow. A man in a black robe and a long beard sat at a center table, eating and drinking and laughing – and occasionally eyeing them from across the courtyard. An'Iniga said that was Lord Su'Fyen, but it was unlikely the man would speak with any of them today. She and Ib'Dignas had received a short audience with him when they first arrived, but theirs was such a small family with such simple needs that he easily assigned one of his officials to care for them. He was a generous man, but he had many duties.

After eating, several of the center tables were pushed aside, and a series of thick, wooden poles were set on end. Concentric red circles were painted on the poles, targets, and Zhava was immediately intrigued. Several men and a few women strode forward, hatchets in hand, and began throwing them at the beams. The crowd cheered or groaned, depending on the throw and the skill of the competitor. One man's hatchet went completely off course, bouncing off the side of the pole and skittering across the ground. After a loud gasp and a moment of silence in which it became obvious no one had been hurt, everyone laughed and jeered the man, and he was promptly ushered back to a table where he sat with a sullen look on his face. Other than that, the competitors were very good, with many of them striking the innermost target.

"Would you like to play?" An'Iniga asked.

"That's very kind of you," Zhava said, "but we are all very tired. We should get some rest."

"No, I insist," she said with a wave of her hand. She turned away and beckoned someone to join them.

Zhava clenched her teeth but did not reply. She was getting so angry at these people for dismissing everything she said. Were all Go'aabites like this?

"Garai," An'Iniga said as the young man stepped to their table. "Ib'Posef and An'Allenka would like to try. Lend them your hatchet and show them how."

"Of course, All'Mother."

"Wait," Posef said, his smile vanishing. "I never said I want to try. I'm fine with not trying."

"Come along, husband." Zhava gripped his arm as she stood from the table. "An'Iniga inists."

They followed Garai around the edge of the crowd.

"I am terrible at throwing things," Posef hissed into her ear. "And I have never thrown a hatchet. How do you throw a hatchet?"

"We're about to learn," she said with a smile. "So act like you're enjoying yourself."

As Garai led them forward, the crowd of players separated, many of them cheering them with their smiles and claps and whistles. A woman reached forward from the crowd and shoved her own hatchet into Zhava's hands, smiling and talking animatedly in her own language. Zhava nodded and thanked her as she followed Garai. The hatchet was shorter than her Felton sword, but it had a hefty weight, far heavier than any sword she had used. The wooden handle was worn smooth where the woman had obviously used it for many seasons. The short, curved blade glinted in the flickering torchlights. A bird was carved into the handle, just behind the blade, the wing feathers so delicately etched into the wood that it must have taken the woman a long time to finish.

Zhava slowed and turned, found the woman's face in the crowd again and smiled her thanks. The woman gave a slight bow of her head in return.

Garai was already instructing Posef how to hold the hatchet and swing his arm. Keep the wrist straight. Keep the elbow bent. Start from behind the head. Swing forward. Release.

Zhava followed along with Garai's instructions, but Posef kept interrupting with questions. Garai was a patient instructor, repeating himself several times. Zhava stepped away and practiced the movement a couple times. It was natural, a hard swing forward and a quick release. Posef was still questioning something about the placement of his feet; he never attended knife-throwing classes, or he would have realized how similar the movements were. She felt ready, so she stepped up to the line in the dirt.

A few of the nearest men crossed their arms and watched, and several others grew quiet. She raised the hatchet, swung her arm forward – and yanked the sleeve of her robe tight against her shoulder. The hatchet flew from her hand, landed on the ground, and spun around in the dirt. No one laughed, but the crowd got quieter.

"You need to...um," Garai said, gesturing at his own robe, which was open wider at his neck, looser across his shoulders. "Yours is too tight."

She retrieved the hatchet from the ground and studied the way the competitors wore their robes. Each person had loosened the neck, and several of the men had actually untied the top so that the cloth draped over the belt and hung around their legs, baring their arms and chest. The few women who were playing had all loosened their robes too, but they wore dark shirts beneath their robes. Zhava wore her red Hibaro shirt beneath her robe – not something she wanted these people to see. She didn't need the entire front loosened, though, just enough around her shoulders to not interfere with her throw....

"Mama," Sanama said from beside her.

She never noticed her "daughter" approach, but she smiled and bent down. "Yes, my dear?"

"I can help. Loosen the neck tie, and turn around." Sanama held her own belt in her hands. Zhava loosened the ties at her neck, and Sanama threaded the belt up Zhava's right sleeve, behind her neck, and down through the left sleeve, then looped it back around and tied it just above the shoulders. It wasn't attractive, but it kept the folds of the robe tied up and out of her way without revealing any of her Hibaro clothes.

She returned her attention to the competition just as Posef leaned forward and threw his hatchet. It bounced against the side of the pole and skittered across the ground. The crowd boisterously cheered and laughed. Posef, in typical style, raised his arms to the air, pirouetted in a wide circle, and smiled at the people.

"An'Allenka," Garai said, stepping up to her. "Let me show you, um...." He stared at her arm as she spun the hatchet in the air and caught it.

"I was getting a feel for the weight," she said with a shrug.

"No, it's just...you're very strong."

"Thank you." She turned and stared at the target. She had listened to Garai instruct Posef, she had thrown one really awful practice shot, and she felt comfortable with the weapon in her hand. It was similar to her throwing knives, but the balance was completely different.

"Allow me-" Garai said.

Zhava threw. The hatchet spun through the air, arced gracefully, and hit the post with a solid thud – just to the right of center.

The crowd burst into cheers, many people slamming their fists to the tables as they yelled their congratulations. Zhava

ducked her head and smiled as she walked to the post to retrieve the weapon. When she turned back, several more people stood in line waiting to compete with her. Feeling the most
comfortable she had with these people since first meeting
them at the sabkha, she threw herself into the competition.
Garai gave her a few tips on better control, but he soon stepped
away and let the competition continue uninterrupted. Her
next couple throws were far off the mark, but then she felt
the rhythm of the throw and the pace of the weapon. She improved at this as quickly as she had at throwing knives, and by
the time Lord Su'Fyen stood and declared the festivities concluded for the evening, she was striking the center of the target on nearly every throw.

Food was collected, litter was picked up from the ground,
and people dispersed to their homes throughout the town.
Zhava wound her way through the crowd to the young woman
who had lent her the hatchet, and she held it out in return. The
woman took a step back, crossed her arms, and began talking
in her language. Her eyes narrowed, and she looked quite un-
happy. Zhava inspected the hatchet, but it seemed as nice as
when the woman offered it to her. She treated it well; there
were no scratches or markings on it, at least not that she noticed.

"It was a gift," Garai said, stepping between them and looking at Zhava. "She wants to know why you would return such a
gift."

"A gift? But why?"

Garai turned to the woman, and they spoke several times.
The woman's face softened, no longer so angry.

"She heard your story," Garai said. "She lost a sister to
northern raiders when she was very young. She blessed this
weapon and gave it to you so you would find your lost family.
She believes your performance in the competition is a mark

that her blessing has already...taken hold, or that it has landed properly."

"That is so kind," Zhava whispered. "Thank you." She turned to Garai. "Thank her for me. Tell her I will keep this with me always."

When Garai finished translating, the woman smiled, stepped forward, and hugged Zhava before turning to leave with her family.

They collected Barae and Sanama at the table, and Garai led the way to a three-story building he described as a temporary home for honored guests of the city Lord. Barae and Sanama had already seen it when they stowed their bags with the armor and weapons. Several rooms were lit, and Garai took them up a narrow set of stairs to a door at the corner of the second floor. He wished them all a pleasant night's sleep, handed them the lantern, and disappeared back down the dark stairwell.

Inside, their bags still sat where they were placed, no evidence of tampering. A table was wedged in the corner, and a longer table stood near the wall. Two open doors led to smaller rooms with sturdy-framed beds of soft down – it was truly a luxurious guest house. Zhava walked across the room to see their view out the shuttered windows – when a movement in the corner startled her. A person sat there. A large man dressed in black robes.

She stepped back and raised her hands, the hatchet held high as she prepared to defend herself. Without thinking, her little flames flared to life across her shoulders and down her arms, bathing the room in bright, flickering light.

Lord Su'Fyen sat in a wooden chair, his head resting in his hand and his eyebrow cocked as he stared at Zhava.

Barae and Posef stood still across the room, too shocked at the intrusion. Sanama, however, had drawn a sword and stood between them and the city's Lord, her eyes narrowed at the potential threat.

"An'Allenka," the man said, his voice deep and slow. "No. I thought perhaps...Sister Allenka. But no, you're far too good with a weapon for that foul-tempered beast."

Zhava stood nervously, watching him. How did he know Sister Allenka? How did anyone in Go'aab know a woman at the Hibaro – and well enough to call her "foul-tempered"?

"But now the pieces fall into place," he said with a nod of his head, the beard brushing across his shirt. "Novice...Zhava."

She couldn't help it. Her eyes grew wide as he recognized her. She opened her mouth, but she couldn't think what to say. No one had even questioned their story as they rode through the desert, but this man, this city's Lord, recognized her immediately.

He turned to the others. "Which means you must be...Novice Posef, Novice Barae, and...ah, the young runaway, Initiate Sanama."

"What do you want?" Zhava said, finally finding her voice.

"I?" He shook his head. "I want nothing. But you have placed yourselves in a most dangerous situation – one that will get you killed."

Chapter 22

"But first," Lord Su'Fyen said with a gesture outside. "The shutters are latched, certainly, but anyone looking at this window will see too much light around the frame. I would not want anyone thinking there is a fire. That would interrupt our conversation."

Zhava didn't move. He was right, the flames would be obvious, but she had no intention of dropping her guard.

"The lamp." He pointed to the table behind her where a large, crockery lamp sat.

She willed one of her flames to leap to the table, climb the lamp's glass chimney, and slide down to light the wick. In moments, the lamp's soft, orange glow filled the shadows behind her. She waited.

He yawned. Straightened his robes. Admired his fingernails.

With a little cough, Zhava doused the rest of her flames — all but a few, though, that remained on her shoulders. She was not yet sure if this man was offering to help them or hurt them, but she wanted him to know she could defend herself.

"That is certainly better," Lord Su'Fyen said. "Less likely to be interrupted."

"What do you want?" Sanama said.

"Let the adults speak," he replied with a glare.

"It's a good question," Zhava said. "What do you want? And how do you know us?"

"I am ligistak, one of only a handful in all of Go'aab. Trained since birth to absorb all information, to make the connections from one piece to another, to observe the whole as well as the parts, and to deduce the truth of any and all situations."

"You're a Salient?" Posef asked.

"Hah!" the man said with a bark. He scowled at Posef. "Those tricksters you employ in Remmli? Children, compared to me." He turned back to Zhava. "You were brought to my city so that I might better evaluate the truth of your claims. I've done so. You have none. Why should I not call immediately for your execution?"

She wasn't sure if telling him the truth would help, but lying to him was obviously not working. If he really was as powerful as a Salient — or more so, according to him — then more lies would only delay the inevitable. They might still end up fighting their way out of this city, but if she could avoid that, she would. "We really are looking for my parents."

"Your parents," he muttered, thinking. He glanced at the floor, his eyes flicking back and forth across the dusty tiles. "Prince Ooleng attacked your parents' farmstead and fled into the desert — into my desert — with only a small group of his remaining mercenary thugs. But your parents were not with him, and they are not in my city." He turned his head. "But you were not traveling to my city. Ib'Dignas brought you to my city. You were not pursuing Prince Ooleng. You were traveling south, and at great speed." He cocked his head to the side and shut his eyes. "You were traveling...to...." He opened his eyes wide and stared at her. "Wui-sha'Olm?"

"That was amazing," Posef whispered with a grin.

"You believe your parents are in Wui-sha'Olm?"

Zhava nodded.

"Why?"

Zhava shrugged. Truth only went so far, and visions of people in the land of the dead was a line she would not yet cross.

"I was given the information," she said. "High Priest Viekoosh has taken them captive."

"In Wui-sha'Olm?" he said, his voice rising in shock. "That is impossible." Then he turned to the side and stared at the wall. "Impossible. Impossible. Viekoosh and Ooleng...and the sengret eggs...."

"Zhava stopped them from getting the eggs," Sanama said.

"The sengret...and the nightly visions...and the voices in the dark." He shut his eyes and leaned his head back on the chair. "And Zhava receiving information...receiving information...information from...someone...."

Zhava shifted uncomfortably. This man was smart, and he really could make connections with disparate pieces of information. It was as if he took it all in and mixed it together, pieced together the parts to discover how they really set – and then uncovered the holes.

"High Priest Viekoosh...wants a war?" He turned back to Zhava, his eyes focused again. "Io Liori was the one who provided the information about Wui-sha'Olm?"

"Um...no."

"Ah. You withheld an important piece of information." He sighed and steepled his fingers before his face. "Why would you withhold that information?"

"She speaks to the dead," Sanama said.

"Shh!" Zhava turned and glared at her.

"But he can help us," she replied.

"The dead," Lord Su'Fyen whispered. He turned his head away, and his eyes drifted again as he began muttering aloud. "The dead...the dead...a student...with an Ability of the dead...."

There was a soft fizzle from Zhava's right shoulder, and she looked as her little flaming men vanished in a puff of smoke. That was weird. She hadn't released them. Why would they leave?

Her throat began to burn, suddenly thirsty for the first time in several nights. As Lord Su'Fyen continued his muttering deductions, she went to their gear in the corner and pulled out her waterskin.

"This man is weird," Barae whispered, leaning in close.

"He's a genius," Posef said.

"But he's not reading our thoughts?" Zhava asked as she replaced the waterskin. Her throat felt better, her thirst finally quenched, but now it was itchy, as if something was lodged deep down. She coughed a couple times, but nothing came loose.

Posef shook his head. "I wasn't thinking of Io Liori. I put Brother Tymare's name in my head to test him. Barae?"

She shook her head. That left only Sanama, but the girl still stood in the center of the room, her small sword drawn against the city's Lord.

"Keep testing him," Zhava said. "Think of random things, anything that makes no sense. See if he uses it." As she returned to Sanama's side, she called a flame to her hand. He appeared instantly, dancing joyously in her palm. She shut her hand over him. Could Lord Su'Fyen have done something to make her flames fizzle away? It was possible, but she hadn't seen him do anything. He seemed unimpressed by her flames, even when they ringed her arms and shoulders.

"Apprentice Emsterold is alive," he blurted. He turned to Zhava. "And you can speak with her."

"How do you know that?" she asked. "How do you learn these things?"

He didn't reply. He turned away and continued his ramblings, his head twitching as he muttered to himself. "High Priest Viekoosh...Salient Kretsch...Prince Ooleng...Apprentice Emsterold...Io Liori-"

"Liori?" Zhava said. "Why Liori? Stop."

But the man didn't stop. "Novice Zhava...Novice Posef...Novice Barae...Initiate Sanama...Novice Plishka-"

"Plishka?" Zhava stepped forward and raised her voice to interrupt. "What about Plishka?"

When he still did not reply, she shook his arm. He jerked in the chair and turned to her, his eyes wide. "What?"

"What about Plishka? You said her name."

"Did I?" He glanced away quickly, then back to her again. "I did, yes. You are all fools." He rose from the chair so quickly that Zhava stumbled backward. Sanama raised her sword and stepped forward, ready to defend them. Barae and Plishka fumbled for their own weapons. Lord Su'Fyen, though, paced the short length of the room, ignoring them all as he spoke animatedly. "Fools, all of you. It's the prophecy of the tyrant, don't you see? The invasion of Wui-sha'Olm by the fool God Coredor and his men. They want to make it come true again, after all this time."

"I'm confused," Posef said.

"You've been confused since you were born," Lord Su'Fyen said in an offhand way. He turned to Zhava. "But you know the power of Coredor's followers. You fought them."

It was true. High Priest Viekoosh himself was a follower of the trickster God, and he had surrounded himself with like-minded believers.

"But the tyrant already ruled," Sanama said.

Lord Su'Fyen turned to her, his eyes wide. "You know the prophecy?"

"I heard it." She lowered her sword as she spoke. "The king would desecrate the sacred shrine, the people would rebel, and a great war would kill most of the desert people. But it already happened, a really long time ago."

"Very good, Initiate Sanama. Quite insightful. You surprise me."

"Well I don't know it," Posef said.

"Neither do I," said Barae.

Lord Su'Fyen turned to Zhava, and she shrugged. She didn't know it either.

"What do they teach at this Hibaro of yours?" Lord Su'Fyen said. He leaned against the wall and stared at the floor. With a quick sigh, he said, "You know the God Coredor. He is consumed with hatred for the Gods-blessed, the ones with Abilities such as yours." He pointed at Zhava. "But he is a trickster God, and a lazy God. He prefers letting others do his work for him. So he declared that the Go'aabite family would be His army against the Gods-blessed. The family was divided in this, however, with some people declaring it a foolish war, and others eager to wipe out the enemies of Coredor. Only a few of the people in the family followed Coredor; there are so many Gods, and the family could not agree on the correct course of action. Coredor knew his cause would be lost if he did not unite the family. He gave a vision to one of the Gods-blessed women of the north, a priestess of Hoap, that she would find her lost daughter within the sacred caves of Go'aab. She crossed the desert alone – a long and dangerous trek – and she found the caves. But her daughter was not there. Another trick of Coredor. Instead, she interrupted a holy initiation. The family killed her for the transgression. The followers of Hoap joined together in the north to march against the family of Go'aab; the family banded together to retaliate, and in the end...the Go'aabites are now a split family, far fewer of us than there were back then."

He stopped.

Zhava stared. "That's it? What does that have to do with...anything. My Papa and Mama? Or Plishka and Io Liori?"

"Wui-sha'Olm is that sacred place," Lord Su'Fyen said with a sad shake of his head. "And the followers of Coredor now number in the thousands across our desert."

"They want to restart the war," Sanama said.

"That makes no sense." Posef stepped forward. "What about all the priests who work and live at this temple of yours? Someone would have noticed already. If this temple is so special, someone would have stopped Viekoosh from taking over."

"Our family is not like you mountain folk. We have no priests who live off the wealth of others. In the heat of summer, when the sun is at its apex, many of us will travel to Wui-sha'Olm. In the depths of winter, when the sun reaches its zenith, many more of us will travel to Wui-sha'Olm. Otherwise, the place is left alone for the Gods to use as they so choose."

"This is winter?" Barae chuckled.

"I don't understand," Zhava said, shaking her head. "How do I fit into all this?"

"You do not." Lord Su'Fyen shook his head as he turned to stare at the floor again. "I admit I was confused, but that is understandable. I was missing information, which you have now provided. Prince Ooleng should not be here. You should not be here. Somehow you fought him off from your farmstead, him and his hired warriors."

"Yeah, we had some help with that," Posef nodded.

"He hid within my city, lied to me about his intentions, abused my hospitality. He knew...he knew of the coming war." Lord Su'Fyen paused, squinted at the floor for several moments, then continued. "Salient Ayaan received poor information."

"How do you know all this?" Zhava asked, more amazed the longer the man spoke.

"I told you," Lord Su'Fyen said with a frown. "I am ligistak. I know all, I see all, and I connect all. Salient Ayaan received poor information and passed that along to Io Liori. Io Liori went in search of the missing twin. The missing twin is irrelevant, though. She was the decoy – yes! The decoy that would bring the soldiers that would invade Wui-sha'Olm that would be there when the solstice begins and the family arrives. A simple plan, but then you-" He pointed at Zhava. "-did not cooperate. You would not be caught by Prince Ooleng. You refused to be removed from the battle. You received your vision from the land of the dead, and now...here you are. Five days before the solstice. Able to give warning." He shook his head and stood up straight. He looked at each of them in turn, then back to Zhava. "You have been of assistance. I will not order your execution."

Zhava tensed. She hadn't realized her execution was still being considered.

"But you will travel to Wui-sha'Olm immediately – tonight. You will clear out the people of Remmli from our sacred mountain, and you will do it before I arrive with my people, and with my army, when we celebrate the winter's solstice five days from now."

Zhava raised her voice in protest. She had no army of her own, she did not know how many hired soldiers were there, she tried once before to stop High Priest Viekoosh – but Lord Su'Fyen simply held up his hand and waited. When she stopped, he continued.

"I hear you," he said. "But anyone remaining in Wui-sha'Olm by the time of the winter solstice will be put to the sword, and the blame for their spilled blood shall be placed upon you, Novice Zhava. You are an apostate of the Remmli Hibaro, a student who went her own way to do her own thing and without the knowledge or consent of her teachers and elders."

"But, Lord Su'Fyen, that is not us," she said.

"You have abused the hospitality of the family of Go'aab, and you lied to Lord Su'Fyen, the magistrate of this pearl of the desert, the city of Ving'Sa-wehn. Your actions are your actions alone, and they in no way reflect upon the Kingdom of Remmli or the rest of its people."

She stood there, stunned. What was she to say? What was she to do?

"If, however," he continued, "you find your people, clear them from our mountain, and return them to your own lands before we arrive to celebrate the winter solstice, then the family will hear a different tale. A band of students traveled from the Hibaro, at great risk to themselves and at the request of the King of Remmli himself, to quickly and decisively remove a dangerous man and his followers from our sacred mountain. These students were known by Lord Su'Fyen, the magistrate of the pearl of the desert, the city of Ving'Sa-wehn, who did, in fact, invite them into his confidence. Who sent them on their way with all haste and with many blessings so that they could fulfill their mission. The names Zhava, Posef, Barae, and Sanama shall be revered throughout the land of Go'aab, honored for the swift, decisive action taken on behalf of the family."

"You're the hero of both stories," Posef said. "You ride in with your soldiers and kill everyone, blame it all on us, or you send us to do your work and then take all the credit."

"I am ligistak," Lord Su'Fyen said, his arms spread wide. "I know all, I see all, and I connect all. Of course, I am the hero."

"You're not giving us a choice," Zhava muttered.

With a sigh, Lord Su'Fyen stepped forward. He turned his back to the other three, leaned in close to Zhava's ear and whispered, "Why are you doing this? You know they are not your parents."

Zhava gasped. She took a step back and stared into the man's face. How did he know?

"Return now to your Hibaro," he continued. "Leave this place, and I will say nothing at all of your involvement. I will say nothing about any of you."

"But...you'll kill them all."

"Yes." He nodded his head slowly, firmly.

"I can't do that. My Papa. My Mama-"

"No. Not your parents. And your 'mama' despises you."

"She was cursed. That's not her fault. And they raised me. Papa, he...he raised me, and he loves me."

"Loves you...yes, he does. Understand me, Novice Zhava. I do not want a war with the King of Remmli. We would not lose such a war, but the losses would be great – for both of our kingdoms. What I do now, I do for the safety and security of the family of Go'aab."

"That's what I'm doing," she said. "I want my family safe."

"Then I make this vow to you: I will delay my arrival until the last possible moment. You will have all the time I can give you, and I will send one of my own men to guide and assist you. But whoever remains at Wui-sha'Olm by the winter solstice, whether fiend or friend – even you and your adopted family – we will kill. I will maintain the peace with Remmli at all cost. That I must do for the good of us all."

Zhava nodded. What more was there to say?

He stepped away, studied Posef, Barae, and Sanama in turn, then said, "Until next we meet, whether on the battlefield or at the dining table, I wish you all peace."

"Wait," Zhava blurted, stepping before him. "You know about my family? You know who my parents are?"

He narrowed his eyes and studied her. Unlike his frantic pacing and mumbling from before, however, his thinking about this question did not require him to look around the room and talk to himself. He simply stared into her eyes.

"Complete the task you have been given," he finally said. "I shall gather more information. Perhaps one day, depending what happens at the solstice, we can speak of this again." With that, he turned and left the room.

Chapter 23

As the door shut behind Lord Su'Fyen, Sanama slid her sword back into its sheath and said, "I don't like him. He thinks he knows everything."

"He knew almost everything," Posef said.

"No mind tricks?" Zhava asked.

"I thought about some weird things from back home, some of my Hibaro lessons, even about the last time I got in trouble. If he was digging through my thoughts, he didn't use any of it."

"Barae?"

"I kept thinking one thing over and over," she said, looking Zhava in the eyes. "Something only you and I would know. He never even noticed."

That hurt, Zhava thought. Barae was a wonderful friend, but that really was Zhava's feeling: friendship, companionship. Why couldn't Barae content herself with that?

"I just thought about killing him," Sanama said.

"That thought wasn't even hidden," Posef laughed.

"He was mean. He wanted to kill us."

"Enough," Zhava said. "He's letting us leave, so let's do it. Gear up. If he's going to tell everyone we're Remmli, then let's be well-armed Remmli."

They stripped from the Go'aabite robes and put on their armor and weapons over their Hibaro clothes. Zhava finally felt more comfortable as she cinched the leather armor tight to her back and chest, the Felton sword at one hip, her newly-acquired hatchet on the other, and the half-dozen throwing knives on her belt. When everyone was ready, they gathered the saddle bags and opened the door.

Garai stood in the dark, his face lit by the soft glow of the room's lantern, and his hand in the air as if he was about to knock. He stared at them all, frozen in mid-motion, and took in their clothes, armor, and weapons. His eyes especially lingered on Zhava, moving from the tightly-cinched, black breastplate to the gauntlets on her arms and the leather greaves covering her legs. He took a step back from them all, though he had almost nowhere to go on the small landing.

"Lord Su'Fyen told me you are all soldiers," he said. "Soldiers in training. And that you are in command...Novice Zhava?" He said her title and name as if for the first time, and found them distasteful. He didn't grimace as he spoke, but he did not look pleased.

She set her hand on the pommel of her sword, unsure if he was there to hurt them or help them. "That is all true. He also said we're free to leave. We have a mission to complete."

"Yes." He glanced at Sanama, frowned, then back to Zhava again. "Lord Su'Fyen assigned me...to your command."

"Of course he did," Barae laughed, shaking her head.

He ignored her and continued. "I am to guide you to Wui-sha'Olm and assist any way I can, except that I am not allowed to fight at your side. I am to bear witness and report on the outcome of your actions."

"You won't fight with us?" Sanama asked. "Then what good are you?"

"I have been given my orders," Garai said, clenching his fists and glaring at them each in turn. "You lied to me and my family, you trespassed into our desert – and yet, I am to assist you. Were I this city's Lord, I would kill you where you stand and throw your bodies into the desert to be picked clean by the vultures and your bones buried by the next storm. Let the Gods deal with your treachery."

Zhava flicked her hand and let a flaming man dance between her fingers. "If you're threatening me or my soldiers, Garai...." She snapped her hand shut, snuffing out the flame.

"Unlike you Remmli," he said through clenched teeth, "I honor my word. Lord Su'Fyen said to guide you and stand by your side, and that is what I will do."

Zhava studied him as he stood there in the dark. She wanted to believe he would keep his word and not harm them, but she would not put the lives of her friends at risk. If he decided to attack them while they slept, or if he tried to lead them astray, they would have to deal with him. She really didn't want to hurt him, though — and not for any of the romantic reasons Barae thought.

"Posef," she said. "What do you think of Garai's intentions?"

"I...think he's telling the truth."

"Then let's leave." She pushed past him and headed down the stairs.

The dusty streets were dark. The storm had blown itself out, and the air was calm and chilled. Lanterns hung from tall poles along the empty streets. It was all eerily quiet, and Zhava hung back, unsure why no one was around. Every shutter was latched tight, and only one had a faint glow of light behind it. Though she lived on a farm, she was familiar with the light and activity around towns. Even the regimented Hibaro was busy with people going about their business late into the night.

"Lord Su'Fyen ordered everyone inside," Garai said. "No one is to interfere as you leave the city, and no one is to even observe you." He pointed to their left. "Your mounts will be ready for you at the stables."

"Wait," Posef said. "You forgot. Where is Prince Ooleng?"

Garai shook his head and stared at the ground. "I did not forget," he spat. "You did not ask."

"Lord Su'Fyen said he was ours to take," Posef continued. "We're taking him."

Lord Su'Fyen said nothing of the kind to them, but Posef obviously heard something of that in Garai's mind.

"We shouldn't have to ask," Zhava said. "We have our orders, and you have yours. Where is Prince Ooleng?"

"Follow me." He sighed, turned to the right, and led them down the wide center street. They crossed the city circle, where the tables and food and festivities had been only a short while earlier, then led them down a much narrower, darker street. Here, too, shutters were closed, but some of these homes did not have shutters, or they had broken window boxes, some had no doors, and others had only a narrow door barely wide enough for a single person turned sideways. This was obviously a poorer part of the city.

As they approached an intersection, they heard a voice – the first voice since leaving their rooms. A man spoke rapidly, animatedly, and seemed to be approaching from an intersecting street.

Zhava knew that voice. She had been betrothed to him, set to ride into the mountains as his wife. That would be her life now, if Io Liori and her people had not arrived and taken her away. She edged forward for a better look.

"I can't seem to find...I just need to find," Ooleng said as he turned the corner, limping along.

That limp was Zhava's doing. She swept his legs out from under him in a wet cave, knocked him to the ground where he struck his head against the stone. She did not feel bad for her actions; he kidnapped her. But he didn't seem quite right in his mind anymore.

A second figure came around the corner behind him, a woman covered in armor and weapons. Jezza, the fighter who controlled water.

Zhava edged deeper into the shadow, hoping she remained out of sight. If Jezza was here, then her giant partner, Nu, must be nearby. Of all the fighters Ooleng hired, those two were his most formidable.

"You make too much noise," Jezza said. "The city Lord will reprimand you again."

"I don't need – I don't need p-p-permission," Ooleng said, though a bit quieter. "Something is wrong. Something is different. Why this night? Why does he require this night?"

"I don't know, but we should return. We've found nothing."

"It is her," he hissed, rounding on Jezza and pointing a finger in her face. "I can...smell it. No, that's not right. Not smell. Not smell. I can taste it, I can think it." He reached up and slapped the side of his head, the side where his hair had been shaved away to reveal the patch of scars. Those scars were Zhava's fault also, the place where his head struck the stones. "I can...hear her."

"Do we take him now?" Sanama whispered.

Zhava turned to look at her friends. They had edged near to her, standing at her back in the dark alley.

"Jezza is powerful," she replied. "We need to be careful."

"Give me your bags," Barae said, reaching forward. "I'll load the camels; you get Ooleng."

They quickly and quietly handed over their supplies, and Barae looked like a lumbering rock loaded down with saddlebags. She wobbled a bit but kept her balance.

"Can you handle all that?" Zhava asked, worried her friend would fall over and get hurt.

Barae raised her hand and turned to go.

That's when Zhava saw it. A slight movement in the alley behind them – behind Garai. A darker shadow moving within the shadows. A person following them.

She drew her sword and slammed a hand against Barae, knocking her aside, but it was too late. The shadow reached

Garai, a darkened hand pressed to his head, and a flash of blue light sparked from the dark fingertips. Garai didn't have time to react. His body jerked sideways, slammed into the wall, and crumpled to the ground as the figure stepped from the shadows.

Zhava gasped. "Plishka?"

Chapter 24

Zhava ran forward to hug her friend, but Plishka held up her hands to stop her – and that's when Zhava saw it. The matted hair flattened against her head, the red dirt rimming her eyes and mouth, the bruises on her cheek and arms, the drops of blood across her armor and tunic, and the two fingers of her left hand wrapped together to mend a break.

"Plishka," Zhava whispered, "what happened?"

"This Go'aabite was sneaking up behind you," she said, pointing at Garai sprawled across the ground. Her deep voice cracked, as if she was too parched to speak.

Zhava shook her head. "No, he was with us. Our guide."

A wave of water drenched them all from behind. Zhava wiped her eyes, and spun around to see Sanama floating in the air at the end of alleyway – but not quite in the air. Her body floated in a pool of water, suspended off the ground, her head sticking out the top and her limbs flailing helplessly within.

"Zhava, help!" Sanama screamed.

Jezza stepped out from behind the floating pool, her jaw clenched, her eyes focused on Sanama, and her fingers splayed and stretched taut at the water.

Ooleng shuffled out from behind her, his hand to his mouth and snickering. "You – should – see yourselves." He waved at Zhava. "Surprise, my wife."

Zhava called to her flames, but as they sprang to life, they almost immediately drowned in the water soaking her clothes and dripping off her armor. Little puffs of steam spread across her body, but no flames.

"Oh, no-no-no-no-no-no-no-no-no-nooo!" Ooleng yelled and stomped his foot to the wet ground. "No fire! No fire, my wife. My...Zhava. That is not allowed. And you-" He pointed at Plishka. "-keep that lightning – under – your clouds." He shook his head vigorously. "Under your...hands. Just, don't do it. You'll kill us all."

Zhava spread her arms wide and glanced from Sanama to Jezza and back to Ooleng again. "Husband...darling."

He frowned.

She smiled. "We should talk."

"I...wanted to talk. I...wanted – you – back again. But you...you...." He tilted his head. "You attacked me?"

"I attacked you? No, I didn't," she said, tensing. Her little flames scratched against her palms, eager to spring forth.

Posef's voice jumped into her head. *Patience,* he said, and then he was gone again.

"Oh, yes, you're right," she continued. She bowed her head. "I attacked you, and that was wrong of me."

"And?" he said with a chuckle and a wave of his hand.

"And...?" What more did he want? Although, knowing Ooleng as she did, he likely wanted much more. "And I'm sorry. I never should have done that." She took a step forward, her hands raised at her sides and away from her weapons. "How can you ever forgive me?"

"Don't trust her," Jezza growled, her face strained with the effort of keeping the water bubble around Sanama.

"Shut up, witch!" Ooleng yelled, his voice echoing into the night. He shut his eyes and clamped a hand over his mouth. "Oh, that was loud. Too loud."

Be ready, Posef whispered into her mind. *When I yell, hit Jezza with all your flames.*

"No, Ooleng, she's right," Zhava said, stepping forward again. She focused on the flames within her, let them build just beneath her skin. Wisps of steam came off her body as she let the heat dry her skin and clothes. "You have no reason to trust me, except that I'm tired of running. I'm tired of trying to protect my friends. I'm ready to be your wife."

"You...are?" He dropped his hand and stared into her face, into her eyes.

"Now!" Posef yelled, and everyone moved at once.

Zhava drew her flames and shot them at Jezza's chest, stumbling her backward and breaking her concentration. Posef threw himself into the water bubble, grabbed Sanama, and flew out the other side in a crashing wave that spread water and mud far into the street. Plishka flung lightning past Ooleng, and he screamed and dropped to the ground – and then scuttled forward and rammed into Zhava's legs. She toppled over him and landed hard on the ground beneath Jezza – who swung her sword in a fast arc, aiming at Zhava's head.

She gripped the hatchet on her belt and brought it up to deflect the strike, but Jezza struck again and again. Each strike a little harder, and each time Zhava blocked it a little slower. Jezza spun the sword point-down, raised it high above her head, and smiled.

"Good bye, little girl," she said.

A bolt of lightning arced through the air and struck Jezza in the chest. She flew backward, slammed into a wall, and crumpled to the ground.

Plishka hurried past, scooped up Jezza's sword from the ground, and held out a hand for Zhava. "Let's go."

Posef and Sanama were soaking wet, but otherwise unharmed. Barae was standing again, adjusting the saddlebags across her arms and shoulders. Garai still lay on the ground where he fell.

Ooleng, however, stood at the other end of the dark, narrow street, his silhouette staring back at them all, one hand tapping the shaved side of his head, and the other hand flicking the air at his side.

Zhava turned to Posef and Sanama. She pointed at Garai's limp form and asked, "Can you carry him?"

"Leave him," Plishka hissed. "We don't need Go'aabite trash."

"He's with us," Zhava replied.

"You...tricked me," Ooleng growled. He cocked his head to the side.

Zhava grabbed Plishka by the arm. "Help me now; debate me later."

"Just go," Posef called. "We've got him."

Without even a backward glance, Zhava tugged Plishka forward and ran at Ooleng. The man darted away. She turned the corner of the dark street and saw his shadow just as he ducked down another street. They raced after him, down one street after another until they found themselves running back toward the city center, with its water well and tables set up from the festivities. Ooleng stood near that well, staring back at them and smiling as they ran down the empty street – but something about his face, something about the little grin she saw in the bright light of the city-center torches, and something about the way his eyes weren't focused on her. He was watching something else.

Someone else.

Zhava dropped to the ground. She reached out to the dirt and sand and willed it to speed her along just as the huge broadside of a sword swung through the air above her head. She loosened the ground under Plishka's feet and made her slip beneath the sword's arc – but not quickly enough, and the edge glanced off her shoulder and sent her sprawling to the ground. Zhava stopped her own slide, called the flames to her arms and shoulders, and turned to face the giant, Nu, standing alongside the building, his body draped in long, heavy robes.

"You again," Nu said, but he was staring at Plishka as she gripped a hand to her bloody shoulder and stood up. "I thought I killed you."

Plishka let the lightning crackle at her fingertips and smirked at the giant. "What happened to that metal armor of yours? My lightning loved that."

The giant roared his fury and rushed at them, his sword swinging wide.

Zhava didn't have time to think. She ran from the spot, leaped onto a table, and started running across the plaza, jumping from one table to the next. Nu, however, ran after Plishka, roaring at her and lunging after her with his sword.

Zhava stopped. She crouched on top of a table and rolled a ball of fire into her hands. She waited as Plishka ran around the edge of the plaza, bringing the giant closer to her, then flung the fireball straight at the giant's chest.

Plishka ducked aside as the fire exploded. The giant screamed and tore at the little flames dancing across his shirt and head.

"Why does he hate you?" Zhava asked as Plishka ran to her side.

"We've had a couple fights," she said breathlessly. "The first time, he knocked me off the city wall. That's how I got hurt. Last night he caught up with me in the desert, and I scorched his armor."

Nu ripped off the remains of his flaming shirt and tossed them aside. Bits of fiery cloth scattered on the breeze, and he swatted at the few flaming men still clinging to his arms and chest. He turned to the two women. "I'm going to kill both of you – I don't care what Ooleng says."

"No!" Ooleng yelled.

He struggled from beneath one of the tables behind them, his arm flailing wildly to get their attention.

"No," he called again. "Not my – wife! Do not – kill – Zhava."

Across the plaza, Barae, Posef, and Sanama were sneaking along the shadows, carrying the bags and Garai's limp body, trying the entire way to remain hidden.

Zhava gripped Plishka's arm. "Catch Ooleng. Let me deal with the giant."

"I can't let you do that. You have no idea how strong he is."

"I fought him before. He broke my foot."

Plishka's eyes went wide at that, and then she grinned. "All right, so it's your turn. But I'll be right back."

Zhava turned to Nu as her friend leapt from the table and chased after Ooleng. She heard her "husband's" frantic cries as he ran across the city plaza, but she kept her attention on the giant before her. She flicked a dozen flames to life across her arms and in her hands and slowly, carefully stepped down from the table on which she'd been standing. His gaze darted from Plishka's noisy pursuit to Zhava circling him, and he squinted at her.

"What do you think you're doing?" he asked. He spun the sword loosely in his hand. "You come to fight me? You think I won't kill you because your prince said not to?"

She had to keep his focus, keep him watching her. Let her friends do what they needed to do. "I think you took me by surprise last time. I think you and I haven't truly sparred."

He laughed at that, his head thrown back and his mouth open wide. She marveled at the size of him. Almost twice as tall as her – his arms were as long as she was tall, and his hands were bigger than her head. She had seen those hands close-up when he held her high in the air against the side of her home.

"Your trick with the fire doesn't scare me." He held his sword before him and tensed, his eyes narrowed on her.

She reached out with her senses, reached for the dirt at his feet and pushed it out from under him. He stumbled forward, the sword swinging wildly, and she tossed the flames at his face as she drew her Felton sword and rushed forward. This was the tactic Sanama had used, quick strikes. Run at him, slash at him, and run away. She flicked the sword up high but only managed a shallow cut across his thigh. As she dashed away, she felt the rush of air as his sword sliced past her head. She spun around and skidded to a halt.

He was brushing flames from his hair.

She reached for the dirt again, but this time she added just a hint of wind and blew it high into his face. She flicked her wrist and sent a flame skittering through the air to his right as she rushed across his left side. He coughed and spit, rubbed one hand at the dust in his face while he swung his sword at the flame – and she gave a backhanded slash of her Felton across the back of his knee.

That cut went deep. He screamed and spun far more quickly, catching the leather armor on her back with the edge of his sword and sending her skidding forward. She stumbled, nearly dropped her sword, and staggered to a halt at the edge of a wall.

She turned – and ducked low as Nu's sword flashed forward and into the wall, slicing across the stones. Bits of rock and dust rained across her, and she skittered aside to get away, to get back out into the open plaza where he couldn't keep her pinned down. She jumped onto a table and turned – just as his sword flashed down before her, and the point wedged deep into the wooden tabletop at her feet.

With one hand, he yanked hard to dislodge the sword while the other hand swept around to grab her. She ducked beneath his reach, rolled off the table, and stood on the other side facing him. He was so fast! How could he be that large and that fast at the same time? Her throat hurt, and she coughed. The dust? The running?

"I will catch you," he said, frowning, "and then I will slice you in three."

She pulled the wind and the sand to her, spun them in her mind, spun them around at the base of Nu's feet. She pulled all the bits of sand and dirt from nearby, everything that had collected beneath the table and through the plaza street and along the edge of the wall far behind him, and she twirled them through the wind at his feet – "kindled it," as Priestess Marmaran would say.

"What?" he said, glancing down.

She spun it up faster and lifted it all off the ground, lifted all the debris to cover his ankles, to cover his knees.

He backed away, and she made the wind and dirt follow him with each step. She added more sand and dirt, made the funnel cloud thicker and darker around his legs. She began to sweat with the effort, and her throat burned as if something clawed at it from the inside, but she didn't stop – she couldn't stop if she was going to make this work.

"What are you doing?" Nu asked, looking up at her. "You stop this."

With more effort – and more sweat on her brow – she pushed the wind and the sand harder, and the funnel cloud lurched upward, enveloped the giant up to his chest. She loosened the sand at his feet, and he started spinning slowly within the funnel cloud, pushed along by the force of the wind.

Nu jabbed his sword through the swirling sand, lashing out and trying to strike at her, but from the other side of the table and far out in the street, there was no way for him to get her, even with his long reach and huge sword. She gave a final push of will and fully enveloped him in the funnel cloud. Her arms began to shake, sweat ran down her back, and her mouth and throat were painfully dry. But she had one more element to add to this mix, one more Ability to throw at the giant to finally stop him. She pulled her little flames to herself, and her body lit with the hundreds of fires spread across her arms and shoulders, dancing across her head, clinging to the armor and sliding down her shirt and pants.

"Go," she whispered. The flames leaped into the air and caught the wind. They fell into the funnel cloud, and the entire thing erupted in a cascade of wind and sand and flames that lit the plaza brighter than a dozen torches.

Nu screamed and ran, and Zhava pushed the funnel along with him, forced the flaming debris to attack him, to punch at him and pierce his skin. This huge man, this giant from the far side of the Purneese Mountains had hurt her, helped Ooleng to hurt her family and their servants, attacked Plishka, and now threatened to kill her and her friends. He had to be stopped.

She felt the attack mounting from behind her before she ever saw anything. She felt the power call, felt the water within the plaza well react to the call, felt it rise from deep beneath the dirt and sand, from where it was buried within the rocks far below the city's streets. It was a subtle call within her, something she had never felt before, and it distracted her just enough that she lost hold of the flaming funnel cloud a moment before the deluge of water struck her in the back. The wave knocked her feet from under her, and she was shoved beneath the table where she desperately grabbed hold of anything, struggled to hold on as the mud and water rushed past her, poured across her, ran into her mouth, and soaked her armor and clothes.

When the wave passed, she gasped for breath and pulled herself up. Her body ached, and not just from the water that knocked her to the ground and bounced her around beneath the table. She felt a weariness within her, an exhaustion she'd never felt before when using her Abilities. Her fingers tingled, her back and shoulders ached, and her throat felt raw.

Nu screamed in pain, and he frantically beat out the little flames still clinging to his singed, ragged clothes.

"Little girl!" Jezza yelled from the other side of the plaza. "Your life is over."

Zhava struggled out from the mud beneath the table, pushed herself up and looked between Nu's half-naked, singed body and Jezza's clenched, furious face. Jezza's leather armor was scorched across the front where Plishka's lightning had struck her, and her hands were clenched tightly into fists at her sides. Zhava opened her palms and called to the little flames, and they sputtered to life in her wet hands. She wasn't sure she could repeat what she attempted against the giant, but she had little choice but to try now against them both.

A bolt of lightning arced across the plaza, flashing brightly and making Zhava squint. Plishka stepped out from between two of the buildings nearby, lightning crackling down her arms and around her hands. She glared at Jezza and opened her mouth to speak –

– and that's when a loud, low horn blared from all around them. The sound echoed off the walls, and Zhava put her hands to her ears to block it out.

The plaza was suddenly filled by at least a hundred people, men and women in uniforms and armor and two men blowing long and loud through rams' horns. Most of the soldiers were positioned atop the buildings and held bows pulled taut and pointed at the four of them. Many others stood in groups of five or six and positioned themselves at the ends of streets, their swords drawn, shields held high to block their faces.

One man strode confidently into the plaza, his long robes rippling around his legs: Lord Su'Fyen.

Zhava's left ear still rang from the horns. She slowly lifted her hands high above her head, the flames all gone, but the mud and water dripping off her to form a small, sticky pool at her feet. Plishka, too, had stopped her lightning and stood still as several of the soldiers pointed swords at her back. Nu grunted and tossed his own sword to the ground with a racket, but his angry eyes remained focused on Zhava, not at the soldiers or the city's Lord. Jezza stood relaxed, watching it all as if she had no care at all.

"Novice Zhava," Lord Su'Fyen called, and Zhava jumped as he seemed to bark out her name. "We came to an agreement, you and I."

"Yes, Sir." She slowly, carefully, lowered her arms and wiped some of the mud from her face.

"So honor it." He stared at her from the front of the plaza, his hands on his hips and his eyes bright in the torch glow. "Take your people. Leave my city. Fulfill your mission."

"Yes, Sir." She reached down and retrieved her Felton sword from the mud.

"Novice Plishka," Lord Su'Fyen continued. "I have tolerated your unwelcome presence in my city these several days, but no more. You will leave with Novice Zhava. Her mission is now your mission, and her fate now your own. "

Plishka said nothing, but she nodded her understanding.

"But Novice Plishka, we do not tolerate theft within our walls." She stopped and stared at him. "The sword you stole from Jezza. Drop it." She flicked her wrist, and Jezza's sword went skidding through the plaza's dirt. She walked on.

Zhava started toward her friend, but she quickly realized her leg throbbed and was bleeding from a gash at her thigh. It wasn't deep, most likely a cut from the table leg, but it made walking painful. She limped forward.

"Nu," Lord Su'Fyen said, turning toward the giant. "You were instructed to remain outside my city. Your people are not welcome within these walls – and yet, here you are."

"I had a contract to finish," the giant grumbled.

Plishka met Zhava in the road and wrapped an arm around her friend's shoulders. Together, they walked away, down the main road to the city's gates – which were now standing open, their camels and their friends waiting for them.

"Jezza," Lord Su'Fyen said from behind them. "You will replace the water in my city's well, and you will take your giant and leave here – never to return again."

Sanama ran up to Zhava, gave her a quick hug, and took her sword. "Your orders?" she whispered.

"Do we have everyone?"

Sanama nodded.

"Including Garai and Ooleng?"

"Ooleng is kind of weird," Sanama said, glancing over her shoulder. "He seems sick, but we have him."

"Good," Zhava said. "Then we ride out of here fast, before Lord Su'Fyen changes his mind and kills us."

As they mounted their camels and rode away, they still heard Lord Su'Fyen barking commands at his soldiers and chastising Nu and Jezza for their roles in the destruction of the city plaza. The wooden gates slammed shut behind them.

Chapter 25

They rode out of the Ving'Sa-wehn valley and then through the Sineise Desert for most of the night. Zhava pulled splinters from between the seams of the armor on her thigh and wrapped the long, deep cut to staunch the blood flow. She still did not remember hitting the table leg, but Jezza had thrown that wave of water at her so hard she didn't remember much about those moments. Her ears were still ringing from the two horns Lord Su'Fyen's men blew in the courtyard. Her body ached, apparently from using all of her Abilities at once, though that had never happened before; it scared her, and she wished she had one of her teachers here to ask. Io Kua might know, or certainly Io Liori. She missed them. She looked up at the sky, traced the paths of the thirteen Gods she could see in the constellations above her. She quickly found her God in the stars, the water nymph Preizhavan with her garland of grape-seed vines wrapped elegantly around her hips. Was Preizhavan watching her now?

Garai awoke soon after they crested the ridges of the Ving'Sa-wehn valley. He was confused and angry and nearly fell from where Posef had hurriedly tied him across a camel. He yelled about his poor treatment, especially when Posef rushed over and untied him, and he grumbled to himself and glared at anyone who rode near him – especially at Plishka because Barae had to tell him she zapped his head and put him to sleep. Plishka only made that situation worse when she flashed lightning between her fingers. Now he rode at least thirty paces behind them. If not for the sliver of moon near the horizon, she probably wouldn't see him back there.

Barae was only too happy to retrieve Captain Redoly's gear and maps from the saddle bags and begin plotting their travels again. With Posef's help, they located their party in the desert by the position of the stars, tracked their distance to Wui-sha'Olm – unfortunately, still a couple days away at a good pace – and marked their direction on the far horizon.

When they settled into the routine of travel again, Zhava edged her camel near to Plishka's.

"What happened?" she asked. "You and Io Liori were going to get your sister."

"Our information was wrong," she spat. "It wasn't a small camp in the middle of the desert. It was 100 soldiers barricaded inside a rock fortress."

"Wui-sha'Olm?"

"We saw it long before we reached it. It's like a mountain stuck in the sand. Io Liori said to take it slow, to watch for any movement, but we never saw anything. It looked empty – until it wasn't. They had soldiers hiding under the sand all around us. I don't know how we didn't step on them. We must have stepped on some of them. Soldiers were hiding in the rocks where we couldn't see them. Their first attack cut us in half." She snapped her fingers. "Like that. A dozen people died, shot by arrows from above or stabbed by those people buried in the sand. I was at Io Liori's side, and she pulled me off my mount before I even knew what was happening."

"So...she lived?" Zhava wanted to know, but she wasn't sure she wanted the answer.

"Oh, she lived. They wanted her alive, and that was their only mistake. I stayed at her side, and I could see it by the way they fought, they weren't trying to kill her. And...and she saw it too." Plishka stopped. She stared into the night, her lips pursed. Her eyes twitched, and a tear glittered down her cheek. "She told me to run."

Zhava waited. The night seemed to grow still as her friend fought with the memories, tried to speak aloud the flow of the battle.

"There were 30 of us," she whispered. "But when she...told me to run...we were down to five. I did not want to leave." She turned to Zhava, her jaw clenched. "I have never run from a fight. But she made me. She pushed me away, and then Brun pushed me away. Terro grabbed my arm and told me to get back to the Hibaro any way I could. To get to the King and let him know what happened, and then he threw me on his camel. He was so strong, and he tossed me onto that camel and told me...to go as fast as I could."

By this time, Posef, Barae and Sanama had edged to Plishka's side as they rode quietly through the night. Even Garai had closed the distance behind them, near enough he likely caught most of what was said.

"The camel was already injured, a cut to its side, and it took a couple arrows as we fled. It was so scared, it just ran and ran, and all I could do was hold on. I tried to control it, but it was too scared. It ran forever, and then it stopped and died. That's how I found that city and that evil Lord Su'Fyen."

"Lord Su'Fyen is a great man," Garai called out.

"Shutup," Barae replied.

"That giant caught me sneaking into the city, and then...then I found you."

Zhava leaned over and squeezed her friend's arm. Plishka did not look, of course. She wasn't the type of person to show her emotions like that, but Zhava felt some of the tension leave her body with that simple gesture.

They rode the rest of the night cold and silent – or at least as silent as it could be with Ooleng alternately muttering and yelling and pouting from his place tied atop a camel. He expressed his love for Zhava, his anger with Zhava, his devotion to Zhava, his desire to kill Zhava, and his regret that he ever met Zhava...and then he started over again. At least twenty times.

There was something wrong with him, and she knew she caused it. Not that she regretted her actions. She did what she had to escape him, and this was the result. He held them prisoner in that mountain cave of his, but when she and Plishka escaped, she knocked him to the ground. The side of his head was now shaved and scarred, and he twitched and slapped at his head and couldn't seem to keep his thoughts moving very long in the same direction. Except he was always focused on her.

Deep into the night, they stopped to make camp. Zhava stepped forward, focused on the sand before her, and willed it away. With a brush of wind, she scattered it to the sides and pulled more sand out of a deep hole. She soon had a long crevasse formed through the sand, a gradual slope leading down into it. They led their camels forward, and as they disappeared into the darkness, Zhava dropped her little flames along the ground at their feet. The path led into a wider area, large enough to store their gear along the wall and let the camels mill around while they made camp against the opposite wall.

Zhava stared up through the cut in the sand, watched the line of stars sparkle in the dark sky.

"I didn't know you could do this," Plishka said, looking up and down the crevasse.

"I didn't either," she replied. "But if the wind could make a valley big enough for Ving'Sa-wehn, then I thought I could make a valley big enough for us."

Plishka ran a hand down the wall of sand. A dusting came loose, but most of it remained in place. "Why doesn't it collapse? It's just sand."

"I told it not to," she said with a shrug.

"No-no-no-no-no!" someone behind them yelled.

They turned to see Ooleng sitting cross-legged against the far wall, Posef offering him some dried fruit. Ooleng clamped his mouth and eyes shut and pointed his face at the sky, obviously unwilling to eat.

"We need answers," Zhava muttered. She pulled some flames into her hands and turned toward them. This had worked for Captain Redoly; maybe it would work for her. "Posef, get ready with that little trick you do."

"Yes, Sir," he said with a grin. He tossed the dried fruit back in a bag and sat on the ground between Sanama and Barae.

Garai looked up from his spot at the far edge, his eyes bright with interest.

"Ooleng," Zhava said. When he didn't look at her immediately, she rolled her hand, and a dozen more flames sprang to life in her palm. "I know you're afraid of me."

"I...am not...afraid of my — wife." He shook his head vigorously but kept his gaze to the sliver of stars far above.

Zhava casually rolled the flames into a tight ball and threw them at the wall above his head. They burst apart and showered down around Ooleng, and he screeched and ducked and covered his head with his hands.

"That was a terrible shot," Barae said, joining in on the game.

"I know," Zhava said with a small cough. She shook her head. "The teachers never let us have any real fun."

"You treacherous," Ooleng spat, "murdering — lying — woman! I should — kill you — where — you stand."

"What's wrong with him?" Sanama asked.

"He's not right in the head," Plishka said.

Barae clucked her tongue. "No, the Gods have loosed one part of his spirit. It wanders away and returns and then wanders away again."

"He acts like he was injured in battle," Garai said. He pointed. "Probably from that scar on the side of his head. I've seen soldiers who act like that. One moment they're fine, and the next they can't figure out which end of a sword to hold."

Ooleng curled into a ball on the ground, pulled his legs toward his face, and began crying.

"Though this seems extreme," Garai finished.

"I may be out of practice, Ooleng," Zhava said, "but I'll bet I can hit you within the next six shots." She tossed another ball of flames in his direction. It arced high in the air, landed on the ground between them, and sputtered out.

"I...loved you," Ooleng said between sobs.

"Oh my Gods, this is painful," Barae muttered. "Just hit him, and let's be done with him."

"Ooleng, I need to know about my parents," Zhava said. She called a dozen flames to rest on her shoulders, brightening the dark crevasse and allowing her to better see the whimpering man on the ground. She coughed and said, "I really don't want to hurt you to get the information."

"You could – never – hurt me more – than you already – have," he whispered. He clenched his teeth and narrowed his eyes at her. Slowly, achingly, he pushed himself back up into a sitting position. "Do it."

Zhava studied him as she rolled another ball of flames in her hand.

"Kill...me."

What really happened to him in that cave? Was all of this from her kicking him to the ground, or did something else happen after she escaped?

"Aim straight and true," Barae called. "Put him out of his misery."

Zhava knew she could hit him. She could have hit him a dozen times already if she had been trying. This was what Captain Redoly did, though. This was how he got Monh to confess to his role in the kidnapping of her parents. Except...Monh wasn't injured in the head.

She glanced at Posef. He shook his head and shrugged his shoulders. Nothing.

"I'm so out of practice," she said, taking a step forward. "Maybe I just need a larger fireball." She pulled several flames to her hand, then a dozen more, and a dozen more. She quickly had more than 50 of the flames swirling between her hands.

"Do – it," Ooleng yelled. He gripped the hem of his robes and pulled them open wide, exposing his chest. "Kill me – as you – killed – my father."

She stared at him, her throat burning, and thought back to her time in that cave. She had knocked Ooleng to the ground. He cracked his head against the wet, stone floor, and she left him there surrounded by hundreds of flames. She left his father in the larger cave chamber, surrounded by so many flames that she hadn't even bothered to count them all. She just kept dropping them from her hands as she walked out. The last she saw, the entire cave was filled with flames all the way to the wide entrance. But he was alive.

"Kill – me!" Ooleng screamed, and something glinted from inside his robes.

She focused on it. Something shoved into an inside pouch was reflecting the light of her flames. It seemed heavy, and it pulled at the seams of the pocket. It had a long, cloudy neck, and it had been stopped up with a charred bit of cloth and wood – and Zhava's breath caught in her throat.

It couldn't be! Could it? Ooleng carried it? She thought High Priest Viekoosh carried it, but – if it was Ooleng.

She lunged forward, tossing aside the ball of flames at her feet.

"Be careful!" Plishka called, jumping up.

Zhava yanked at Ooleng's robe and pulled the stoppered bottle from the pocket. She turned and strode away, the flames on her shoulders all leaning forward, each one as curious about the thing in her hand as she was. The smoky glass reflected the flames' eager faces, just as the spiderweb cracks embedded in the glass splintered their reflections, as if a thousand geometric flames stared back at them.

Her blood drummed through her body as she peered deeper into the glass container – and she saw the necklace inside. Still in one piece. Still trapped within. The burning within her throat seemed to intensify, and the high-pitched flute resounded in her ear, drowning out the questions from her friends.

Without a second thought, she pulled the Felton sword from its sheath, spun the blade, and smashed it upon the smoky, cracked glass. It shattered, and the necklace within came free, tumbling slowly to the ground.

Priestess Marmaran, her eyes clear, her hair long and wavy and vibrant blonde, flashed before Zhava's eyes. She held her cane in her hands, but she snapped it in half across her knee, turned to Zhava, and gave her a fierce smile.

"I will not be contained by the forces of this world," Marmaran said. "Neither will you." She gripped Zhava's arms and yanked her forward – and they fell into the thunderous, flashing abyss.

Chapter 26

The wind and rain spattered Zhava's face and soaked her armor and clothes. She blinked at the lightning strobing the sky, met the stern eyes in the faces far above, and tried to shut her ears to the resounding tone echoing all around. The now-familiar, winding path stretched out both before and behind her, and she wasn't surprised to see two people at her side. Emsterold stood hunched over, her thin clothes soaked and clinging to her back, her wet hair hanging down her face, and her hands clamped tightly over her ears. Her eyes were shut tight, pained by that same ominous tone that rang all throughout the land of the dead.

Priestess Marmaran, though, stood straight and tall, the driving rain somehow blowing around her. The wind blew her vibrant blond hair and made the folds of her red cloak whip and crack behind her, but she did not falter. She casually tossed aside the two halves of her broken cane and strode toward Zhava, arms outstretched. She placed a hand on each of Zhava's ears, muttered something to herself, and pressed hard.

The ear-splitting tone died away on the wind. Zhava relaxed and stood a little straighter, only now aware she had been hunching against the overwhelming sound. Emsterold lifted her head and slowly, cautiously moved her hands away from her ears.

"Oh, my child," Marmaran said with a grin. "It is wonderful to see you again."

Zhava wrapped her arms around Marmaran and squeezed. This was a different Marmaran, though. A younger, stronger woman who held herself upright, who didn't feel fragile, who did not totter backward.

Voices rumbled high above, the voices of the dead thundering away as they watched the reunion unfold beneath them. Zhava did not care she was being watched. She only cared to have her teacher returned to her, to be able to speak with her again – to be held by her again.

"We have much to do, my child, and only a short time in which to do it."

Reluctantly, Zhava released her grip and stepped back, but she kept one hand firmly wrapped around her teacher's hand and squeezed, thrilled at being able to do that again after so many moons.

"Why did you return?" Emsterold asked. "You said you were coming for me – for the real me. So why are you here? Now?"

Priestess Marmaran ignored her and studied Zhava. She looked her up and down, eyes narrowing as she lingered on Zhava's neck and head.

"What did you do?" She brushed away the strands of hair around Zhava's right ear and studied it, seemed almost to peer inside Zhava's head.

So she explained the injury, how Nu, the giant, hit her across the head, somehow injured her ear, and how that awful, piercing tone now stabbed at her when she least expected it.

"Yes, my child, I see the damage." Marmaran took a step back. "You should have been to a healer immediately for that. You should have asked Sister Tegara."

"She...." How to tell her of Sister Tegara's injuries? How to tell her that Sister Tegara might never wake up, or that she might already be dead. "Yes, you're right. I should have done that."

"But, what is this?" She bent down and peered at Zhava's neck.

She wasn't sure what Marmaran saw, and she reached up to touch her neck, to feel under her chin and around her collar. Nothing.

"Why did you let that get inside you?" Marmaran asked.

"Let what inside?" She felt nothing.

Marmaran chuckled as she looked Zhava in the eyes. "That's going to hurt coming back out." Then she frowned, leaned forward, and whispered, "And you make sure it comes back out. That will hurt even more if you let it remain."

"Listen to me," Emsterold said, gripping them each by an arm and yanking them around. Her glowing eyes were wide, and her hands shook as she gripped them. "I'm dying. High Priest Viekoosh hasn't let me back into the living world in at least nights, and my body is dying. I can feel it. You have to do something. You have to come get me. Come get us all."

"Come here," Marmaran said. She spread her arms wide, and Emsterold shuffled forward, her wet, bare feet scraping along the mud-soaked road. She wrapped her arms around the cold, wet girl and hugged her. Emsterold's body shook as she grabbed at Marmaran's robes and buried her head in the folds of cloth.

Marmaran beckoned for Zhava to join them. She hugged Emsterold as Marmaran made quiet "shushing" noises. "Child, we are coming," Marmaran whispered.

"Please," Emsterold said between sobs, "I don't want to die. Come quickly."

"Yes, child. We're coming." She turned her eyes toward Zhava – but there was something different about those eyes, something...not quite right. They were Marmaran's eyes, brown with little flecks of green around the edges, but the dark center, where the black of her eyes should have been, Zhava could see something else. Something deeper. Something moving. A...pool.

Zhava's body seemed to fall forward into that pool, but it wasn't water she found within. She found power. A vast storehouse of power swirling through Priestess Marmaran's body. It linked the woman's arms and legs, her head and heart, all together and through each other. It pulsed through her body, moved her forward, pressed her onward.

As quickly as Zhava saw it, the pool vanished, and she was left staring at Marmaran's young, smiling face. Marmaran's gaze narrowed, and she studied Zhava a moment before whispering, "That was impressive, my child. Now, go. Complete our work."

Something yanked at her body, and she was flung backward through the darkness. The huddled forms of Priestess Marmaran and Emsterold vanished into the distance as the wall of black enveloped her –

– and she fell back into her body. She heard voices all around, people speaking in harsh whispers, arguing. She heard her name, and she listened more closely. A woman spoke quickly, animatedly, about their trek across the desert, meeting Ib'Dignas and his family, and venturing into the valley city of Ving'Sa-wehn. That was Barae.

Someone laughed, a deep, slow laugh, and said, "I know Lord Su'Fyen. He is a good man."

Zhava knew that voice, too, but she did not expect to hear it. Captain Redoly? She opened her eyes, the deep blue sky high above and a few stars twinkling.

"She's awake," a woman called, and a face appeared above her – Brii. Dressed in her robes and with a sword belt secured at her waist, she smiled at Zhava, shifted the weapon to the side, and knelt in the sand. "Welcome back."

Zhava shifted, felt the blankets beneath her and the small, clay jar in her hand. She clenched her fingers, gripping the jar and the leather cord wrapped around it.

Brii glanced at it, then back at Zhava. "That's a powerful necklace." She might have said more, but several more faces crowded in: Barae, Plishka, Posef, and Captain Redoly all stared down with varied expressions of fear, surprise, or relief. Barae was the first to speak.

"Thank the Gods you're alive," she said, dropping to the sand and hugging Zhava around the shoulders. "When you collapsed like that I thought you were dead, but then Posef said you weren't dead, that you were deep in some kind of dream he couldn't see, and that's when Ooleng tried to run away, and Plishka hit him with her lightning –"

"Stop," Zhava mumbled. "What did she do?"

"And that was too much talking," Captain Redoly said as he pulled Barae back.

She clung to Zhava's robes, though, and held on tight. "No, it wasn't all that bad. She didn't kill him."

"Let go of her," Redoly said, pulling a little harder until Barae finally stepped back, tears in her eyes. Then he waved the others away, and when they were alone he knelt in the sand with a sigh. "Don't worry; Ooleng's alive, and we have him."

She stared into the sky. It had grown a little darker, and she could see several more stars. "How long was I asleep?"

"Very good," Redoly said with a smile. "We arrived at midday, and your panicked friend back there said you collapsed just before dawn, so...most of a day."

Zhava sighed and shut her eyes. It could have been worse.

"Why? Do you have someplace to be? Wui-sha'Olm, perhaps?"

"How do you know?" she asked, turning to him.

"And that was the wrong question."

She bit her lip and stared at him, thinking through every-thing that happened. Of course he knew where they were going; she announced it several times to her brothers. Once the captain awoke and found them missing, he probably loaded up the remaining camels and followed them into the desert. He would have caught them sooner if she and her friends hadn't been taken to Ving'Sa-wehn. So far she had seen Captain Redoly and Brii, but what about...?

"Sister Tegara? How is she?"

"Ah, that is a better question," he said with a nod. "She awoke just before we left your parents' farm. She was weak, but your sister-in-law assured us they would nurse her back to health. Next question?"

Zhava rolled over and pushed herself up on her elbows, scanned the narrow campsite. Posef and Garai sat against the near wall quietly talking; Barae was stirring something in a pot suspended above the fire; Brii stood with her arms crossed watching the cookpot; Plishka stood beside her; and Ooleng sat against the far wall, his hands tied behind his back as he muttered to himself and shook his head. She didn't see Redoly's other soldier, Ravid – or Sanama. The captain had probably sent them up top to act as lookouts...something Zhava should have done.

She dragged her friends through the desert to catch Ooleng and rescue her parents, but the reality of the situation was far more dangerous. Ooleng was nothing more than a distraction, a way to get Zhava away from the Hibaro and across the Purneese Mountains. It might have worked, too, if Captain Redoly and his team hadn't been such skilled warriors, and if Sanama hadn't shown up to distract the giant. Attacking the farm and kidnapping her parents was only part of High Priest Viekoosh's plan, however. He had enticed Io Liori into the desert, leaked information about Plishka's sister and drawn them out so he could capture her. But why? If it was all to start a war, then why capture Liori?

It wasn't just a war, though. It was also about her Abilities, about the gifts the Gods had given to her and her friends. It was about the God Coredor and his hatred of those gifts, the way he despised the women who wielded them, those women who stood against him. High Priest Viekoosh followed that God, and now he was recruiting others to his cause. That's why it wasn't just a war he wanted. He wanted the extermination of all those who displayed the Abilities of the Gods.

"This is bigger than me and my parents," she whispered.

Captain Redoly nodded and waited for her to continue. She turned and stared at him, suddenly realizing....

"You and Brii and Ravid – you're too good to just escort me home. You knew that was a trap, and you walked us right into it."

He nodded again, this time with a smile.

"But, why? That was so reckless – you lost one of your own men on that trap."

"My team and I, we are a special force," Redoly replied, "and we report directly to the King. Our mission was simple: The King read about your adventure in the Purneese Mountains, how you escaped capture and freed those students, and he wanted to know more about you – what you are capable of achieving. You and your friend over there, Plishka. Salient Ayaan assigned me to you, to field-test you, to take you up into the Highlands, and he assigned Io Liori to test Plishka. Mission took a turn, however. There was nothing to indicate that recovering Plishka's sister was in any way related to what happened at your family's farm. In that, our information was...lacking."

"You never intended to return us to the Hibaro. You wanted us to run away."

"Io Liori is, let me say, too fond of you. Her reports show too much praise of your Abilities and your training, but one thing seemed quite clear in all of her reports, as well as the reports of your Mentor, Io Kua: When you are pushed too hard, you push back harder." He turned and stared at her, his voice dropping a bit. "It is a weakness of yours, something you will have to train hard to overcome. I am not the only one who can use that against you."

"Then you want us out here? You want us doing what we're doing?"

He opened his mouth to reply, but before he could say anything more, Sanama came running down the hill of sand, waving her arms to get everyone's attention. She saw Zhava sitting up, though, and darted straight for her. She leaped to the ground, spraying sand across the blankets, wrapped her arms around Zhava and held on tightly. Zhava braced one arm to keep from falling over, but she used her other arm to return the hug.

"Sanama," Redoly said, "you interrupted us, and you were supposed to–"

"Ravid said to get you," Sanama breathlessly replied. "Something's coming fast."

Redoly jumped to his feet and started pointing at people and giving orders. "Brii, stay with the prisoner. Posef and Plishka, with me. Garai, keep the camels settled. Barae, douse that campfire." He turned to Zhava and Sanama. "You two, enough hugging, and let's go."

Sanama pulled away, but she wrapped one hand around Zhava's and wouldn't let go. As Zhava shifted off the blankets, her free hand slid into the sand, and she felt a rhythmic pulsing. It ebbed through the ground, touched her hand, and made her fingers tingle. As if the world slowed down, she saw the people around her slide to a halt, some in mid-stride, others in mid-sentence. Sanama was stopped in mid-turn, her body contorted as she reached back to help Zhava stand. Her friends looked like statues, and it was unnerving.

The pulses continued against her hand, and as she shifted her fingers, she felt the grains of sand slide across her skin. Their sharp angles prickled as they bounced and slid, and she heard...voices. She couldn't even describe them as real voices so much as...echoes of voices. Impressions of voices. Without it ever speaking words to her, she knew what the sand thought, what the sand felt...and it was beautiful. It sang into the night. It grew chilled with the setting sun, but it seemed content. Much of the sand had traveled throughout the heat of the day, and it felt good to settle for the night. To rest. The sand had been disturbed at the dawn, disturbed by her – by Zhava. Disturbed by the rough way she pushed it aside, the way she burrowed down through it to create this crevasse and the small cave so deep within it...but now that was also fine. Now the sand had come to peace with the difference, had grown accustomed to this new shape and did not want to lose it. The sand would become sad if it lost this new shape...but the sand also knew it was destined to lose this new shape, that it would be disturbed again at some later time. That change would happen. That change was inevitable, and that change was all right. That was the way of the world of sand.

She pulled her hand out, and the sensation stopped. The world crashed back around her with its noises and talking and bustling around the camp. Sanama yanked on her arm to get her up from the ground, and Captain Redoly swiftly led Posef and Plishka up the steep ramp. Barae scooped up a handful of sand and tossed it into the fire –

– and Zhava cringed as the cookfire flames cried out in pain, and then went silent. She studied the place where the flames had been, where the sand smothered them, and she felt...sad. They had been doing their dance, as Barae asked of them, and then she suddenly stopped them. Killed them.

"Zhava, what's wrong?" Sanama asked, tugging harder.

She said she was fine, that she was simply distracted by the fire, but then she caught a glimpse of Sanama's eyes. She had something in them, something just at the corners of her eyes, and Zhava couldn't quite tell what it was.

"Stop," Zhava said, peering closer. "What is...that?" The brown of Sanama's eyes seemed normal, but something swam through the black center, something long and sinewy. Zhava fell forward into that black center, fell deep into Sanama's eye, just as she had done with Priestess Marmaran. She tumbled into the blackness and felt the power swimming around her, circling her. The power opened its jaws and snapped, barely missing her arm, and Zhava had to retreat. The thing was long, like a snake, and it rippled through the black, eyeing her as it swam. She felt the power even when she couldn't see it, even when it dipped down into the black or swam behind her, she always knew where to find it. The longer the snake moved, the better Zhava understood it, the more she was able to learn from it. It lived within Sanama, and it directed her, guided her, provided her Gods-given Ability. Zhava gasped as she realized – though Sanama believed she had no Ability, though the teachers at the Hibaro saw nothing within her, she most certainly was Gods-blessed. She had the power of...the sword. It was raw, and mostly untapped, but Zhava could tell that if Sanama nurtured this power, if the Ios trained her and a good Mentor made her study the Kandor, that Sanama could become a powerful warrior. Her fierce fighting and her weapons techniques weren't simply learned from watching her brothers; it lived deep within her.

The snake-power-thing lunged forward again, and Zhava pushed herself away, pushed herself out of Sanama's eye and back into her own body again with a gasp.

Sanama frowned. "What happened?"

"You have an Ability," Zhava blurted out.

"No, I don't." She laughed.

"You do, and...I want to train you." She hadn't realized it until she said it, but it was true. This girl, this Candidate who had been cast off by her brothers and was now being shuffled aside by the teachers at the Hibaro, who called herself "Zhava's Little Soldier" – she had an Ability within her, and Zhava wanted to do something to nurture it. Anything. "When we get home, I'll talk with Io Kua. I'll work with you on the Kandor and on your weapons training. You have an Ability – I saw it – and we'll make sure the others see it, too, and we'll get you promoted to Initiate."

The more she talked, the more certain she was that she wanted this to happen – and the wider Sanama's eyes grew. The girl sprang forward and wrapped her arms around Zhava's neck and squeezed.

"Oh, thank you," Sanama said. "I love you!"

Zhava returned the hug, then stood and headed up the sloping ramp, Sanama holding her hand the whole way. The girl said nothing more, but she walked a little straighter, held her head a little higher, and kept that huge grin the whole way. She was so cute, Zhava had trouble not reaching down and hugging her again.

When they reached the top, everyone – Captain Redoly, Ravid, Posef, and Plishka – was lying on the ground and staring to the north. Sanama joined them, but Zhava was distracted by a rustling in her ears, a small voice that seemed to whisper on the breeze...or that, maybe, was the breeze. She shut her eyes and turned her head, and she clearly heard the voices of the wind, though she couldn't make out what they were saying.

"Zhava, get down," Redoly hissed.

She opened her eyes and dropped to the ground. The sand seemed to shiver beneath her, and the wind continued its muttering. She shook her head and tried to focus. Everyone else was watching something. Ravid held up the glass eye and stared through it into the distance.

"This is the second I've seen," he whispered, handing over the glass eye to Redoly.

"Definitely a sengret," the captain said after a moment's observation. "My Gods, that thing's big."

"May I see?" Sanama asked.

Redoly passed along the glass eye, and Sanama held it up and studied the horizon.

The voices of the wind kept whispering to Zhava, and she shut her eyes again to listen. It wasn't many voices, she realized, but one voice speaking over itself, talking and muttering and laughing and arguing. It wanted to go fast, but it was so tired; it went a little east, but then it decided to travel south; it was too cold, and the sand was too hot. Most interesting of all, however, was that something large was disturbing to the voice. Something beat against it and sliced through it, something that traveled from far north: the sengret and the bulky basket it held in its talons. The wind was disturbed by the sengret, and a little angry at it for being so big and noisy this late in the day.

"It's coming fast," Redoly said. "Let's get back underground."

Zhava did not want to go back down. She wanted to listen more to the wind, and she wanted to know what it thought of the sengret. She wanted to feel the rhythmic pulsing of the sand beneath her. Better yet, she wanted that sand to be pulsing around her, for the wind to be directed. She wanted to stay up here, and she did not want the sengret see her.

"Captain...?" Ravid said. "What's going on?"

"It's Zhava," Sanama whispered.

She opened her eyes. The sand swirled around them, carried along by a wind that blew from the east and the west at the same time. The sand was picked up, spun above their heads, and twirled high above them, completely obscuring them from view.

She still felt the sengret on the wind, but it shifted its flight, it drifted farther to the east to avoid the swirling dust that rose higher into the air. And as it flew past, she directed the wind to shift course, to blow the sand around them so they remained hidden.

In a moment, the sengret passed them by, and Zhava released her hold on the wind and sand. With a sigh of relief, the wind went back to its muttering complaints. The sand's pulsing rhythm quickly returned.

Everyone stared at her. Sanama's grin grew even wider. Barae and Posef both seemed shocked, their eyes wide and their mouths open. Ravid was annoyed and brushed sand from his hair. Captain Redoly, however, squinted at her with a look that Zhava could only describe as...conniving.

"We need to talk," he said. "What you just did? We can use that."

Chapter 27

As the sun set on the following evening, Zhava and Barae walked through the desert, Barae holding the ropes that kept Ooleng walking bound at their side. Zhava stirred the sand all around them, loosened it off the dunes, and made it want to fly, to leap off the ground and into the air. She also caught the wind around her, directed it to her will, and spun it up and around to catch the loose sand and send it flying before them. The farther they walked, the more dust and wind she was able to bring together until it seemed that curtains of blowing red and brown flowed everywhere. It was an incredible feeling to be following behind a dust storm, to know that the elements preceded them into this fight, that she could call upon and build up such power.

"Doesn't it make you tired?" Barae called over the rushing wind and sand.

"Not at all," she yelled in return, a bit of dust catching in her throat. She coughed, then flashed a grin at her friend. "I can feel the sand all through me, and I can hear the voices on the wind. It's beautiful!"

When Captain Redoly explained his plan to them all, Barae immediately volunteered for this part of it – to be at Zhava's side. Sanama yelled and complained it was unfair she couldn't join them, but Redoly calmed her down with a mission of her own, something that would put her very near to Zhava. His overall plan was simple, though reminiscent of his assault on Zhava's farm: They road hard through the day to get as near to Wui-sha'Olm as they could without being seen. Then Zhava built up a sand storm, and she and Barae walked it up to the sacred mountain to surrender themselves to Viekoosh and his forces. That part was the distraction, though. Redoly, Brii, Sanama, and Posef followed the dust storm from the east, and Ravid, Garai, and Plishka did the same from the west. Redoly had a small set of maps showing the network of tunnels that ran through Wui-sha'Olm, though he casually dismissed with a wave and a grunt Zhava's question of how he got those maps. He muttered something about secrets and continued giving instructions.

Zhava and Ooleng would undoubtedly be taken to Viekoosh; Barae would likely go there or be corralled with the other prisoners. Either way, Barae was to start talking the moment they arrived and keep talking the entire time – loudly. Redoly said this part of the plan played to one of Barae's strengths, her ability to maintain an incessant stream of chatter, and though Zhava thought the comment was rude, Barae grinned and said it would be fun. Redoly and his team from the east would take the high tunnels into the mountain; Ravid and his team from the west would take the low tunnels. One team or the other would hear Barae, and that would lead them to either the prisoners or to Viekoosh himself. Zhava was impressed with Captain Redoly and his ability to lead people. Though her friends followed her willingly into the desert, she still did not feel like a leader.

"When you said I was beautiful," Barae said, breaking Zhava from her thoughts. "Did you mean it?"

"Did I mean it?" Ooleng yelled. He started laughing. "Did I mean it? Did I mean it?"

Zhava called a flame to her hand and flicked it at Ooleng. It flew past his head, and he screamed and jumped aside, but it shut him up.

Barae glanced quickly at her, then returned her attention to the ground before them. "You said I was beautiful."

"Barae, you are one of the most beautiful people I know." Zhava had to yell above the rushing wind, and it made this particular conversation even more uncomfortable. How was she to express such complex feelings when she had to be so loud? "You were the first person to accept me when I arrived at the Hibaro. You showed me around, and you introduced me to the most wonderful people I ever met."

"No, you don't understand." She shook her head and turned to look Zhava in the eye. "When I had that...awful dye running through me – when I was blue. You said I was beautiful. You looked right at me and called me beautiful. I have never heard you say that about anyone, but you said it to me."

"Well, yes. That was incredible, and it was beautiful. You were beautiful."

"But that's the only time you're...you know...attracted to me?"

Zhava had a moment to realize exactly what Barae was saying to her, that this was about their feelings toward each other – actually, about Barae's feelings toward Zhava – before Ooleng screamed, spun around, ducked his head, and ran straight into Barae's stomach. They fell into the sand, and though Ooleng's hands were tied behind his back, he repeatedly slammed his head into Barae's stomach and chest, yelling at her.

"You can't have her!" he screamed. "She's mine – she's my wife! My father bartered for her, and he promised her to me, and she is mine. Mine!"

Zhava almost lost her concentration on the dust storm, and the wind and sand paused, hovering in the air before her. She shut her eyes, shut out the screaming of Ooleng and Barae for just a moment, and listened to the wind, felt the pulsing of the grains of sand swirling through the air. The storm shifted,

burst in its intensity, and grew louder and fiercer than before –
as Zhava poured her own anger and frustration deeper into it.

Ooleng still thrashed and kicked at Barae, but she was struggling out from beneath him. Zhava gripped her Felton sword,
kicked Ooleng off her friend, and knelt at his side, the blade
pressed against his throat. He stopped struggling and stared at
her, his eyes wide with disbelief.

"You listen to me," she hissed. "I am not your wife. I was
never your wife, and I will never be your wife. I didn't kill you
in that cave, but I wish I had. If you were dead, I would have
my parents right now. If you were dead, my friends and I would
still be at the Hibaro. If you were dead...none of this would
have happened. But if you try to hurt us now, if you attack us
again, I will run you through with this sword, and I will bury
you in so much of this desert sand that no one will ever find
your bones."

His eyes darted back and forth between Zhava and Barae,
but otherwise he did not move.

She stood and slid the sword back in its sheath. She returned her attention to the weakening dust storm and churned
it up again.

Ooleng shut his eyes, curled up his legs, rolled over into the
sand, and started crying. His sobs carried even over the rushing wind, and his coughs spit up sand beneath his face.

"Oh, just get up," Zhava said with a shake of her head.

Barae dusted the sand from her robes as she stepped closer.
"What is wrong with him?"

"I don't know. You said he has two spirits at war within him,
but I don't think it's anything like that. I think I hurt him a lot
when I kicked him over in that cave."

"Is that the...." She pointed at the scars covering the left side
of his shaved head.

Zhava nodded, pulled Barae in close and hugged her tightly.
"Listen to me," she whispered. "You and Plishka, Posef and

Sanama, you are my best friends. You're each so special to me – I love you all."

"I'm attracted to you," Barae whispered back.

"I know you are." She took a step back. "And I like you, but...I am not attracted to you. Not like you want me to be."

"Yeah, that's, um...." She shook her head and laughed, looked at the sand. "I guess it's obvious. 'Garai is a god' after all."

"I did not say that," Zhava laughed back.

"That is what you said."

"I do not remember saying that." She thought about it, though, about Garai on his camel, his back straight and his dark, strong arms exposed to the sun. About Garai holding that hatchet. Or standing in the dark hallway. Sitting on the floor of the cave. Leaning forward and listening to Redoly...she sighed.

"You're thinking it now."

"I am not!" Zhava turned to the dust storm, the wind slowly settling, and she pressed her will into it again. "We have to leave. We're on a schedule."

"You were thinking about Garai," Barae said with a smile as she leaned down to get the sobbing Ooleng standing again.

They continued through the desert, Zhava driving the dust storm forward and Barae chattering at her nonstop. It felt good to Zhava, comfortable, as if their friendship was returning to the way it had been several moons ago. Barae changed topics numerous times as they walked, but Zhava didn't care. They discussed everything from the taste of their favorite foods to the locations of the Gods in the night sky. They even agreed to visit Barae's father on his fishing boat at their earliest opportunity.

When they reached the rocky incline that preceded the mountain, they embraced and wished each other all success, and Zhava released her hold on the wind and sand. The dust storm shifted, began drifting away, but it wasn't quick enough for Zhava. Captain Redoly said to make their entrance "dramatic." The dust storm slowly spilling off wasn't dramatic. So she reached back for the wind and the sand, pushed her will into them – and flattened the storm to the ground. In one moment, the rushing wind and pounding dust ceased, and Zhava, Barae, and Ooleng stood staring at the mountain of rocks and caves. They stood at the main entrance of Wui-sha'Olm.

"That should get their attention," Barae whispered into the sudden silence.

Zhava smiled. The sacred mountain fortress was massive. It stretched far to the east and west, and it was far taller than anything Zhava had ever before seen. The rocks themselves were a bright brown, glinting from seasons of the wind and sand polishing them. The edges were sharp and pointed, and they stuck out at weird angles. Surprisingly, a few things grew between the stones, some flowering plants and even a couple short trees. If anything, though, that tiny bit of vegetation made the entire rock fortress appear more forbidding, as if the life that grew was in danger of being snuffed out at any moment.

Zhava cupped her hands to her mouth and yelled, "We're here to see Viekoosh! I come to barter for my parents."

Silence answered back.

Ooleng snickered and shuffled his feet in the sand.

Barae leaned in close to Zhava. "What do you think? Are they in there?"

Zhava shrugged. She wondered the same, but she didn't want to voice it. She didn't want her worst fear to be true: that she wasted everyone's time.

"Hm," Barae said, stepping forward and putting her hands on her hips. "I wonder what Captain Redoly would do."

What would Captain Redoly do? He would call out to the people inside, which Zhava had already done, but he wouldn't stand here and wait. He would do something. He would force them to act. She turned to Ooleng, his hands tied behind his back, and watched him shuffling through the sand and wobbling to keep his balance. When Captain Redoly led the assault on her farm, he used Posef to keep everyone's attention; he made everyone think Posef was expendable...and that gave her an idea.

"It's your choice," she called to the rocks. "I want my parents, and I'm willing to barter. But if you're not." She flicked her hands and called to her flames. They sprang to life across her shoulders and arms, a display she knew would be dramatic, especially as the sun was setting so quickly. She probably lit up the sand for half a day's ride in every direction with this many of her little flames. She turned toward Ooleng.

"Zhava?" Barae asked. "What are you doing?"

"I know Ooleng is your contact for the sengret eggs," she continued. She let the flames drop from her hands and dance upon the sand. Ooleng flinched. "I know you used me as payment for those eggs." More flames upon the ground. "And I know you had my parents kidnapped to lure me out of the Hibaro – so that he could take me to his home across the Purneese." She stopped. She made a circle around Ooleng and surrounded him in little dancing flames. He shut his eyes to the sight, and he stood whimpering and tossing his head from side to side. A part of her felt bad for what she was about to do to him – but only a small part. "If I'm wrong, then I guess you don't need him."

She raised her arms above her head and clapped her hands together. She didn't need to do that, but as Redoly instructed, "be dramatic." The clap sent dozens of flames scattering through the air above and around her. The rock face lit up as if it was the middle of the day. She lowered her flaming arms, balled up a group of her flaming men, and took a step back to aim at Ooleng.

Someone laughed.

Zhava turned to the rock face and saw a single torch being held high and a man stepping carefully toward them. It was hard to see him, even with so much firelight, but he walked steadily forward, chuckling the whole way...so maybe her display hadn't been as impressive as she thought.

"Who are you?" Barae called.

"I'm a friend of Viekoosh," he said, "but don't mind me. Please, Zhava, continue. Send this sad, little man to a flaming death."

He stopped, planted his torch in the ground beside him, and stood with his arms crossed, watching.

"I'm here to see Viekoosh," Zhava said. She dropped the fireball but kept her flaming men dancing along her shoulders and arms.

"Well, he's busy right now, so you have me." He gestured at Ooleng. "Please, continue. Burn him up."

Barae looked back and shrugged. She didn't know what to do either. Zhava took a couple steps forward, and she could see a little more of the man's features. He was older, with thinning, gray hair. His stomach stuck out far, barely contained by the rope keeping his robes secured across him. He was also barefoot, and he carried no weapon – that she could see. No telling what was beneath those robes of his. His grin was wide, though, as if he was truly enjoying himself.

"I am Zhava of the western plain of Remmli," she said. "Viekoosh has taken my parents captive, and I am here to negotiate their release."

"Yes, yes, I know all that." The man waved a hand through the air. "I told you. I'll take you to Viekoosh. But right now, this." He pointed at Ooleng. "You were about to burn him up. Do it. I want to watch."

"Who are you?" Barae asked.

"I don't think you understand," Zhava said, not waiting for an answer. "This man works with Viekoosh. He sells him sengret eggs. Viekoosh will want this man returned to him, and I want my parents returned to me. I want to make a deal." Why would this man not work with them? Did he really want Ooleng killed instead of returned to Viekoosh? This was not the way Captain Redoly said this would go.

The man heaved a huge sigh, reached down and picked up his torch, and said, "So, the show's over. Fine. Follow me." He turned and trudged back up to the rock face of Wui-sha'Olm.

Barae stared, open-mouthed. Zhava turned and waved a gap into the flames encircling Ooleng, and they followed this strange man inside. The cave system curved and turned at odd angles, as if some had been dug by people and others by animals. The man with the torch led the way along a narrow passage sparsely lit by lamps and occasional torches shoved between rocks. They passed one large room filled with at least 15 people, all of whom were seated around the walls and listening to one man who stood in the center and read from a scroll. She recognized it as a story of Coredor, the God of these people. The God who declared death to anyone with a special Ability. The God who declared death or servitude to all women. He was not a nice God, and Zhava whispered a quick prayer to her own patron Goddess, Preizhavan, that she might be protected.

Barae performed her part of the plan perfectly. She started talking the moment they entered the caves, and she continued incessantly – and loudly – as they walked. She ordered Ooleng to walk faster, commented on the size of the tunnels, asked their guide several questions he refused to answer with anything more than a laugh, recounted their journey across the desert, and even sang a short song.

Zhava, however, ignored her friend and kept track of their path through the tunnels. It was long, and it twisted a bit, but she was confident she could find her way out again. Other than the roomful of devotees reading about Coredor, they also passed a few men and women in armor, their weapons at their sides, who gaped or glared at them.

They climbed a set of carved-stone stairs that ended in a massive room with dozens of oil lamps set on tables with chairs pulled up to them. Only two people sat in this room: the giant, Nu, and his water-witch partner, Jezza. They each tensed, scraped their wooden chairs across the stone floor, and stood from their spots as the man led Ooleng, Zhava, and Barae into the room. Nu's head almost scraped the ceiling, and he had to bend forward, which made him look even more imposing this close up.

"What is this?" he rumbled.

"Sit down, sit down," their guide said with a laugh. "This is no time to fight. It's time to celebrate! They are returning your prince, and he seems mostly unharmed."

"We were hired to capture that one," Jezza said, pointing at Zhava.

"Yes." The guide stopped, turned to look at Zhava, and grinned. "And if I was your employer, I wouldn't pay you – not after the crappy way you did your job." He burst out laughing, but Jezza flicked her hands and called forth a ball of water.

In an instant, the old man stopped laughing and drew a sword from somewhere. It happened so fast that Zhava didn't even know where he'd gotten it. Was it hidden in his robes?

"You sit," the man said, and there was no more laughter in his voice.

Jezza closed her hand, and the water dripped to the floor. She narrowed her eyes at the guide, but she and the giant slowly sat down again and scooted their chairs to the table.

"You had your chance," the guide said, that harsh edge still in his voice. "Now I'm dealing with Zhava and Ooleng."

"Whatever you say," Jezza replied with a shrug.

The giant nodded.

The guide set the sword on a nearby table and walked across the vast room. They stepped up to a closed door – the first Zhava had seen in the entire cave system – and he slipped the bolt and pushed it open. They entered another large chamber, this one built into a circle with a fire pit at its center and a large, flat stone behind it: an altar. Behind that altar stood Viekoosh.

Zhava wasn't sure how she would feel seeing the man again – and so the anger that boiled up within took her by surprise. He wore a loose-fitting robe that draped across his thin body, and his hair and beard looked as if he hadn't trimmed them in at least a moon. He was writing something on a scroll laid upon the altar before him, and he didn't look up. That casual calm enraged her further, that he could be so completely unaware of her after all the damage he had done to her and her friends, that he set upon her family. She felt the little flames tickling at her palms, begging to be set free upon him, upon this entire room. She forced them down, forced herself to remain calm.

Captain Redoly has a plan, she reminded herself. Stay to the plan.

"Yes, Kretsch," Viekoosh said, as he glanced up. "What can I...oh." He stared across the room at Zhava, his mouth open in mid-sentence.

It was that one name that caught Zhava's attention, though. The name of the man guiding them through the caves, the man who met them on the sand: Kretsch. She had heard that name, "Salient Kretsch," for the first time just a few moons ago, when she learned that her Papa and her Mama were not her birth parents. Several men dropped her off as an infant. They contracted for her care – but then Viekoosh and Kretsch went one step further. They placed a cruelty upon her Papa and Mama. Kretsch had gone inside Mama's head and planted a false memory of the infant Zhava abandoned on their doorstep, and they set it within Mama that she would despise that infant. It was Kretsch...the man standing beside her at this very moment...who was responsible for that cruelty.

And she wasn't sure she could keep control of her anger and her flames.

Kretsch laughed at her as he ambled away. "Oh, Zhava, if only you could see your face. You look just like you did as a baby. Those puffy cheeks all spread out wide, and those eyes so tight and mad."

"Kretsch," Viekoosh said, "that's enough."

"Oh, no, I think it's going to get better," he said, glancing across the room.

Zhava turned to look – and her heart stopped. A woman stood there, framed by the cave door. She seemed just as shocked as she stared back, a set of blue robes wrapped loosely around her body, and a sword belt secured at her waste. She cocked her head and made a silent "Oh" at them all.

"Io...Liori?" Barae gasped.

Chapter 28

Zhava could only stare. So many emotions ebbed and flowed so quickly, and the questions raced through her mind. She was thrilled to see Liori, and glad Liori was safe, but.... She wasn't a prisoner? She was walking around – free? And wearing her sword?

Zhava's heart raced, and the high-pitched tone sounded in her ear. Could Io Liori be working with High Priest Viekoosh and Salient Kretsch? No, that couldn't be true. Could it? Was this part of some elaborate plan to rebel against the King and destroy Remmli? If so, why?

She couldn't think those things. She couldn't let herself believe the worst that was floating through her mind. Except...what if it was true? Then what was she supposed to do?

Salient Kretch's annoying laughter filtered through the questions and the tone-noise, slowly bringing Zhava back into the moment. Captain Redoly had a plan, and Zhava was a part of that plan. She had to remember that, had to keep that in mind.

Fortunately, Barae's part of the plan played to her natural tendency – talking – and she started immediately.

"But, Io Liori," she said, "what happened? Plishka said you were captured, and she wasn't sure if you were even alive – she was barely alive, and that giant was trying to kill her. And why are you working with these evil people? You're not evil – are you? I don't think you're evil. You could never do the things these other people have done. But, if you aren't evil, and if you're not working with these people, why didn't you try to get away?"

Liori shut her eyes and held up a hand to stop the questioning.

Viekoosh, however, was less patient. "Barae, shut up."

"Is she always like that?" Kretsch asked with a laugh. "I don't think she stopped talking long enough to take a breath the whole way here."

"That is mean," Barae said, putting her hands on her hips and spinning around to Kretsch. "Are you always so mean? Is that what they taught you when you were young? Because my father taught me to respect other people, and he's captain of his own ship, and he has a whole crew of people who respect him. They listen to him and do what he says because they respect him."

"Shut up!" Kretsch and Viekoosh both yelled.

Barae took a breath, preparing to launch into another tirade, but Liori softly said, "Novice Barae, you've said enough."

Zhava stepped forward. "You never answered her question. What happened?"

Liori glanced at Viekoosh, who gave a quick shrug, then back to Zhava and said, "High Priest Viekoosh has shown me the truth. The world must be cleansed of the meekly powerful."

Zhava blanched at the quote, at the words of one of the most evil Gods, Coredor. It wasn't even that he was trying to be evil. He was most often a trickster, and he truly believed he was doing the right thing. He saw the way the other Gods blessed some people – people like Zhava and Barae, Plishka and Posef – but He thought those blessings were dangerous. He thought the Gods-blessed would one day overthrow the Gods themselves, that the "meekly powerful," as he called them, would take over the world, and he feared that day. He fought against that day. His followers, like High Priest Viekoosh and Salient Kretsch, fought against that day. And apparently...so did Io Liori?

"Yes, that's all a wonderful sentiment," Kretsch said, staring with narrowed eyes at Liori. "You've said all the right things. All has been forgiven by your beloved Viekoosh."

"Beloved?" Barae said. "She hates him."

"Hah!" Kretsch bent over, laughing, then said to Barae, "You should have seen them 15 seasons ago!"

"Kretsch, that's enough," Viekoosh said.

"They were in love, if there even is such a thing."

"Kretsch," Viekoosh said, his voice rising. "Stop."

"No, brother, you stop. And listen." He pointed at Liori. "I still don't trust her, especially now that two of her children have arrived."

"I do."

"I'm so happy for you. That means she'll have the perfect answer." Then, frowning and turning to Liori. "What do we do with the girls? What do we do with Zhava?"

Zhava and Liori stared at each other, and Zhava could see the pain in her teacher's eyes, that she was struggling with what to say and do next. Her hand hovered above the pommel of her sword, and Zhava mirrored her, preparing to draw her own Felton sword to defend herself – though she had no idea how she could do that. Liori wasn't just a teacher and an Io. She was First of the King's Third Salient, a group of warriors trained so thoroughly they could take on a dozen regular troops at a time.

"The answer is simple," Liori said. "Novice Zhava and Novice Barae must die."

Barae yelled, "Io Liori, no! You can't do this."

Zhava, however, expected that and called her flames as she drew her sword. They burst to life across her back and shoulders, and she let them cling to her arms, some of them dropping to the cavern floor and dancing at her feet. Captain Redoly would be proud.

Io Liori smiled as she drew her own sword – nearly three times longer than Zhava's – and stepped forward slowly. "Your Gods-granted Ability does not frighten me, Novice," she said. "In fact, it's one more reason you must die."

"Io Liori, please," Barae continued. She drew her sword and stood nearer to Zhava. "You are one of the best teachers at the Hibaro – no, you're probably the best teacher there. You can't do this. Please, just listen. Stop."

Liori drew a second, smaller sword from a scabbard hidden within her robes. She flicked the sword in her left hand, swishing it sharply through the air.

Barae gripped her sword in both hands, a useless gesture for such a short sword.

"Control yourself," Zhava said to her.

"We can't fight her."

"Calm," Zhava said. "Focus. Remember your training."

"I remember my training – I lose all the time. Io Liori, please."

Zhava shifted her weight, balanced on the balls of her feet. Liori circled around the edge of the room, her head down as she walked, and her swords held loosely at her sides. Kretsch chuckled and leaned against a table, his arms crossed over his chest.

"Liori," Viekoosh said. He shut the book in which he had been writing and stepped away from the table. "I know you. You don't want this, not even for Coredor. Not even for me."

"If this is what Coredor demands," Liori said, "then this is what I must do."

She lunged.

Barae shrieked, but the strike was aimed at Zhava. She parried, Liori's sword crashing into her own with a resounding clang. The blow jolted Zhava's entire arm, and her hand shook as Liori sidestepped and slowly, calmly, stepped back and continued circling.

"Oh, my gods!" Barae yelled. "Io Liori, please, no."

Jezza burst through the door with a crash of wood against the rocks, her own sword drawn. She took in the room in one quick glance, smiled, and lowered her weapon. Nu squeezed his bulky form through the same door, crossed his arms, and stood there watching. A snickering Ooleng poked his head through the door, his hands now freed, and he watched wide-eyed.

"Why did you have to bring Barae into this," Liori said with a shake of her head. "You know she's not a fighter."

Another quick lunge, but this time Zhava was ready. She caught the swing and angled away, and she sent a dozen of her flames through the air at Liori – who sliced in with her second sword and caught Zhava in the leg. The sword bit through the robes and cut into her thigh, just enough to sting and draw a line of blood.

Liori backed away again, half a dozen flames clinging to her. She spread her arms wide, and a ball of water angled through the air and doused the flames before they could do any damage.

Zhava turned to see Viekoosh lower his dripping hands. She hadn't forgotten his Ability to manipulate water – he used it to fight her in that cave – but it would make this fight far more difficult. She coughed at the tickle in her throat, that little scratch that bothered her for more than a dozen nights. She did not need the distraction right now.

"That is not fair," Barae said, glancing from Liori to Viekoosh and back again.

"We need to stop this," Viekoosh said. "She is too important to both of us."

"I wanted her trained," Liori said with a sigh. "I see now that was wrong."

"What are you two talking about?" Barae said.

Liori turned on Barae, swung one sword high and the other low. The first struck Barae in the head, but Liori had turned it broadside, and it smacked across the girl's cheek. The second sword struck broadside into her knees, knocking her off balance. Barae's sword crashed to the cave floor moments before Barae herself tumbled to the ground in a heap. Liori stepped forward and kicked the sword away, then turned her attention back to Zhava. It was over so fast that Zhava could only blink.

Now she started to really worry.

"Barae, talk to me," she said, stepping away from Liori.

Barae lay on the ground, gasping for breath as two lines of blood ran down her cheek. Her eyes were wide and full of fear as she crawled across the ground.

"You didn't have to get her killed," Liori said. She slid the smaller sword back into its sheath, raised the longer one before her, and locked eyes with Zhava. "You could have left her at the Hibaro where she was safe. But now she'll die with you. Here."

She lunged so quickly that Zhava barely had time to react. She raised her sword, called more of her flames, and prepared for the worst – but Liori didn't stab or slash. She swiped aside Zhava's Felton with a clang of metal-on-metal, wrapped her other arm around Zhava's back, and yanked her forward. Their bodies pressed together, and the flames across Zhava's robes sizzled as they came in contact with Liori's dripping wet clothes. Liori reached inside Zhava's robes and gripped one of the throwing knives from the belt at the small of her back.

She pressed her face to Zhava's cheek and spoke straight into her ear. "You distract the giant and his friend; I'll handle Kretsch and Viekoosh."

Liori yanked out the throwing knife and shoved aside Zhava. She flung the knife, and it arced across the room – straight at Kretsch's chest. He started to turn aside, but he wasn't quick enough, and the knife sank into his shoulder.

The next moment was pandemonium. Kretsch screamed and staggered into the table, one hand clutching at the knife protruding from his shoulder. Viekoosh threw up a wall of water from floor to ceiling and seemed to vanish behind it. Nu crashed his fist into his shield, and the explosive sound echoed off every wall around them. Jezza raised her sword and leaped across the table, her eyes on Zhava – who had just enough time to understand this new situation.

Io Liori never joined Viekoosh and his people worshipping Coredor; she only fooled them into thinking she was with them. Now that Zhava was here, Liori was ready to get back into the fight. That sounded so much more like Io Liori.

The sword came at her a moment later, and Zhava ducked and rolled. The spray of water followed close behind, but she loosed a dozen of her little flames to deflect that. She sprang up, her Felton drawn, just as Jezza slammed into her and shoved her backward. Zhava staggered, nearly dropped the sword, but kept herself from falling as she skidded to a stop.

"You have been the hardest person to catch," Jezza spat. She pushed out with her hands and sent another spray of water at Zhava who knocked it aside with her flames.

"Save some for me!" Nu yelled. He gripped the edge of a long bench and shoved it aside with a rumble of wood-on-stone as he stormed forward.

"Don't hurt her!" Ooleng screamed, but neither of the mercenaries seemed to hear that as they rushed at Zhava.

She lowered her arm and spun in a circle, dropping dozens of little flames and surrounding herself in fire. She needed a moment to think, just a moment for these two to back off so she could defend herself.

Jezza called up a stream of water and poured it across the flames, drowning them in sputtering jets of steam, and she swung her sword high.

Zhava twisted and blocked the sword, but Nu swung his fist at her from the side, and she had just a moment to jerk back.

Jezza swung again, harder this time, and Zhava's hands ached from the blows to her sword. Sparring with Plishka was one thing – this, though, was an intensity she never experienced in any of her training, and the hits kept coming. Jezza seemed to switch up her style with each attack, at once coming in high, then low, then stabbing, then slicing. The few times Jezza stepped back, Nu stepped forward and took a few swipes at her with his enormous, powerful fists, so that she was either blocking Jezza's strikes or dodging Nu's blows – and it was exhausting. Sweat ran down her back, and her hands were beginning to slip on her sword's hilt. She couldn't keep this up for long. If she could only get a moment, she knew she could think of some way to turn this around, some way to best them in this fight, but they wouldn't stop.

She reached deep inside her, to all the frustration she felt in this moment, to all the anger she felt at these two for trying to kidnap her – for Nu hurting her so badly she almost died. She thought of how much pain Ooleng caused her – and for what? Because she wouldn't bow down and be his wife? Because she wouldn't abandon her studies of the Kandor and follow him across the Purneese Mountains? Because she slipped from his reach at just the moment his parents negotiated the bride price for her? She didn't belong to him. She didn't belong to anybody, no matter what he might think. No matter what her brothers might think – no matter what Caleb might think. All of those feelings deep within her rose up and joined the frustration she felt in this moment, at being so brutally attacked by these two mercenaries, and she let those feelings wash over her. She embraced them, and in that moment her little flames burst to life across her body, the sand and rocks at her feet trembled to life, and the very air around her seemed to suck in a deep breath –

– and she let it explode. Little flames caught on a violent wind. The dust and rocks at her feet shot up. She pushed them all away and directed her rage at these two, at Nu and Jezza – and at Ooleng cowering behind them. She wanted him to go away, and to take his two hired thugs with him.

The force of the explosion knocked those three backward. Ooleng flew out the open doorway, his face contorted in shock, but Nu and Jezza crashed into the rock wall behind them, their armor clanging.

"Are you all right?" Liori yelled.

Zhava turned. The Io's sword flashed around her as she fought Viekoosh. He wielded a long, thick staff with both hands, which he used to parry her attacks, and he tossed blobs of water at her face and dripped water across the stone floor, making her footing slippery and uneven. Zhava wanted to scream back, "No! I am not all right. These two are much better fighters, and I don't know how to win this!" But watching Liori, seeing her sword flash through Viekoosh's attacks and her feet dancing across the wet floor, she could not say that. Liori fought against only one man, but that man had also been trained in the King's army.

She looked around and saw Barae kneeling on the floor and cradling her sword – and a set of keys. They were large, metal keys on a cord of rope tied together.

"Zhava?" Barae said, holding up the keys. "These were by my sword. Did you...?"

Hope stirred. In her vision, her parents and the other captives were locked behind metal bars with thick chains and locks. For Barae to find a set of keys here, in this particular chamber. Io Liori had kicked aside Barae's sword, but she hadn't kicked her out of the fight; she gave Barae another mission. Slipped her those keys somehow and got her out of the main fight so she could –

"Take them. Release the prisoners. Go!" She pointed at the far end of the room, where Io Liori had entered, then turned her attention back to the fight as Barae raced away.

She called to her little flames, and they ringed her arms and shoulders and climbed onto her sword. She kept them coming, and as more piled on her, some fell off and splattered to the floor, creating circles of flames around her as she stepped forward again. Against most opponents, this little display would have been intimidating, but Jezza had far more control of her water sprites than Zhava had of her flames. As Jezza had done before, she would likely try to wash away the flames and drown them, and Zhava was ready for that.

Nu staggered back up, his heavy armor clanging and his sword swinging wildly. He tossed his shield to the floor with a crash and punched at the air with his free hand. His head nearly brushed the cave's ceiling, and his face contorted in rage as he glared at her from across the room.

"I'm going to kill you!" Nu raged.

Jezza raised her sword and ringed herself in water sprites along her arms and shoulders, mimicking Zhava with a snide smile. She said nothing, but slowly, deliberately stepped forward.

Zhava took a deep breath. She recalled the lessons from her swordmaster, Io Suleenuo, and placed her feet a bit apart, left foot forward, leaned forward on the balls of her feet. She squared her shoulders and focused on her opponents, held her sword confidently – not too tight, but not too loose. She wished she had a shield, but Io Suleenuo's lessons came to mind again: "The sword is both your weapon and your shield." She could do this. She had to do this, she thought as she heard the crash of weapons from across the room. Io Liori needed her to do this.

If anything, Jezza's attacks came faster this time. Her sword flew in a blur, and Zhava barely kept up.

Nu stepped to the side, tried to flank her, and punched forward, his immense fist aiming at her head. She ducked and rolled, anticipated Jezza's next attack and deflected it.

Little flaming men and water sprites littered the ground at their feet, each popping and sizzling as they met.

Jezza leaped forward, her sword arching down in a powerful strike. Zhava deflected it and stumbled a bit, her footing slipping across the steaming, damp floor.

Nu's sword sliced at her, and she ducked beneath it, pirouetted, and cut him across the arm. He was powerfully strong, but she was much faster. She darted away in time to deflect Jezza's next attack – but Nu roared in pain and anger, and he punched his fist into her shoulder.

It was as if her arm vanished off her body. Her sword fell from her grasp and clattered to the floor as she lost all sensation from her fingers to her shoulder. She stumbled backward, the force of the blow nearly knocking her off her feet and sending her sprawling across the ground.

Jezza's water sprites pounced, jumping onto her body, soaking her clothes, and trying to snuff out her little flames. She rolled toward her sword and dropped several dozen flames behind her, the ground sizzling and popping as steam swirled through the air behind her. She started coughing on the heat, gripped the sword in her weaker hand, and floundered back up – just in time to duck beneath Nu's sword.

He screamed at her and swung again, his face contorted in rage. She stumbled against the edge of a table but ducked out of his way.

"Stand still!" he yelled.

She rolled a ball of flames in her hand and tossed it at him. They clung to his armor, and he flailed around, tried to knock them off.

Someone stepped to Zhava's side and she spun to see a woman in full armor and carrying a bloodied sword: Captain Redoly's soldier Brii!

"Need some help?" she asked, panting. Sweat poured down her face, and the front of her armor was spattered in blood. Behind her, Captain Redoly stood at Io Liori's side, both of them now fighting Vieshook – and beating back his attacks.

Posef's voice broke into Zhava's mind, and he said, *Don't worry – we made it. Sanama's with me and Barae, and we're going to set the prisoners free.*

Zhava laughed at the good news and rubbed her tingling arm. One team made it through. Captain Redoly said they could do this, and he was right. They could stop this horrible plan to spark a war between the countries, a war between Remmli and Go'Abb.

Be safe, she thought back to him. *Keep them both safe.*

I always do, he said, a tinge of humor in his voice. *Trust me.* But his voice suddenly changed. He gasped, and he anxiously whispered, *Where did she-? No, she shouldn't have....*

What's going on? Zhava said, but before she heard the reply, Brii gripped her arm.

"Focus!" Brii yelled.

The spray of water flew at them from above, and Zhava had just a moment to call dozens of flames and throw them high. They met the water sprites and exploded in a shower of steam – from which Jezza and Nu came running forward. Jezza slid on the wet stone and met Brii's sword. The clash of metal rang through the room as they furiously began fighting, but Zhava had only a moment to spare for their exchange before Nu slammed into her with his shield. The heavy, banded wood knocked her back, and she crashed into the wall behind her. Her head pounded from the shield up front and the rocks at her back, and she struggled to stay standing. The room seemed to spin. The edges of her vision darkened just a bit, and she had trouble focusing. Nu stood before her and raised his sword high, preparing to strike at her from above.

She knew she should do something, but she wasn't sure what. That high-pitched whistle echoed in her ear. Nu was prepared to attack, and she knew she should defend herself. Her sword had been ineffective against this giant of a man who hit with the force of five men and towered above her. Her flames seemed only to annoy him and slow him down – so what could she do?

He grinned. His muscles twitched, and she prepared for the strike, prepared to call hundreds of her little flames to her. She would pour out her fire on him and knock him backward, and then she would keep throwing more of her little flames at him –

– but a shriek distracted her. Distracted them both. A high-pitched voice yelled from across the room, screaming Zhava's name.

Sanama ran at them. She had her small sword raised high above her head as she ran for them. Ran at Nu.

The entire room seemed to stop at the girl's piercing call. Even Viekoosh and Liori and Redoly stopped their fight and jerked their heads toward her.

Jezza stumbled backward at the distraction, and Brii pressed the advantage, sliced across Jezza's sword arm.

But Sanama's focus was on Nu. She ran straight for him and brought her sword forward to slice across his leg – just as she had done at the farm. Just as she had done when she first rescued Zhava.

Nu spun to meet her. He brought that solid shield around from the other side of his body, and he slammed it into the girl.

"No!" Zhava yelled.

Sanama's head jerked backward. Her feet flew out from under her, and she spun through the air, water flying off her boots. Her short sword went spinning away. Blood gushed from her nose.

Nu roared in triumph.

Sanama's limp body crashed to the ground. Her head struck the rock floor first, and she skidded to a halt. Her arms lay crooked at her side.

It was as if the entire world vanished, and all Zhava could do was stare at the little girl on the ground. The rocks beneath her feet thrummed with the pulses of battle. The air in the room swirled around them all, bodies and swords and gasping breaths creating currents around them. But nothing moved around Sanama. The ground beneath the girl could not feel her muscles twitch. The air above her did not get sucked into her body, did not get breathed in or out, did not get swirled into a current. In one moment she had been running into battle, and in the next.... In the next moment...she had simply...stopped.

"Switch," Jezza yelled.

It happened in slow motion. Jezza ducked beneath Brii's sword, spun backward and out of her reach, and slid along behind Nu. The giant took a huge step to the side and met Brii's sword with his shield – and in that moment they exchanged places.

Zhava knew they moved, but she kept her eyes on Sanama – kept waiting for the girl to get up again, to pick up her sword again, to run again. She focused on the rocks of the cavern and the air swirling through the room, but nothing changed. The rocks never felt the girl move, and the air never entered her body.

The cold spread up Zhava. It was so cold and wet as it climbed up her ankles, past her knees and up her thighs. The water encircled her waist, gripped her chest and her shoulders, washed across her arms. As it fully enveloped her head, the water distorted her view of Sanama lying on the floor, seemed to make the room ripple around the girl – as if the girl might actually be moving. But of course she wasn't. Sanama was dead. She had rushed into battle to be at Zhava's side, and the giant stopped her. Killed her.

The water sprites wrapped themselves tightly around Zhava. They climbed into her ears and stopped her from hearing. They climbed inside her mouth, washed themselves down her throat, and poured into her lungs. She felt the air being sucked out from within her by the little drops of water...and she felt herself drowning. Felt herself suffocating. Her throat started to burn. That place deep within her, far down her throat where she had swallowed something earlier, when she first fought Jezza at the farm. That spot tore at the inside of her throat.

She tried to gasp – but nothing. No air.

She tried to reach up, to reach out through the water, but the little sprites climbed all over her and wouldn't let go. They washed down her body and climbed deep within her and swallowed up every last bit of air she had inside of her until...she died. Just like Sanama.

Chapter 29

The path of the dead flashed in a dazzling array as lightning crisscrossed the clouded sky. Zhava stood on that path that seemed to stretch before her in a never-ending line to the horizon. Rain poured down. Thunder rumbled. The air crackled with the sense of impending death – but not just her death. Someone else was here, someone special to her.

A hand clamped on her shoulder, and she turned to see Priestess Marmaran standing there. It was the young Marmaran, though, the woman Zhava did not know. Her long hair blew back in the wind coming from above, the breaths of the dead who lived in the clouds and acted as sentries to the straight path. The ones who watched now.

"Do not speak, child," Marmaran whispered. "It will only hurt more."

Zhava turned to see, and she gasped. Sanama – tiny, smiling Sanama – stood on the path before them. But she didn't simply stand there. She floated. Just off the stone path, her feet did not touch the ground. She stood in the air and grinned at them. She reached behind her back and pulled out a sword and swung it wildly before her.

"Zhava, will you teach me now?" she asked. "Will you teach me to be a strong warrior like you?"

"Do not answer her," Marmaran said, squeezing Zhava's shoulder. "You cannot keep promises to the dead."

The girl floated higher, level with Zhava's eyes, and her grin was huge. "We killed that giant, didn't we? He couldn't stop us."

Zhava shut her eyes and nodded.

"I saw him knock you down, and I knew you were hurt. I had to help. I had to save you."

Another presence appeared, a person Zhava knew only here, on the path of the dead, and she opened her eyes to Emsterold standing with them. Her wet, stringy hair lay flattened to her head and shoulders, and her body was tiny and skinnier than when Zhava last saw her.

"You see?" Sanama called. "We make a great team. We are fighters. I can be an Io!"

Emsterold stepped back and watched Sanama slowly ascending. "Who is she?"

Zhava couldn't speak through the lump in her throat. The sadness that threatened to overwhelm her. Sanama loved her so much, and she had failed the girl. She promised to take Sanama back to the Hibaro and train her, to act as a Mentor to her – but instead, she led the girl to her death deep in the desert. Her death at the monstrous hands of a mercenary who didn't care at all about the lives he snuffed out, so long as the gold was good. So long as he accomplished Ooleng's mission.

"Zhava, come with me," Sanama called, her smile beginning to falter. "We can train together."

"Oh, Zhava," Emsterold whispered. She bowed her head and folded her hands before her. "I'm so sorry."

"Zhava, come up here. You have to teach me how to swing a sword like you – how to fight like you."

Zhava tensed. She wanted to go with Sanama, join her in the air above and float away and spend the rest of eternity showing the girl how to fight.

Marmaran leaned over and whispered, "Sanama's fate is sealed, but yours is not. That is why you remain on the path while she drifts away."

Zhava opened her mouth to speak, but nothing came out. She coughed, and the thing in her throat dug in. It gripped the inside of her as if tiny, sharp claws held on tightly and refused to move.

"Why are you getting smaller?" Sanama said, her own voice beginning to disappear in the rain and thunder. "Where are you going?"

Zhava tried again to call to her friend, but no sound came. She wanted to tell Sanama that she loved her, that she would always love her and remember her. That if there was any way to help, she would do it. If there was any way for her to save Sanama, she would do it in an instant, but that it simply wasn't possible. Sanama was dying, and Zhava...might be dying also. She wasn't sure.

She thought back to the fight, that horrible fight with Jezza and Nu. She was losing, and no matter what she did, she couldn't get the better of those two warriors. Nu knocked her down, and Jezza wrapped her in a water cocoon so she couldn't breathe. She was drowning...or she had drowned. Why wasn't she floating toward the dead?

"Oh!" Emsterold exclaimed. She lifted a hand into the air – a translucent hand – and turned it around before her wide eyes. "They found my body. They're waking me up!"

Zhava smiled. At least someone was able to leave this place. All it took was waking up again.

"Thank you," Emsterold said. She stepped forward and gripped Zhava's arms, though the hand felt slippery, as if it couldn't quite make contact. "Thank you so much. I thought I would die here, but you –"

She vanished. One moment Emsterold stood on the path, and the next moment she was gone.

"You did this, child. You made this happen, and I am so very proud of you. Without your strength, without your determination, Emsterold and all the other people would have died here."

Zhava looked up. Through the rain and the lightning and the wind, she could just make out the rising form of Sanama's small body. The girl slashed her sword through the rain, yelled something to the ground, and vigorously waved. Zhava waved back, tried to say something in return, but was stopped by the thing lodged in her throat. She coughed, but it would not come loose.

Priestess Marmaran said this was a good thing she had done. It was good to bring her friends into the desert to rescue her parents, to rescue Emsterold and the others that Viekoosh captured. But right now, it didn't feel good. It hurt. She watched her friend die, watched her friend be taken up to be with all the other dead, and she couldn't even say, "Good bye." Could barely speak around this thing in her throat. She pressed her hands to her neck, wanted to rip the thing out.

"Leave it alone, my child," Marmaran said. She had transformed back into the elderly woman again, the old woman who lived with them for two wonderful seasons on the farm, taught Zhava every day about the Kandor, how to speak another language, and how to harness her Abilities.

But it was all so useless now. So senseless. What good were her Abilities if she couldn't even protect a little girl?

"Zhava, do not do this thing."

It took a moment to realize what she was even doing. She was pouring her frustration into herself, pulling her Abilities deep inside and trying to crush this thing in her throat. If she could at least do that. If she could at least be free of this thing that had gotten inside of her, then maybe she could...do something. She could at least call to her friend, tell her how sorry she was for failing her.

"My child, if you leave the water sprite alone, it will die on its own. It has been there for so many nights, and it is so weak that it will not harm you – if you stop right now."

A water sprite? Inside her throat? She fought Jezza only twice before, once in Ving'Sa-wehn and once at...her farm. Jezza used the water to capture Zhava, to keep her from moving. When Zhava got free, her throat burned, and that burning stayed with her all the way through the desert – where she never drank any water. Where the water sprite simply quenched her thirst and kept her alive.

"Hear me, my child. Do not crush it. That will harm you more than you can imagine."

But what else was she to do? Jezza was drowning her right now back in the real world, and she had no way of fighting back. The sprite would not allow her to speak, to at least wish Sanama a blessing for the afterlife. It clawed at the inside of her throat. She had trouble breathing around it.

"Zhava, listen to me. Stop what you are doing."

She shut her eyes and cupped her hands to her ears. She focused all her attention, all her energy on the water sprite lodged in her throat. She wanted it gone, out of her body. She wanted it destroyed so it would never come back, and then she could use her little flames to free herself from Jezza, to free herself from the path of the dead. She could speak again. She could...avenge Sanama's death.

That was what she wanted. Right now. Jezza and Nu had to be stopped. Viekoosh and Kretsch and Ooleng had to be stopped. All of this – all of the death and the kidnapping and the hatred – it all had to stop.

"Zhava, you must not."

She clenched the muscles in her body, knelt to the ground, and pulled every one of her Abilities into herself. She called her flames, she drew on the wind around her, and she raised up the dust and rocks from the path of the dead. She would free herself of this water sprite, and she would return to the real world, and she would stop all of these evil people from ever doing this again.

"Zhava!" Priestess Marmaran yelled, but her voice was almost lost in the buzz of the flames and the roar of the wind and sand.

She opened her mouth and let her Abilities pour back inside her, let them attack the water sprite directly. She would be free of it. Free to do as she wanted. The thing clawed at the inside of her throat. She couldn't hear its cries, but she felt them, felt the thing trying to get away from the flames and the wind and the sand pouring down into her.

The sprite snapped. One moment it was there, and the next moment it was gone – as quickly as Emsterold had vanished before her. But something didn't feel right. Where the creature had been in her throat, the spot now tingled. It almost vibrated.

She swallowed, and there was no more lump in her throat. She hummed. She whispered her name, and she heard herself.

"Oh, my child," Marmaran said, and her voice was surprisingly close.

Zhava opened her eyes to see her teacher kneeling beside her on the path of the dead.

"You should not have done –"

The path vanished, and Zhava was back in the real world. Jezza stood before her.

Chapter 30

Zhava didn't hesitate. She pushed aside Jezza's water sprites and hit her with a blast of wind that knocked her over and sent her skidding across the stone floor until she bounced against a table leg. The mercenary lay on the floor, panting, and stared open-mouthed at Zhava.

"You should be dead," she called as she struggled to stand. She rolled a ball of water in her hand and threw it at Zhava's head.

Zhava flung out a hand – and caught the water sprites. She stared at them. They danced in her hand, rolled between her fingers, twisted around each other, and some even stared back at her – and they smiled. She could hear them talking with each other. They laughed, and one of them was singing.

She felt the rush of water coming at her before she saw the second ball Jezza threw, and she reached out and caught it in her other hand.

"No!" Jezza screamed. She was standing now, her sword in one hand and a ball of water swirling in her other. She threw the water, and Zhava caught it, mixed it with the other two, and let the water sprites spread up her arms. "How are you doing this? How?"

Jezza advanced on her, pulling all the water from the air that she could. She built a wall of water that flowed before her, then expanded it until it blocked Nu and forced Brii to back away. The water rose up before them, churning and dancing all the way to the rock ceiling and cutting off both Zhava and Brii from the rest of the room.

"The ones with Abilities are really hard to fight," Brii said with a shake of her head. She slashed at the water, but the little sprites danced across her blade.

Before it even happened, Zhava knew the water would attack. She felt it inside her, just as she knew the dance of her own little flames. She felt the water lunge forward, and she willed it to stop.

The water stopped. It held suspended in the air between her and Jezza, the water sprites confused and unsure what to do, which way to go.

Zhava didn't hesitate. She called to her little flames. She called dozens of them, a few hundred to her in a moment's breath, and she tossed them into the air just as she called up the wind to push them forward. The little flames struck the water sprites, and they exploded in a burst of boiling steam propelled onward by the wind.

The force of the explosion knocked Jezza across the room. It was even enough to push over Nu and shove him across the ground. Across the room, Io Liori, Captain Redoly, and Viekoosh staggered from the explosion. They stopped their own fighting long enough to stare in shock at Zhava.

Jezza and Nu, hit by the full force of the explosion, yelped in pain, knocked aside the smoldering remains of the fire-water sprites, and staggered back up. Jezza gripped her sword and stood against the far wall, her hair and armor soaking wet, and steam wafting off her skin. Nu slammed his fist against a table as he pushed himself back up, the noise echoing around them.

"She's one girl," Viekoosh yelled at the two mercenaries. "Do I have to do this myself?" He tossed a jet of water at Zhava –

– who caught it, rolled it into a ball of her own, and flung it back at the high priest. She sent a burst of wind behind it, and the water struck Viekoosh in the chest and knocked him back. He slammed against the wall, cracked his head into the rock, and fell forward. He landed on his hands and knees, his staff clattering to the ground and rolling away, and he shook his head and groaned in agony.

Zhava didn't stop, though. This man had tricked her — tricked everyone at the Hibaro — and he must be stopped. She stepped toward Viekoosh, walked up the small dais where he, Liori, and Redoly had been fighting, and she called to her little flames. With each step, she tossed more of them to the ground and let them run ahead of her, let them encircle the priest as he struggled to sit upright.

"Zhava, you did great," Captain Redoly said. He lowered his sword and stepped to her side. "You caught him. That's what we need."

But catching him might not be enough. He had worked with Ooleng twice to kidnap her and send her away. He had bartered with Ooleng's family, trading her for a shipment of sengret eggs. He caught her Papa and Mama and locked them in cages deep in the desert. He did all of that...and what might he do next? No, simply catching him would not stop him. It might not even stop his movement, all those people worshipping his God, Coredor. He could rally people together again and cause even more problems next time, maybe even kill her parents or her friends...just as Nu killed Sanama. Perhaps the best thing would be to stop him here, now. Perhaps the best thing would be...to kill him.

"Novice Zhava," Io Liori said. She stepped forward, her sword raised between them, and her hand outstretched. "You will stop and back away."

Zhava took another step, let a few more flames drop from her hands. They joined the flaming circle around High Priest Viekoosh, dancing and shouting and spitting embers at him. She turned to stare into Io Liori's eyes, to look deeply into them. That was the first thing Io Liori had done when they met, look into Zhava's eyes. She dismissed Zhava immediately, not seen what she was hoping to see – what Zhava could now see in other people. That shine. That blazing well down which she could fall and learn about a person's Ability. Learn about the person herself –

"You do not hurt him," Liori whispered. She dipped her head just a bit, tensed her muscles, and shifted her sword to a slightly better angle, an angle that would strike at Zhava's arm.

She didn't need to dive into Liori's eyes to know the woman would fight her. She did not want to fight her teacher, but...Viekoosh was dangerous.

"Trust me," Liori said. "He's going to the King's prison."

The clang of metal echoed behind her, Brii still fighting. Captain Redoly glanced over, then back at Zhava. Io Liori's eyes never wavered, focused on Zhava the entire time.

"Make up your mind," Redoly said. "Fight with us or against us, but I want to get it over with and help my soldier. She's tired, and that giant's strong."

The giant. Nu. The one who killed Sanama.

Liori and Redoly were correct. High Priest Viekoosh moaned in pain, struggling to sit up and bleeding from the back of his head. He wasn't going anywhere. The mercenaries, though, and that little snake, Ooleng, could still escape. She had to stop them.

Zhava's anger flared, and she spun on her heels. She reached for the water sprites again, and, surprisingly, they came to her. She thrust her hands forward and sent them sailing across the room. Several arched over Brii's head, and a few dropped to the ground and rolled past her, but they all struck Nu. Most hit him in the chest, shoulders, and head, and he staggered back, nearly dropping his sword. The ones on the ground slid past his feet and up his legs, loosening his footing and making him slip on the wet stones. He yelled and flailed, his arms windmilling at his sides.

Brii lunged forward with her sword and sliced down the inside of his flailing arm. His yells of frustration flashed to screams of pain. He dropped his sword, tripped over his feet, and tipped backward. His head crashed into the chiseled rock and knocked his helmet spinning into the air, and he fell through the doorway in a cacophony of screams and crashing metal. Brii pushed through to follow him, but a jet of water blasted through from the other side and knocked her to the ground.

That had to be Jezza, Zhava thought. Her little flames flared to life, and she ringed them across her shoulders, around her neck, and down her arms as she moved to chase the mercenaries.

"Leave it to us," Captain Redoly called from behind. "We can wrap this up."

"You do not pursue them!" Liori said.

But Zhava would finish this. Jezza. Nu. Ooleng. She would stop them herself. She needed to stop them, especially for what they had done to her friends, to her parents...to Sanama. She lowered her hands as she ran, and she let the flames drip off her body with each step. They piled in behind her, rolled around each other, and blanketed the damp floor in writhing, steaming little bodies of fire.

"Novice Zhava," Liori yelled. "Stand aside! We will finish this."

She didn't reply. She didn't even turn around. She glanced at Brii long enough to see the soldier was all right, though she coughed up a spray of water as she rolled to stand again. Zhava turned aside and kept going, the flames rolling down her arms and dropping behind her. Io Liori yelled something else, but the anger rose so fast in Zhava that she didn't hear the words.

A second stream of water blasted through the doorway, but Zhava thrust her flames through it. The water exploded in a torrent of steaming jets that spattered the walls and ceiling and shrouded the doorway in a cloud of mist. She stepped through the steam and dropped another dozen flames into the doorway. She did not want anyone following her. She would not be responsible for anyone else getting hurt.

Jezza stood by Nu, her sword drawn and facing Zhava. The giant grunted from his place on the floor as he frantically bound his bleeding arm with a torn cloth. He had tossed aside his shield, and his sword lay on the floor in the other room, so he was essentially defenseless – except for his huge size and powerful arms, and for Jezza standing protectively at his side.

"This was a job, little girl," Jezza said, panting. She stole a quick glance at Nu, who was tying off the bandage on his arm, then back at Zhava. "Snatch you, and deliver you to the crazy man. But Nu and I, we never signed up for this kingdom war, not for any of that priest's crazy chanting to Coredor. I don't even like Coredor. I'm more of a Tecta woman, if I have to worship anyone."

Zhava didn't know the God Tecta, and she didn't care. She threw a ball of flames at the mercenaries, and Jezza met it with another blast of water sprites. The sprites and flames exploded through the air, but Jezza didn't hesitate. She lunged through the explosion, sword flying. Zhava gripped the hatchet from her belt and met the attack. The hatchet was heavier than her sword, and the balance felt wrong for a fight like this, but it was either this or the small throwing knives at her back.

Jezza was fast with her sword, faster than Zhava could be with the hatchet, and she pressed the advantage. Within moments, Zhava was against a wall with nowhere to go. She pulled at the wind around her, sent a gust at Jezza's legs, and knocked her feet out from under her. Jezza landed hard on her chest and slid away on the slick rocks.

Zhava caught a quick breath, leaped forward and landed on Jezza's wrist. She felt a bone snap, and was about to roll on top of the woman when Nu's fist came at her head. She ducked aside but caught the impact in her shoulder. The hit sent her sprawling across the floor, that shoulder numb.

"Get up," Nu said.

Zhava looked, expecting the next strike, but instead Nu was helping Jezza stand again. Jezza cupped her broken arm to her chest and stumbled at Nu's side, and the two of them rushed from the room.

Zhava pushed herself up, her right arm still tingling from the giant's first strike and now her shoulder beginning to throb from this second strike. She knew the throbbing was good, though. The throbbing meant she could still use that shoulder, just as she could still use her right arm. The pain might bring tears to her eyes, but she could fight through it.

As she stood, she saw Jezza's sword lying on the ground where the mercenary dropped it. In the middle of the fight, Zhava hadn't noticed how beautiful it was. The grip was bound in oiled-leather bands, deep brown near the guard and lightening to a tan near the pommel. The guard itself tapered outward, and a water sprite had been etched into each side. The blade was long and sharp, beveled to two fine edges and narrowed to a sharp point at the end. No wonder she'd had such trouble fighting Jezza; the mercenary was an excellent fighter, but this sword was beautifully designed for thrusting and slashing, better than any Zhava used at the Hibaro.

Someone behind her laughed, a wet, throaty laugh that made the hairs on the back of her neck stand on end. She knew that laugh. She'd first heard that laugh more than six moons ago, and it had gotten sicker each time the man came near her: Ooleng.

She raised the sword and turned around. The man sat in the far corner of the room running his hands through what there was of his disheveled hair. His robes were soaking wet, dirty and torn. He scraped his bare feet against the damp, rock floor

– when did he lose his shoes? He watched her from the corners of his eyes, his mouth turned up in snarling grin.

"They brought you to me – again," he chuckled.

"What?"

"My wife. My beautiful...wife."

Zhava's anger rose. This man had been hounding her this whole time, arranging for her to be kidnapped, attacking her family and home, carrying away her parents. And all for what? Because he could not live with the fact she didn't want him. That she found a life apart from him. That the Hibaro was her life now, and that the King gave her a calling she could not refuse – that she did not even want to refuse. That Io Liori and Io Kua and all of her teachers were training her to be something more than she ever dreamed possible for herself. He could always find another wife, someone to travel with him on his trading errands, to keep his home for him, to bear his children. But she could never turn her back on the life she now had. It had been more than six moons since she first met Ooleng. Papa was right when he said she was not the same girl who left her farm back then. In those six moons, she had grown to be a Novice at the King's Hibaro. Ooleng needed to learn that.

She strode forward, dropping her little flames to the ground with each step. Ooleng flinched as the fire got nearer to him, but his laughter grew more intense. He shuffled his feet, pressed himself even more against the rocks at his back, as if he could push himself through them and escape the fires. He twisted so that the shaved, scarred side of his head was turned to her, and he tried to hide his smile behind his shaking hands.

"Hear me, Ooleng," she said, waving the sword between them. The little flames ringing her neck and arms all stared down at the man, and she knew the effect was intimidating. She wanted the man intimidated, and his nervous laughter and darting eyes showed it was working. She brought her flaming left hand nearer to his face and let the little flames dance before his eyes. "I am not your wife. I will never be your wife. It is time for you to...let...me...go."

The laughter ceased as he stared at her fiery hand, and he jerked his head in a nod. Zhava backed away, dropped all her flames to the ground, and willed them to remain there until Io Liori could collect Ooleng.

Chapter 31

Rushing through the narrow cave, she followed the sounds of fighting and people yelling. She called her flames, and several dozen shot to life across her right arm and shoulder. Her left arm, however, was ringed in water sprites. She was going to send them away when one of those soldiers ran around the corner of the cave and skidded to a halt, nearly losing his footing on the slippery rocks. His eyes huge, he gaped at Zhava and worked his mouth soundlessly.

She raised Jezza's sword in one hand – her sword now, she thought with a smile – and the hatchet in the other and rushed at the soldier. He jerked from his shock in time to meet her attack. The little flames went skittering off her arm from the blow, several flying at the man's face, and he stumbled back. Zhava loosened the rocks beneath his feet and sent a gust of wind at his chest, and he tripped, struck his head against the rock wall, and fell to the ground, unmoving.

As Zhava turned, a second man sprinted around the corner, his own sword drawn and ready to fight. She had just enough time to raise her sword again and block his swing, but he followed through with the shield and smacked her in the face. She staggered, and he came at her again, this time clipping her arm. The cut burned, and her head throbbed. The high-pitched whistle in her ear came back louder than ever, and she shook her head trying to clear out the distracting noise.

The soldier pressed forward, and she tossed a spray of water as she stumbled. The water hit him in the face, and she tossed her hatchet at his legs. It was a wild throw, but it cracked across his knee and clattered into the distance. The soldier yelped and hopped back – and a burst of blue lightning encircled his body. He shook in place for several moments before falling to the ground.

Plishka rushed around the fallen soldier to Zhava's side, reached for her hand, and yanked her up. Plishka was breathing hard, and lines of blood criss-crossed her armor, but she wore a determined smile as she pulled Zhava close and wrapped an arm around her.

"I know we're late," she said. "Ravid sent me ahead. Are you hurt?"

"No, but what about the giant? Did you see him?"

"He and that woman ran past me. They didn't even look at me. What happened?"

"Sanama's dead. They did it."

Plishka's eyes narrowed, and the smile vanished. "Let's go. We can still catch them."

Zhava gripped her sword tightly and prepared to charge down the stone passageway, but instead she stared at her friend. Plishka was a good fighter – with a sword, she was better than Zhava – but she controlled only the one Ability. Plishka had fought the giant and the water witch twice already, and she barely escaped with her life. What if she was not so fortunate this third time? What if the giant landed a solid blow to Plishka, as he had done to Zhava. What if she suffered the same fate as Sanama, and they killed her?

Papa said something important to her after she led Plishka and those children down from the mountain, and she hadn't realized how important it was: These people followed her. They deferred to her – even Plishka, just a little older than Zhava, was willing to charge into a dangerous fight simply because

Zhava said it was the right thing to do. Sanama did that. Sanama was one of "Zhava's Little Soldiers," and it was cute for a time, back at the Hibaro. Back where nobody would actually kill them. Where it could be a game. But here....

"Wait," Zhava said, placing a hand on Plishka's shoulder.

"Why? We have to go. We have to catch them."

She pointed her sword back down the narrow passageway, back to where she'd left Liori and Redoly secure behind a wall of flames. But she wouldn't tell Plishka that. "We can't leave. Io Liori is back there, and she needs our help. She's...hurt. I think we should go back."

The clash of swords and the yells of battle echoed like tiny voices to them from the passageway beyond, obvious sounds of the fighting still happening. Behind them, it was silent. Plishka looked back and forth, torn between her duties to the battle and her duties to Io Liori.

"We will get the giant, but later. He's not getting away, but Liori needs our help." She remembered Barae and the set of keys. "And the prisoners are back that way. We need to find my parents – and your sister."

"Vinaara?" Plishka said, suddenly focused on the path behind.

"Yes. Barae was going to rescue them. We need to help her."

The moment of decision was clear on Plishka's face. If there was anything to motivate her, it was finding her twin sister. To be so close, she would do anything to get her back. She rushed down the cave toward the large room, fully expecting Zhava to follow.

But Zhava stood there, watching her friend slip around the corner of rocks. She willed her flames to the ground, had them pile on top of each other until they formed a mound of fire, and told them to guard this passageway. No enemy soldiers were allowed through, and Plishka was not allowed back out – but they couldn't hurt her. They mustn't hurt her.

"Please forgive me," she whispered, knowing Plishka wouldn't hear, but she needed to speak the words, if only for herself. "I can't lose any more friends."

Chapter 32

Zhava bolted away from the fire mound before she could change her mind. It was worth Plishka's wrath, she told herself. Worth it to keep her safe, and to keep Io Liori, Captain Redoly, and Barae all safe. They all risked so much for her, and she couldn't ask them to do more. She couldn't ask them to give up their lives as Sanama had done.

Zhava swiped at the corners of her eyes, clearing away the tears threatening to cloud her vision. She stopped short as a mercenary staggered into view from a narrow passageway to her right. He quickly recovered and pushed himself back into the passageway where quick, sharp raps of metal resounded. He hadn't even seen her.

She ringed her arms and shoulders in flames, let another dozen cling to the blade of her new sword, and stepped up behind him. He was one of two soldiers in the narrow passageway who pinned Garai between piles of barrels stacked against the far wall. The passage was wide enough that the two soldiers blocked his escape, yet narrow enough that neither of the soldiers was swinging his sword, simply thrusting forward and wearing down Garai a little at a time. The leather armor across his chest kept him alive, but his bare arms were marked by bloody spots where he hadn't been quick enough to deflect their attacks.

Zhava's flames lit the passage bright as the evening sun — and that got her noticed. Garai squinted and nearly took a sword point in the face, but he ducked aside. The two soldiers hesitated, and the one nearer to Zhava turned and gaped.

She didn't hesitate. She loosed a deluge of water sprites at their feet, knocking over both of them as the sprites slid beneath their boots, their swords clattering across the wet stones, and they toppled over in a heap. Garai thrust his sword down and killed them both before they could recover.

He staggered forward, out of the narrow passage, and sank to his knees. "Praise you, great Goddess," he began, then glanced into Zhava's face and stopped.

"Get up," she said.

"But...." His gaze followed the dancing flames ringing her arms and shoulders and prancing atop her head. The remaining water sprites still clung to her palms and drip-dropped off her finger tips. "How are you...?"

"You have no one among you who can do this?" she quipped. "Now go find a place to hide until this is over."

She turned and strode toward the sounds of fighting – but Garai followed close behind.

"Wait," he demanded. "I must speak."

"Get away from me." She kept focused on the sounds down the cavern. She was getting closer.

"I see now why I am here."

"Go away."

He gripped her arm and pulled, and her anger flared with the light of her little flames. The cavern lit brighter than the high sun, and she knocked Garai off balance as she yanked her arm from his grip.

"Do not touch me," she snapped.

"I – I don't know what you are, but you have my thanks-"

"I don't want your thanks."

"-and I would be your soldier."

She stared at him in the piercing light of the flames. His head was bowed, his hands outstretched. He was dirty and blood-stained and sweating – and he was asking to be led. Just as Sanama had asked to be led.

"I am not a soldier or a captain or an Io. I do not command people. I am a Novice of the Hibaro Reverie under the leadership of Io Kua and Io Liori" – whom she'd just locked in a room – "and I am here to get my parents back, and to kill a giant."

"I will fight by your side."

"Oh, Gods above!" In frustration, she dropped every little flame clinging to her body and willed them to keep Garai contained. She would not be responsible for anyone else dying on her behalf. If she had to lock up every last one of her companions and friends, she would do it to stop them from dying, to stop them getting killed simply because they followed her. When a mound of flames solidly blocked the way, she turned and continued on, Garai calling her name.

Within moments she found the fighting: the side room where she and Barae had seen a dozen soldiers praying. Ravid now stood in the center of that room, fighting four soldiers at once. He slashed and punched and kicked at each in turn, somehow keeping them from rushing and overpowering him. It was a beautiful display of fighting skills, but Zhava could see he was wearing down. His responses lagged, and his sword drooped a bit. He needed help.

She poured her flames upon the ground and willed them to attack the soldiers. Climb them, bite them, distract them – anything that would give Ravid an edge as she prepared to –

The punch to her back came from nowhere. She stumbled forward, barely remaining upright, and tried to suck in a breath her body did not want to hold. Her sword clattered to the ground, and the flames scattered before her, tumbling and bouncing across the cold floor. She cracked her leg into a wooden chest near the wall and kept her head from being split open by throwing up her arms and taking the fall on her elbows and shoulders. The enemy soldiers all jolted at the racket, and that allowed Ravid the moment he needed to stab one of them and knock him to the ground before the others resumed the fight.

A wave of water slid across the ground and at Zhava's face, dozens of water sprites pouring over each other to catch her, to drown her. Instinctively, her little flames gathered from across the room and rushed at the wave to leap onto it, sending sprites scattering away or exploding in bursts of steam.

Jezza stood in the doorway, one arm cradling the other, her leather breastplate marred and scorched, and cuts bleeding through her robes. She glared at Zhava and seemed determined to fight, but Nu pulled her back, and they disappeared.

Furious, Zhava struggled back up. Her back throbbed where the giant hit her, and the leg she'd cracked into the chest did not want to support her weight, but she would not let those two escape. Sanama's murderers!

She flicked her hand and sent a dozen of her own water sprites at the feet of the enemy soldiers fighting Ravid, then sent a gust of wind at them. Two of the soldiers slipped in the water and fell over from the wind – and both tumbled to the floor in a heap, one of them striking his head on the rocks.

Zhava had no more time for Ravid and the soldiers of Coredor. She helped him enough, and now Nu and Jezza were escaping. She retrieved her sword, rushed into the deserted passageway, and turned in the direction they'd run – the direction that sloped down and back to the open desert. Their fleeing steps echoed back to her, and she raced after them. As she rounded a corner, a ball of water flew at her head, and she dodged aside just in time.

"Return my sword," Jezza said, "and we'll let you live."

"You killed my friend!"

"We killed many people," Nu chuckled. "It's business."

"And when you took my parents and killed their servants? Was that just business?"

"Little girl," Jezza said, balls of water swirling in each hand, "you do not want to push us. Be smart, return my sword, go on your way."

"We're wasting time," Nu rumbled, stepping forward. "I'll get your damn sword."

"No, wait!" Jezza yelled, but Nu thrust forward with his sword.

Zhava spun away and slashed at his bare arm – and connected. The sword cut deep, and Nu shrieked and jerked back.

Jezza flung her water sprites, and they landed on Zhava, snuffing out her flames in puffs of smoke. Nu backhanded her across the head and sent her reeling, stars of pain exploding before her eyes. A punch to her side, a kick to her legs, another strike to her head, and more of those water sprites streaming across her body. The pain came fast and hard, and Zhava didn't even have time for a breath. She poured her will into the water, wrestled away control of the sprites, and turned them back on the two mercenaries. With yelps of surprise and pain, Jezza and Nu staggered back, swatting away the water sprites now biting into them.

Anger boiled within her, and Zhava struggled against the pain to stand straight again. She blasted wind at them both. Jezza fell to the ground, surprised at the sudden turn of events, and slipped backward down the sloping cave floor. Nu, however, leaned into the wind and knocked aside the last of the water sprites clinging to his body and armor. He reached forward with the sword in his bleeding arm and swiped at Zhava's face, but she blocked it and sent a few dozen of her little flames at him. They flew forward on the wind, grabbed hold, and held on tightly – long enough for her to send water sprites right behind them. The sprites and flames exploded in bursts of steaming, boiling water, and Nu finally lost his footing and fell backward also.

Zhava let go of the wind and ringed herself in fire. Little flaming men along her shoulders, down her arms, clinging to her legs and her sword, and she rushed forward. Jezza knelt on the ground, just beginning to stand again, when Zhava rushed at her and swung hard. The blow knocked the mercenary to the ground, and Zhava swung again and again and again, raining down strikes on the woman's armor-covered body. With each blow, more of her little flames tumbled forward, falling to the ground and covering Jezza, biting holes through her leather armor.

The flames screamed a warning in Zhava's ears, and she tucked and rolled just in time to avoid Nu's sword. She pelted him with more bursts of steam – flames from her left hand, water sprites from her right – and he staggered back against the onslaught, stumbling farther down the tunnel toward the harsh light of the high-sun desert beyond.

Zhava whirled back on Jezza, who was coughing up blood and struggling to sit up. She raised her sword and prepared to swing, but the woman ducked her head, held up a hand, and gasped, "I yield! I yield."

Zhava hesitated, the sword held high. She hated her. This woman who hurt so many of the people she loved, hadn't flinched when Nu killed Sanama – and yet she asked for mercy. She offered to surrender.

A voice echoed through her mind, the voice of her mentor, Priestess Marmaran. The voice was a little sad, barely a whisper as she reminded Zhava of the teachings of the Kandor, and the teachings of her mentors at the Hibaro. Strength through justice. But was it justice to kill Jezza now, or to accept her surrender and deliver her to the Ios?

The little flames yelled their alarm, but Zhava didn't react quickly enough to avoid Nu's fist to her head. She saw it coming at the last moment and started moving away, but it wasn't enough. The blow knocked her aside, felt as if her head would explode as she crashed into the wall and stumbled to her knees. The rocks bit into her legs, hands, and face as she scraped across the ground. Her right ear rang louder than ever before, and her whole body shook from the trauma.

"Jezza, let's go," Nu called.

The ringing in Zhava's ear and the thrumming of pain through her body drowned out whatever answer Jezza gave. But she no longer cared. She no longer felt any compassion for these two, any reason to let them live. She drew on her Abilities, called everything to her, every last bit of fire and water, every bit of loose dirt and rock, every breath of wind in the tunnels of the caves all around. She drew them all to herself, embraced the ringing of the trumpet in her ear as a soldier would follow a battle call – and punched everything out from herself and down the tunnel entrance in a stone-shaking explosion.

Jezza and Nu flew out the cave's twisting entranceway in a jet of steaming rocks and cyclonic wind. They tumbled across the desert sand, the little flames and water sprites scattering around them.

Zhava pulled herself up from the cave floor and staggered down the sloping passage, her sword scraping behind her where she dragged it across the stones. She limped into the blazing sun and squinted at the sight before her. Jezza lay splayed across the sand to her left, unmoving. Maybe dead, maybe not. The dust-blown dunes stretching before her were alternately ablaze or awash in muddy-red pools of water. Nu was pushing himself up and stripping off the metal armor that had become dented, cracked, and misshapen around his massive, bulky form. He stripped down to his tunic, cursing at the metal clasps that would not release, yelping in pain at the metal cutting into his body.

Zhava advanced on him. She barely noticed when hundreds of her little flames sprang to life across her body.

"Stay away from me!" Nu yelled as he hopped on one leg, desperately trying to untangle himself from the busted cinches of his reinforced boot. "You – are evil!"

"And you're a murderer," she croaked. She didn't know if he heard her, and she didn't care.

She reached deep within herself and called to the wind. It answered immediately in the open desert, and she twisted it into a tall, swirling mass. It spun between her and Nu, eating the red sand beneath it and spewing it high above. Within moments, the red funnel cloud roared with an energy of its own, rumbling into the open sky and thundering against the ground.

Nu's mouth moved, and his face contorted in anger, but whatever words he spoke were lost in the pounding of the wind and sand.

Zhava gave the funnel cloud a nudge of her will, and it pounded forward – scooping up Nu as it rumbled away into the open desert. She watched it slowly recede from view, felt a grim satisfaction as it pulsed and jostled over the dunes and wound its way through the little valleys of sand until finally she no longer heard it. Her vengeance could never bring back Sanama, but at least Nu would never again hurt another person.

Sanama.

She shut her eyes and felt the grief begin to take hold.

Sanama....

Chapter 33

Her heart felt empty. Hollow. The funnel cloud had almost disappeared, yet she remained where she stood, trying to feel anything. She thought she should feel something. She thought it would make her feel better to get her vengeance on these people who hurt her so much, the people Ooleng hired. But she didn't feel much different. If anything, she felt a little lost. The rage burned so brightly just moments ago, but now...nothing. The world was now as the world had been – empty without Sanama.

Zhava could almost hear the girl speak. The last real conversation they'd had together, deep in that ravine beneath the sand: Zhava saw the Ability within her, saw the power of sword fighting floating untapped and untrained within Sanama, and she offered to train the girl. Sanama wrapped her arms around Zhava's neck and squeezed, and she said, "Oh, thank you. I love you!"

That was what she heard now. Sanama's words echoed through her mind.

"Oh thank you. I love you!"

"Oh, my child," Marmaran said, and Zhava jerked her head to see the priestess, old once again and leaning on her cane to watch the funnel cloud in the distance. "What you have done, it will hurt you so much."

"Why are you here?" Zhava rasped.

"To guide you. To support you in your times of greatest need."

"No," Zhava said, suddenly realizing a new direction. Suddenly seeing a way to fix this – or at least make it a little better. "You died, but...you're here."

She turned her old, blind eyes to Zhava. "Oh, child, do not go there."

"But you came back." The rage began to swell in her again, and the little flames clinging to her armor and clothes buzzed their excitement. "There's a way. Before you died, you taught me the way. Death is not the end – it wasn't the end for you. It doesn't have to be the end for Sanama."

"It does, child. Listen to –"

"No!" She spun on her heels, ready to storm back into the rocky fortress, but stopped short at the sight outside the mountain caves. Garai stood several paces before her, his head bowed and his hands folded reverently beneath his chin. Ravid and Plishka were helping the bloodied and battered Jezza sit upright in the sand. So. Not dead. Jezza cradled one arm to her chest, and the other shakily gripped Plishka's arm. Barae and Posef ran to the cave's entrance and stood there in shock, and that's when Zhava really took notice of her surroundings.

Sand and rocks had been blown from the cave, and the blast pattern showed clearly in the surrounding area. Several of her flames still burned as they bounced and rolled across the ruts in the sand, and many of the water sprites were busily forming red, muddy pools where the flames left them alone.

"Forgive me," Garai said, quickly dipping his head in a deeper bow. "I thought Lord Su'Fyen made a mistake assigning me to your command. I should have known better. He does not make mistakes, and you are such a powerful warrior. A leader."

"Great," Zhava said, limping forward. She didn't care what Garai thought of her before, and it didn't matter what he thought of her now. She had to get back to Sanama's body.

"Please," Garai said, reaching out. Zhava tensed, but he simply indicated the sword she dragged behind her. "May I?"

"Sure, whatever." She handed over the sword, and slowly, painfully climbed the steep slope back to the cave system. No one spoke to her as she trudged past, the flames buzzing across her bruised and bloodied body. She proceeded as quickly as she could through the now-empty passageways, stepping over and around remnants of the fighting, including bodies of the mercenaries she and the others had slain. On a side table, likely used for some Go'aabite ceremony, she spotted a small cup with a lid, and she scooped it up on her way past; she would need it for the ritual. Many of the little flames she'd left behind had been scattered aside, and those that remained she willed to follow her, so that by the time she reached the central chamber again, she had a long, fiery wake trailing behind her.

Sanama's body lay near the side of the room, her arms folded across her chest and her eyelids shut. Someone had cared for her when Zhava sought vengeance against her killers. She knelt by Sanama's head and began recalling the chants Priestess Marmaran taught her all those moons ago.

"What are you doing?" Io Liori said, stepping out of a side door and glaring at Zhava.

"She cannot die," Zhava growled.

"No." Liori strode toward her. "You did this to your teacher. You cannot do it to your friend."

"Stay away." She willed a line of flames between them. "I must do this."

Liori raised her sword and pointed it at Zhava – the first time the Io had ever done such a thing. "You must leave that body alone. Sanama will receive the proper rites, and her body will be returned to the Hibaro for a proper burial."

Zhava ignored her and recited the first line of the resurrection chant from memory.

"Zhava, back away."

She continued the rest of the first stanza, scowling as she tried to focus her attention on Sanama. That was difficult with Io Liori yelling and threatening.

"I do not want to hurt you, Zhava."

She began the second stanza, the words flowing more smoothly now.

"Gods-dammit, you are stubborn." Io Liori took a step.

Zhava willed more of her flames to pile on top of each other, forming a small, fiery wall blocking them apart. The third stanza, and she felt a little jolt of energy at the words themselves. She didn't remember that when she'd performed this on Priestess Marmaran's body, but maybe it happened and she didn't notice.

"Plishka," Liori called. "Get in here – now."

Marmaran's face shimmered in the heat of the flames, her blind, gray eyes staring into Zhava's very soul. "Child, do not do this."

"Plishka!" Liori yelled. She sheathed her sword and rushed away.

Zhava knew she had only moments to complete this before Liori returned with Plishka in tow, likely to zap her lightning through the flames and knock Zhava aside. She couldn't let that happen. She had to complete this ritual. She had to bring back her friend. Her little soldier, Sanama.

She rushed through the remaining stanzas, calling out the final words just as Liori and Plishka burst through the doorway. Plishka's eyes grew huge.

Zhava pushed all of her little flames – every flame covering her body, all the flames forming her wall, and the dozens of flames that trailed behind her through the caves – and she set them to devouring Sanama's body. They piled atop the girl and blazed and buzzed and danced.

Zhava set the cup and lid on the floor and sprang back from the blaze. She lifted her chin defiantly at Liori and slowly, painfully scooted back across the floor to lean against the wall, her chin resting on her knee. It was complete. There was nothing she could do for Sanama in the physical world, but if she could bring her back from the land of the dead, that would be something. She could still show the girl how to wield a sword, how to be a fighter, and how to study the Kandor. Sanama might not become the warrior she dreamed of, but she could still experience the world with Zhava. That would be real.

Io Liori said something to Plishka who rushed away, and Liori stepped slowly, purposefully forward and stood above her. She glanced at the flames devouring Sanama's body then back to Zhava, a scowl on her face.

Garai stepped away from the wall – Zhava hadn't even realized the Go'aabite warrior followed her.

"Who are you?" Liori asked, glaring at him. "What do you need?"

He introduced himself and explained that he was part of Captain Redoly's team that infiltrated the cave system, and that he was proud to serve under An'Zhava. He reached forward to return her sword, but Io Liori held a hand to stop him.

"'An'Zhava?'" she said. "No, Garai, she bears no Go'aabite honorific. She is Novice Zhava, a student of the Hibaro Reverie – and she is under my command. I'll hold this." She jerked the sword from his grip, dismissed him with a wave, and knelt at Zhava's side. She leaned forward and with a shake of her head whispered, "The things you have done here...I don't even know where to begin with you."

Zhava said nothing. What was there to say? She did all that she had to do, though it was not enough.

Captain Redoly strode into the room with a smile on his face and a bounce in his step, even as he eyed the blazing fire nearby. He saluted and said, "Yes, Io Liori?"

"Take Novice Zhava to the holding cells in the back and re-unite her with her parents."

Zhava sat a little straighter. Her parents were still alive.

"Yes, Sir," Redoly said. He narrowed his gaze at Zhava, taking in the cuts and bruises and streaks of blood that covered her body, armor, and robes. "Er...there's a healer among the hostages. Should I try and locate him?"

"No." Liori stood and dusted off her knees. "When Brii is available, have her patch up Novice Zhava with bandages and salves. If anything's broken, it can be wrapped and restrained like every other soldier. We need something to clip this girl's wings." With that, she strode away, disappearing through the doorway that led outside.

He helped her stand, then supported her as she limped from the room. She glanced back once to see that her little flames were still burning Sanama's body, and Garai stood to the side, transfixed by the dancing flames. They would die down and collect some of the bones and seal them inside that small cup. She wasn't sure how or when she would be able to retrieve that cup, but there was nothing to do about it now.

The going was slow. Now that the frenzy of the battle was over, she felt every injury. The cuts across her arms, legs, and face. Amazingly, most of them were from the ground and rock walls; only a few cuts seemed to come from anyone's sword, a testament to how well she used her training. Every part of her ached, however. Her back and head were throbbing where the giant landed a few solid hits. Her arm tingled – Nu also hit her there. The knuckles of her sword hand bled, though she wasn't sure when that happened. She wiped the blood on her robes and wrapped her hand to staunch its flow.

"For what it's worth," Captain Redoly said, his voice low in the dark passageway, "you're a good fighter."

She didn't reply. It was a nice thing for him to say, but if she had been better, things might have gone differently.

"I don't know what the Hibaro has planned for you, or what the King might want you to do, but I could use a soldier of your skill."

She stared at him and almost tripped, then watched where she was going as she limped ahead.

"You would, of course," he continued, "have to learn to follow orders."

She scowled. That wasn't fair. "I couldn't let anyone else get hurt," she mumbled.

Redoly burst out laughing, nearly knocking her over as he stopped and turned to face her. "This was a fight – a significant battle!" he said, one arm sweeping around to encompass the whole of the mountain. "What did you think would happen?"

She shrugged.

He leaned in close. "You're not the only one to suffer loss on this campaign, Novice Zhava. We lost Tomaath when we retook your farmstead – or did you forget him already?"

"No." She lowered her head. Actually, in all that happened since the farmstead, in her grief at seeing Sanama killed in front of her...she had forgotten.

"Tomaath's death was on me," he continued. "I was his commanding officer, and he died carrying out my orders. Sanama's death, however...is also on me."

She jerked her head to stare up at him.

"Not you, no. I almost left her behind – I should have left her behind – but I saw her devotion to you. My Gods, she chased after you on foot for days when we left the Hibaro. I could have tried to leave her behind when we came here, I could have tied her up and left her sitting in that sand cave you made, and maybe that would have been best. Maybe she would still be alive. Maybe, somehow, Tomaath could still be alive. Or maybe...." He gripped her hand, narrowed his gaze, and whispered, "Maybe we could stop second-guessing the past. Maybe we could learn from our mistakes and become better leaders. Hm? What do you say?"

She didn't know what to say. She had watched Captain Redoly deal with the loss of his soldier, Tomaath, but she hadn't given it enough of her attention. They had a memorial and a burial, and Redoly was quiet and contemplative...and then he moved on to the next phase of the mission. He dealt with his loss, but it didn't stop him from moving forward. Most importantly, he didn't let it consume him. He did not seek vengeance.

"Well," he said, returning to his boisterous attitude as he led her forward again. "It seems I've given you something new to think about. That's good. It's not all books and training, you know, but you get out into the field and learn something new, and you become a new person. You learn who you are."

They turned one final corner and entered a large cavern filled with more than two dozen people standing, sitting, or leaning against the far walls. A few wore the simple dresses or pant/shirt combinations of her native Remmli, but most of the people wore the elaborate robes and head coverings of Go'aab. Quiet conversations were happening throughout the room, and everywhere she looked, she saw smiles on people's faces.

Plishka sat on a rock across the room – but Zhava did a double-take when she saw the woman's skinny form, her matted and dirty hair and clothes, and the way she wobbled as she nodded and spoke with Brii. That wasn't Plishka; it was her twin sister, Vinaara. She'd obviously had a rough time in captivity the past four moons, but now that help arrived – and now that she could be reunited with her sister – she would undoubtedly get better.

Zhava also recognized Emsterold lying on the ground near Vinaara. If anything, Emsterold looked even worse. Her cheeks were sunken, and the skin of her arms pressed tightly against her bones. Did they never feed her? Apparently not much, though, if they relied on her to communicate with people in the Land of the Dead. But then...why? What was Emsterold doing for Viekoosh and Kretsch all that time she spent in the Land of the Dead? She never asked. Why had she never thought to ask?

"Zhava!" a man called out. Her Papa hurriedly pressed past several people to reach her, his own dirty robes billowing around him. He wrapped his arms around her, and hugged her tightly – and Zhava gasped at the pain shooting through her body. He released her with a jolt and stepped away, suddenly realizing what he had done.

Zhava clenched her jaw at the pain and nearly collapsed into Captain Redoly who caught her and kept her standing.

"She was hurt in the fighting," Redoly explained to Papa. "I think all over, pretty much her entire body is hurt. If you can take her – gently – while I get someone to tend to her injuries."

"Of course," Papa said. Slower this time, he took her weight and let her limp at her own, slow pace. "They told me you led the fighting, and I was so worried, but also...." He glanced around, then leaned down and whispered, "Also so proud of you. So proud."

She felt the tear burning at the edge of her vision, threatening to spill out. If only he knew what she had done. Would he be so proud?

Chapter 34

The cleanup of the Go'aabite holy mountain took far less time than Zhava expected. By the following morning the bodies had been carried away and buried far off into the desert; the fallen weapons were collected; the blood washed away; all the prisoners released and their medical issues tended; and Viekoosh, Kretsch, Ooleng, and Jezza were secured and kept under strict guard. Captain Redoly, Ravid, and Brii would be taking those four immediately to the King's guards for interrogation; the Go'aabites were free to return to their respective homes; and Io Liori would be leading the students and Zhava's family straight north and back to Zhava's farmstead. From there, Zhava was unsure where she would end up. With Io Liori still so angry, she might be sent back to the fields to herd sheep. The rush to leave the desert, however, had little to do with their desire to return home. Lord Su'Fyen was due to arrive with his army at dawn.

Zhava's Mama, of course, blamed all of their problems on Zhava.

"None of this would have happened if you'd married that trader's son like you should have," she muttered from behind her as Papa lent a supporting arm down the twisting cavern. "I knew from the moment those Ios arrived that they would cause trouble for us. We never should have let them take you. We should have told them you already left, that you were perfectly happy marrying Ooleng – or we should have told them you were dead. That would have made things so much better for us, if you were dead."

Papa said nothing. Not because he agreed with Mama, but because there was nothing that could be said that would make Mama say anything else. This was the curse acting on her, the curse that had been planted inside Mama 14 seasons ago, when Zhava was left with her and Papa. The curse that Kretsch had given her, to despise Zhava all the days of her life. To argue made it worse, and so Papa and Zhava said nothing.

"I don't know why I have to carry our bedding," Mama said. "She still has one good arm."

Papa gave that one good arm a squeeze and turned a pained expression toward Zhava, who smiled in understanding. Her other arm, the one Nu struck early in the fighting, had what Brii called a "fool's break." It hurt for Zhava to use it, to twist it or lift anything with it. Brii easily found the focal point of the fool's break, but no matter how much she poked and prodded, she could not feel any spot where the bone was actually broken. The examination hurt worse than Nu's initial hit, and Brii wrapped the arm tight against Zhava's chest and said she would examine it again later. Until then, she couldn't use it – not even for hauling the bedding.

There wasn't much of her that didn't hurt. Her back felt as if a herd of horses had stampeded across it. She had cuts and scrapes across almost every part of her arms, and one long cut on her leg that she didn't even remember. Brii liberally rubbed healing salve across that one and bandaged it for her before she fell asleep. Her head ached, though Brii assured her there was no permanent damage, and that flute sound rang in her right ear for half the night. The knuckles of her sword hand stung – and most annoying of all, that hand kept dripping bits of water, sweating. She flicked it away for the third time this morning and wiped her palm on her dirty shirt.

They exited the cave to the chill and pre-dawn glow of the desert plains. Many would be forced to walk so that the severely injured could ride or be pulled behind on cloth-bound runners that Barae spent all night sewing together. Those runners were, of course, skillfully designed and beautifully made. Two cloth runners attached by poles to a center joint could be pulled gracefully, one on each side of a camel, across the desert dunes. Emsterold and Vinaara, each too weak to ride or walk, were already loaded into runners.

"Well?" Barae asked, running up to meet Zhava. "Which will it be? On top of a camel or to the side of a camel?"

"Zhava will walk," Mama said.

Before anyone could respond, Io Liori stepped up from behind and interrupted. "No. Novice Zhava will ride. She will only slow us down if she walks, and the few runners we have left are needed for those more badly injured."

Zhava's heart sank. She hoped to lie in a runner and sleep. Sitting on top, every jolt of the camel's steps would feel like another punch to her back. She didn't argue, though. She wasn't certain that Io Liori, as angry as she was, wouldn't simply leave her behind.

Everyone loaded up their supplies, and the procession soon left behind the Go'aabite holy mountain, Wui-sha'Olm, to head into the open desert. They fell into a slow rhythm, painful though it was for Zhava.

As the sun crested the eastern dunes, they saw flashes of light far to the north. Io Liori slowed their pace even more and let the caravan approach them. It wasn't even the second hour before Lord Su'Fyen and his soldiers led a procession of pilgrims that must have numbered over a hundred. Io Liori, Garai, and Plishka rode ahead to meet him. Zhava settled into her saddle a bit more, her butt already sore and her back aching worse than last night, and she watched the conversation. Lord Su'Fyen greeted them, Io Liori returned the greeting, and they all dismounted, met at the crest of a small dune, and talked. It was all very anti-climactic and boring as Io Liori talked, occasionally gesturing back to Wui-sha'Olm, and Lord Su'Fyen stood in his sharp-cut, black robes, one hand stroking his beard, and listened. Zhava's eyes were falling shut in the rising heat of the desert morning. Waiting was painful – until Plishka gave a quick nod and ran back to the group and straight for Zhava on her camel.

"Lord Su'Fyen's requested you."

"Why?"

"He didn't say, but I think he wants to reward you."

That seemed unlikely, but she wasn't about to make anyone else angry by refusing. Even with Plishka and Papa's help, she struggled from the saddle and hit the sand with a jolt that made her wince. She limped forward. It was a long, painful slog through the sand to reach the little group standing atop the dune, especially with everyone in their group silently watching her. Her legs ached, and it felt as if a bandage on the back of her thigh might be coming loose, but when she and Plishka finally reached them, she bowed to Lord Su'Fyen.

"Greetings, Lord."

"And to you, Novice Zhava." He returned a shorter bow to her and smiled. "I received Io Liori's report, and I understand all."

She didn't doubt that. He was probably the most brilliant man she had ever met.

"I was informed of the tragedy that struck, and I am deeply saddened by your loss. Candidate Sanama had a warrior's heart."

"Thank you, Sir."

"Now, however, you will know that Lord Su'Fyen keeps his promises." He turned around and walked a little away from them, spread his arms wide at the nearby soldiers, likely the captains of his own army, and spoke.

"Know this, my family: A band of the most talented students traveled from the Hibaro of Remmli, at great risk to themselves and at the request of the King of Remmli himself, to quickly and decisively remove a dangerous man and his followers from our sacred mountain. These students were known by Lord Su'Fyen, the magistrate of the pearl of the desert, the city of Ving'Sa-wehn, who did, in fact, invite them into his confidence. Lord Su'Fyen sent them on their way with all haste and with many blessings – and in the guidance and counsel of our very own cousin, the honored warrior Garai – so that they could fulfill their mission. The names I now speak to you, the names of Novice Zhava, Novice Posef, Novice Barae, and Novice Plishka are to be revered throughout the land of Go'aab, honored for the swift, decisive action taken on behalf of the family of Go'aab and the king of Remmli. Furthermore shall it be decreed that all remember the youngest warrior of their party, Candidate Sanama, who nobly sacrificed her young and promising life in the heart of a raging battle to protect Novice Zhava from the terror of the giant, Nu. Lord Su'Fyen recognized the warrior's heart beating within Candidate Sanama, and though she was still so young, he foresaw the important role she would play in the fight that was to come, the fight that could only be won if Novice Zhava remained standing until the end." He bowed his head. "So let it be decreed."

"It has been decreed," the warriors murmured in reply.

Lord Su'Fyen lowered his arms and returned to face Zhava. "Novice Zhava, warrior sent into battle by Lord Su'Fyen, I thank you for your service to the family of Go'aab. You are now released from my charge and back into the care of your commander, Io Liori."

"Thank you," she said with another bow, but she did not want to thank him. She wanted to correct him – on so many parts. He did not send them on their mission. The Remmli King had not sent them on their mission. They didn't even have a mission. His decree was filled with falsehoods that would be repeated, things that would make their entire journey sound like a magnificent bedtime story.

Lord Su'Fyen leaned down and whispered into her ear, "In this way, we are both the heroes." He winked, stood up straight again, and returned his attention to Io Liori. "As always, it is my sincere pleasure to be with you again. Your students have provided a noble service to us, and I hope that you will reward them as they most deserve."

"Thank you," Liori said with a bow. "I will see to their appropriate rewards."

Zhava knew there was more to that response than Io Liori said. Possibly sending Zhava back home forever or making her scrub the kitchen with Posef for the next few seasons.

Lord Su'Fyen and his men turned and led their camels aside. Garai, however, approached Zhava. Several of the nearby Go'aabite soldiers stopped to watch, but Lord Su'Fyen simply walked on.

Garai stood up straight, took a deep breath, and stared into Zhava's eyes. "An'Zhava," he loudly declared.

She could almost feel Liori's rage at that.

"When Lord Su'Fyen assigned me to your command, I had no idea the powerful warrior I would serve. You are magnificent on the battlefield." He bowed, extended his closed hands, and opened them to reveal the cup she left on the floor of the cavern, the cup in which she instructed her flames to leave some of Sanama's bones and ashes. "The importance of this item is unknown to me, but its value to you was unmistakable. I return it to you now."

She smiled so hard that tears threatened to escape, and she gently retrieved the sealed cup from his hands. "Thank you," she said.

Garai turned to join his fellow Go'aabites, one of whom seemed to question him as they walked away.

The meeting now concluded, everyone returned to their camels and continued on their way. Within moments, they passed by the Go'aabite warriors and pilgrims and proceeded into the open desert. Zhava heard her Mama speak up soon after they departed.

"I don't know why they're making such a fuss about Zhava. She didn't do anything."

Chapter 35

Zhava and her Papa sat in the sand, a small, thin table on short legs set between them and filled with some delicious provisions generously provided by Lord Su'Fyen, some smoked meats, a little pile of dates, and two small scoops of pomegranate seeds. It was their evening meal, and as Io Liori had restricted Zhava to remain inside her family's tent – and with no visitors – Papa agreed to eat with her. She did not know where Mama had gone, and Papa did not offer. Their meal had been, in fact, rather silent.

"We should be home in a few nights," he said between bites. "Yes."

"Will you be staying a while, as you did last time?"

After rescuing the kidnapped children, she and Plishka brought everyone to her farmstead to recover. This time, however, she was not free to make her own plans. Io Liori made it clear she was not free at all. She had to ride with her family – not her friends – and remain inside the tent with her family. They were returning to the Hibaro by way of her farmstead to allow her Papa and Mama to remain behind...and possibly to leave her behind as well, she wasn't sure. Io Liori had not said anything to Zhava throughout the entire ride that wasn't an order: "Zhava, dismount." "Zhava, tend to your family's rides." "Zhava, go to your tent and remain there."

She shrugged at the question. Io Liori would decide how long they remained at the farmstead and who stayed behind.

She wiped her damp, right hand on her robes, annoyed that she couldn't seem to stop that hand from dripping sweat.

They sat quietly and ate. It was a good silence, though. A companionable silence that Zhava rarely enjoyed with her Papa, especially when Mama was with them and making critical remarks every few moments. It almost made her wish that Mama had never been around as she grew up. Perhaps she and Papa would be closer now. But, as Captain Redoly said, that was the past, and the only thing to do with the past was to learn from it.

"The desert is not so hot this time of year," Papa said.

"Yes. The ride down was pleasant. Ving'Sa-wehn was fun." She told him about the party, the feast and the music and the hatchet-throwing contest. She described the hatchet she had been given, then wondered what might have become of it. None of her weapons had been returned to her, so she did not know which were forever lost and which were simply confiscated.

"I would like to have been there," Papa murmured. "I have not thrown in ages, but I'm certain my old hatchet is somewhere in the back barn. Perhaps you can show me sometime how well you throw, and we can have a little competition of our own."

She smiled. "That would be fun."

"Good evening," came a woman's voice from outside the tent. "This is Io Liori. May I enter."

"Certainly, Io," Papa said. He and Zhava stood from the little table that was now nearly empty and bowed as Io Liori pushed aside the tent flap and entered.

"Greetings," she said, "and peace to you both."

"Greetings," Papa said.

"Peace to you," Zhava replied, hoping Liori and she were both speaking the truth of that statement.

"I believe our project has been a success," she said to Papa.

He took a sharp breath and covered his face in his hands.

"There is only so much I can tell, however," she continued. "I would need you to speak with her and gauge her responses. Will you do that for me now?"

"Certainly," Papa said, and Zhava noticed his eyes glittering even in the dim light. Were those tears? He turned to her and smiled – a bigger smile than she had seen from him in many seasons. Possibly ever. "Oh, Zhava. This...." He shook his head.

"Novice Posef is outside," Liori said, and Zhava's heart leapt at that. To have one of her friends so close. "He will take you there."

"Yes, thank you," Papa said, striding forward. "Thank you." He flung back the tent flap and gestured for Posef to lead the way. Posef gave a quick wave to Zhava before the flap shut again, and she smiled.

Liori sighed and crossed her arms to stare at Zhava. She wore her armor and an array of weapons. Her short hair was pulled tight and tied at the back. She looked ready to fight, and Zhava did not like that idea. Who was the enemy inside this tent?

"What am I to do with you?"

Zhava didn't think she wanted an answer, so she kept quiet.

"When I left, you were headed for the Proving Cove, but then we meet again in the middle of the Sineise Desert – and suddenly you're controlling water with as much skill as Viekoosh. Possibly more."

Zhava surreptitiously wiped her sweaty hand on her robe. She kept her head high, though, her eyes on Liori. She couldn't change the past, she told herself, but she could learn from it. One thing she learned was she had strength, more strength than she ever knew, and right now she would show that strength to Io Liori – even if it was the last thing she ever showed her before being sent home.

"Sit," Liori said.

"Sir, if I'm to be reprimanded, I prefer to do it standing. I'm a Novice, not a child."

Liori almost smiled. Zhava noticed the corners of her mouth twitch, but then the woman's face grew stern again. "Ah. A Novice, are you? This is an official reprimand, is it? Speak to you as one of my soldiers, and not as a child? A little girl who has spent a handful of moons at the Hibaro and was promoted too quickly? Is that what you prefer?"

Zhava kept her gaze steady. She had strength. She could endure.

"Then let's have that conversation." She reached behind her back, and Zhava tensed when she brought forth two throwing knives. They were Zhava's. She flicked one at the ground, and it lodged into the wooden serving tray – splitting a date in half, Zhava noticed. She flicked the second one, and it landed right beside the first. "You have talent – incredible stores of raw talent. The Gods have certainly blessed you, Zhava, but I've watched you with those talents. I've read Io Kua's reports of your training these past few moons. You can't control them."

She opened her mouth to protest. Of course she could control her Abilities. She was using her Abilities when she overcame Jezza and Nu.

"No," Liori said, one finger in the air between them. "You don't speak. Your commanding officer hasn't finished." She reached behind her back and brought forth a hatchet – Zhava's hatchet. "I heard about this from all your friends." With a flick of her arm, she threw it to the ground – where it lodged in the wooden tray next to the two throwing knives, the tip of the blade straight in, and the wooden handle pointing at a perfect angle. "You performed very well. Impressed an entire Go'aabite town, and that is no easy thing to accomplish. But you did it with your skill. You did it with your control."

She drew a sword and held it between them. Zhava recognized it, not as Io Liori's sword. It was the sword Zhava took from Jezza. The one with the oiled-leather bands on the grip, the water sprites etched into the guard, and the long blade.

"I saw you fight with Jezza," she said, swishing the sword through the air. "You showed great skill with that hatchet, disarming and subduing her." She shoved the point of the blade into the sand between them, her fingers white from gripping it so tightly, and her jaw set firm. "If you hadn't turned your back on Nu, you might have actually stopped them both right there. But that's part of your problem. You did turn your back. You allowed yourself to be distracted by one enemy while the other flanked you and got in a position to strike you from behind and nearly broke your arm when he knocked you to the ground!" She was yelling by the time she finished.

Zhava rocked back on her heels at the outburst but kept her gaze steady. She had strength. She could endure. She could learn from this.

"After that you...." She threw her hands into the air. "Well, I don't know what you did. You stopped listening to anyone. You stopped taking orders. You dropped enough fire in those caves I thought the walls would melt, and you locked me and Captain Redoly behind you. You locked up one of your best friends, Plishka – who could have helped you with that lightning of hers. I've watched you two spar, and you are natural partners. You feed off each other in a fight as if you can hear each other's thoughts. She could have helped you, but you left her behind. Ravid could have helped you, but you left him behind. You fell back onto the same weakness we have seen in you from the beginning: you let your opponent, your enemy, goad you into action. The same thing you did with Posef in the dining hall when you first arrived – and yes, I heard about that too – is the same thing you did in those caves, except you didn't stop at your enemy. You did it to your friends too. You stormed through those caves in a rage, fighting everyone by yourself – and for what?" She stepped back and looked Zhava over from head to feet. "You're a mess. I'm surprised you're alive."

"I couldn't let anyone else die," she blurted out. "Sir."

"We are soldiers, Zhava. Sometimes that happens." She clenched her fists and shook her head. "My Gods, I don't know what you're thinking. I should know what you're thinking, I'm you're –" She stopped, squeezed her eyes shut, and took a slow, deep breath. "I'm your commanding officer, and...I should know you better than you know yourself. But right now, I don't have any idea what you might do next. Which order you might disobey next."

"Sir, I –"

Another hand to stop Zhava speaking. Liori gestured at the array of weapons between them, the throwing knives and hatchet embedded in the serving tray, and the sword stuck into the ground. "Do you want this?"

"Sir?"

"You don't know this, but I paid your bride price from my own savings."

Actually, Zhava knew that. When she wasn't supposed to be listening, she overheard that very conversation.

"I did that because I saw the potential in you. Priestess Marmaran saw the potential in you. But what you did back there...." She shook her head. "As Captain Redoly reminded me, repeatedly, you won us the battle. But the way you did it. The way you went off on your own, put yourself in danger, refused to follow orders.... I can't use a soldier like that."

Zhava's heart stopped. Here it was. She would be kicked out of the Hibaro, sent back home to live with her Papa and Mama and her brothers to do...what? Find some other trader's son who would have her? Live out the rest of her days in isolation? Too much a fighter to be anyone's wife, but not disciplined enough to be anyone's soldier?

"The weapons are yours," Liori said, her voice much quieter, though her hands were still clenched into fists. "And the choice is yours. When we reach your farmstead, you may remain behind. As I said, I paid your bride price, and I...will set you free, if that is what you desire." She turned and looked intently into Zhava's eyes. "Or return to the Hibaro with me, and I will personally oversee your training. I should have done that moons ago, but that damn Viekoosh denied me that. Ordered me not to do that."

Zhava knew that piece of information also, but now wasn't the time to mention that.

"Know this, however: If you return with me, I will work you harder than anyone else has ever done. I will pass along every piece of information and every skill I have ever learned, and Io Kua and I will shape you into the kind of soldier who is disciplined, who fights with her companions, not against them. The kind of soldier who understands her Abilities — and how to use them. Not how to be used by them, which is your greatest weakness. You will become a finely-honed weapon in the King's arsenal. That's what I offer you. That is your choice."

Io Liori turned away before Zhava could respond, and again Zhava thought there was a tear in her eye. But out of frustration with Zhava, or out of sadness?

"You are confined to quarters, to your family's tent, for the duration of the trip. Your family may come and go as they please, and they will be allowed to bring your meals, but you will have no contact with your friends. When we ride, you will ride with your family or beside me — nowhere else." She walked slowly toward the tent flaps, her head down. "If you remain behind, at your family's home, I will of course give you time to say your good-byes." With that, she flipped open the tent and was gone, the canvas flaps falling shut behind her.

Zhava stood alone in the tent and stared at the weapons arrayed before her. Her remaining two throwing knives; the hatchet that a kind Go'aabite woman gifted to her; and the beautiful, shining sword she took from Jezza. Her Felton was missing, the one Io Kua gave her when he began training her. People had rushed to clean out the Go'aabite sacred mountain, to wipe away all signs of the fighting that happened within, and they could have easily missed one small sword. Or perhaps someone picked it up who didn't know it belonged to Zhava. Perhaps someone simply kept it. What would it matter, one little sword, if she chose to remain at home...or if she chose to return to the Hibaro.

She liked that word, though: Choice. Io Liori gave her a choice. She had no choice about marrying Ooleng; Papa met the prince and his family on a trading route over the mountains. Papa decided for Zhava that Ooleng was a good match, and he invited Ooleng's family to negotiate the bride price.

Instead, Io Liori paid Papa the bride price – more than the price he asked of Ooleng. The family profited from that deal, gained a great deal of wealth: cattle, horses, camels, sheep, and even a little more land for crops. Several things happened because of those decisions, but none of them involved Zhava. The choice had not been hers, and the rewards had not been hers either.

Her time at the Hibaro these past several moons had been the most liberating of her entire life – even more than her lessons with Priestess Marmaran. Her studies were difficult, her lessons hard, especially the fighting lessons and the endurance training, but it taught her what she could do. She could fight, and she could use her Abilities in service to the King. She made friends, and.... She glanced at her bedroll in the corner, at the blanket wrapped tightly around the sealed cup that contained Sanama's remains. She made friends, certainly, and she lost a friend. Lost someone who respected her, looked up to her as more than a friend. As a mentor. As another teacher.

Captain Redoly said she should learn from the past. Could she really do that? Could she become better than she was? She felt she was very good, better than she had ever been, and Lord Su'Fyen praised her before all of those people, so she must have been doing something right.

But her friend died, and Io Liori said there was so much more for her to learn. So much more for her to do, and to do it better. Could she really go further and become someone better?

Choice. It was her...choice.

Her thoughts were interrupted by Io Liori speaking to someone outside the tent. Zhava couldn't hear it all, but someone was crying, and someone else – Papa? – was making shushing sounds, and Io Liori sounded...happy?

The tent flaps parted, and Liori stepped through, shutting them tightly behind her. She had a smile on her face. That was weird.

"I wasn't certain of this," she said. "I thought it might be possible, and it seems to have worked."

Zhava stared at her, too confused – and stunned by that smile – to know how to respond.

"Zhava, your father made me aware of the abuse you suffered these 14 seasons," she said, stepping forward. "And I've seen it myself since you've been together. Your mother was cursed – and you learned of that curse only a few moons ago?"

She nodded.

"Salient Kretsch was the one who cursed her. Did you know that?"

Again she nodded.

"We have him in custody now. I told him to rid your mother of that curse." She chuckled. "I also told him I would run him through with my sword and pin him to a dune for the buzzards to eat if he didn't do it, so...he agreed."

Zhava didn't know what to say. She wasn't even sure what to think. Was it possible?

Liori stepped aside and pulled back the tent flap, and Papa led a weeping Mama through the open door and into the tent.

"Zhava," Papa said, and he barely held back tears of his own. "This is...your mother."

Mama's face was streaked with tears, but she smiled. The day's dust had been washed away in wet lines down her cheeks, and she gripped Papa's arm like it was a lifeline.

"Zhava," she said, and she took a step closer.

Zhava stood rooted to the spot, unsure whether to stay or go running from the tent. She couldn't remember ever seeing her Mama cry, and certainly not about her.

"You don't really know me," Mama said. She shut her eyes and shook her head, and her mouth opened and shut several times before she continued. "And...I'm still having trouble with these...thoughts...that you are...evil."

Liori stepped forward and placed a hand on Mama's shoulder. "It will pass. Kretsch said that after so many seasons, the thoughts have become rooted, but the impulse to express them will pass. Be patient." She glanced at Zhava. "Patience."

Mama sucked in a deep breath, stood up straight, and looked at Zhava again. She tried to speak, but the words had trouble coming forth. "Zhava, I lo –" She cringed, as if in pain. "Zhava, I lo –" She grunted and clamped her eyes shut, and Papa wrapped his arm more tightly across her shoulders. Another deep breath, and she stepped up to Zhava and took her hand.

Zhava flinched at that touch. A touch from Mama usually involved a slap, or sometimes a wooden spoon across her fingers. Or her head. At Io Liori's encouraging nod, however, she let her hand remain.

"Zhava," Mama started again. "I remember you coming to us in the caves and hugging your Papa, but it feels like a dream.

A nightmare. I thought you were late. I thought it was all – the soldiers and that evil giant and our imprisonment. I thought it was all...your fault."

Mama expressed that clearly. This wasn't new; it wasn't different. It was painful, and Zhava did not want to relive it.

"But I know...mmm," she grunted and clamped her eyes shut. "I know...it...was not...your...fault." She gasped for breath and smiled at Zhava. Actually smiled. Zhava could not remember Mama smiling at her. Ever. "Not your...fault. And I want to say...mmm." She shook her head, took a step closer – and Zhava almost backed away at that, but she held her ground. If she could stand toe-to-toe against Jezza and Nu, she could certainly face Mama without flinching. "I want...to say...." She gasped. "I'm proud – mmm. I'm proud...of...you." With a gasp, she opened her eyes and grinned.

Papa smiled at Mama, then turned and smiled at Zhava. He reached forward and wrapped his other arm around Zhava and brought her in close.

Zhava wanted to run. She wanted to tear herself away from this moment, from this embrace and all the tears and the smiling and laughing and utter weirdness of it all. Mama did not act like this. Mama was not nice – she certainly was not proud, especially not of Zhava.

But Papa was so happy. His strong arms, even after so many nights imprisoned, held on tightly to Zhava and Mama. She could do this, she thought, for him. She could endure the strangeness of the situation if it made Papa happy.

Io Liori dropped her gaze, and Zhava was certain this time that she wiped away a tear. She quietly parted the tent flaps and slipped through without a backward glance.

"We're finally together," Papa whispered, and they both hugged Zhava. "We're finally whole again. A family."

Epilogue

Two moons later....

Zhava ran along the snowy path, her boots crunching with each footfall, and her breath steaming before her. She veered to the left, between two of the larger trees alongside the path, two trees she remembered from yesterday. They were good trees for what she had in mind, large trees with low, thick branches. She leaped, gripped one of those branches, swung her legs forward, and flipped up and around to land on the branch. She let the leather breastplate take the impact, but it still hurt. No time for that now. She pushed herself up and crouched on the branch, a smattering of dead leaves and loose snow drifting to the ground. She cringed. That could be noticed.

With a quick glance back down the path – empty! – she jumped to another branch in a nearby tree, swung around the trunk, and leaped over the path. With one hand extended, she grabbed for the nearest branch – and missed. She tumbled to the ground, twisting one ankle, and rolled across cold, hard ground. That should have worked. It looked like it would work, and it should have worked.

She spun around, ready to loose a dozen flames upon the ground to cover her mistake, but stopped herself just in time. Against the rules.

She jumped back up – and flinched as the knife blade flashed around her head and pressed against her neck. She stood there, panting into the frigid air and feeling the man's presence at her back. The chill wind blew lightly through the trees, making her body shiver. Or perhaps that was the frustration of losing.

"Looks like I win again," Io Kua whispered into her ear, and she could hear the smirk in his tone even if she couldn't see him.

That was probably the most aggravating thing about this fighting game, that Kua was such a bad winner. Seven of these so-called "games" in a row, and he got cockier and more obnoxious each time he won. Which was every time.

However.... She eyed the path. No Io Liori yet.

She stomped on his right foot, slipped her hands into the crook of his elbow and yanked down, and just as he cried out and lost his balance, she spun around and kneed him in the groin.

He shrieked, collapsed to the ground, and curled into a tight ball.

Zhava picked up his sword from where he'd dropped it, stepped up to him lying on the snowy ground, and poked him in the back of his armor. "Yield."

"Yep," he wheezed.

"Novice Zhava, stand down," a woman's voice called, and Zhava cringed. She turned around and saw Io Liori walking between the trees toward them. No wonder the path was clear; Liori cut through the forest.

Zhava lowered her sword, stepped back, and stood stiff and at attention as Liori walked up and crooked an eyebrow at Io Kua's wheezing form upon the ground.

"Will you live?" she asked.

"Yep," Kua said between breaths. "Sir."

"Novice Zhava, I saw it all. Io Kua caught you, but you continued the match after it was completed."

"Sir, Io Kua did not request that I yield. He said...um...." He had stopped wheezing and was now struggling to roll over and push himself up. This would get him into trouble, but it was the truth, so she continued. "He said, 'Looks like I win again.'"

Liori's eyebrows shot up at that, and she turned to watch him slowly sit back on his knees. "You actually gloated?"

"Yes, Sir," he said with a wince and a sigh.

"Novice Zhava, I award you this win. Congratulations on your first combat point."

She smiled and handed Kua's knife to Liori. "Thank you, Sir."

"Too early for that," she said, "because you would be dead if this was a real battlefield. Your acrobatics through the trees were exhilarating, but Io Kua still got a knife to your throat. If he had been a real enemy – instead of a gloating Mentor – you would be lying at his feet instead of the other way around."

"Yes, Sir."

"Two laps through the forest, then meditation until the evening meal. You can spend your afternoon pondering your mistakes."

"Yes, Sir," she said, trying not to sigh.

"And one more thing," Liori said, more quietly. She pointed at Zhava's hand. "You're leaking again."

She put her right hand behind her back, hiding the drops of water falling from her fingertips and splattering to the ground. What she thought in the desert was merely sweat in her hands turned out to be the water sprites shoving their way out from inside her. She had to press a significant amount of her will against the sprites to get them to stop flowing, but they finally did. Both Io Liori and Io Kua knew about the problem, and they were patient with her lack of control. They encouraged her to study the Kandor more deeply to learn how to exert her will over the water sprites as definitely as she did over her natural Abilities, the little flaming men, the wind, and the dirt, but it was so hard.

"Thank you, Sir," she mumbled, and sprinted away.

By the time she finished her two laps along the forest path, she was sweating through her clothes and armor, shivering from the cold and wind, and wanted nothing more than to collapse in her warm bed. Instead she cleaned her armor, washed herself, changed clothes, and sat on the floor of her room to meditate as she had been instructed. The Novice House was built in the style of the western Remmli plains, so it was a rectangular house surrounding a center courtyard – just like home. Her room looked out on the Hibaro stables, but as it was the heart of winter she kept the shutters closed and a pile of her little flames in the fireplace to keep the room warm. They played and danced and sang joyously, and their buzzing activity was a nice background to her meditations.

She set the two canop jars on the floor beside her, the tall, narrow one that contained Priestess Marmaran's ashes and a few bones, and the short cup that contained the remains of Candidate Sanama. She crossed her legs and shut her eyes and began running through her favorite Kandor, a song of strength and encouragement. Within moments the young version of Priestess Marmaran sat on the floor nearby and recited it with her. Her long hair was parted down the sides, and her eyes were bright and aware. When she appeared as her older self, the slow, blind woman Zhava had known, Marmaran was most often teaching Zhava or chastising her for something. This younger version was conversational, more of a friend.

They completed the recitation of the song and sat in companionable silence for some time. Zhava kept her mind open and her eyes shut as the images of the day fluttered before her. She let them come and go, the run through the woods, Io Kua attacking her from behind, Io Liori's chastising instructions.

She saw Vinaara and Plishka briefly on her way back to the Novice House, and that brought a smile to her face. Vinaara healed so well from her time in captivity that Io Liori allowed her to remain at the Hibaro as an actual Initiate in training to be a soldier. That was a far better outcome than Emsterold. She was so weak she had to be sent to the King's own healers, and she had not yet returned. No one knew if she ever would. Weclin, the boy who could speak to the giant birds, the sengret, had also been sent to the King's castle, but he would be mentored by one of the gamekeepers in the capital city. That would be good for him. And her own Papa and Mama, now acting like little children in love, were back at the farmstead and putting things back in order. Her brothers returned from their trek across the mountains, embarrassed and cursing Zhava – and Mama actually chastised them for being so foolish. That bit of information was in a letter from Caleb that Zhava still had on the side table, the same letter in which he apologized for treating her so badly. He asked to visit her again, but she had yet to respond. She couldn't decide when she wanted to see him again – or if she even did. It was her choice, and she would take her time in making that choice.

Stiff and noticing the room had become brighter as the sun set against the shutters, she shifted and opened her eyes – and started at what she saw. A little girl with hollow eyes sat across from her, mirroring Zhava with her crossed legs. Her short hair was curled tightly, and her mouth hung open a little, as if caught in mid-thought.

The elder Priestess Marmaran now sat beside Zhava, and she also stared at the little girl through her cloudy eyes.

Of course this had to be Sanama, though she had never appeared to Zhava in the entire two moons she meditated around the canop cup that contained her remains. Zhava reached forward and lightly brushed a finger across Sanama's cold hand. That was weird; Marmaran's spirit flesh was never cold.

Sanama cocked her head at the touch, shut her mouth, and narrowed her hollow gaze at Zhava. "I think...," she croaked, as if the effort to speak was almost overwhelming.

"Oh, child, what have you done?" Marmaran whispered.

"Sanama, it's all right," Zhava said, ignoring Marmaran.

"I think," she tried again, "something...happened. Something...bad."

"It did, but it's better now." Zhava smiled. "You're better now."

Sanama slowly tilted her head down and stared at herself, then turned and looked at the room. "Something happened, and now...I'm here."

"Yes, Sanama," Zhava said. She sat forward and wrapped her arms around the girl. Her skin was cold, but Zhava knew she could warm her up. She was overjoyed at having her friend finally returned to her, even if only in spirit form, and now nothing bad could happen to Sanama ever again. "I have missed you so much. Thank you for coming back to me."

"I'm here," Sanama whispered, and she held on a little more tightly to Zhava. "I'm here."

Glossary

- *Aayan, Salient*: First of the King's First Salients; a man specializing in the discipline of the mind, and the foremost mind warrior and tactician of the Kingdom of Remmli
- *Ability*: a Gods'-granted, innate specialization of a person; most often exhibited by one trait through any individual person, and most often something useful that allows that person to perform a valuable task for his/her family or community; some individuals exhibit two traits, and rare individuals will exhibit three traits, such as Zhava (wind, earth, fire); there is no record of anyone ever exhibiting more than three Abilities.
- *Allenka, Sister*: a high-ranking member of the Kingdom or Remmli's priestly order; Allenka holds the rank of the second-in-command at the Hibaro Reverie, though she is rarely called upon in any official capacity.
- *Alxindra (Xindr)*: Zhava's oldest brother; he and his wife and children live down the valley from Zhava's family farm.
- *An'Iniga*: Go'aabite family matriarch; wife to Ib'Dignas; the "An" is an honorific denoting her status as the family's matriarch.
- *Apprentice rank*: the third-highest ranking of students at the Hibaro; at this rank each student is assigned to

an individual teacher who trains that student in one particular discipline.

- *Barae, Novice*: one of Zhava's best friends; her Ability is to work with cloth.
- *Bec*: Alxindra and Yenl's oldest son; Zhava's nephew.
- *Brii, Captain*: a member of the Remmli King's elite fighting force.
- *Caleb*: Zhava's brother, and the youngest son in the family.
- *Castinthai*: a seaport city across the Purneese Mountains; well-known as a sea-trade destination and port city.
- *Coredor*: one of the Gods worshipped throughout the region; a trickster God who does his own actions for his own reasons; worshipped by a growing number of people who prefer a return to traditions in which those with Abilities were kept as slaves, women did not hold positions of authority, and individuals exercised personal freedoms without worrying about military interventions from the King.
- *Emsterold, Apprentice*: a young woman whose Ability was to commune with the dead; she was thought killed ("The Initiate: The Tales of Zhava Book 1") until Zhava met her in the Land of the Dead and claiming to still be alive somewhere.
- *Felton sword*: a short sword highly prized for its quality of construction and balance; Zhava received one as a gift from Io Kua ("The Initiate: The Tales of Zhava Book 1").
- *Garai*: a young warrior in Go'aab; assigned by Lord Su'Fyen to accompany Zhava and her friends through the desert.

- *Go'aab (Go'aabite)*: the desert kingdom to the south of Remmli; organized in a loose confederation of interrelated families; quite insular and distrusting of strangers, but exceptionally loyal and kind-hearted to those they know and love.
- *Goodspring*: the small stream that runs around the edge of Zhava's family farmstead; at one edge of the property, the stream runs along the planted fields, but nearer to the house it is down a short bluff.
- *Hibaro*: the school set up within the Kingdom of Remmli to train young people discovered to have Gods'-granted Abilities; students are divided into Candidates (who may or may not continue in their training), Initiates, Novices, Apprentices, and Mentors; once graduating from the Hibaro, students often choose between a further career in the basic military, the Io service, the Priestly ordination, or sometimes even to achieve the rank of Salient.
- *Highlands*: the region in the northern edge of Remmli marked by the high, forested mountains and bands of traveling families who frequently herd sheep or goats.
- *Ib'Dignas*: Go'aabite family patriarch; husband to An'Iniga; the "Ib" is an honorific denoting his status as the family's patriarch.
- *Initiate rank*: second ranking of Hibaro students, immediately after Candidates; Initiates have been recognized as having potential and chosen to continue their training.
- *Io rank*: the highest military rank in specialization; Ios have trained extensively, most often in combat and strategy, and are formidable warriors on the battlefield.

- *Jezza*: a mercenary from across the Purneese Mountains who has an Ability with water; she and her partner, the giant Nu, take jobs for money.
- *Kandor*: the holy book of the Kingdom of Remmli; it contains history, poetry, tales of the Gods, and military strategy and tactics; all students of the Hibaro are required to study it and often focus on a particular specialization from within its pages.
- *Kretsch, Salient*: Third of the King's First Salients, Kretsch is one of the masters of the mind.
- *Kua, Io*: a recent graduate of the Hibaro, specializing in fighting techniques under the supervision of Io Liori; Io Kua was scheduled to begin a tour of duty patrolling the border regions when Zhava requested him as her Mentor ("The Initiate: The Tales of Zhava Book 1"), a request granted by High Priest Viekoosh that ended up delaying his opportunity to lead a group of soldiers.
- *Lhumir*: a strong wine of the Go'aab; each family uses its own secret recipe, and recipes are rarely shared, but many aspects remain the same from one group to another: the wine is always made with fruit of the region in which the family resides, the taste is always quite sharp but pleasant, and the alcohol content is masked by the fruity aroma, allowing people to become quite drunk very quickly; Go'aabite families will often challenge each other to lhumir-drinking contests to determine which family brewed a more potent batch.
- *Liori, Io*: First of the King's Third Salient; a highly decorated and skilled warrior; recruited Zhava and placed her in the Hibaro for training.
- *Ligistak*: name of a group of rulers in Go'aab; trained in the science of deduction and reason, they are capable of taking disparate pieces of information and com-

ing up with a solution or explanation; the Go'aabite spy networks feed all information they receive directly to ligistaks to assist them because any incomplete or inaccurate data can produce incorrect conclusions.

- *Marmaran, Priestess*: a teacher at the Hibaro for most of her life; about 15 seasons ago, she retreated from life and lived as a hermit for many years before suddenly showing up at a farmstead on the western edge of Remmli where she began tutoring Zhava; she died on the journey accompanying Zhava to the Hibaro ("The Initiate: The Tales of Zhava Book 1"); her spirit is tied to a talisman that Zhava keeps with her, allowing Priestess Marmaran and Zhava to speak with one another through their spiritual connection.
- *Mentor rank*: the highest rank of a student at the Hibaro; at this rank students are expected to act as teachers to as many as three of their fellow students, though they most often mentor only one or two students; students at this rank are evaluated primarily through their interpersonal and teaching skills under the theory that a good teacher is more likely to become a good leader.
- *Mitsel*: one of Zhava's brothers; the second oldest son in the family.
- *Monh*: servant who claimed to have seen Zhava's Mama and Papa abducted; escaped to the Hibaro to alert Caleb and Zhava what had happened at the farmstead.
- *Novice rank*: rank at which students at the Hibaro are expected to have mastered the basics of their lessons in the Kandor and are ready to begin implementing those lessons and applying them to real-life situations.
- *Nu*: a warrior giant who travels with Jezza, a woman with an Ability to control water; together they accept mercenary jobs for pay and glory.

- *Ooleng*: son of a traveling merchant who transports wagons of goods over the Purneese Mountains; he and his father struck a deal with High Priest Viekoosh to exchange sengret eggs for child slaves abducted from the Hibaro; it has not yet been uncovered where the father and son meant to take the prisoners or to whom they planned to sell them.
- *Priest/Priestess*: titles of those in the Kingdom of Remmli who father a religious order after their training at the Hibaro; they are spiritual seekers who specialize in knowledge about the Gods and Goddesses, their ways, and how to interact with them; many Priests and Priestesses also have a secondary specialty they use or teach within the Hibaro, such as Priest Qi who oversees the students' physical endurance training or Brother Tymare who organizes the Hibaro's library collection.
- *Purneese Mountains*: the mountain range at the western edge of the Kingdom of Remmli.
- *Plishka, Novice*: twin sister of Vinaara; Plishka has an Ability to control lightning; she is a fierce fighter with a natural affinity for many different weapons; she is one of Zhava's closest friends.
- *Posef, Novice*: from the Highlands, Posef is a prankster and a braggart, though he is a loyal friend to Zhava and Barae; he has an Ability to read minds.
- *Preizhavan (Goddess)*: a water nymph and Goddess, she is also responsible for bringing forth great harvests; Zhava's favorite Goddess.
- *Proving Cove*: a test that all students at the Hibaro must go through at least once, though many students endure the Proving Cove multiple times before graduating; it is a cave on the northern edge of the Hibaro

grounds in which students must enter and fight an animal (and its cubs); Zhava realized ("The Novice: The Tales of Zhava Book 2") that the bites from the animals produce visions or hallucinations, and she guessed that the teachers want the students to experience and analyze those visions or hallucinations; Zhava would prefer the Proving Cove be destroyed and the animals within it killed for the danger the entire thing poses to the people living at the Hibaro, but the teachers insist it is safe.

· *Ravid, Captain*: a member of the Remmli King's elite fighting force.

· *Redoly, Captain*: a member of the Remmli King's elite fighting force; he led a mission to Zhava's farmstead and then deep into Go'aabite territory to test and observe Zhava ("The Novice: The Tales of Zhava Book 2").

· *Remmli, Kingdom of*: the kingdom in which Zhava lives; it stretches from the western edge, just off the Purneese Mountains, to the Storm Coast on the east and the Highlands to the north.

· *Sabkha*: a spot in the Go'aabite desert in which water from occasional thunderstorms and rain showers will congregate; frequent stops for desert travelers as well as places for many of the animals of the region to congregate at night.

· *Salients*: a group of trained thinkers, tacticians, and warriors of the minds, Salients most often report directly to the King of Remmli and do his bidding in research, planning, and war.

· *Sanama, Initiate*: one of Zhava's "little soldiers," Sanama is a skilled fighter who adores Zhava and wants to grow up to be just like her.

- *Sengret*: a breed of birds out of legend, Sengret grow taller than an average person, and they are strong enough to carry large animals in their talons; though fierce and terrifying in appearance, Sengret are very smart and capable of being trained for a variety of duties, especially if they are raised by their trainers from the time they hatch.
- *Sineise Desert*: the desert region to the south/southwest of the Kingdom of Remmli; Go'aab claims the entirety of the Sineise Desert as well as many of the rockier regions to the south of the desert.
- *Storm Coast*: the eastern edge of the Kingdom of Remmli, so named for its continuous bad weather and endless thunderstorms; the inhabitants of the Storm Coast are expertly skilled sailors, though casualty rates for those sailers are quite high.
- *Su'Fyen, Lord*: a Ligistak of Go'aab and ruler of the desert city Ving'Sa-wehn.
- *Suleenuo, Io*: weapons master at the Hibaro; she trains students in various fighting techniques.
- *Tegara, Sister*: overseer of the Initiate House at the Hibaro; she has a healing Ability and frequently uses it on the students after the return from the Proving Cove.
- *Tomaath, Captain*: a member of the Remmli King's elite fighting force.
- *Tsiftoolio dance*: an energetic, fun dance with complex movements of the hands and feet; most Hibaro students know the dance and will compete with each other to see who can go the longest without missing a move.

- *Tymare, Brother*: overseer of the Hibaro library; Zhava worked for him when the campus library was located within the 9-story tower.
- *U'Sholm, Sabkha*: an oasis in the Sineise Desert; frequent spot of travelers for resting and watering animals.
- *Vek*: most powerful and ruler of the Gods.
- *Viekoosh, High Priest*: former leader of the Hibaro; devout follower of the God Coredor who struck a deal to gather Segret eggs in exchange for selling children into slavery; wants to lead a rebellion against the Kingdom or Remmli and install a religious order based on the ideals of Coredor.
- *Vinaara*: twin sister of Plishka; does not display any Gods'-granted Abilities, but is a very smart, dedicated student; kidnapped by High Priest Viekoosh's forces and not seen again in many moons ("The Initiate: The Tales of Zhava Book 1").
- *Ving'Sa-wehn*: major city in southeast Go'aab; ruled by Lord Su'Fyen.
- *Weclin, Initiate*: rescued by Zhava from Ooleng's mountain prison where he had been held for several moons ("The Initiate: The Tales of Zhava Book 1"); has an Ability to speak with many animals, most useful in working with a captured Sengret.
- *Wui-sha'Olm*: a mountain fortress in the south of Go'aab; a holy site in which the Go'aabites celebrate the Spring and Fall equinoxes.
- *Yenl*: Alxindra's wife, Zhava's sister-in-law.
- *Y'Mey, Brother*: a Duhaang from an island across the sea; his skin lacks any pigmentation, instead being quite white, and he sunburns easily; he is an engineer

for the King of Remmli assisting in much of the restoration of the Hibaro.

H. Dean Fisher
*Photo by: John
Kilker at
JohnJKilker.com*

H. Dean Fisher is author of the fantastic, the scientifically fictional, and the macabre. He has been writing since he was 5: first comic books, then short stories, and now novels. His fiction and photography has won awards at various conferences and regional competitions throughout the southwestern United States. He currently chairs a mass communication department at a private university in Pennsylvania.

Books by H. Dean Fisher
The Tales of Zhava series:
    "The Initiate: Book 1"
    "The Novice: Book 2"

"A Revelation of Our Savior, with Translation and Commentary by Dr. Michel S. Curllen"

"The Jungle God" (forthcoming, 2021)

Website: www.HDeanFisher.com - sign up for the monthly newsletter
Facebook: www.facebook.com/SeventhBattlePublishing
Twitter: @HDeanFisher1
Instagram: HDeanFisher

www.ingramcontent.com/pod-product-compliance
Lightning Source LLC
Chambersburg PA
CBHW070644310726
48982CB00001B/405